BUREAU FOR PARANORMAL · RESEARCH AND DEFENSE ·

GARDEN OF SOULS

Created by MIKE MIGNOLA

ABE SAPIEN

An amphibious man discovered in a primitive stasis chamber in a long-forgotten subbasement beneath a Washington, D.C. hospital. Recent events have confirmed a previous life, dating back to the Civil War, as scientist and occult investigator Langdon Everett Caul.

CAPTAIN BENJAMIN DAIMIO

A United States Marine whose distinguished thirteen-year career ended in June of 2001 when he and the platoon he was leading were all killed during a mission. Exactly how it was that he came back to life is an outright mystery.

LIZ SHERMAN

A fire-starter since the age of eleven, when she accidentally burned her entire family to death. She has been a ward of the B.P.R.D. since then, learning to control her pyrokinetic abilities and cope with the trauma those abilities have wrought.

DR. KATE CORRIGAN

A former professor at New York University and an authority on folklore and occult history, Dr. Corrigan has been a B.P.R.D. consultant for over ten years and now serves as Special Liaison to the enhanced-talents task force.

JOHANN KRAUS

A medium whose physical form was destroyed while his ectoplasmic projection was out-of-body. That essence now resides in a containment suit. A psychic empath, Johann can create temporary forms for the dead to speak to the living.

MIKE MIGNOLA'S

B.P.R.D.™

GARDEN OF SOULS

Story by
MIKE MIGNOLA and JOHN ARCUDI

Art by
GUY DAVIS

Colors by
DAVE STEWART

Letters by
CLEM ROBINS

Editor
SCOTT ALLIE

Assistant Editor
RACHEL EDIDIN

Collection Designer
AMY ARENDTS

Publisher
MIKE RICHARDSON

DARK HORSE BOOKS®

NEIL HANKERSON ♦ *executive vice president*
TOM WEDDLE ♦ *chief financial officer*
RANDY STRADLEY ♦ *vice president of publishing*
MICHAEL MARTENS ♦ *vice president of business development*
ANITA NELSON ♦ *vice president of marketing, sales & licensing*
DAVID SCROGGY ♦ *vice president of product development*
DALE LaFOUNTAIN ♦ *vice president of information technology*
DARLENE VOGEL ♦ *director of purchasing*
KEN LIZZI ♦ *general counsel*
DAVEY ESTRADA ♦ *editorial director*
SCOTT ALLIE ♦ *senior managing editor*
CHRIS WARNER ♦ *senior books editor, Dark Horse Books*
ROB SIMPSON ♦ *senior books editor, M Press/DH Press*
DIANA SCHUTZ ♦ *executive editor*
CARY GRAZZINI ♦ *director of design & production*
LIA RIBACCHI ♦ *art director*
CARA NIECE ♦ *director of scheduling*

Special thanks to Jason Hvam

www.hellboy.com

Published by Dark Horse Books
A division of Dark Horse Comics, Inc.
10956 SE Main Street
Milwaukie, OR 97222

First edition January 2008
ISBN: 978-1-59307-882-9

1 3 5 7 9 10 8 6 4 2

Printed in China

This book collects the *B.P.R.D.: Garden of Souls* comic-book series, issues 1–5,
published by Dark Horse Comics.

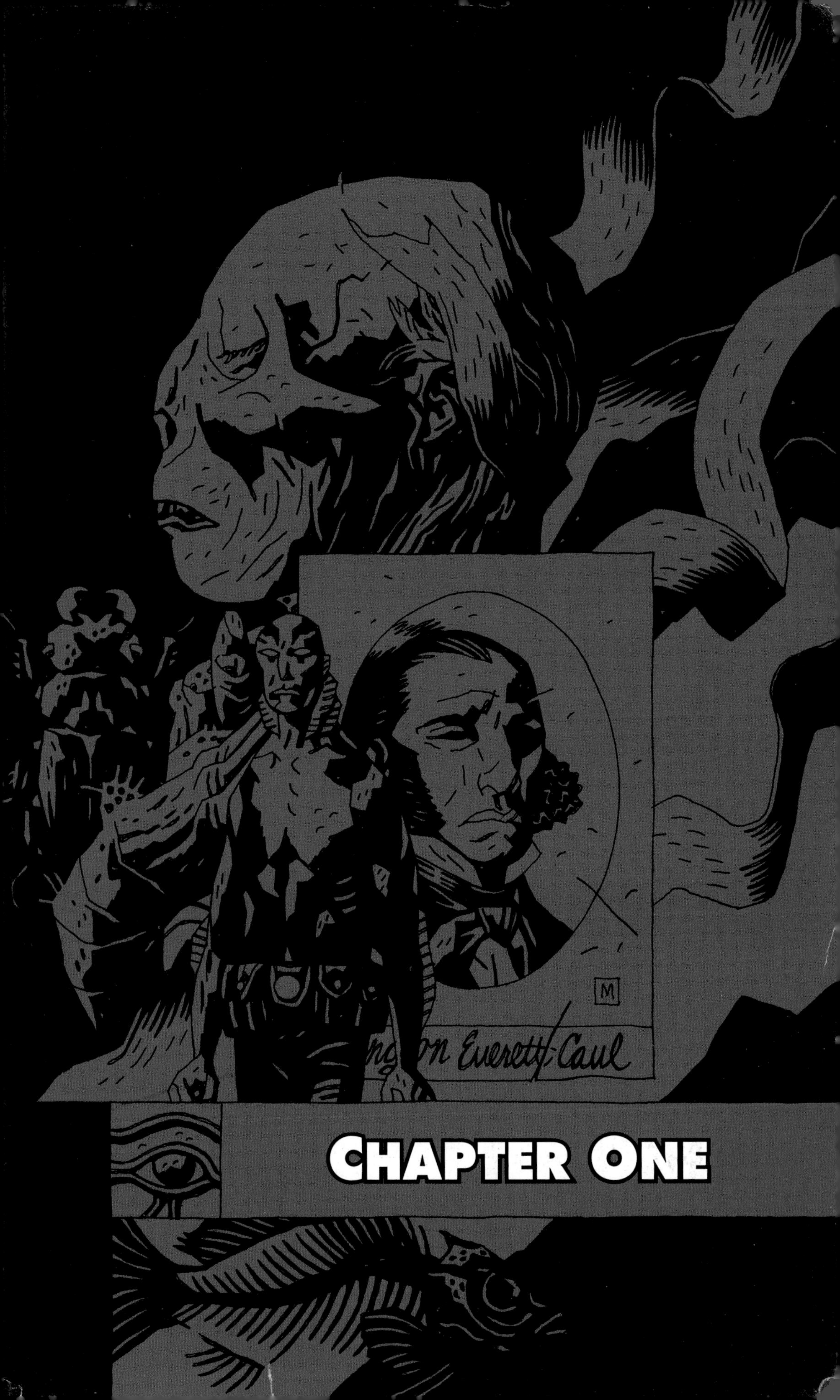
Everett Caul

CHAPTER ONE

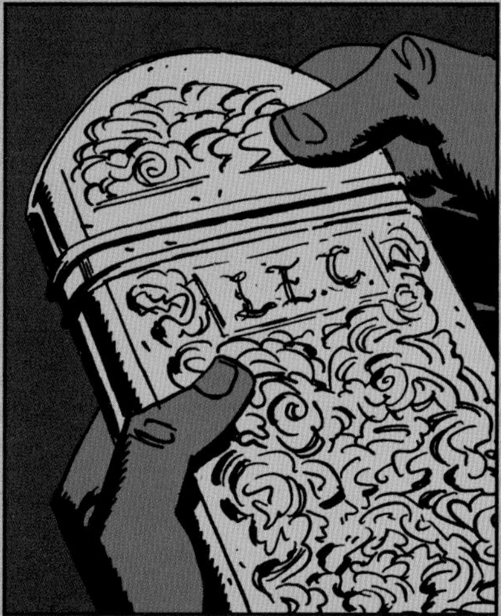

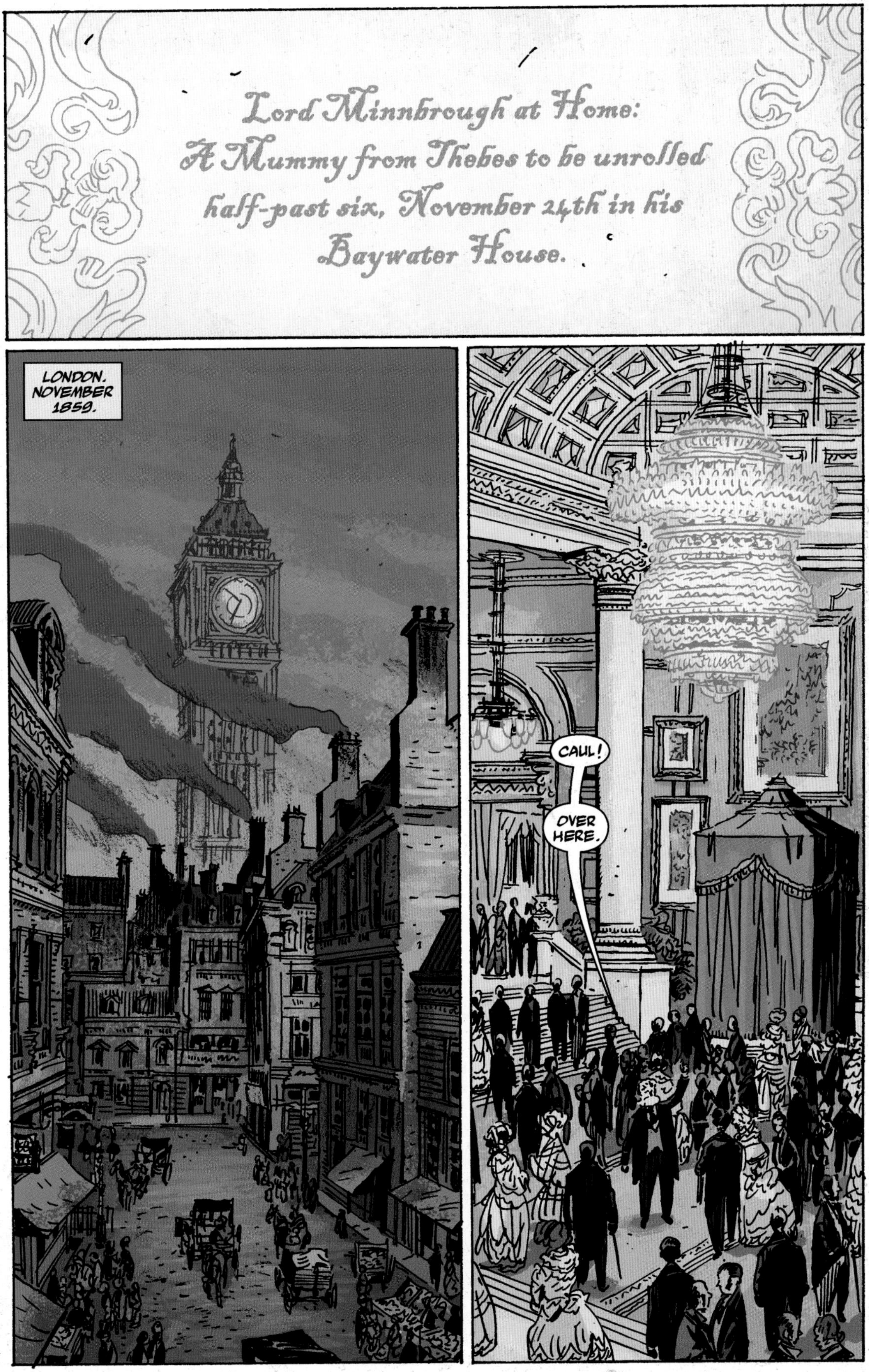
Lord Minnbrough at Home:
A Mummy from Thebes to be unrolled
half-past six, November 24th in his
Baywater House.
LONDON. NOVEMBER 1859.
CAUL!
OVER HERE.

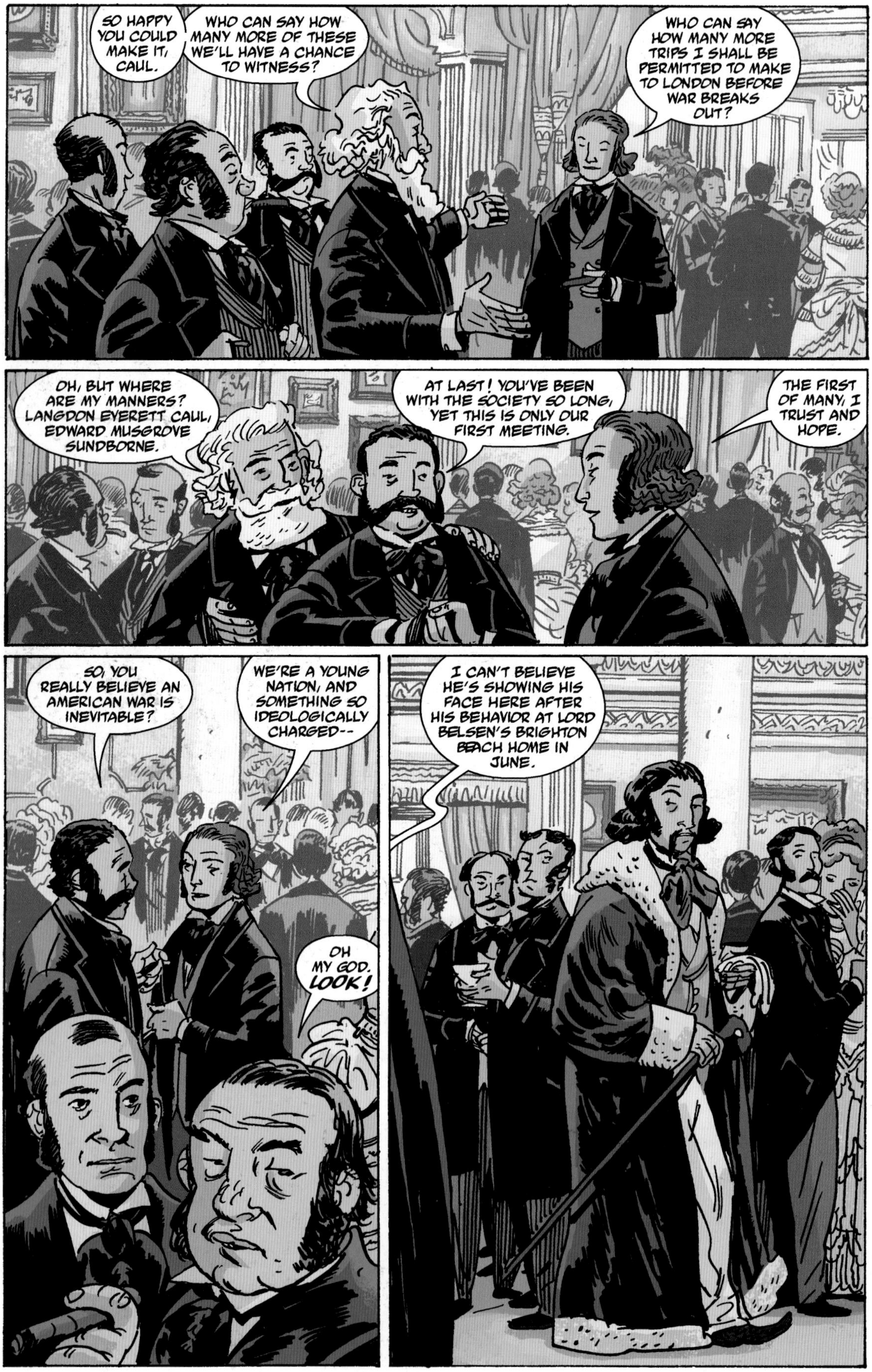
SO HAPPY YOU COULD MAKE IT, CAUL.
WHO CAN SAY HOW MANY MORE OF THESE WE'LL HAVE A CHANCE TO WITNESS?
WHO CAN SAY HOW MANY MORE TRIPS I SHALL BE PERMITTED TO MAKE TO LONDON BEFORE WAR BREAKS OUT?
OH, BUT WHERE ARE MY MANNERS? LANGDON EVERETT CAUL, EDWARD MUSGROVE SUNDBORNE.
AT LAST! YOU'VE BEEN WITH THE SOCIETY SO LONG, YET THIS IS ONLY OUR FIRST MEETING.
THE FIRST OF MANY, I TRUST AND HOPE.
SO, YOU REALLY BELIEVE AN AMERICAN WAR IS INEVITABLE?
WE'RE A YOUNG NATION, AND SOMETHING SO IDEOLOGICALLY CHARGED--
OH MY GOD. LOOK!
I CAN'T BELIEVE HE'S SHOWING HIS FACE HERE AFTER HIS BEHAVIOR AT LORD BELSEN'S BRIGHTON BEACH HOME IN JUNE.

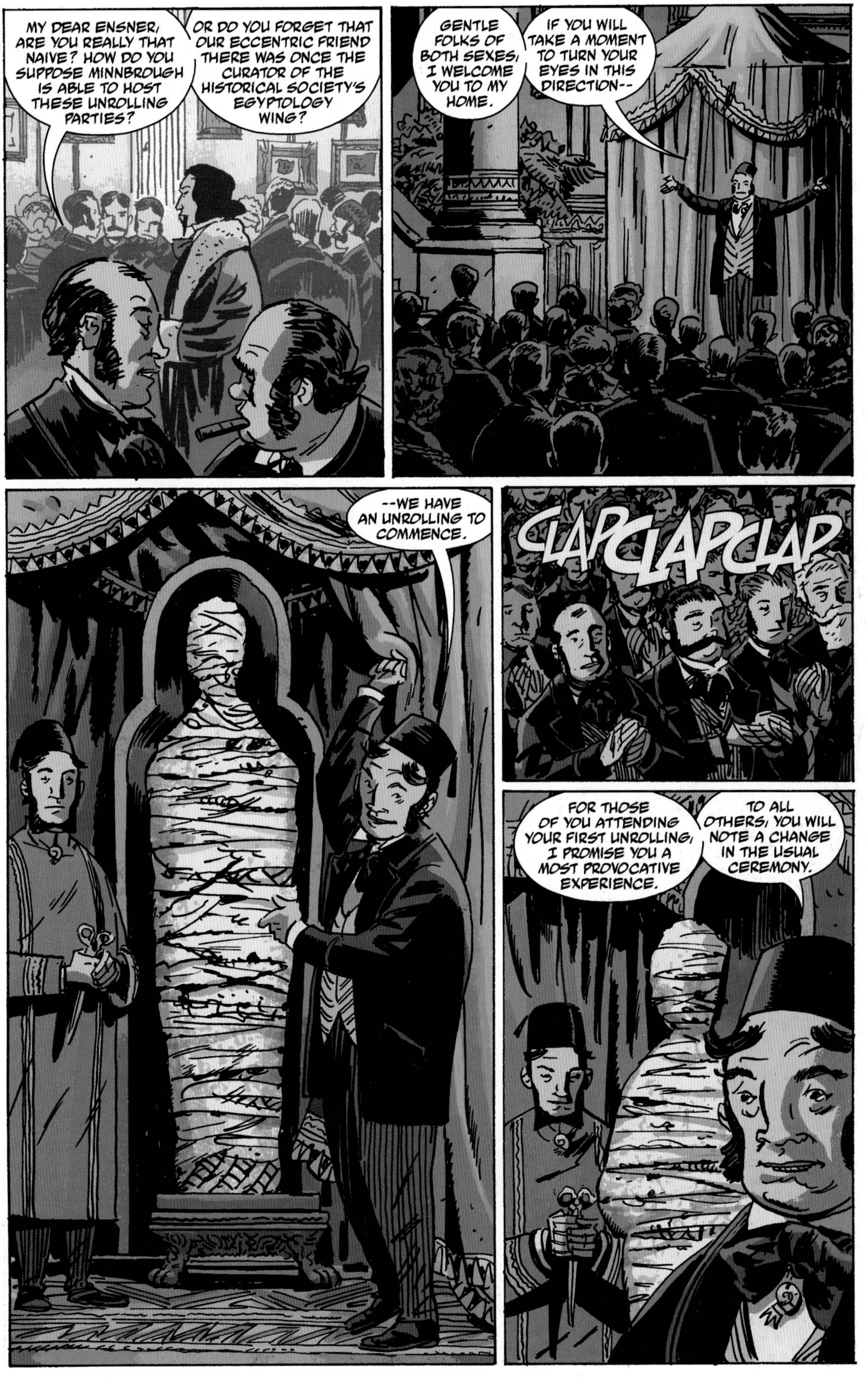
MY DEAR ENSNER, ARE YOU REALLY THAT NAIVE? HOW DO YOU SUPPOSE MINNBROUGH IS ABLE TO HOST THESE UNROLLING PARTIES?
OR DO YOU FORGET THAT OUR ECCENTRIC FRIEND THERE WAS ONCE THE CURATOR OF THE HISTORICAL SOCIETY'S EGYPTOLOGY WING?
GENTLE FOLKS OF BOTH SEXES, I WELCOME YOU TO MY HOME.
IF YOU WILL TAKE A MOMENT TO TURN YOUR EYES IN THIS DIRECTION--
--WE HAVE AN UNROLLING TO COMMENCE.
CLAPCLAPCLAP
FOR THOSE OF YOU ATTENDING YOUR FIRST UNROLLING, I PROMISE YOU A MOST PROVOCATIVE EXPERIENCE.
TO ALL OTHERS, YOU WILL NOTE A CHANGE IN THE USUAL CEREMONY.

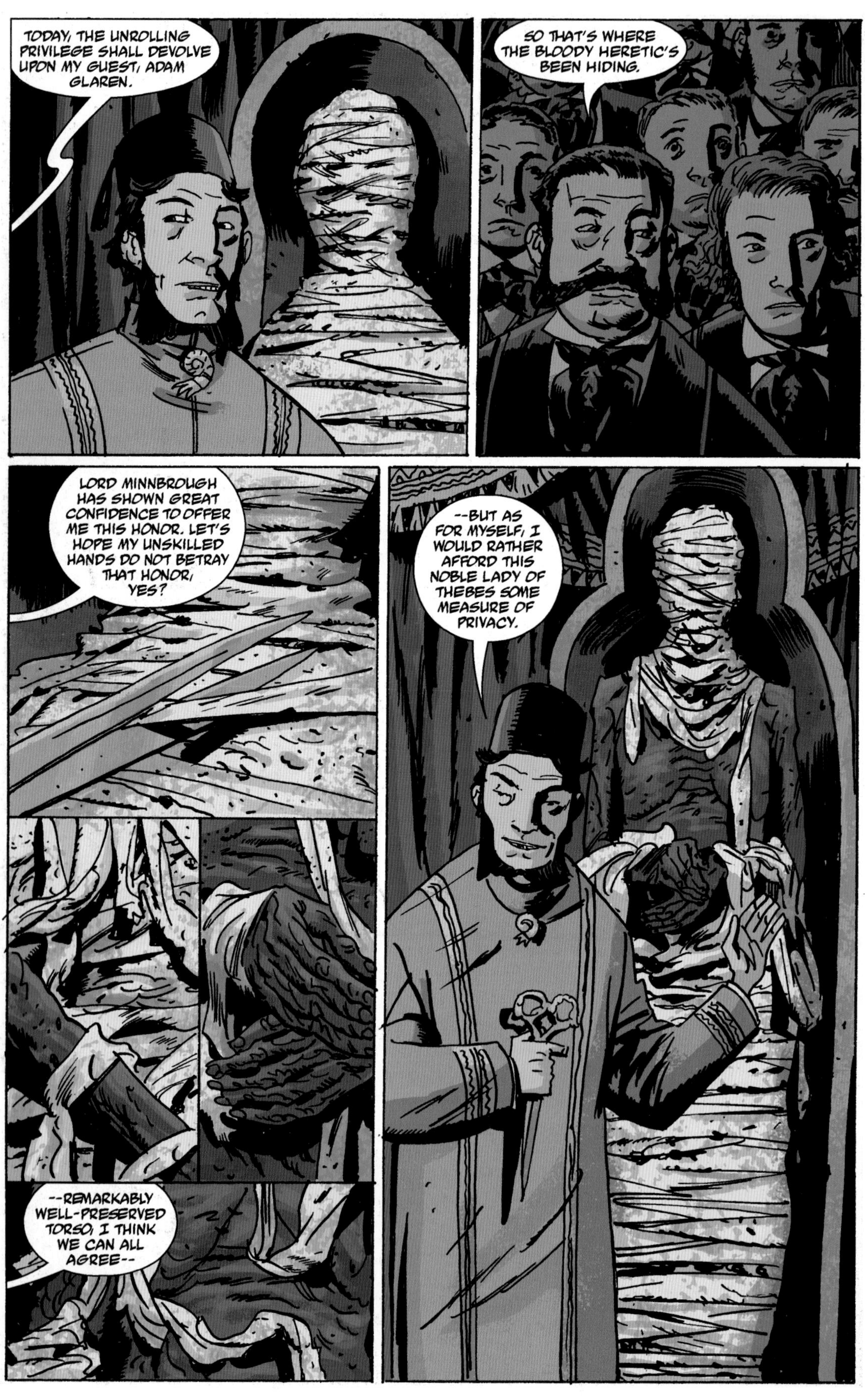
TODAY, THE UNROLLING PRIVILEGE SHALL DEVOLVE UPON MY GUEST, ADAM GLAREN.
SO THAT'S WHERE THE BLOODY HERETIC'S BEEN HIDING.
LORD MINNBROUGH HAS SHOWN GREAT CONFIDENCE TO OFFER ME THIS HONOR. LET'S HOPE MY UNSKILLED HANDS DO NOT BETRAY THAT HONOR, YES?
--REMARKABLY WELL-PRESERVED TORSO, I THINK WE CAN ALL AGREE--
--BUT AS FOR MYSELF, I WOULD RATHER AFFORD THIS NOBLE LADY OF THEBES SOME MEASURE OF PRIVACY.

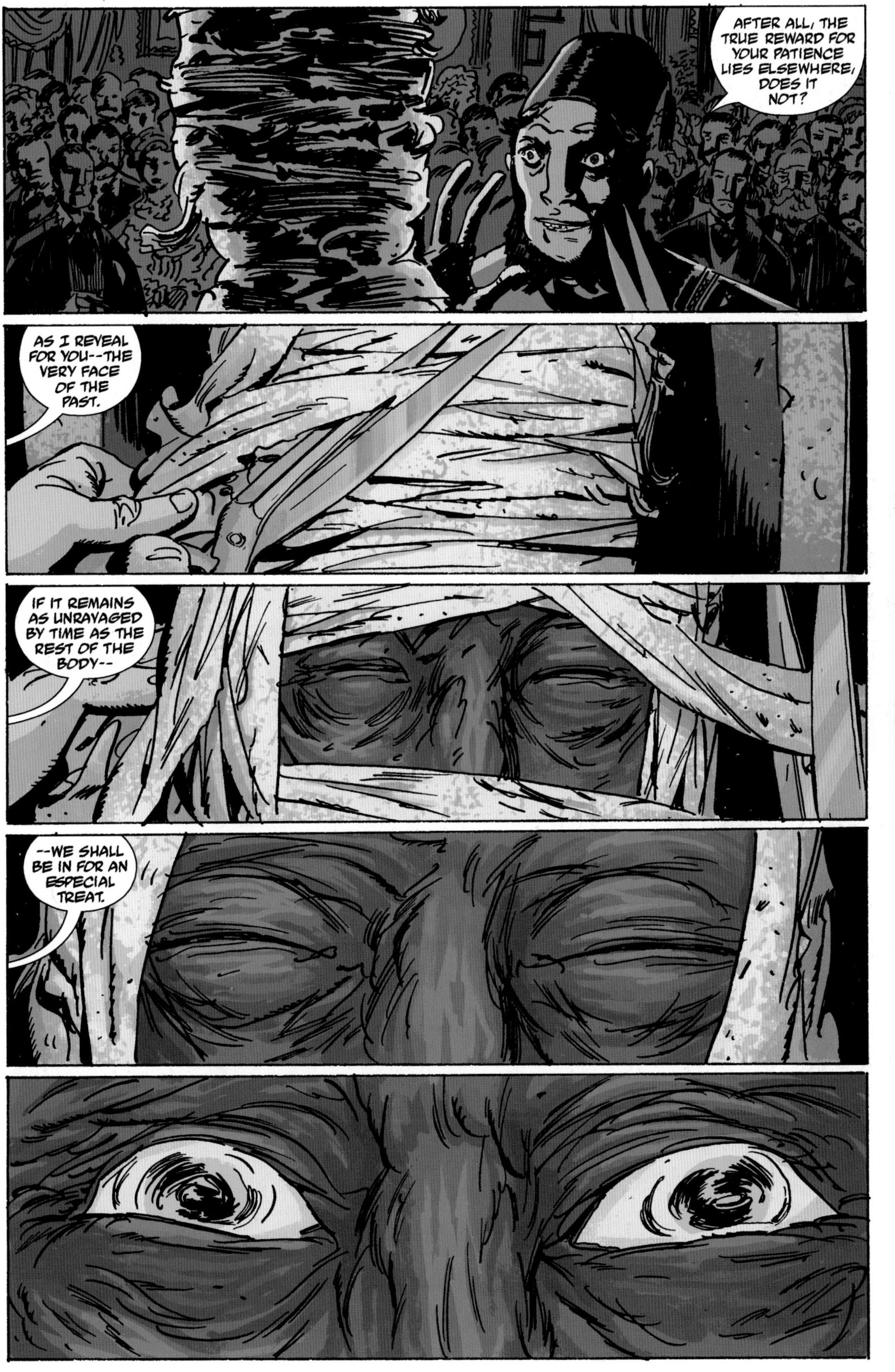
AFTER ALL, THE TRUE REWARD FOR YOUR PATIENCE LIES ELSEWHERE, DOES IT NOT?
AS I REVEAL FOR YOU--THE VERY FACE OF THE PAST.
IF IT REMAINS AS UNRAVAGED BY TIME AS THE REST OF THE BODY--
--WE SHALL BE IN FOR AN ESPECIAL TREAT.

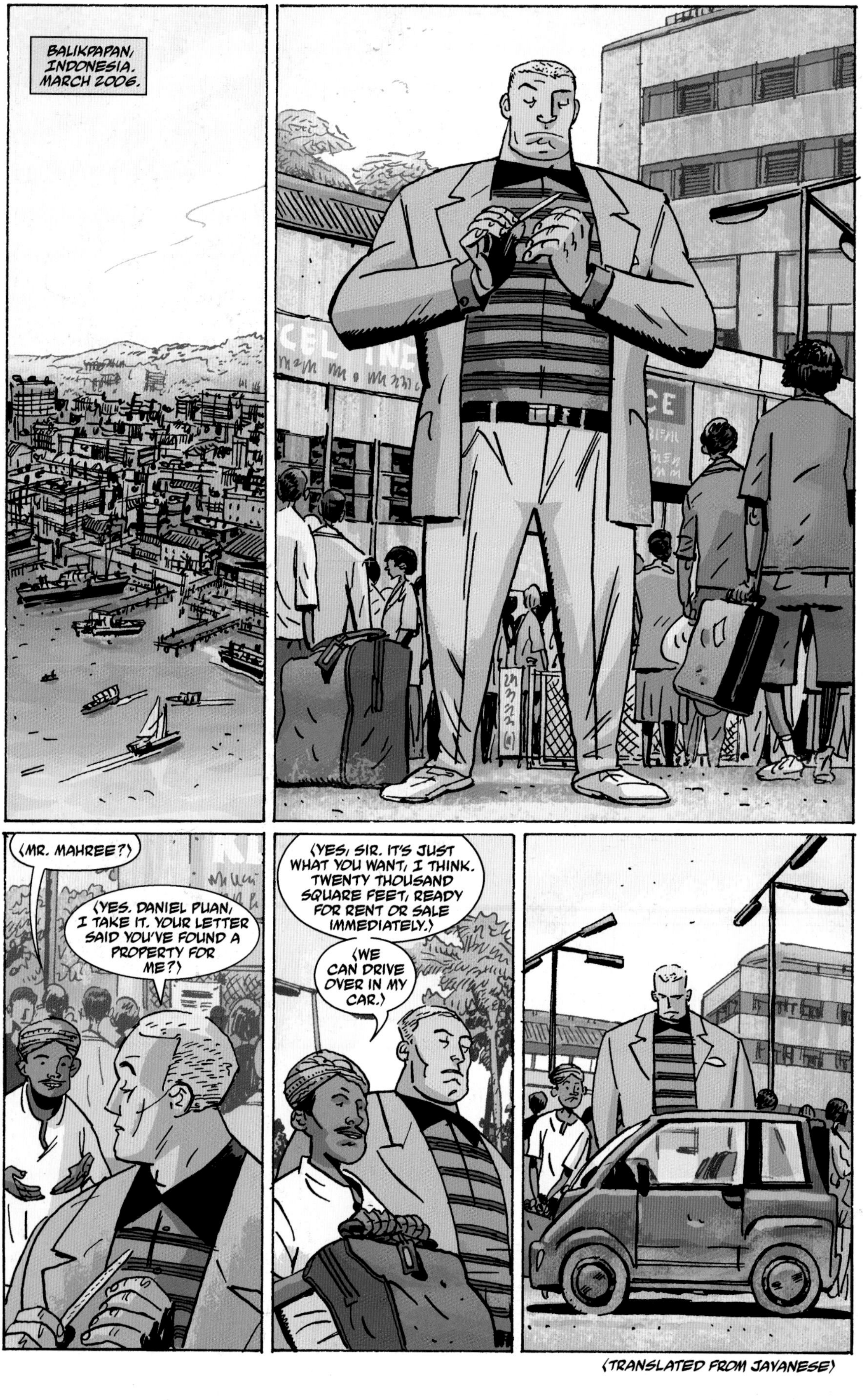
BALIKPAPAN, INDONESIA. MARCH 2006.
⟨MR. MAHREE?⟩
⟨YES. DANIEL PUAN, I TAKE IT. YOUR LETTER SAID YOU'VE FOUND A PROPERTY FOR ME?⟩
⟨YES, SIR. IT'S JUST WHAT YOU WANT, I THINK. TWENTY THOUSAND SQUARE FEET, READY FOR RENT OR SALE IMMEDIATELY.⟩
⟨WE CAN DRIVE OVER IN MY CAR.⟩
⟨TRANSLATED FROM JAVANESE⟩

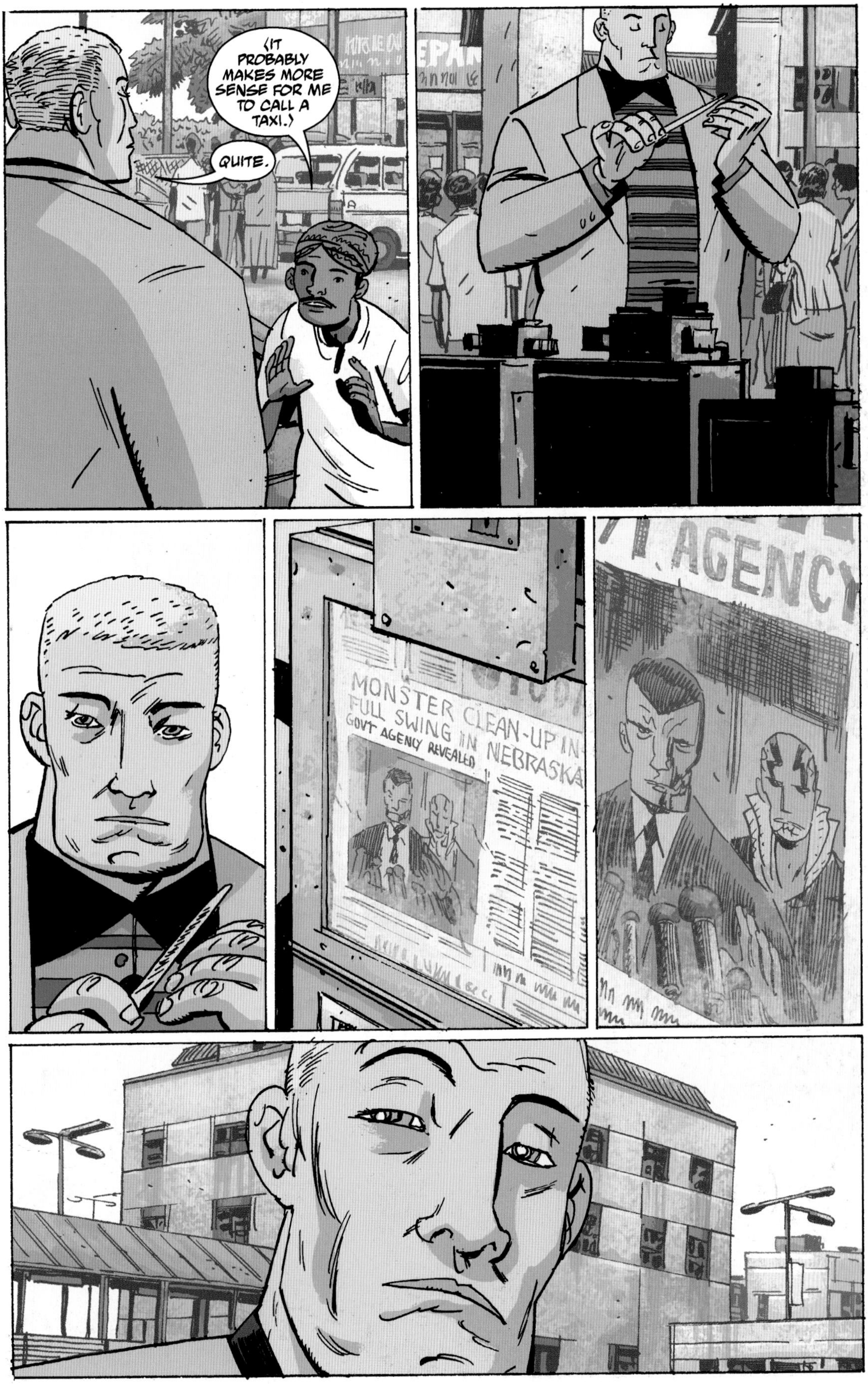
‹IT PROBABLY MAKES MORE SENSE FOR ME TO CALL A TAXI.›
QUITE.
MONSTER CLEAN-UP IN FULL SWING IN NEBRASKA
GOVT AGENCY REVEALED
AGENCY

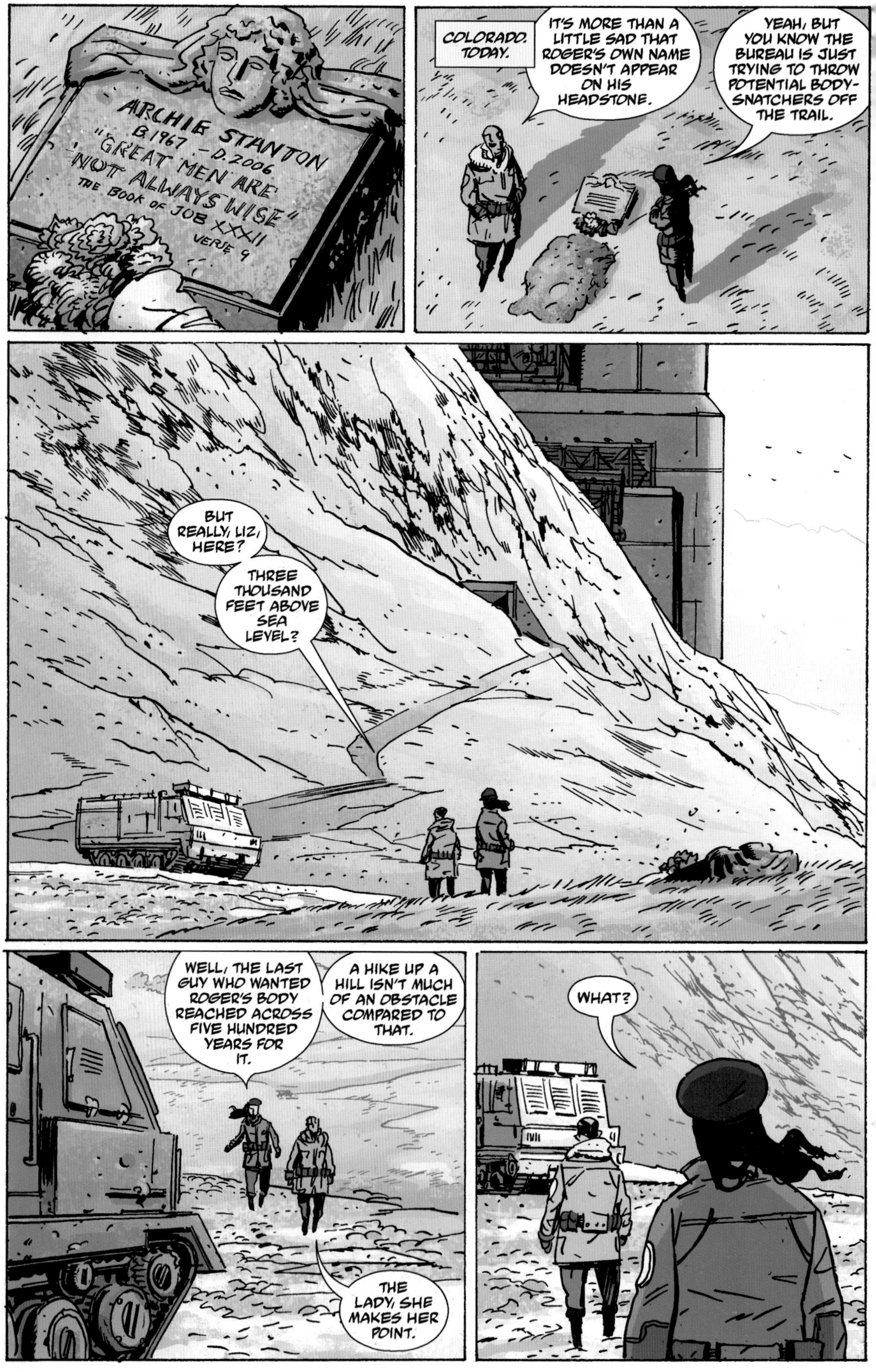
ARCHIE STANTON
B.1967 - D.2006
"GREAT MEN ARE
NOT ALWAYS WISE"
THE BOOK OF JOB XXXII
VERSE 9
COLORADO. TODAY.
IT'S MORE THAN A LITTLE SAD THAT ROGER'S OWN NAME DOESN'T APPEAR ON HIS HEADSTONE.
YEAH, BUT YOU KNOW THE BUREAU IS JUST TRYING TO THROW POTENTIAL BODY-SNATCHERS OFF THE TRAIL.
BUT REALLY, LIZ, HERE?
THREE THOUSAND FEET ABOVE SEA LEVEL?
WELL, THE LAST GUY WHO WANTED ROGER'S BODY REACHED ACROSS FIVE HUNDRED YEARS FOR IT.
A HIKE UP A HILL ISN'T MUCH OF AN OBSTACLE COMPARED TO THAT.
THE LADY, SHE MAKES HER POINT.
WHAT?

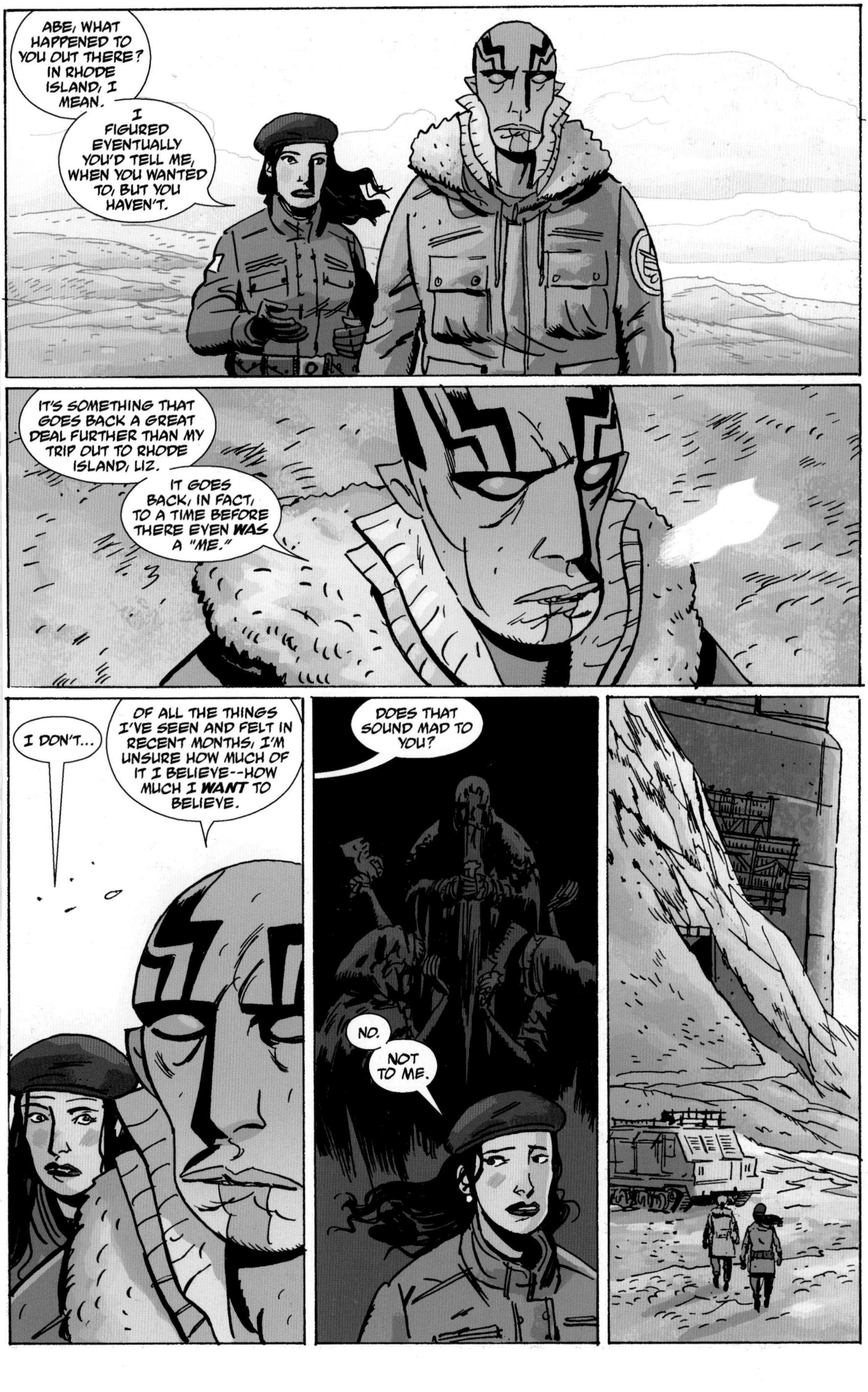
ABE, WHAT HAPPENED TO YOU OUT THERE? IN RHODE ISLAND, I MEAN.
I FIGURED EVENTUALLY YOU'D TELL ME, WHEN YOU WANTED TO, BUT YOU HAVEN'T.
IT'S SOMETHING THAT GOES BACK A GREAT DEAL FURTHER THAN MY TRIP OUT TO RHODE ISLAND, LIZ.
IT GOES BACK, IN FACT, TO A TIME BEFORE THERE EVEN **WAS** A "ME."
I DON'T...
OF ALL THE THINGS I'VE SEEN AND FELT IN RECENT MONTHS, I'M UNSURE HOW MUCH OF IT I BELIEVE--HOW MUCH I **WANT** TO BELIEVE.
DOES THAT SOUND MAD TO YOU?
NO.
NOT TO ME.

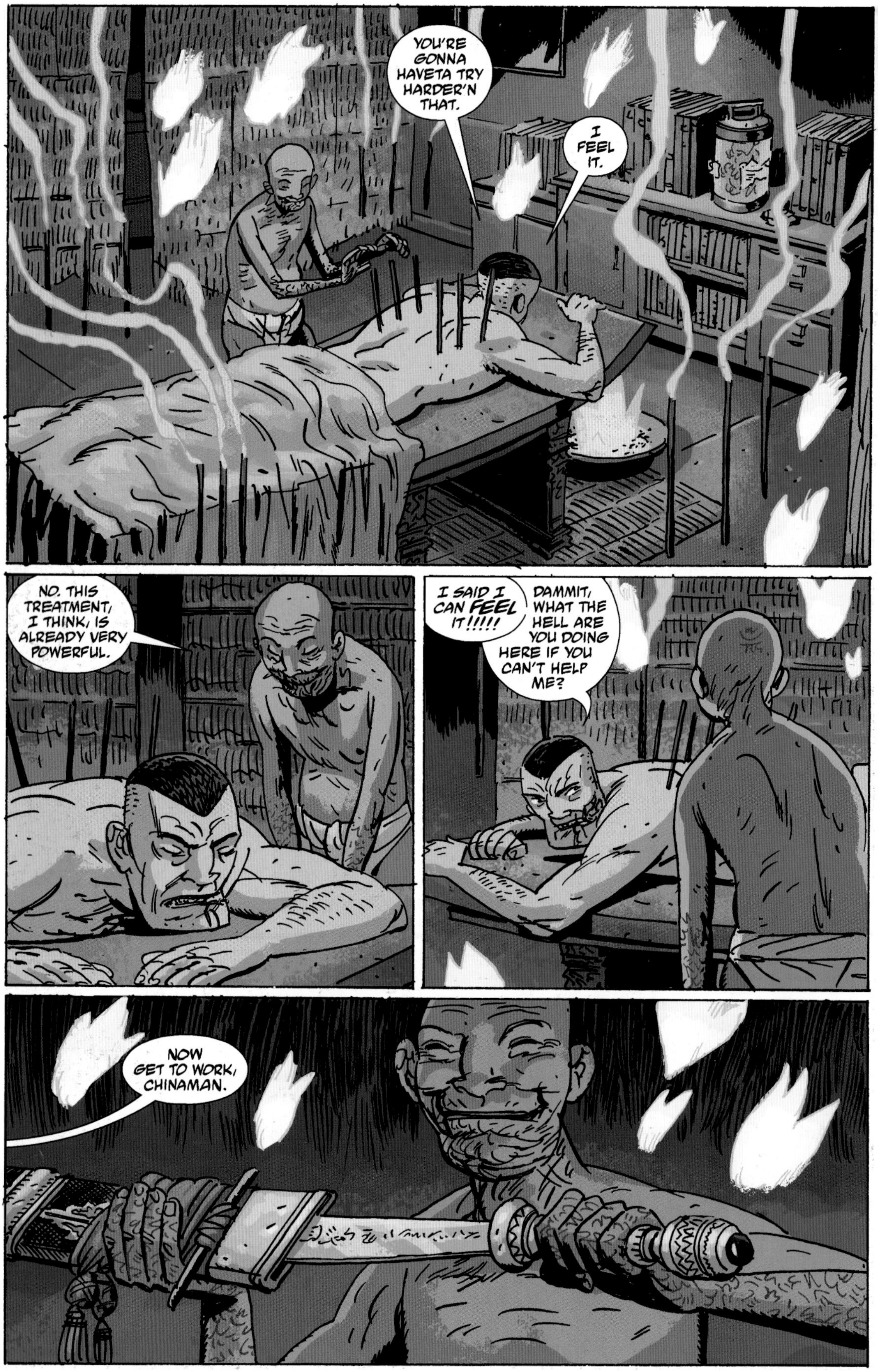
YOU'RE GONNA HAVETA TRY HARDER'N THAT.
I FEEL IT.
NO. THIS TREATMENT, I THINK, IS ALREADY VERY POWERFUL.
I SAID I CAN FEEL IT!!!!!
DAMMIT, WHAT THE HELL ARE YOU DOING HERE IF YOU CAN'T HELP ME?
NOW GET TO WORK, CHINAMAN.

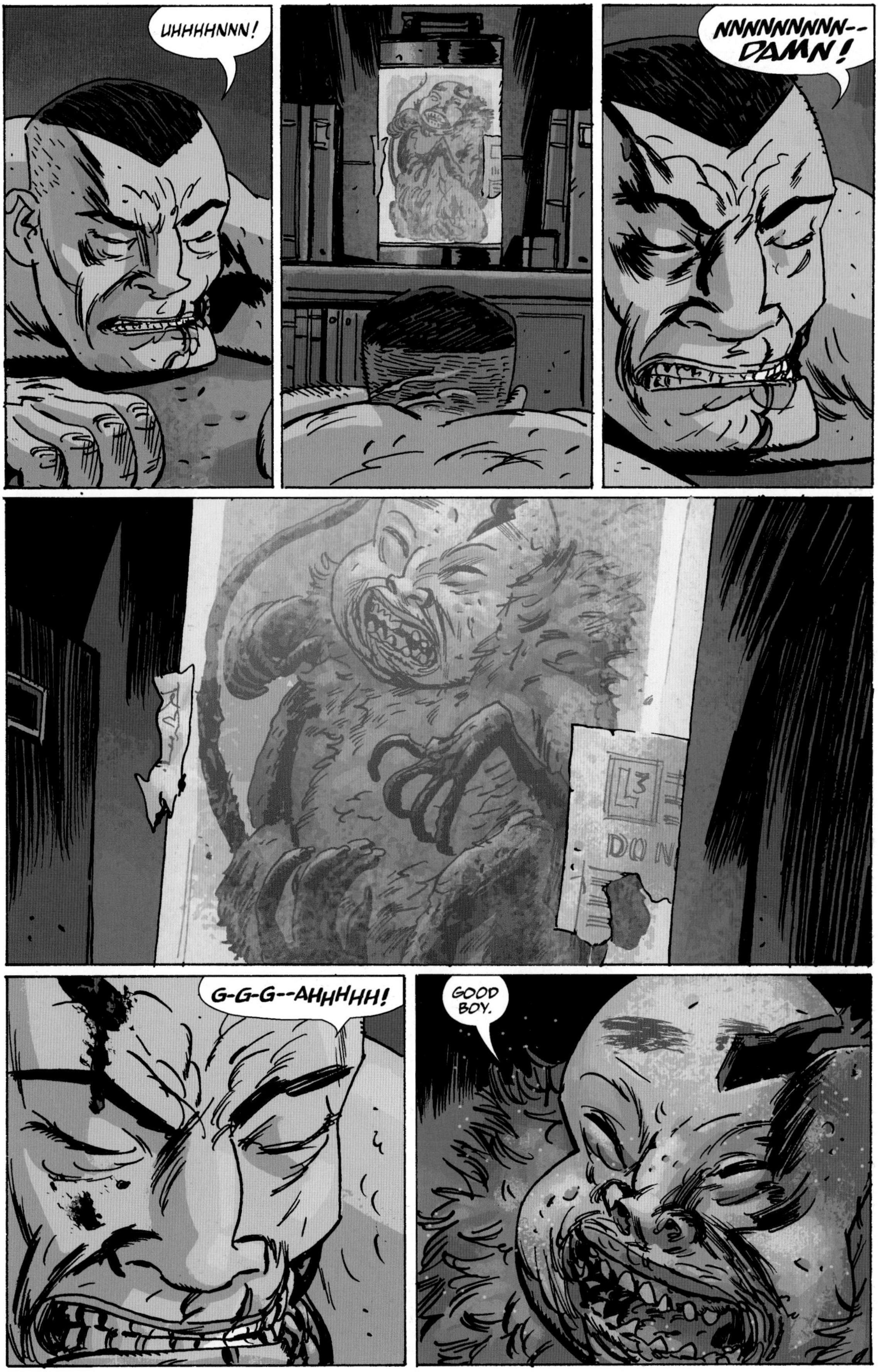
UHHHHNNN!
NNNNNNNNN--DAMN!
G-G-G--AHHHHHH!
GOOD BOY.

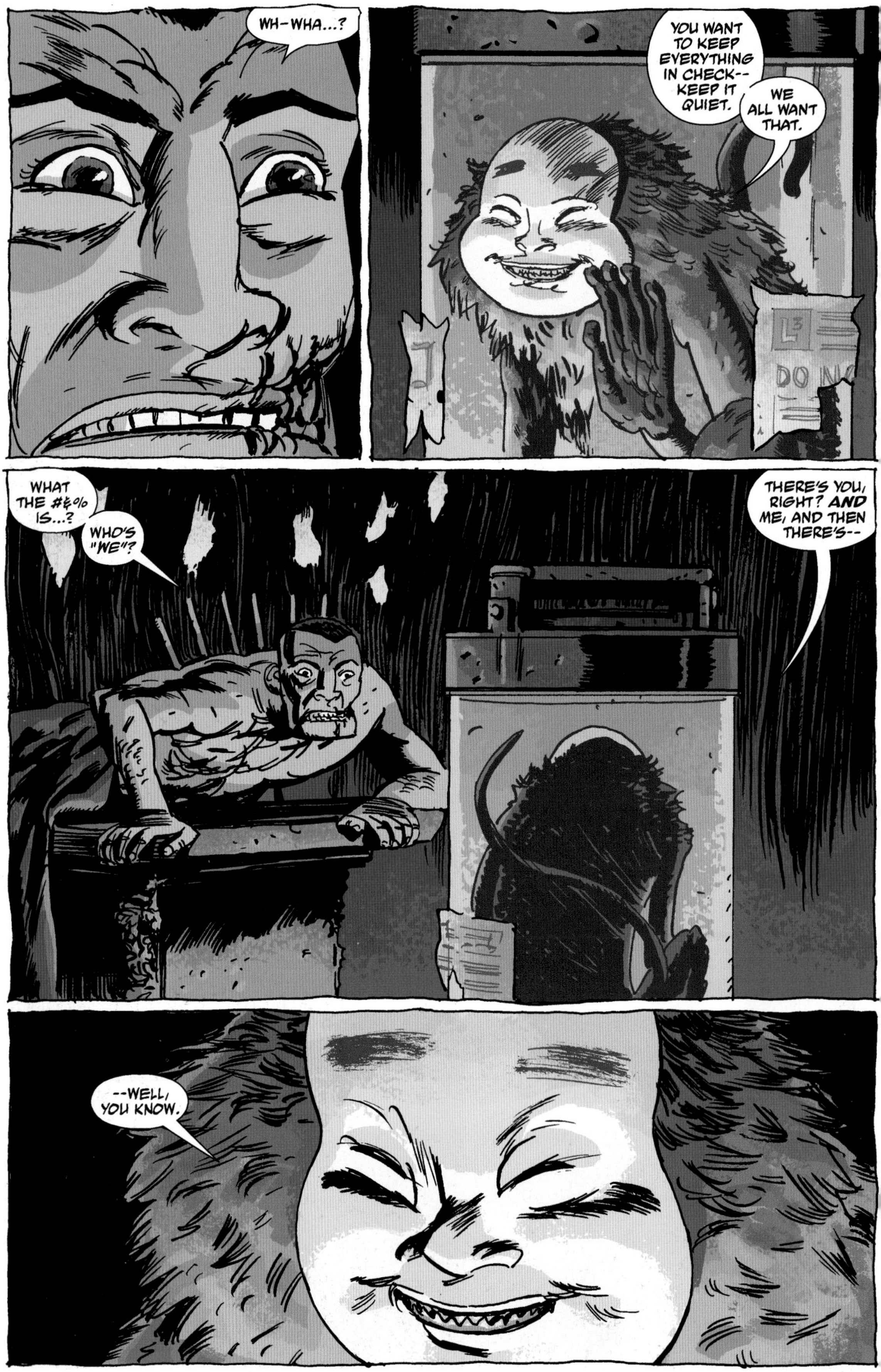
WH-WHA...?
YOU WANT TO KEEP EVERYTHING IN CHECK-- KEEP IT QUIET.
WE ALL WANT THAT.
WHAT THE #&% IS...?
WHO'S "WE"?
THERE'S YOU, RIGHT? AND ME, AND THEN THERE'S--
--WELL, YOU KNOW.

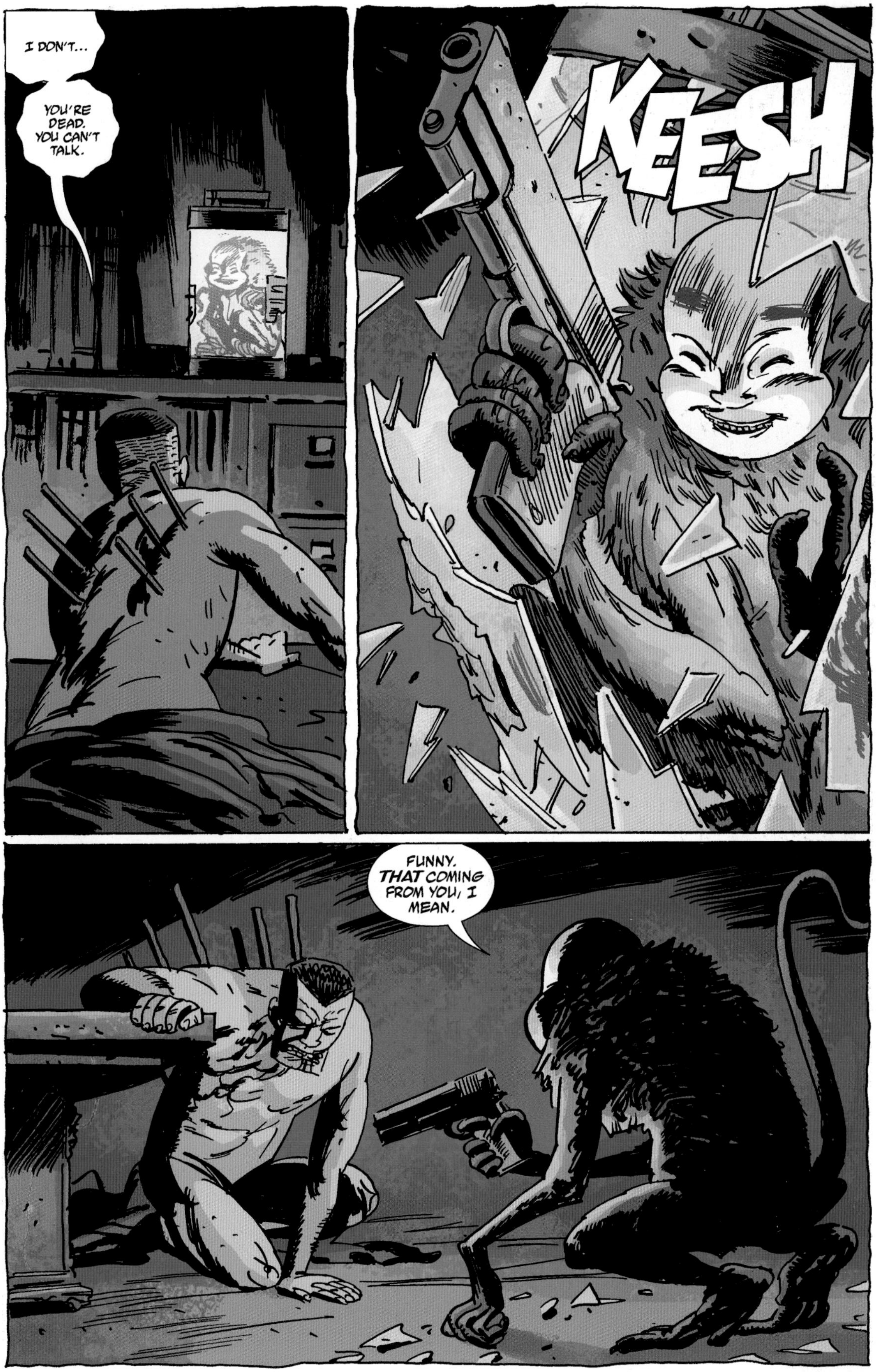
I DON'T...
YOU'RE DEAD. YOU CAN'T TALK.
KEESH
FUNNY. THAT COMING FROM YOU, I MEAN.

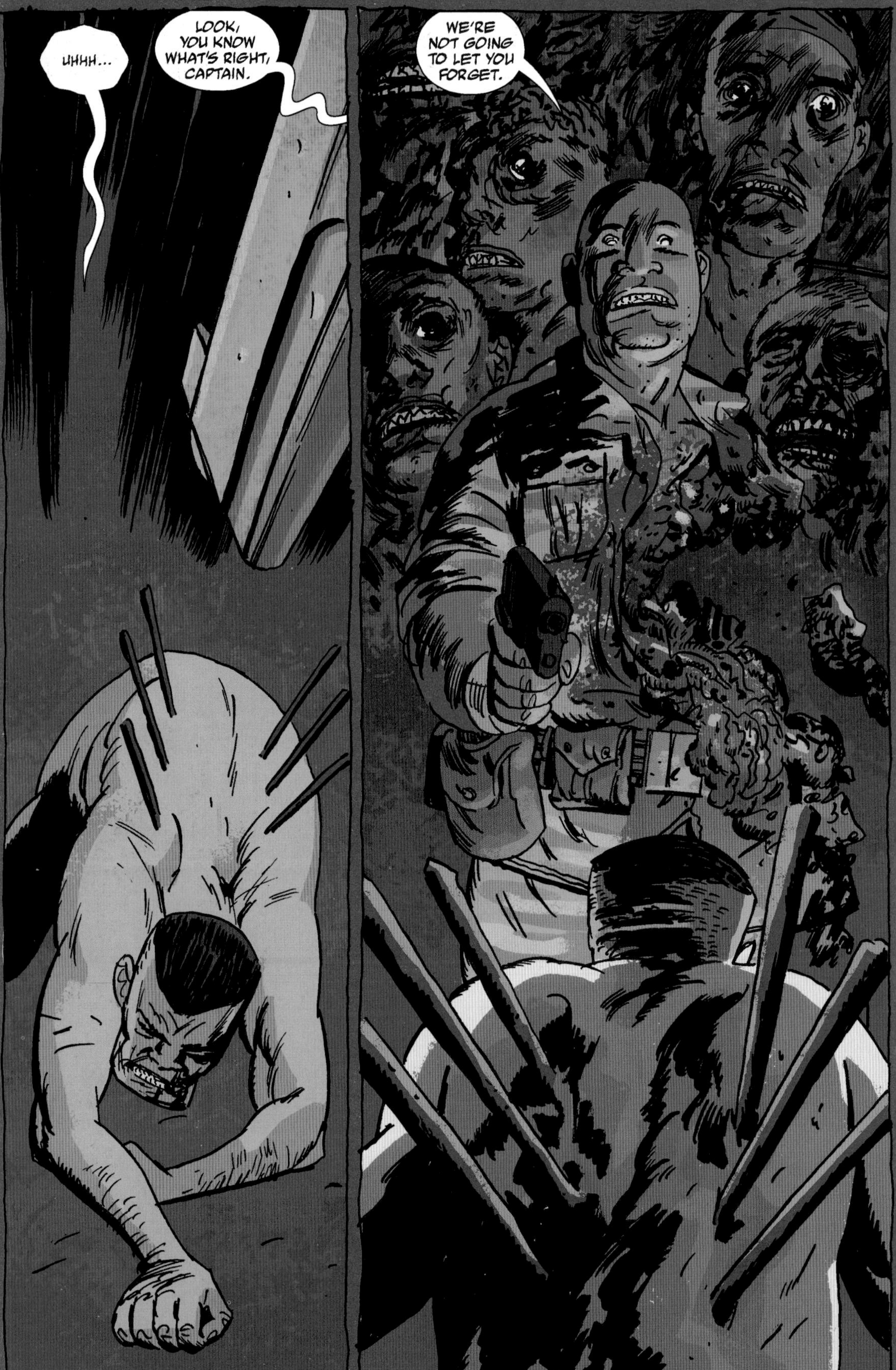
UHHH...
LOOK, YOU KNOW WHAT'S RIGHT, CAPTAIN.
WE'RE NOT GOING TO LET YOU FORGET.

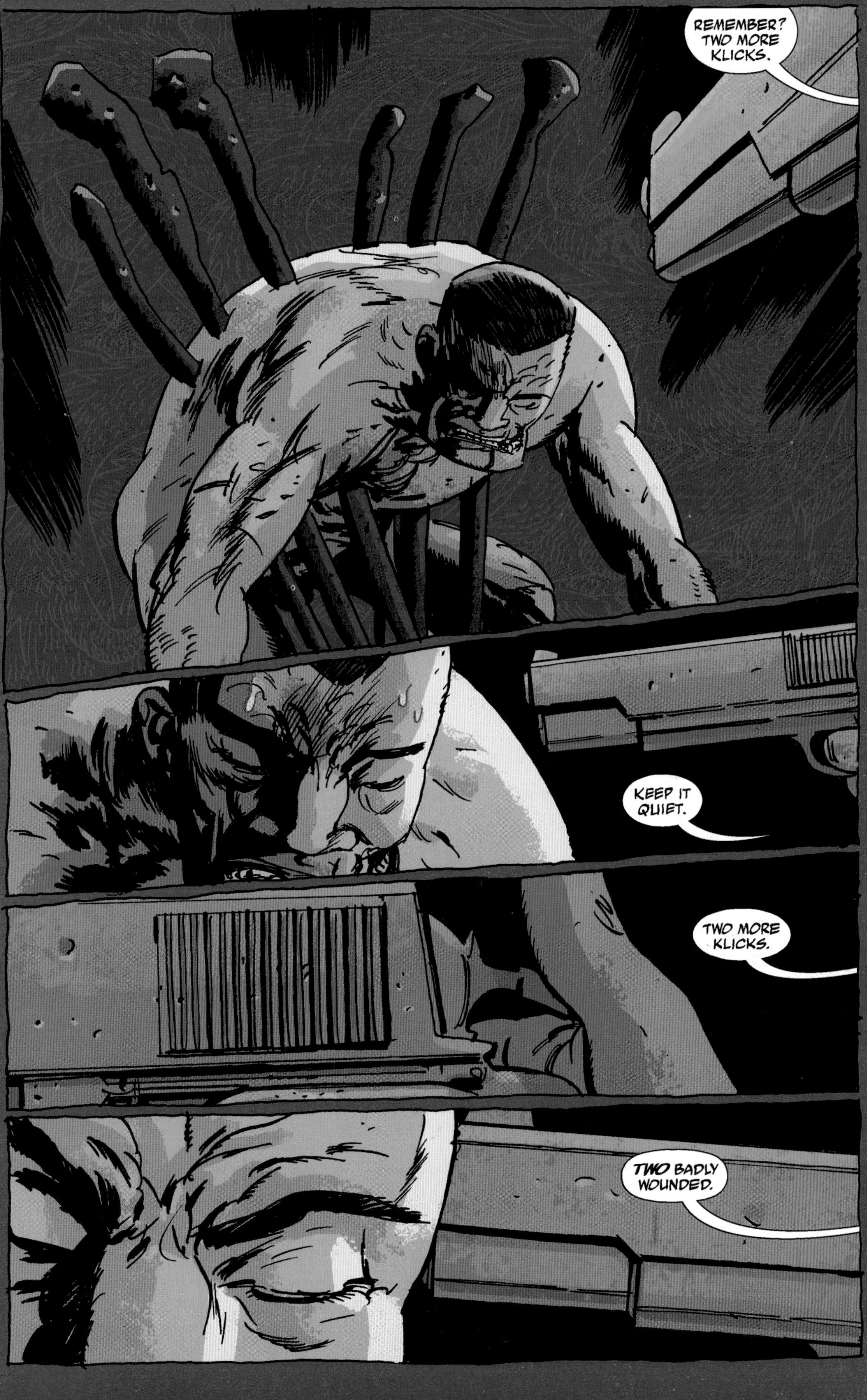
REMEMBER? TWO MORE KLICKS.
KEEP IT QUIET.
TWO MORE KLICKS.
TWO BADLY WOUNDED.

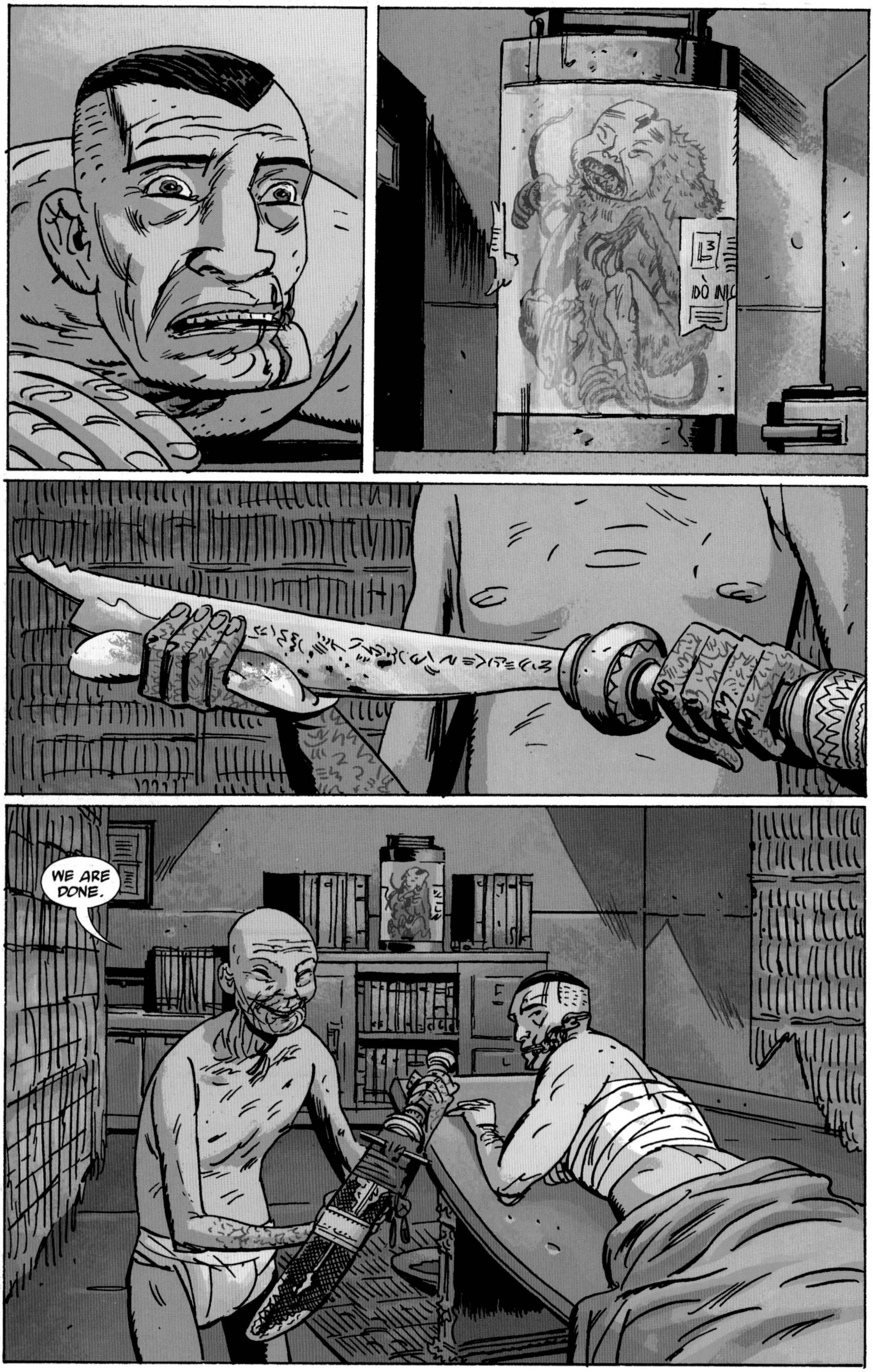
WE ARE DONE.

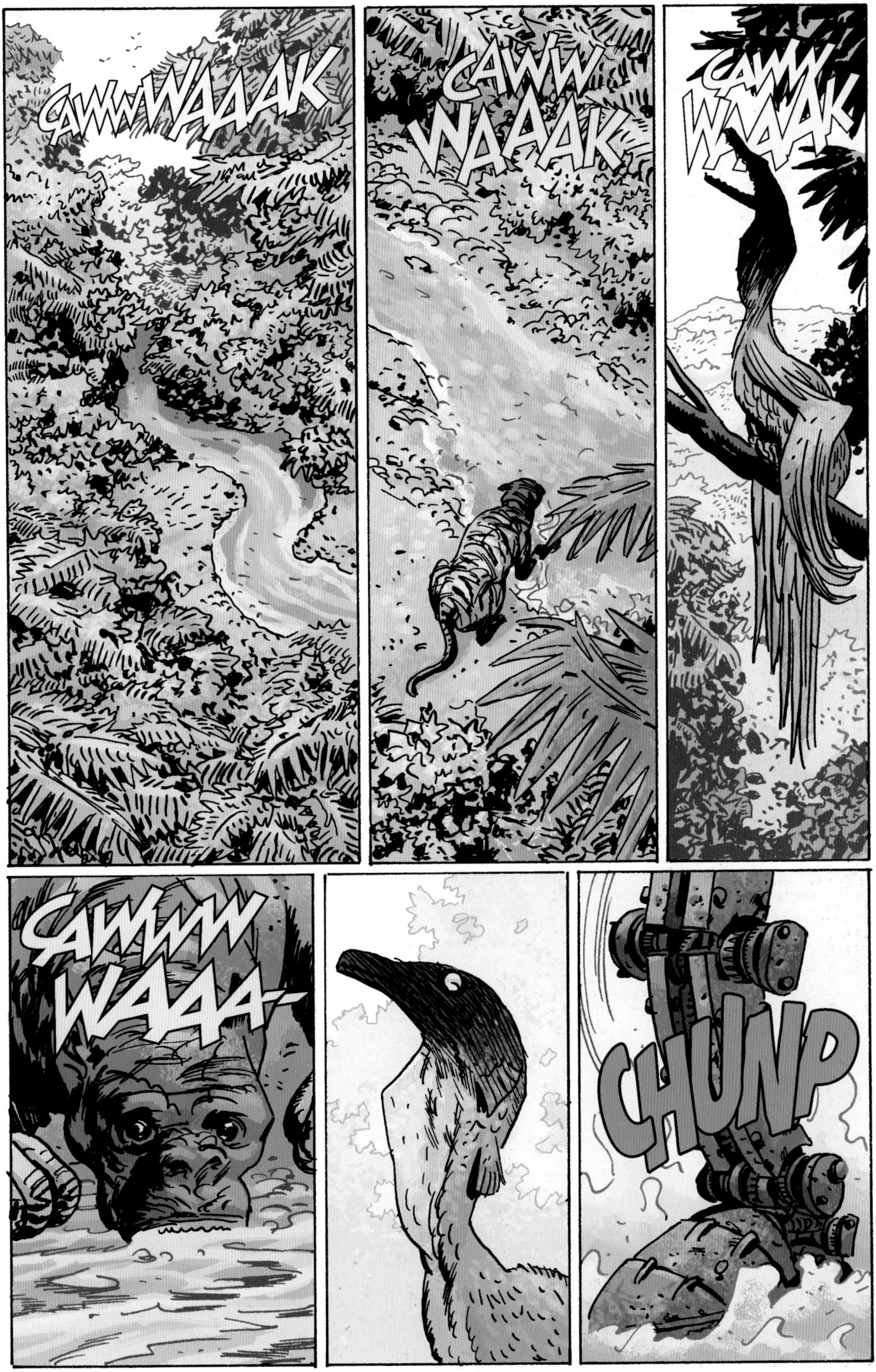
CAWWWAAAK
CAWW WAAAK
CAWW WAAAK
CAWWW WAAA-
CHUNP

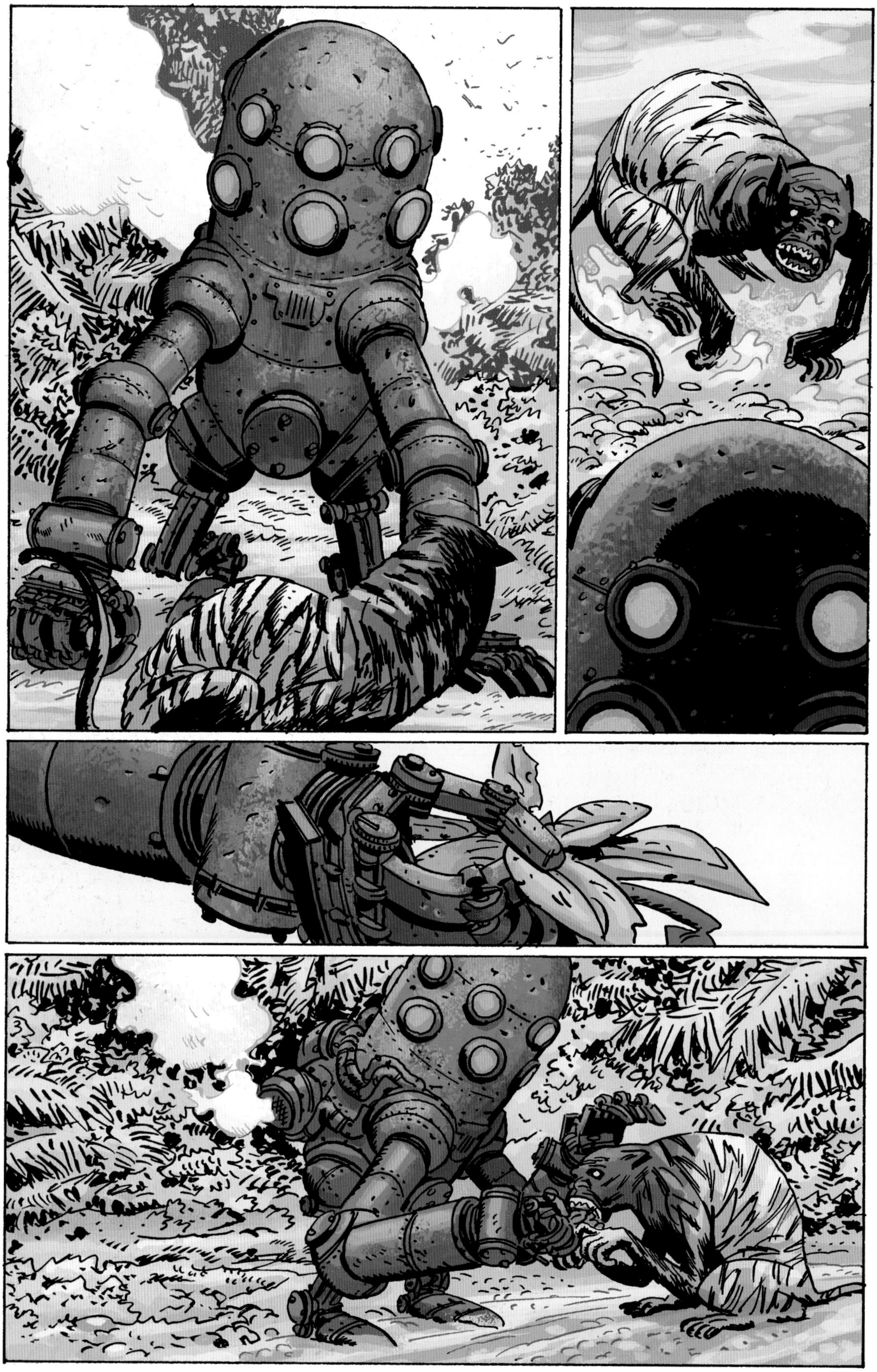

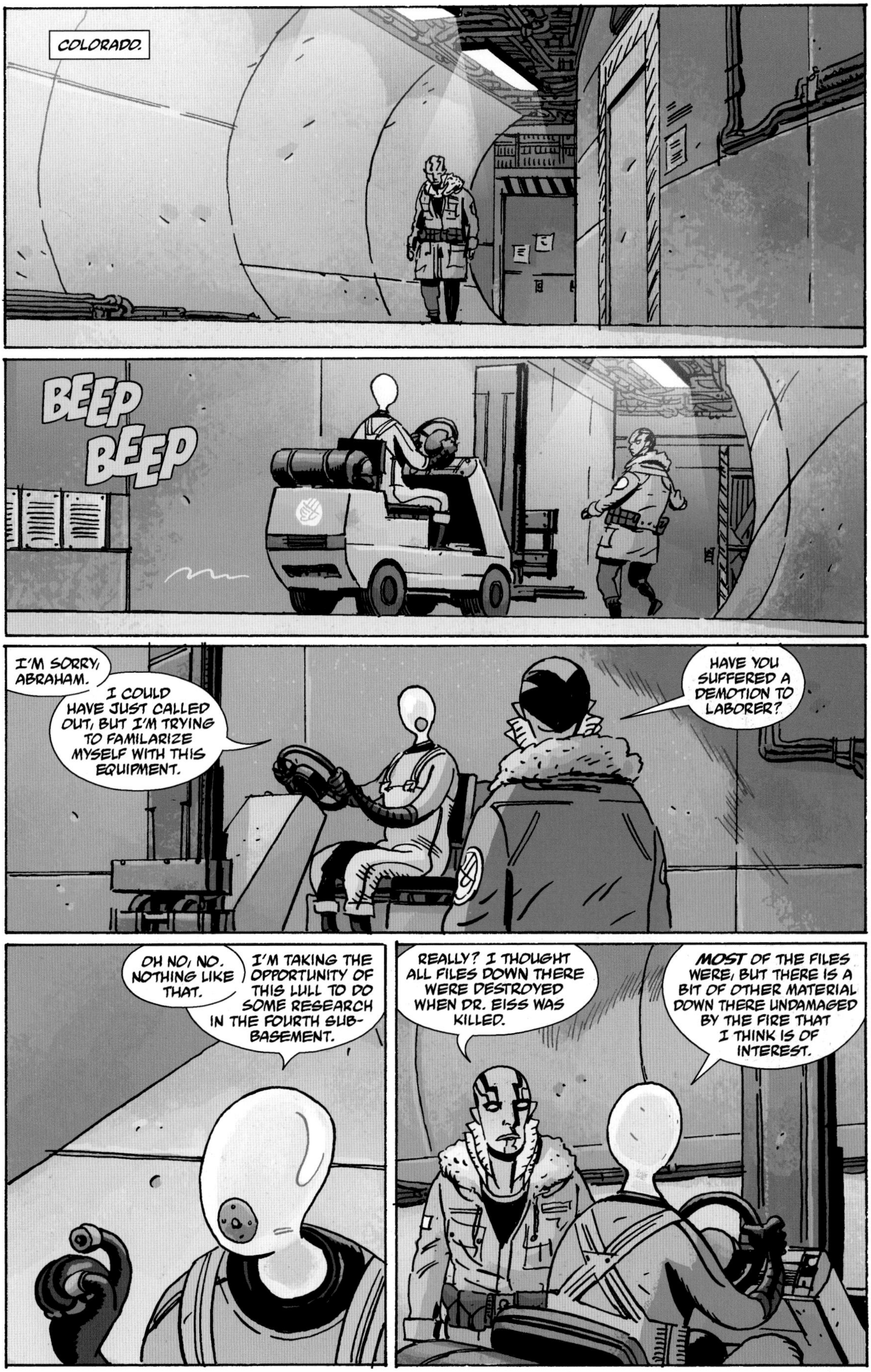
COLORADO.
BEEP BEEP
I'M SORRY, ABRAHAM.
I COULD HAVE JUST CALLED OUT, BUT I'M TRYING TO FAMILARIZE MYSELF WITH THIS EQUIPMENT.
HAVE YOU SUFFERED A DEMOTION TO LABORER?
OH NO, NO. NOTHING LIKE THAT.
I'M TAKING THE OPPORTUNITY OF THIS LULL TO DO SOME RESEARCH IN THE FOURTH SUB-BASEMENT.
REALLY? I THOUGHT ALL FILES DOWN THERE WERE DESTROYED WHEN DR. EISS WAS KILLED.
MOST OF THE FILES WERE, BUT THERE IS A BIT OF OTHER MATERIAL DOWN THERE UNDAMAGED BY THE FIRE THAT I THINK IS OF INTEREST.

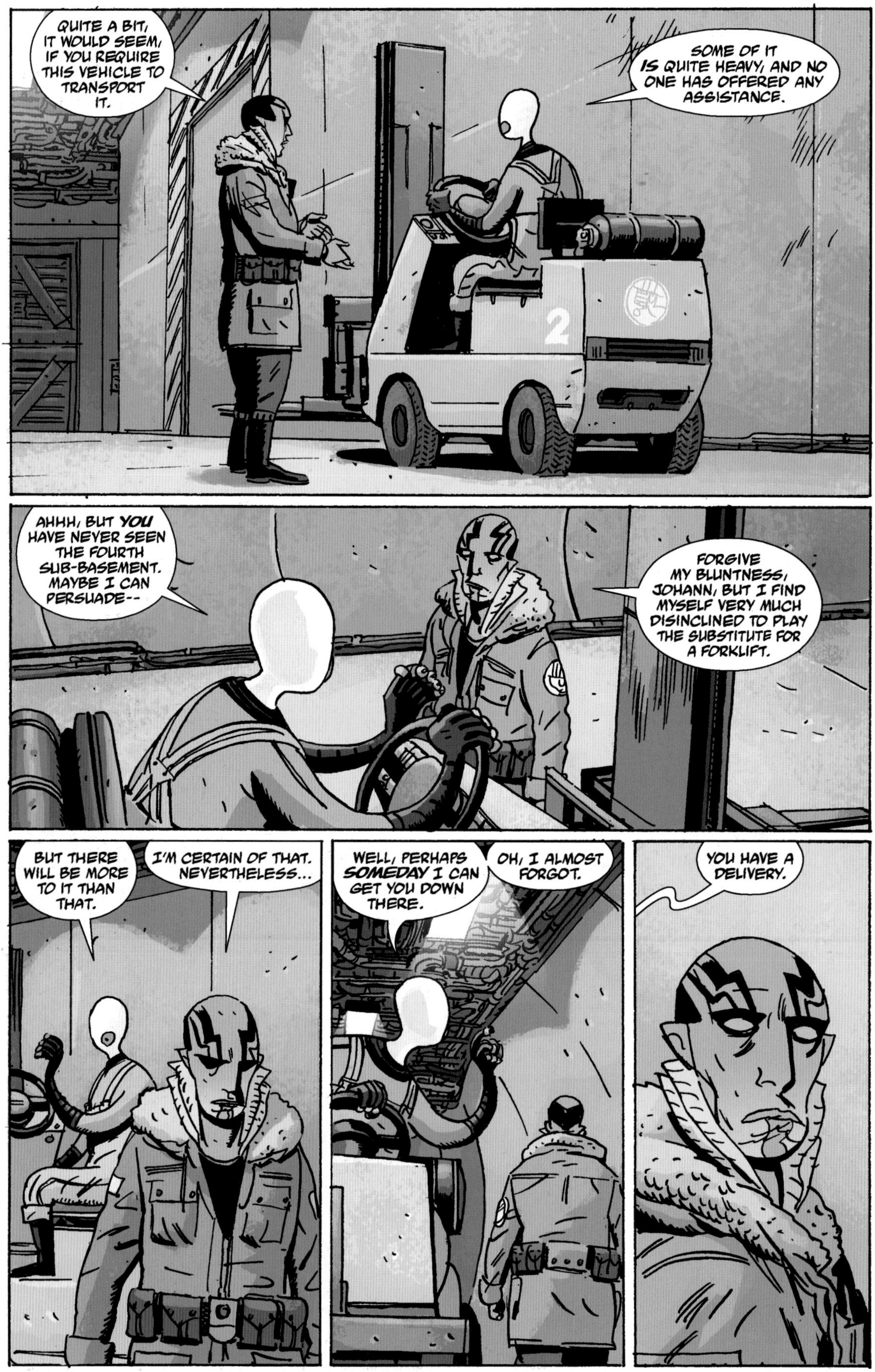
QUITE A BIT, IT WOULD SEEM, IF YOU REQUIRE THIS VEHICLE TO TRANSPORT IT.
SOME OF IT *IS* QUITE HEAVY, AND NO ONE HAS OFFERED ANY ASSISTANCE.
AHHH, BUT *YOU* HAVE NEVER SEEN THE FOURTH SUB-BASEMENT. MAYBE I CAN PERSUADE--
FORGIVE MY BLUNTNESS, JOHANN, BUT I FIND MYSELF VERY MUCH DISINCLINED TO PLAY THE SUBSTITUTE FOR A FORKLIFT.
BUT THERE WILL BE MORE TO IT THAN THAT.
I'M CERTAIN OF THAT. NEVERTHELESS...
WELL, PERHAPS *SOMEDAY* I CAN GET YOU DOWN THERE.
OH, I ALMOST FORGOT.
YOU HAVE A DELIVERY.
2

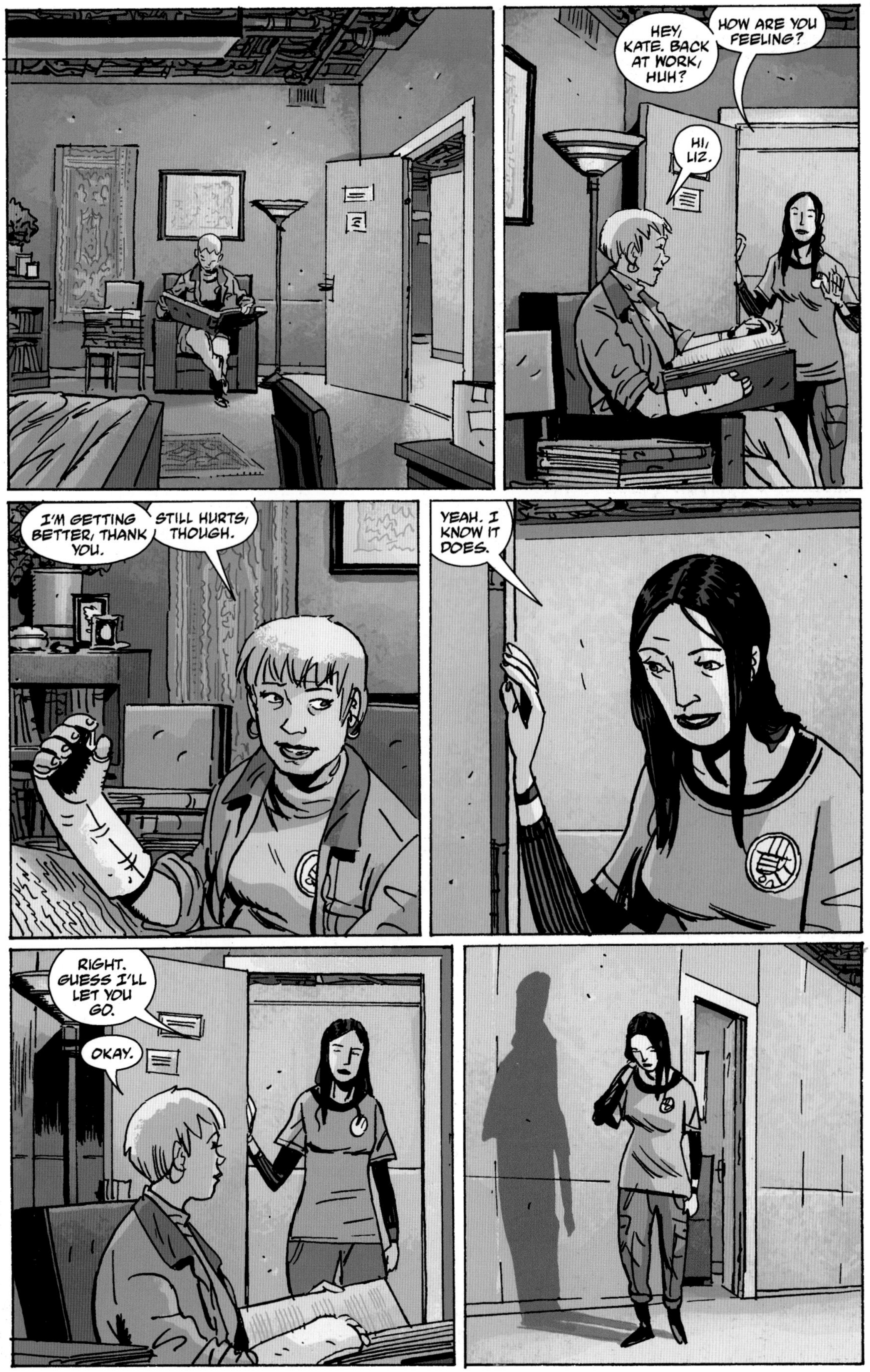
HEY, KATE. BACK AT WORK, HUH?
HOW ARE YOU FEELING?
HI, LIZ.
I'M GETTING BETTER, THANK YOU.
STILL HURTS, THOUGH.
YEAH. I KNOW IT DOES.
RIGHT. GUESS I'LL LET YOU GO.
OKAY.

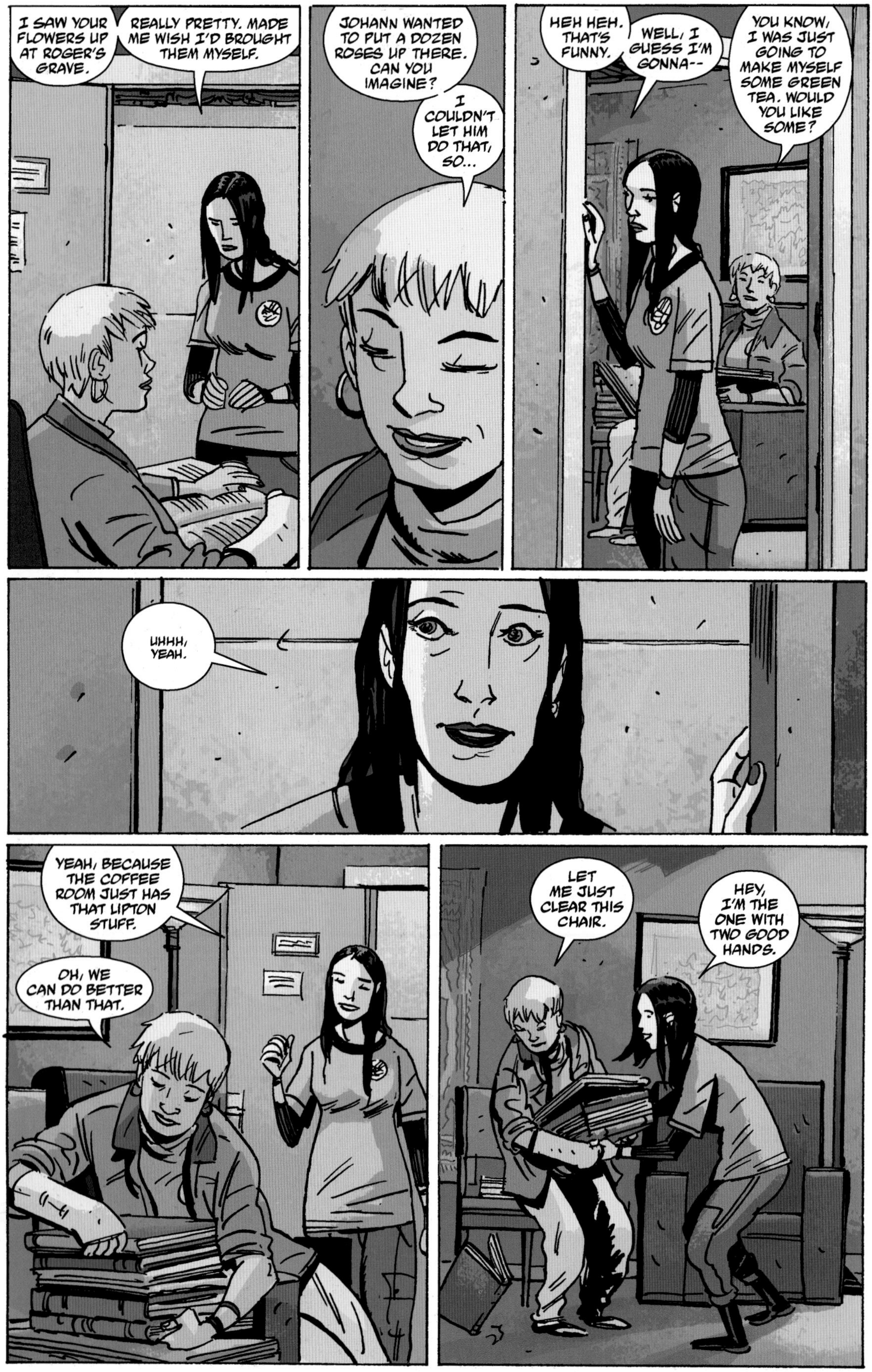
I SAW YOUR FLOWERS UP AT ROGER'S GRAVE.
REALLY PRETTY. MADE ME WISH I'D BROUGHT THEM MYSELF.
JOHANN WANTED TO PUT A DOZEN ROSES UP THERE. CAN YOU IMAGINE?
I COULDN'T LET HIM DO THAT, SO...
HEH HEH. THAT'S FUNNY.
WELL, I GUESS I'M GONNA--
YOU KNOW, I WAS JUST GOING TO MAKE MYSELF SOME GREEN TEA. WOULD YOU LIKE SOME?
UHHH, YEAH.
YEAH, BECAUSE THE COFFEE ROOM JUST HAS THAT LIPTON STUFF.
OH, WE CAN DO BETTER THAN THAT.
LET ME JUST CLEAR THIS CHAIR.
HEY, I'M THE ONE WITH TWO GOOD HANDS.

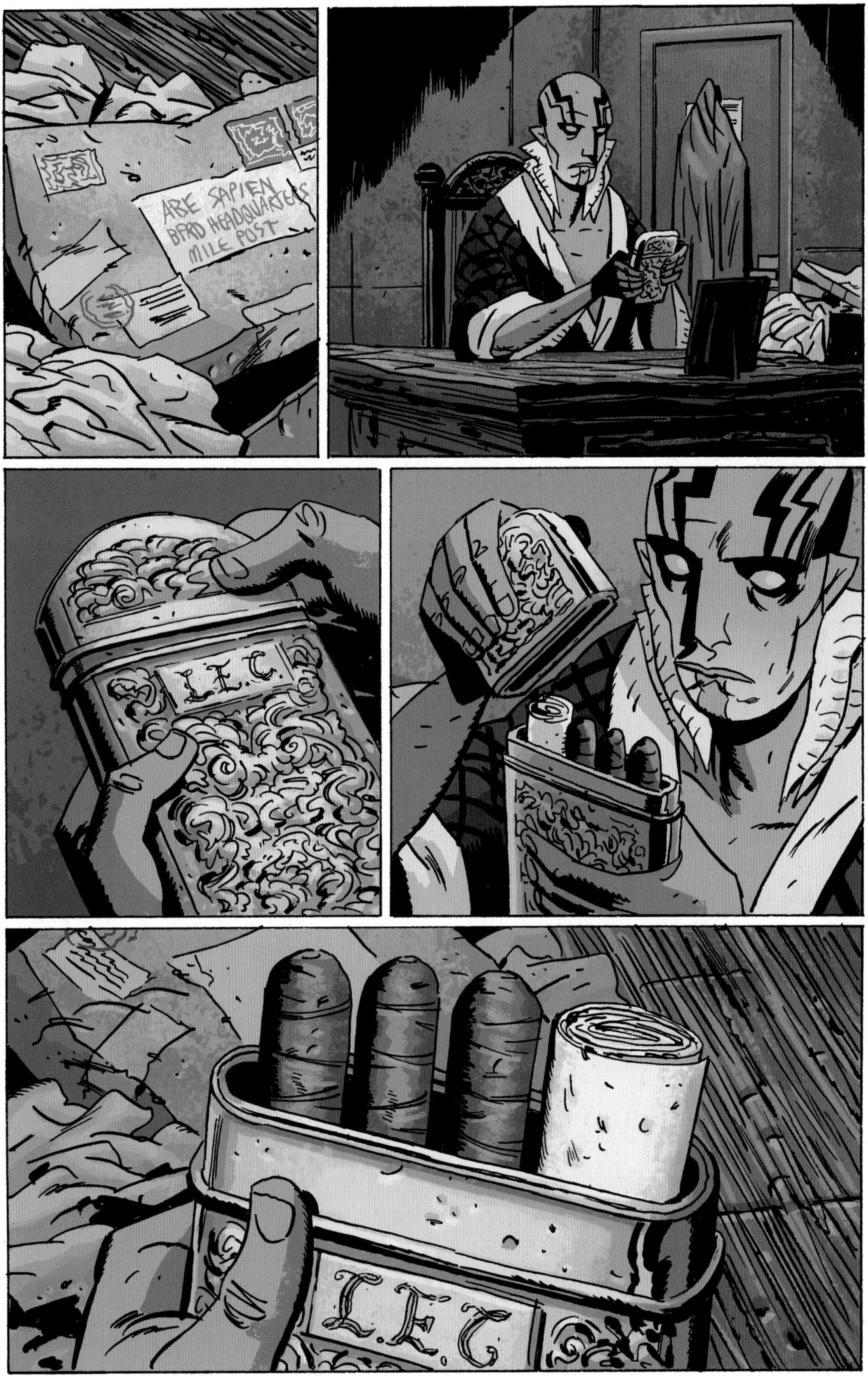
ABE SAPIEN
BPRD HEADQUARTERS
MILE POST
L.E.C.
L.E.C.

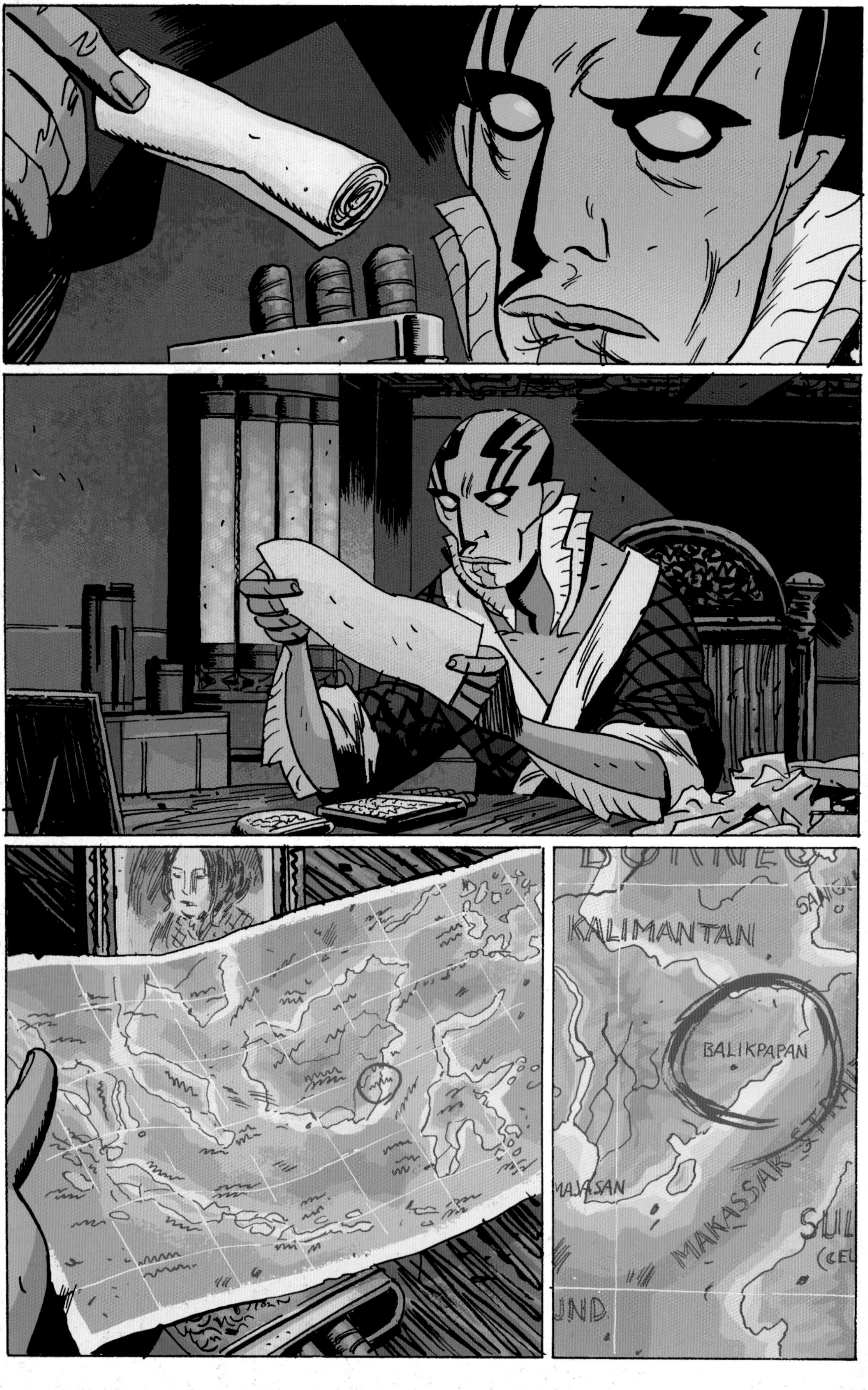
KALIMANTAN
BALIKPAPAN
MAKASSAR

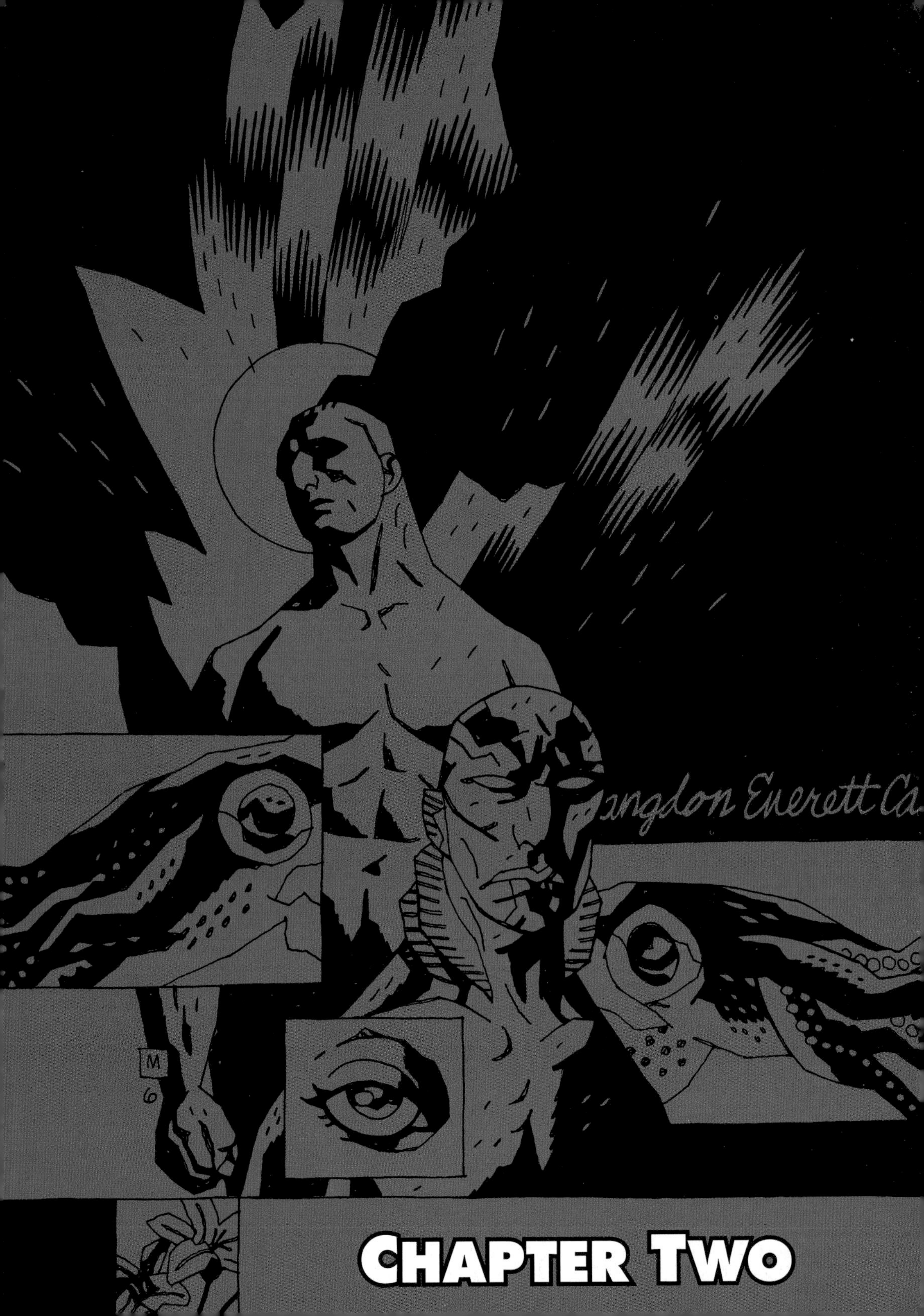
angdon Everett Ca

CHAPTER TWO

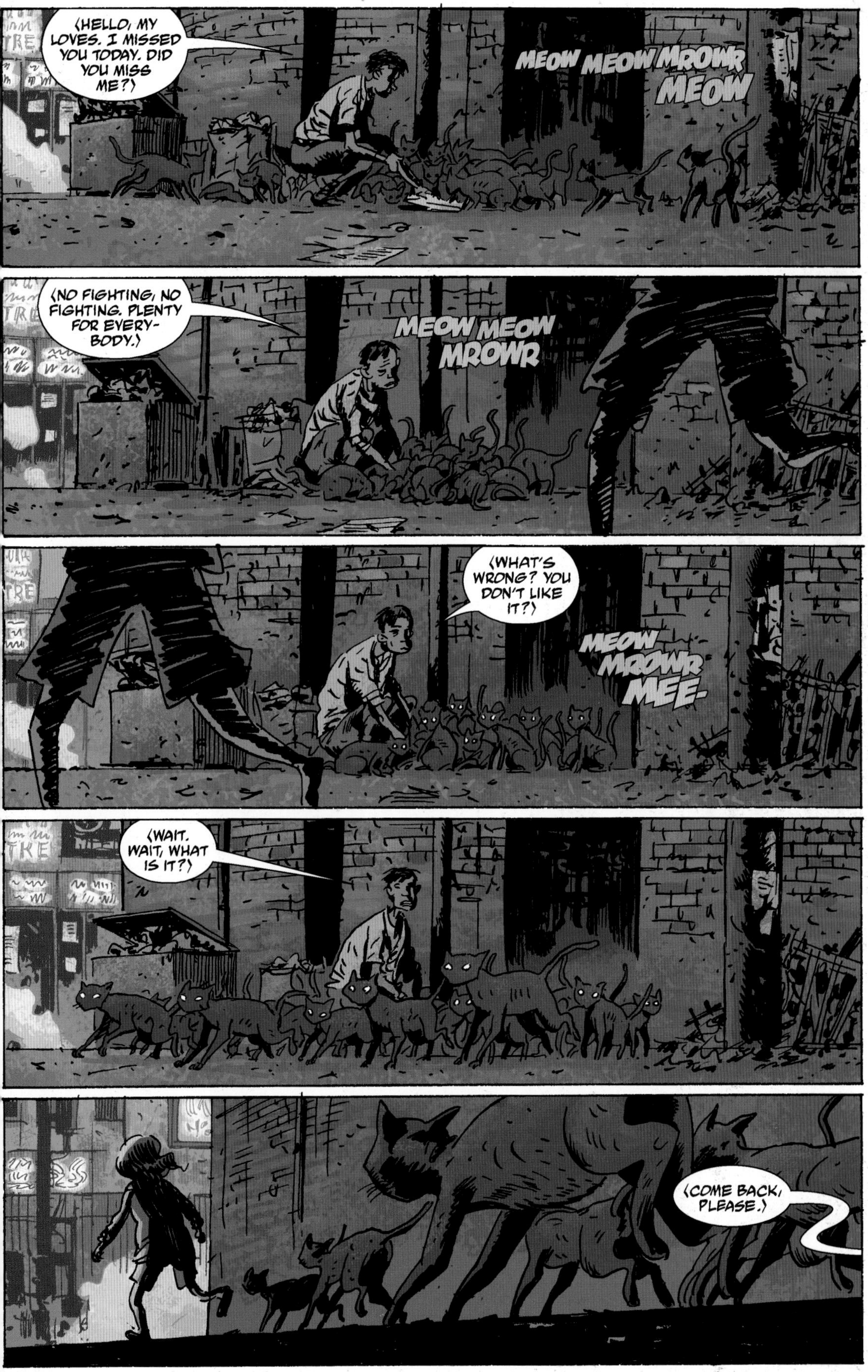
‹HELLO, MY LOVES. I MISSED YOU TODAY. DID YOU MISS ME?›
MEOW MEOW MROWR MEOW
‹NO FIGHTING, NO FIGHTING. PLENTY FOR EVERY-BODY.›
MEOW MEOW MROWR
‹WHAT'S WRONG? YOU DON'T LIKE IT?›
MEOW MROWR MEE-
‹WAIT. WAIT, WHAT IS IT?›
‹COME BACK, PLEASE.›

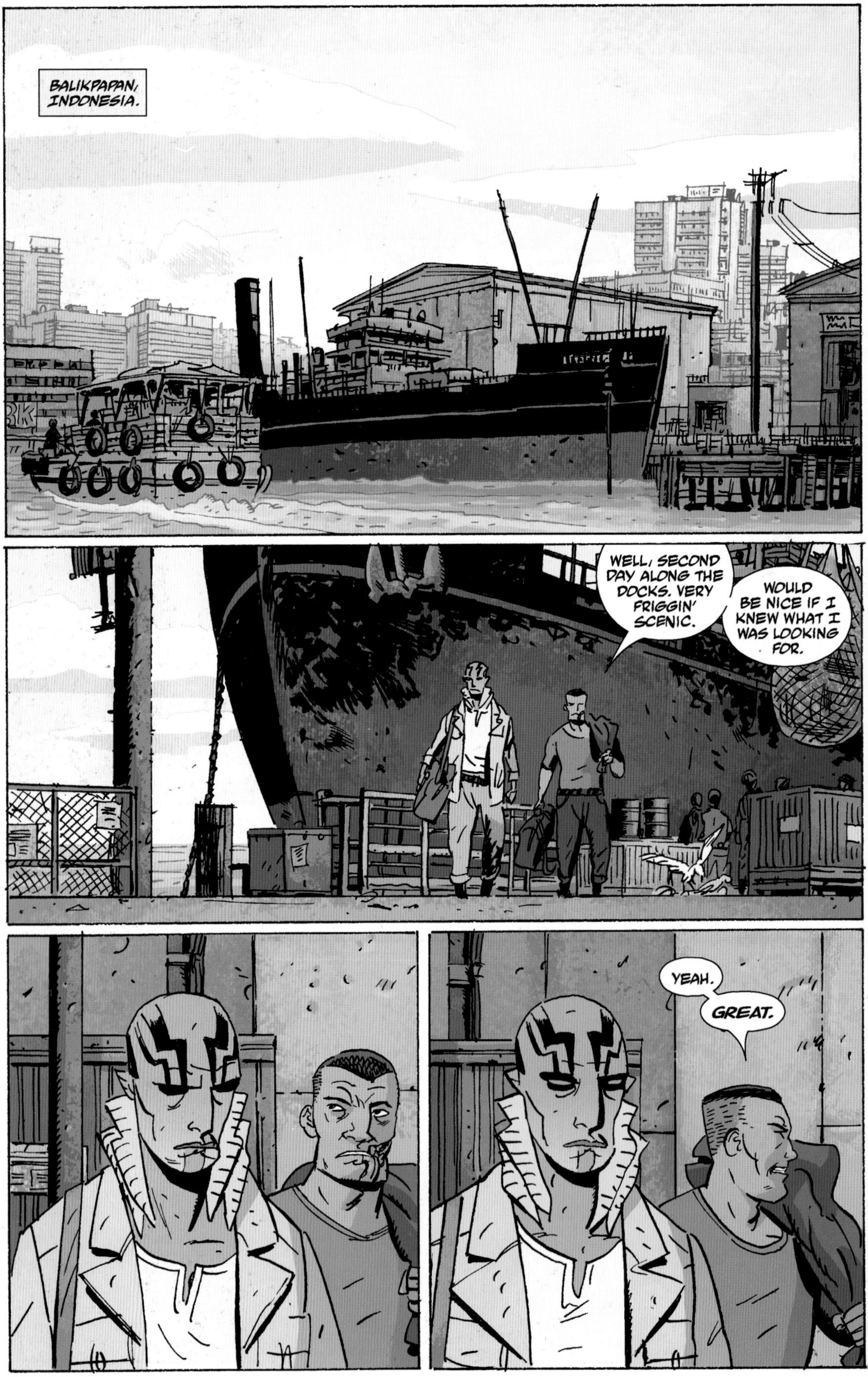
BALIKPAPAN, INDONESIA.
WELL, SECOND DAY ALONG THE DOCKS. VERY FRIGGIN' SCENIC.
WOULD BE NICE IF I KNEW WHAT I WAS LOOKING FOR.
YEAH.
GREAT.

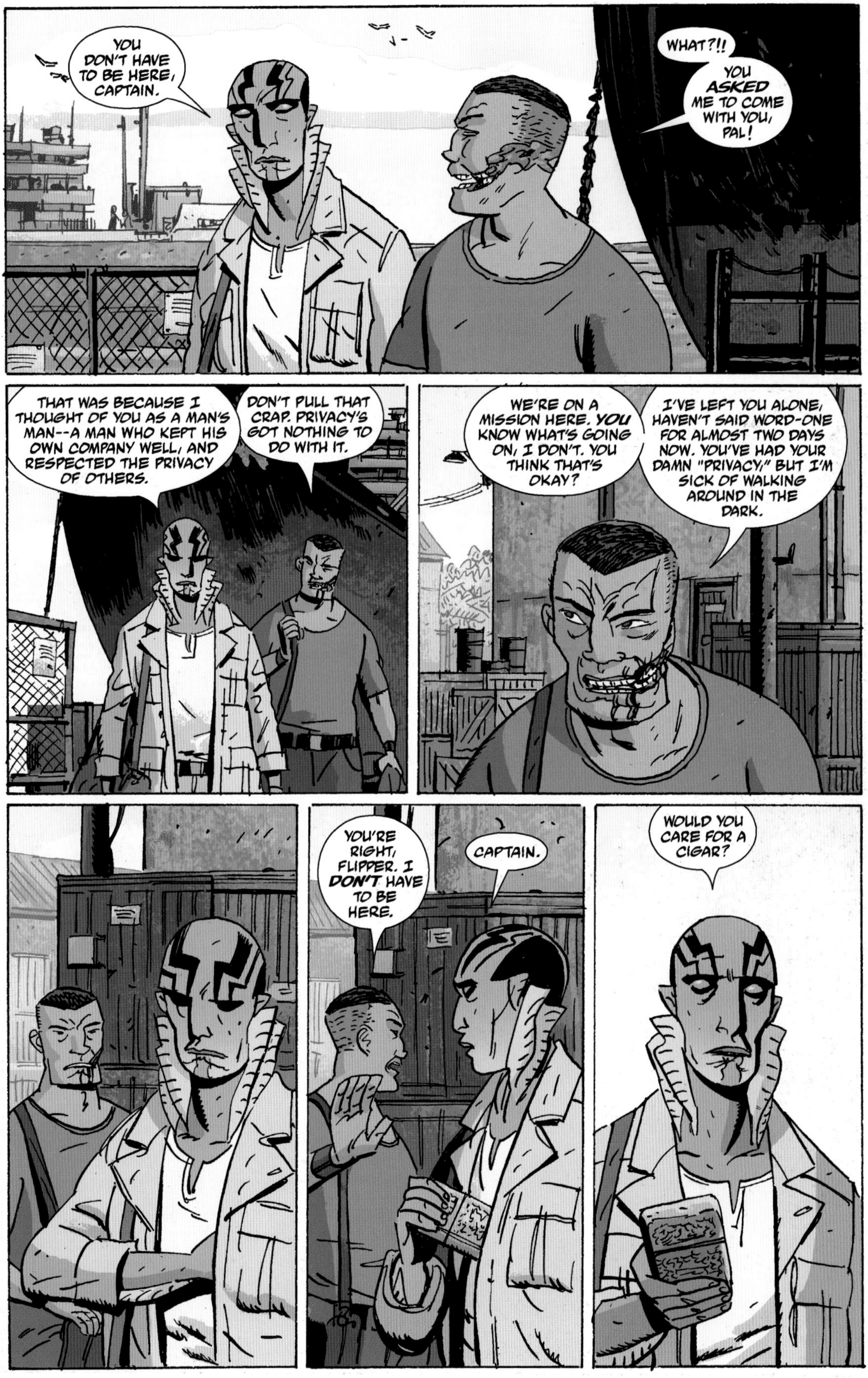
YOU DON'T HAVE TO BE HERE, CAPTAIN.
WHAT?!!
YOU ASKED ME TO COME WITH YOU, PAL!
THAT WAS BECAUSE I THOUGHT OF YOU AS A MAN'S MAN--A MAN WHO KEPT HIS OWN COMPANY WELL, AND RESPECTED THE PRIVACY OF OTHERS.
DON'T PULL THAT CRAP. PRIVACY'S GOT NOTHING TO DO WITH IT.
WE'RE ON A MISSION HERE. YOU KNOW WHAT'S GOING ON, I DON'T. YOU THINK THAT'S OKAY?
I'VE LEFT YOU ALONE, HAVEN'T SAID WORD-ONE FOR ALMOST TWO DAYS NOW. YOU'VE HAD YOUR DAMN "PRIVACY," BUT I'M SICK OF WALKING AROUND IN THE DARK.
YOU'RE RIGHT, FLIPPER. I DON'T HAVE TO BE HERE.
CAPTAIN.
WOULD YOU CARE FOR A CIGAR?

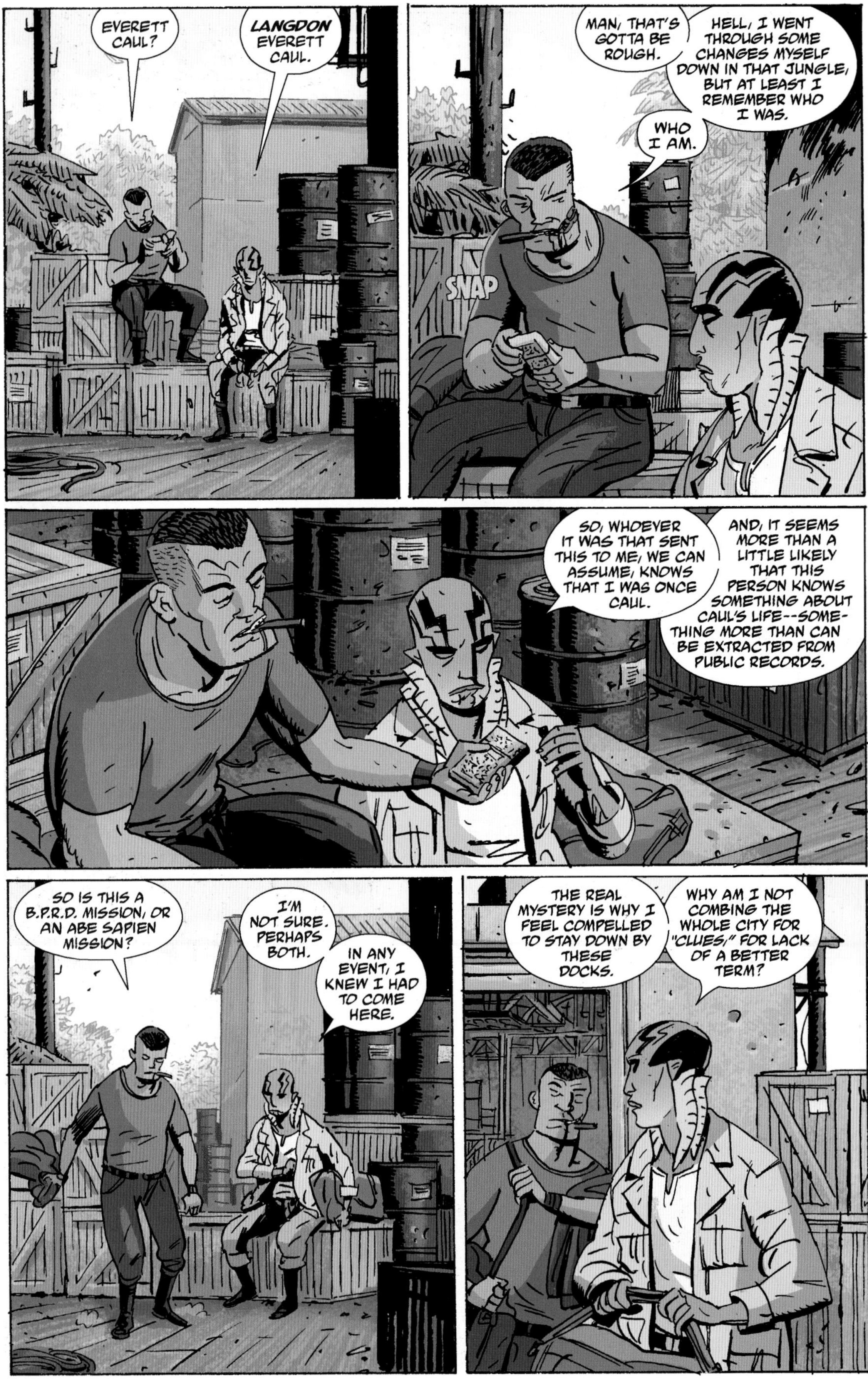
EVERETT CAUL?
LANGDON EVERETT CAUL.
MAN, THAT'S GOTTA BE ROUGH.
HELL, I WENT THROUGH SOME CHANGES MYSELF DOWN IN THAT JUNGLE, BUT AT LEAST I REMEMBER WHO I WAS.
WHO I AM.
SNAP
SO, WHOEVER IT WAS THAT SENT THIS TO ME, WE CAN ASSUME, KNOWS THAT I WAS ONCE CAUL.
AND, IT SEEMS MORE THAN A LITTLE LIKELY THAT THIS PERSON KNOWS SOMETHING ABOUT CAUL'S LIFE--SOMETHING MORE THAN CAN BE EXTRACTED FROM PUBLIC RECORDS.
SO IS THIS A B.P.R.D. MISSION, OR AN ABE SAPIEN MISSION?
I'M NOT SURE. PERHAPS BOTH.
IN ANY EVENT, I KNEW I HAD TO COME HERE.
THE REAL MYSTERY IS WHY I FEEL COMPELLED TO STAY DOWN BY THESE DOCKS.
WHY AM I NOT COMBING THE WHOLE CITY FOR "CLUES," FOR LACK OF A BETTER TERM?

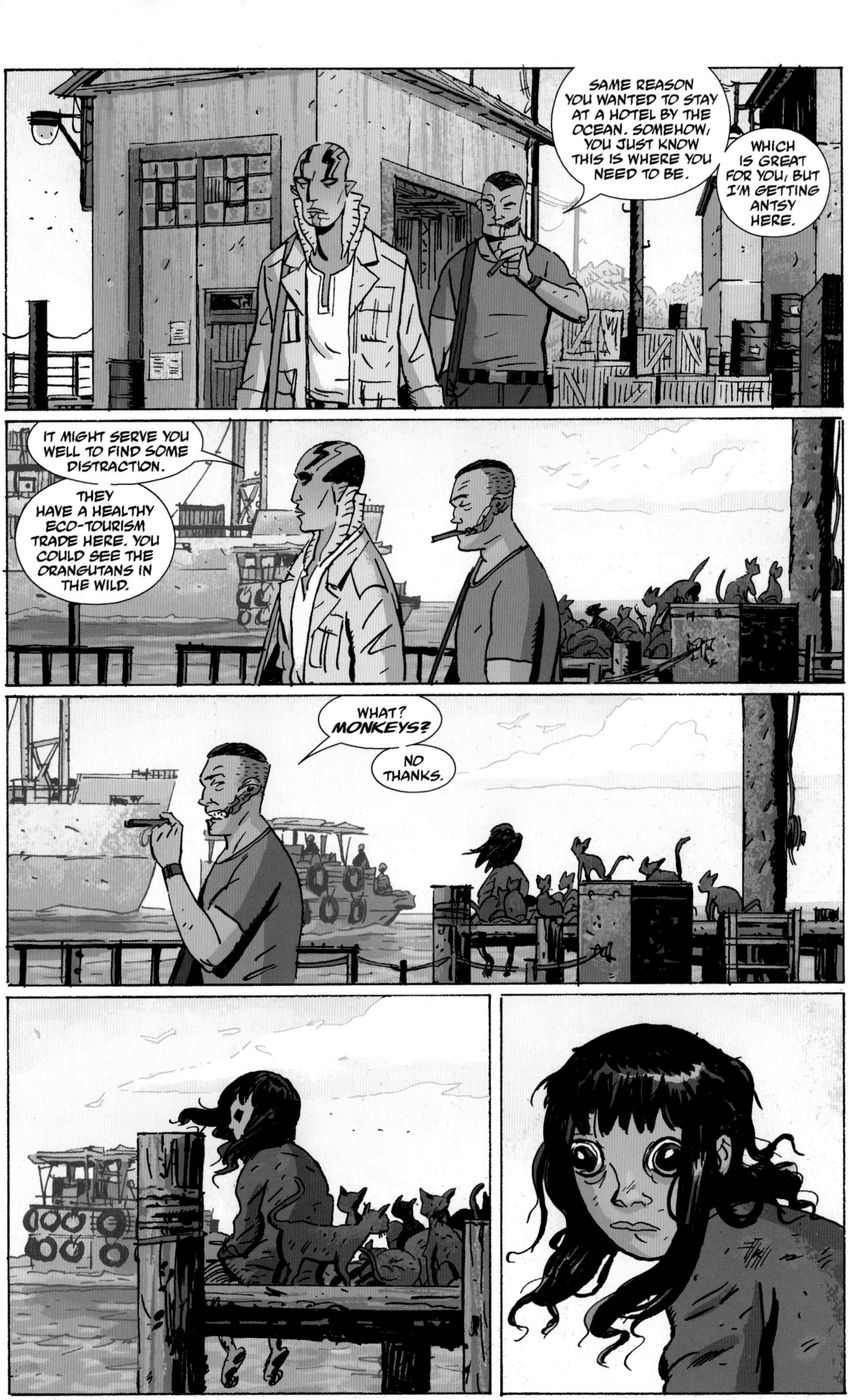
SAME REASON YOU WANTED TO STAY AT A HOTEL BY THE OCEAN. SOMEHOW, YOU JUST KNOW THIS IS WHERE YOU NEED TO BE.
WHICH IS GREAT FOR YOU, BUT I'M GETTING ANTSY HERE.
IT MIGHT SERVE YOU WELL TO FIND SOME DISTRACTION.
THEY HAVE A HEALTHY ECO-TOURISM TRADE HERE. YOU COULD SEE THE ORANGUTANS IN THE WILD.
WHAT? *MONKEYS?*
NO THANKS.

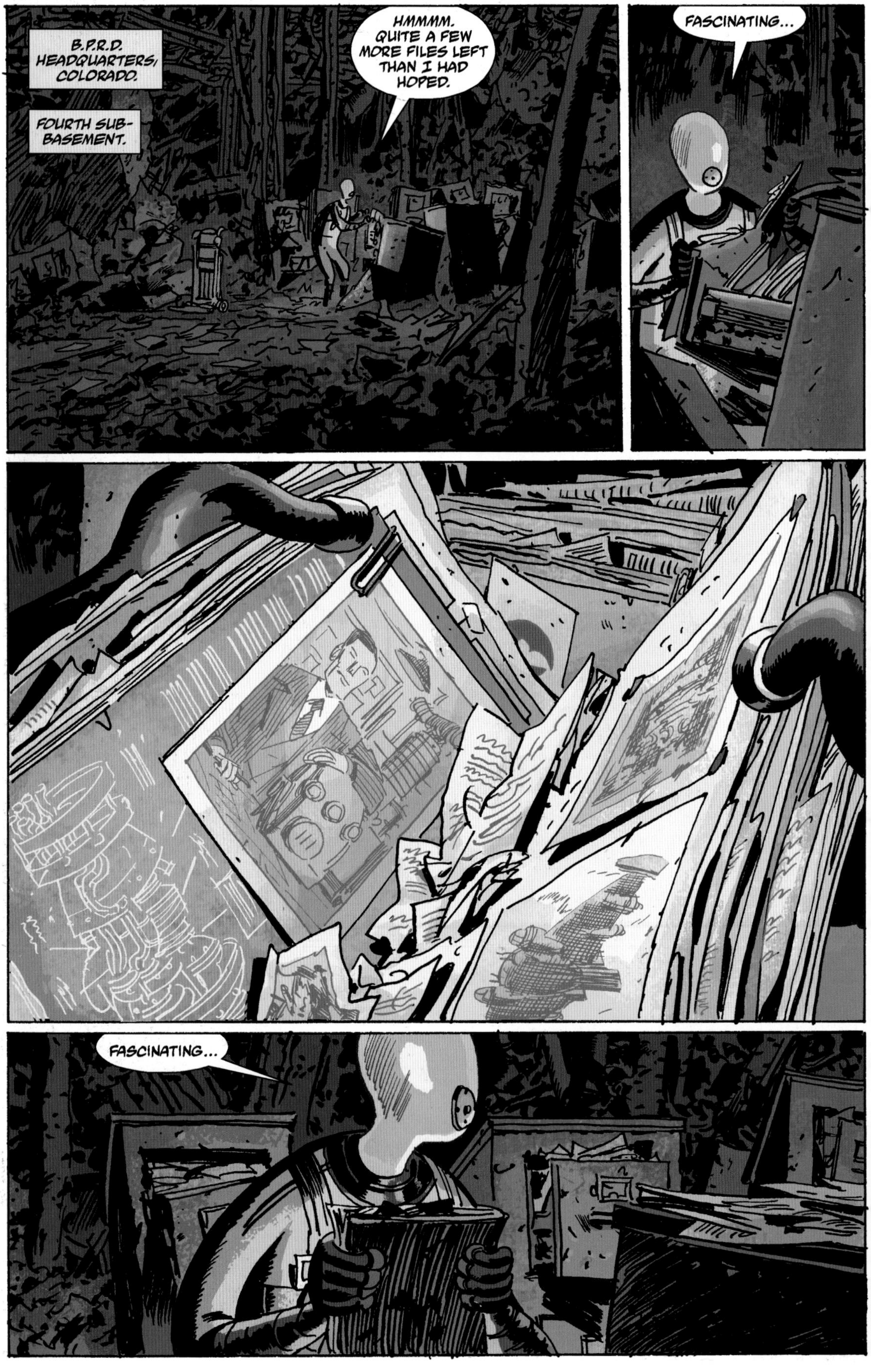
B.P.R.D. HEADQUARTERS, COLORADO.
FOURTH SUB-BASEMENT.
HMMMM. QUITE A FEW MORE FILES LEFT THAN I HAD HOPED.
FASCINATING...
FASCINATING...

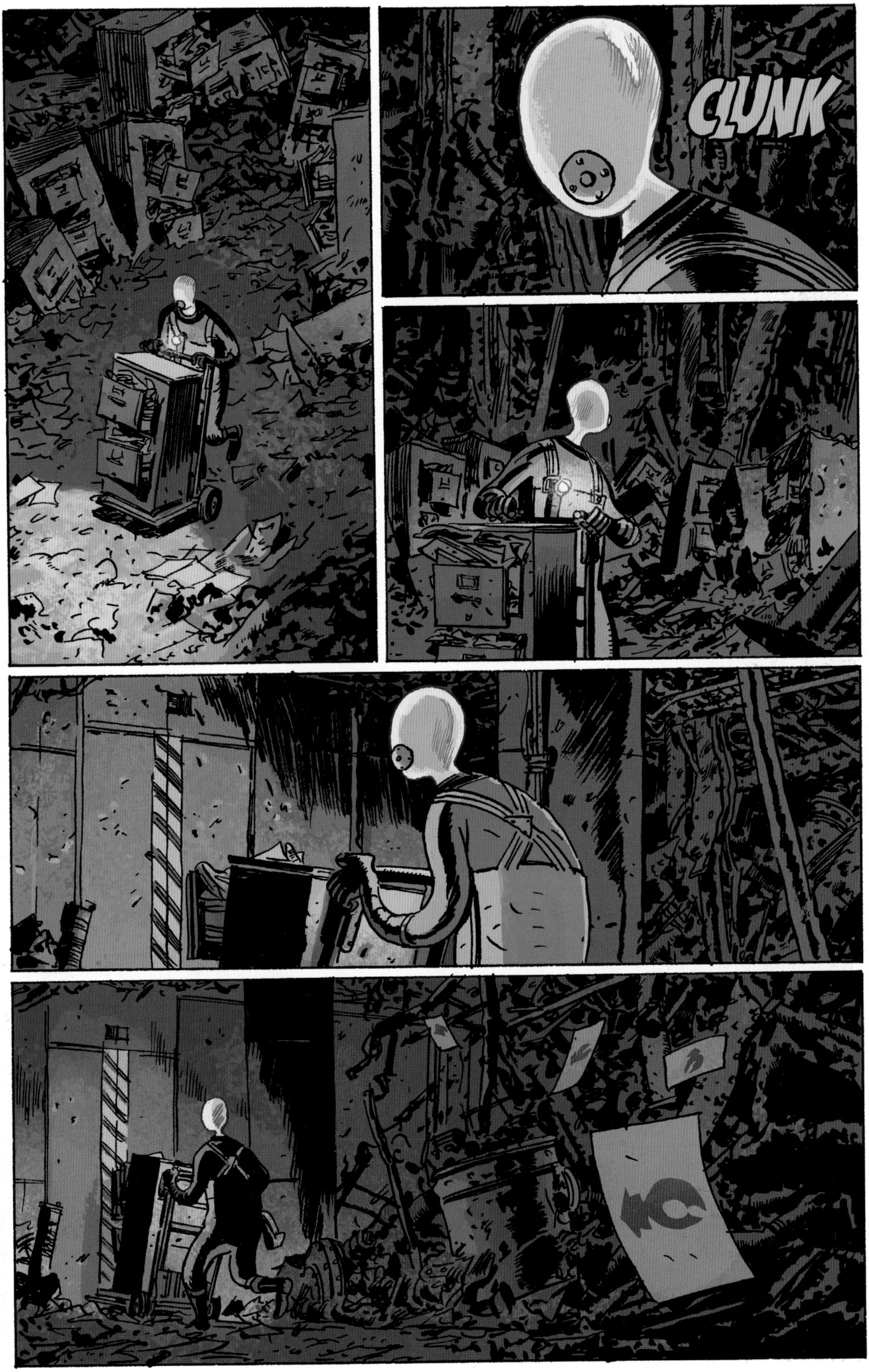
CLUNK

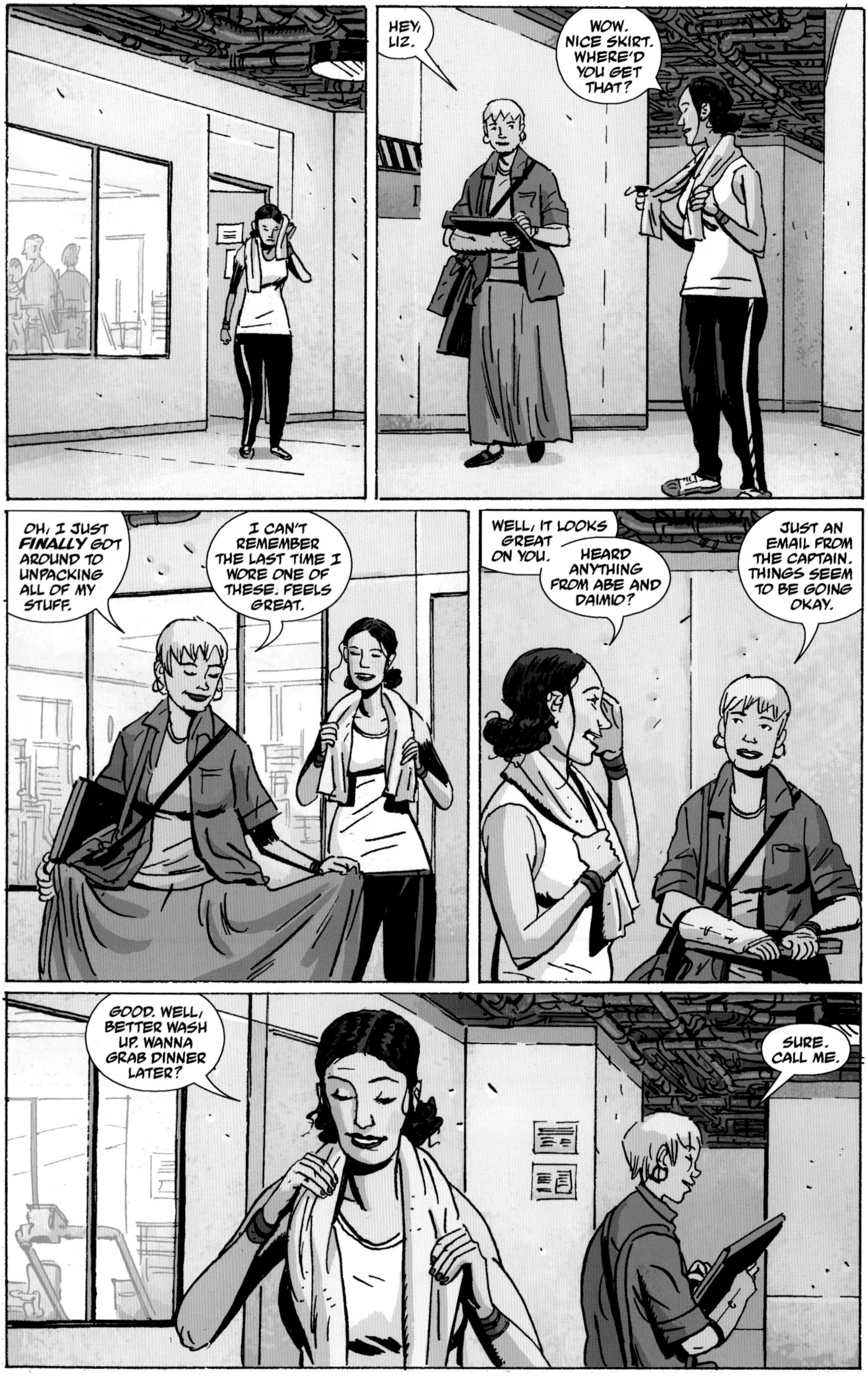
HEY, LIZ.
WOW. NICE SKIRT. WHERE'D YOU GET THAT?
OH, I JUST **FINALLY** GOT AROUND TO UNPACKING ALL OF MY STUFF.
I CAN'T REMEMBER THE LAST TIME I WORE ONE OF THESE. FEELS GREAT.
WELL, IT LOOKS GREAT ON YOU.
HEARD ANYTHING FROM ABE AND DAIMIO?
JUST AN EMAIL FROM THE CAPTAIN. THINGS SEEM TO BE GOING OKAY.
GOOD. WELL, BETTER WASH UP. WANNA GRAB DINNER LATER?
SURE. CALL ME.

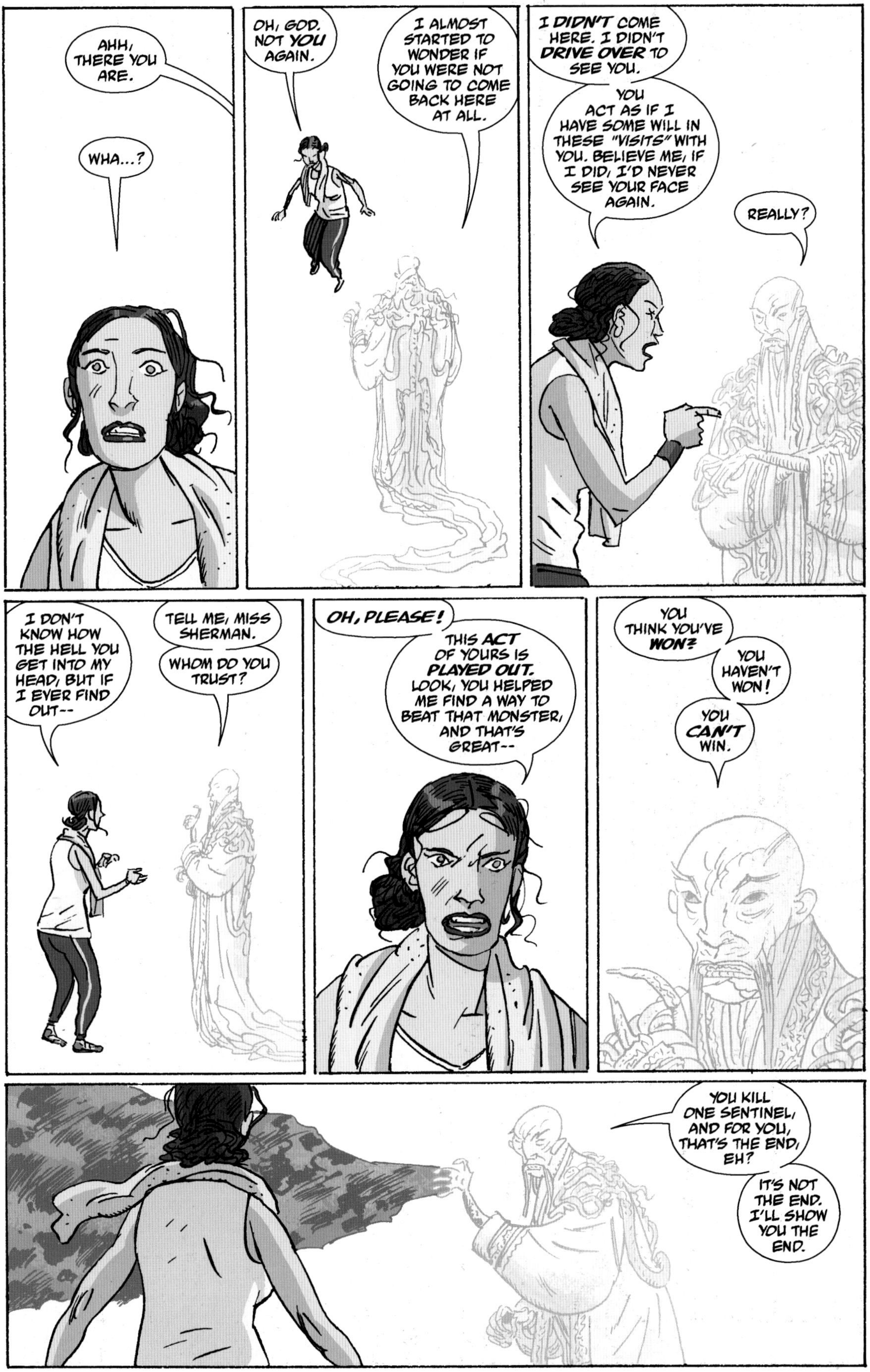
AHH, THERE YOU ARE.
WHA...?
OH, GOD. NOT YOU AGAIN.
I ALMOST STARTED TO WONDER IF YOU WERE NOT GOING TO COME BACK HERE AT ALL.
I DIDN'T COME HERE. I DIDN'T DRIVE OVER TO SEE YOU.
YOU ACT AS IF I HAVE SOME WILL IN THESE "VISITS" WITH YOU. BELIEVE ME, IF I DID, I'D NEVER SEE YOUR FACE AGAIN.
REALLY?
I DON'T KNOW HOW THE HELL YOU GET INTO MY HEAD, BUT IF I EVER FIND OUT--
TELL ME, MISS SHERMAN.
WHOM DO YOU TRUST?
OH, PLEASE!
THIS ACT OF YOURS IS PLAYED OUT. LOOK, YOU HELPED ME FIND A WAY TO BEAT THAT MONSTER, AND THAT'S GREAT--
YOU THINK YOU'VE WON?
YOU HAVEN'T WON!
YOU CAN'T WIN.
YOU KILL ONE SENTINEL, AND FOR YOU, THAT'S THE END, EH?
IT'S NOT THE END. I'LL SHOW YOU THE END.

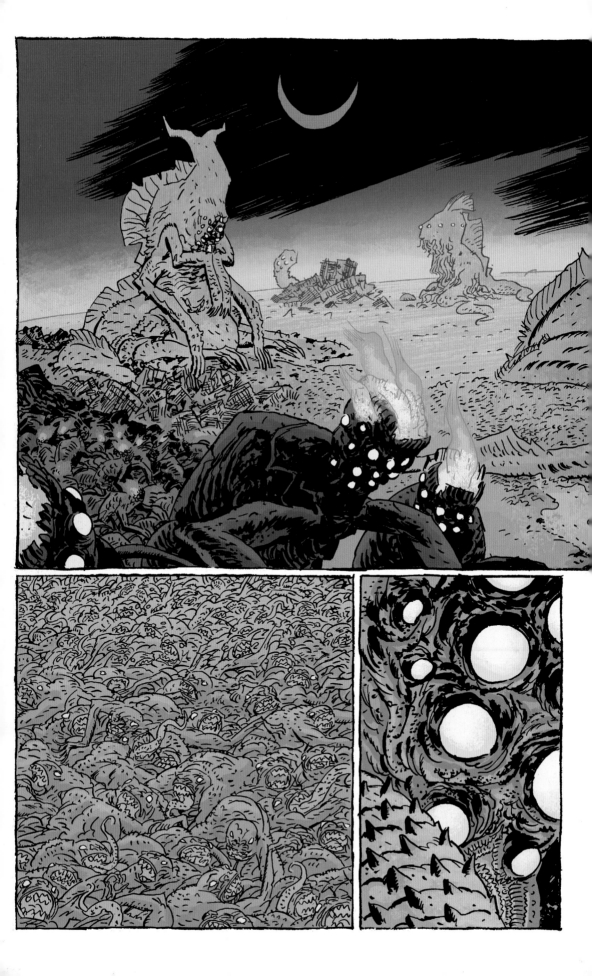

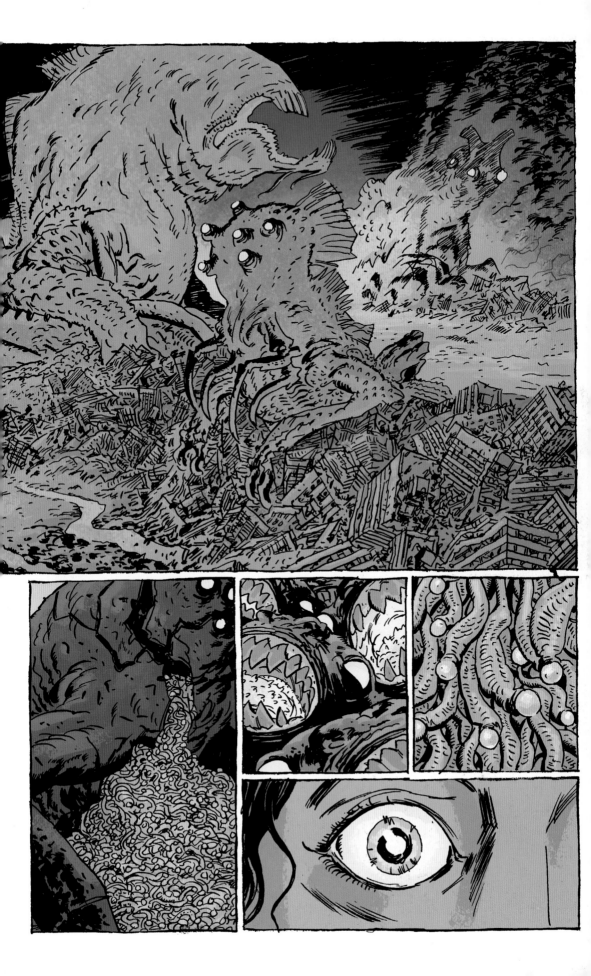

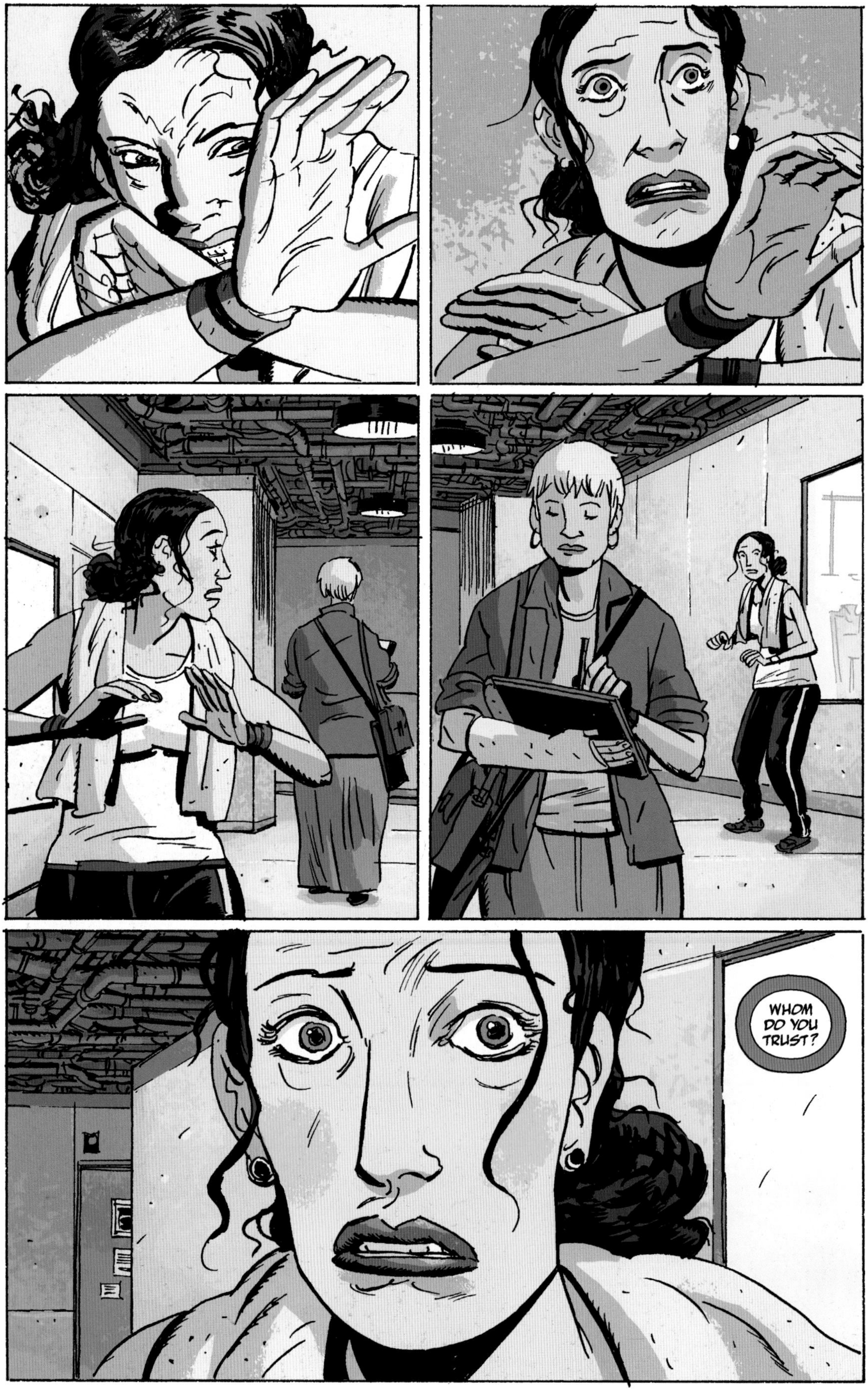
WHOM DO YOU TRUST?

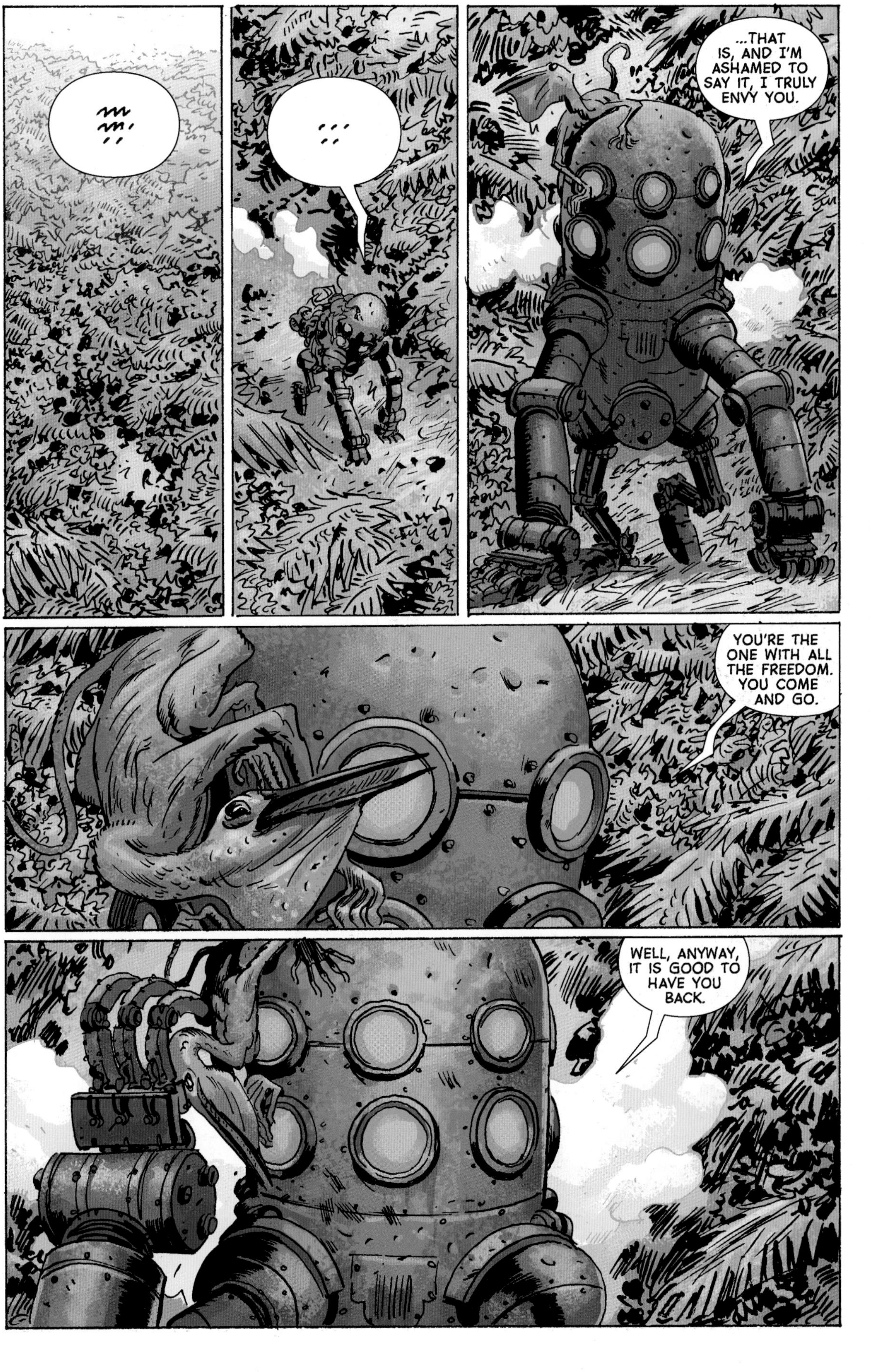
...THAT IS, AND I'M ASHAMED TO SAY IT, I TRULY ENVY YOU.
YOU'RE THE ONE WITH ALL THE FREEDOM. YOU COME AND GO.
WELL, ANYWAY, IT IS GOOD TO HAVE YOU BACK.

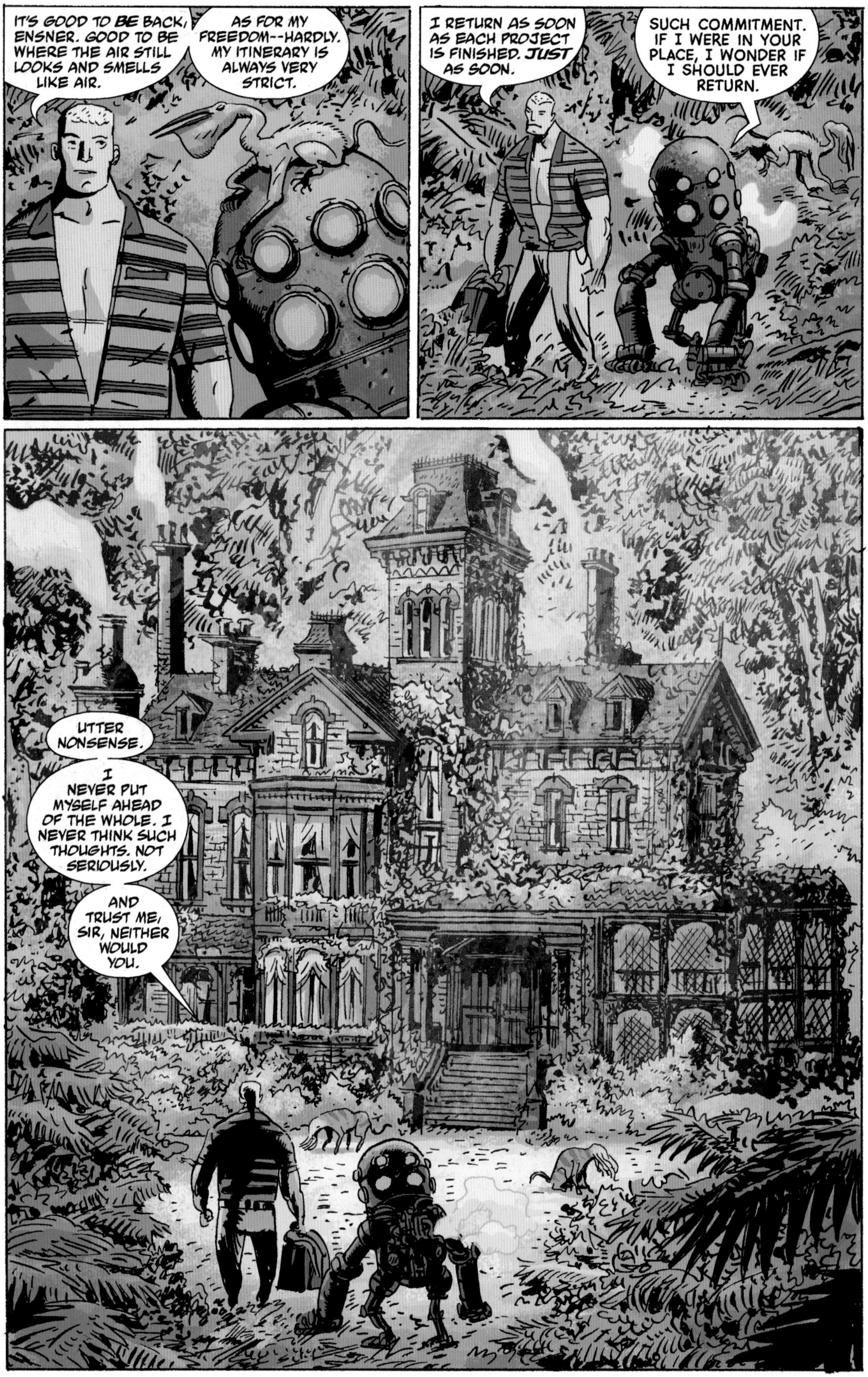
IT'S GOOD TO BE BACK, ENSNER. GOOD TO BE WHERE THE AIR STILL LOOKS AND SMELLS LIKE AIR.
AS FOR MY FREEDOM--HARDLY. MY ITINERARY IS ALWAYS VERY STRICT.
I RETURN AS SOON AS EACH PROJECT IS FINISHED. JUST AS SOON.
SUCH COMMITMENT. IF I WERE IN YOUR PLACE, I WONDER IF I SHOULD EVER RETURN.
UTTER NONSENSE.
I NEVER PUT MYSELF AHEAD OF THE WHOLE. I NEVER THINK SUCH THOUGHTS. NOT SERIOUSLY.
AND TRUST ME, SIR, NEITHER WOULD YOU.

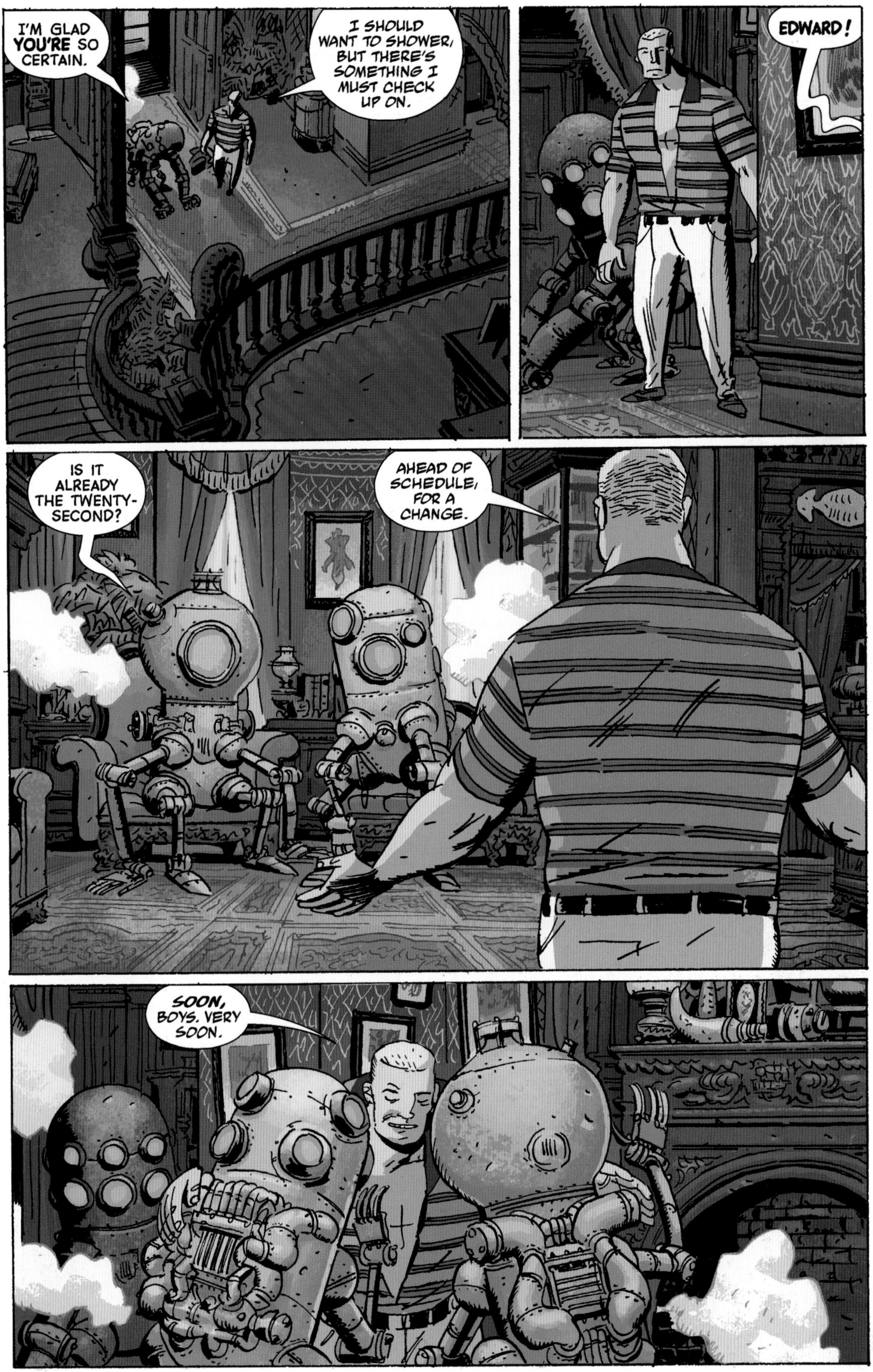

I'M GLAD **YOU'RE** SO CERTAIN.
I SHOULD WANT TO SHOWER, BUT THERE'S SOMETHING I MUST CHECK UP ON.
EDWARD!
IS IT ALREADY THE TWENTY-SECOND?
AHEAD OF SCHEDULE, FOR A CHANGE.
SOON, BOYS. VERY SOON.

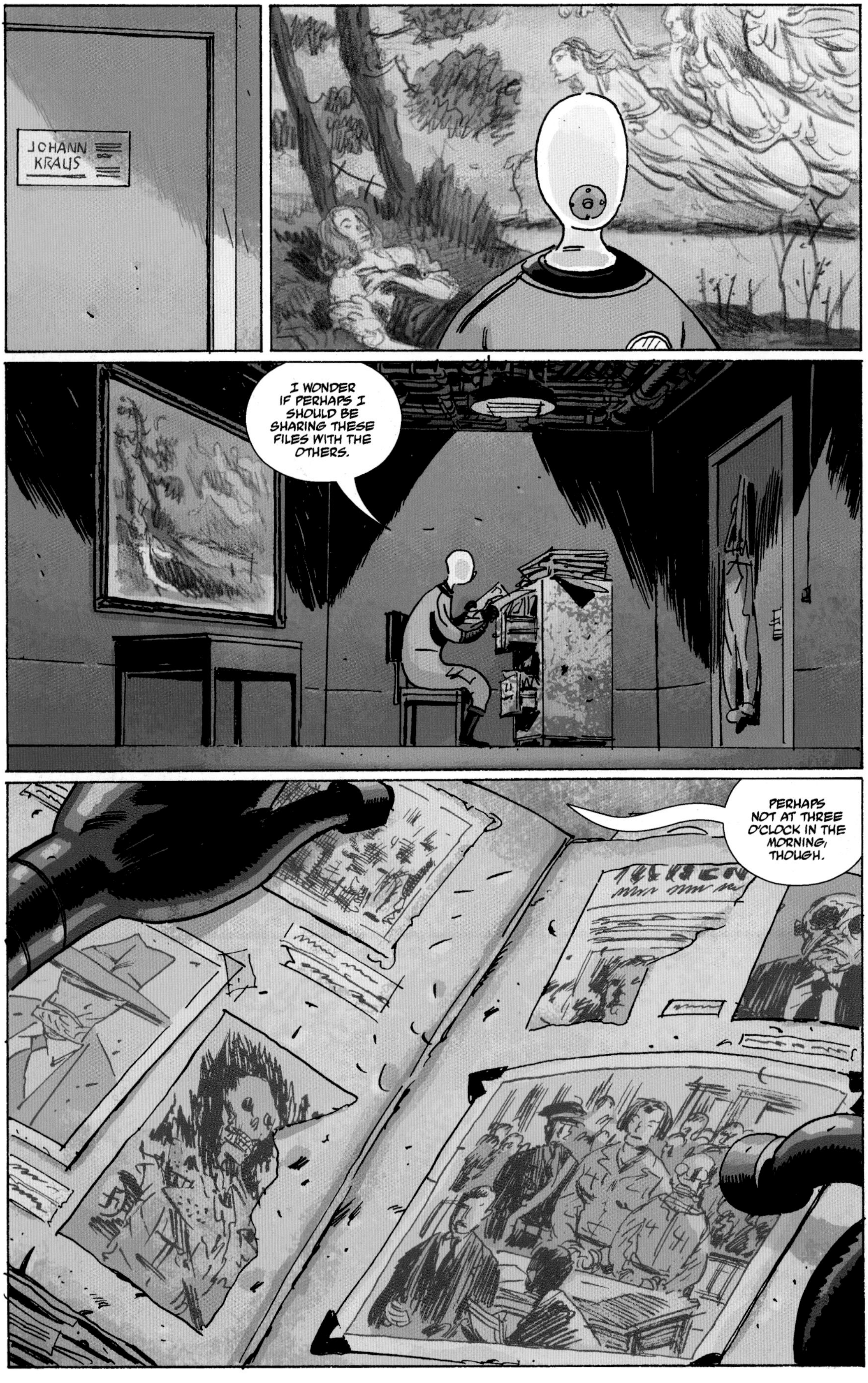
JOHANN KRAUS
I WONDER IF PERHAPS I SHOULD BE SHARING THESE FILES WITH THE OTHERS.
PERHAPS NOT AT THREE O'CLOCK IN THE MORNING, THOUGH.

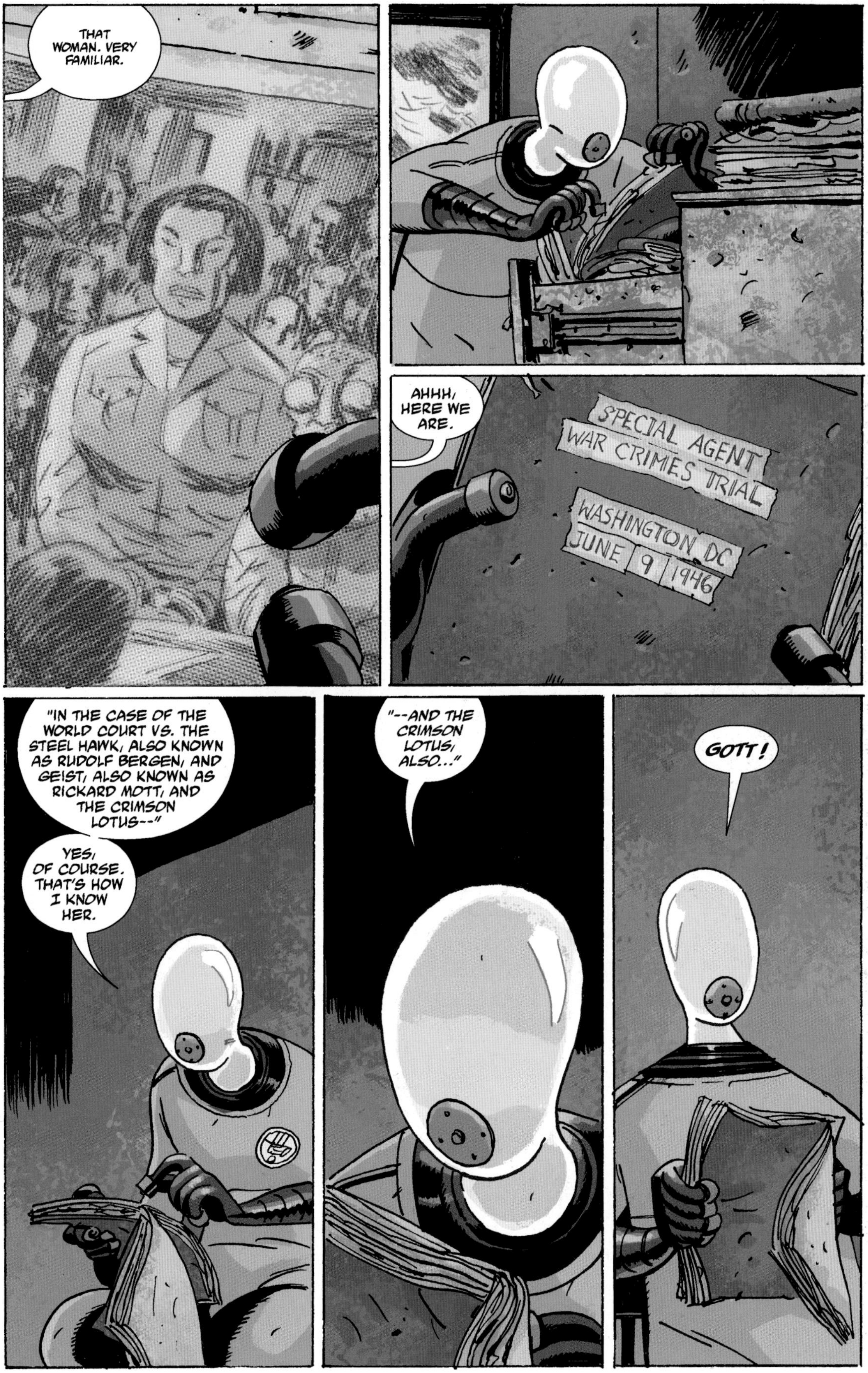
THAT WOMAN. VERY FAMILIAR.
AHHH, HERE WE ARE.
SPECIAL AGENT
WAR CRIMES TRIAL
WASHINGTON DC
JUNE 9 1946
"IN THE CASE OF THE WORLD COURT VS. THE STEEL HAWK, ALSO KNOWN AS RUDOLF BERGEN, AND GEIST, ALSO KNOWN AS RICKARD MOTT, AND THE CRIMSON LOTUS--"
YES, OF COURSE. THAT'S HOW I KNOW HER.
"--AND THE CRIMSON LOTUS, ALSO..."
GOTT!

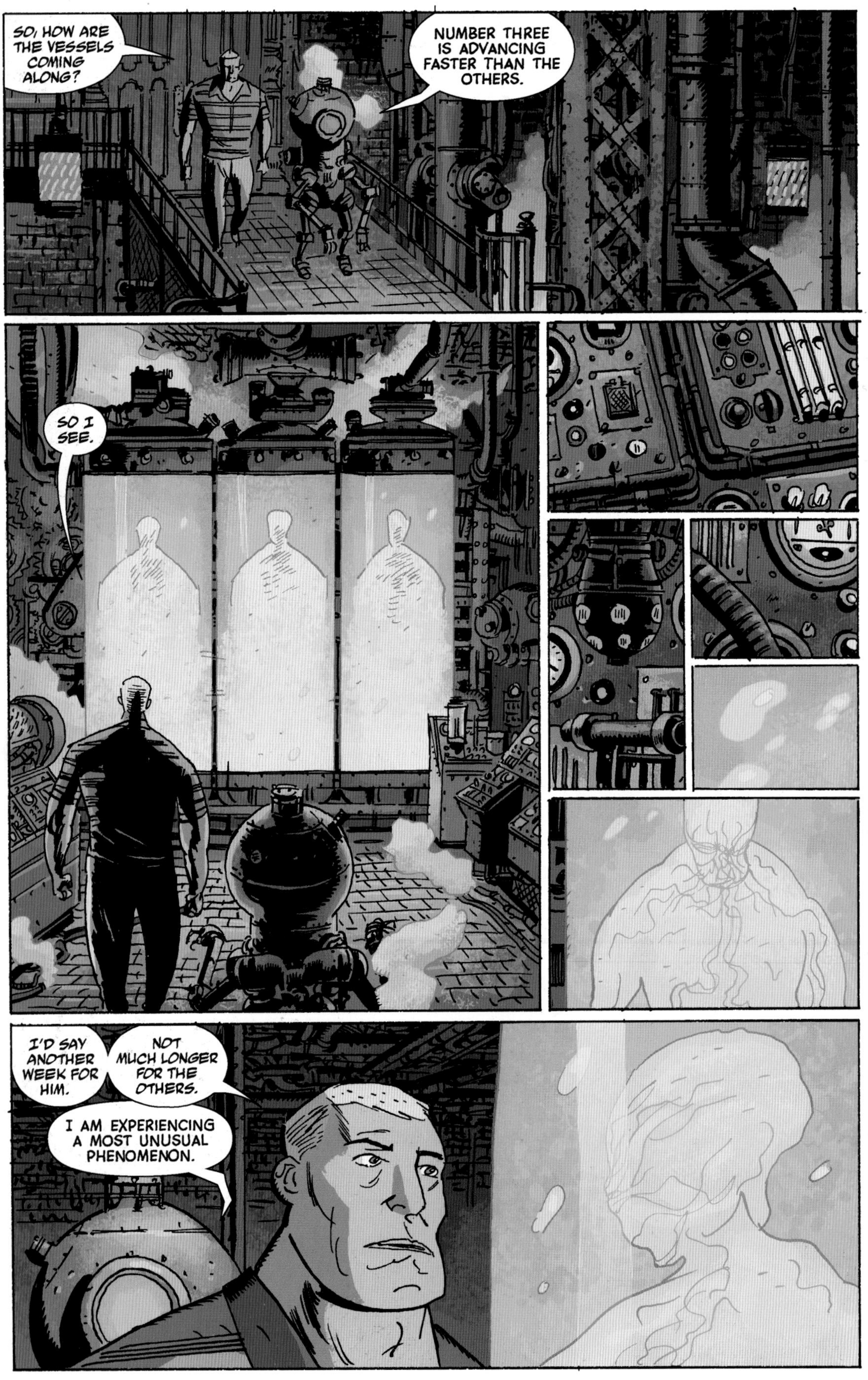
SO, HOW ARE THE VESSELS COMING ALONG?
NUMBER THREE IS ADVANCING FASTER THAN THE OTHERS.
SO I SEE.
I'D SAY ANOTHER WEEK FOR HIM.
NOT MUCH LONGER FOR THE OTHERS.
I AM EXPERIENCING A MOST UNUSUAL PHENOMENON.

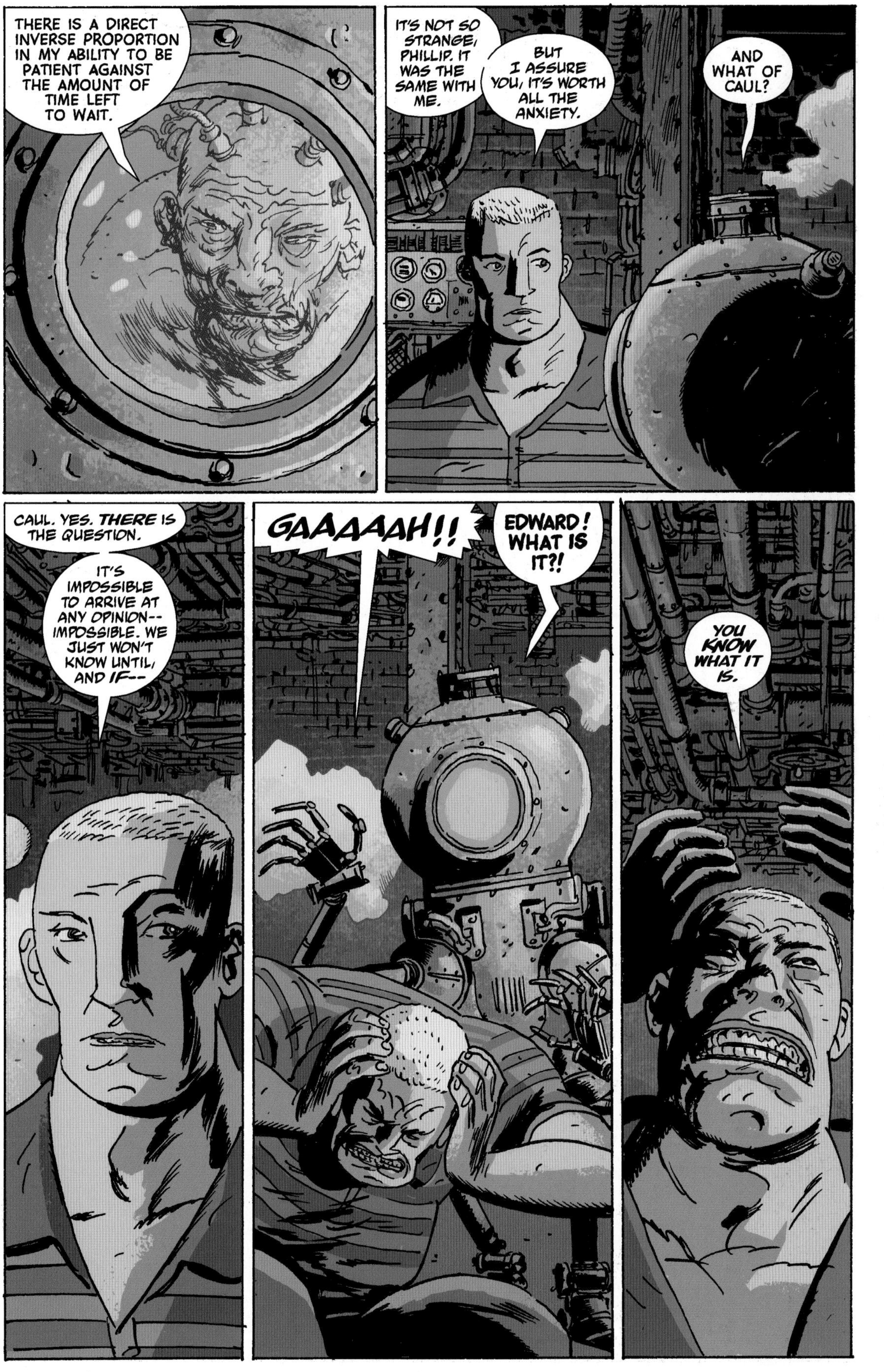
THERE IS A DIRECT INVERSE PROPORTION IN MY ABILITY TO BE PATIENT AGAINST THE AMOUNT OF TIME LEFT TO WAIT.
IT'S NOT SO STRANGE, PHILLIP. IT WAS THE SAME WITH ME.
BUT I ASSURE YOU, IT'S WORTH ALL THE ANXIETY.
AND WHAT OF CAUL?
CAUL. YES. THERE IS THE QUESTION.
IT'S IMPOSSIBLE TO ARRIVE AT ANY OPINION-- IMPOSSIBLE. WE JUST WON'T KNOW UNTIL, AND IF--
GAAAAAH!!
EDWARD! WHAT IS IT?!
YOU KNOW WHAT IT IS.

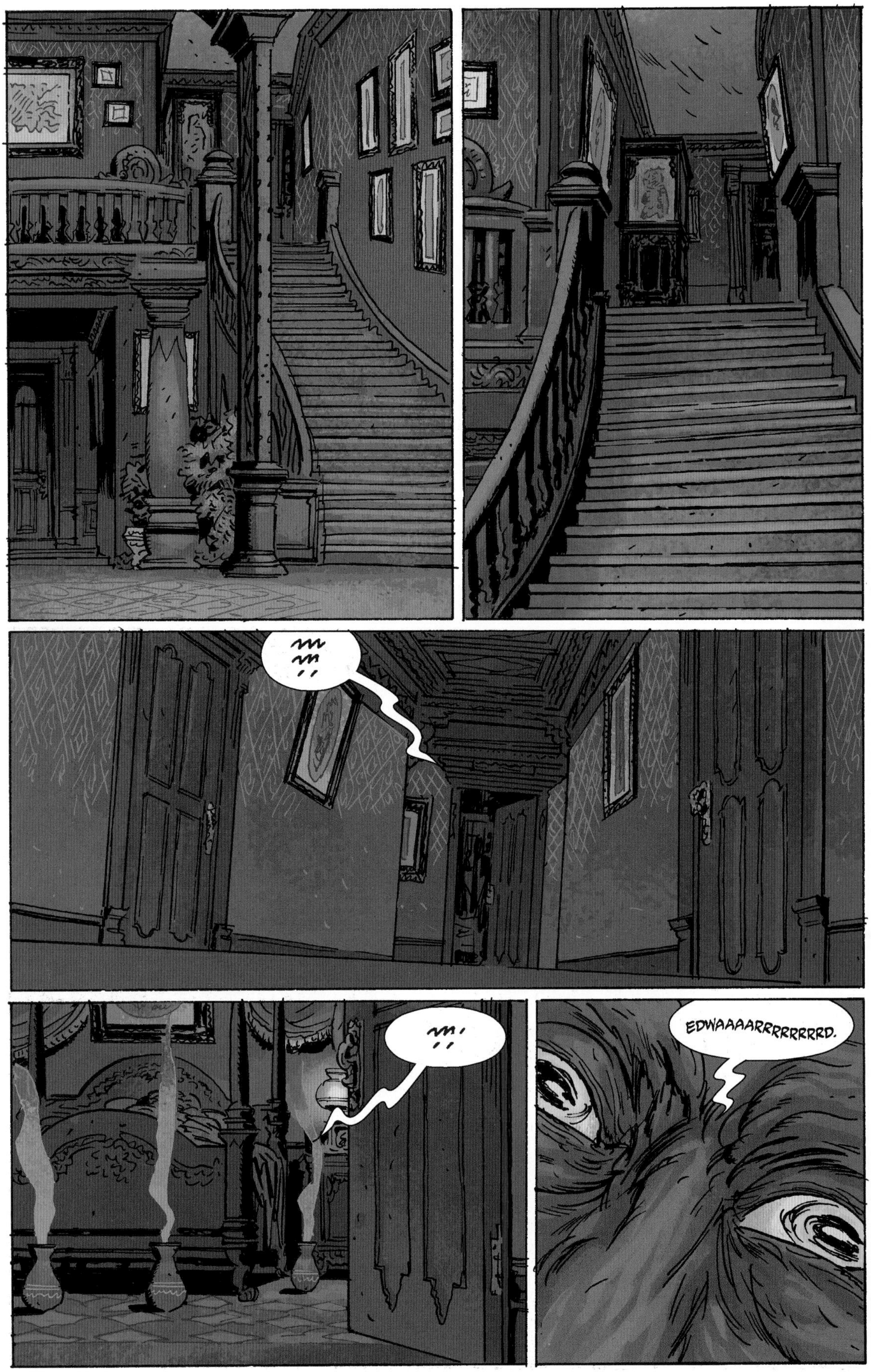
EDWAAAARRRRRRRRD.

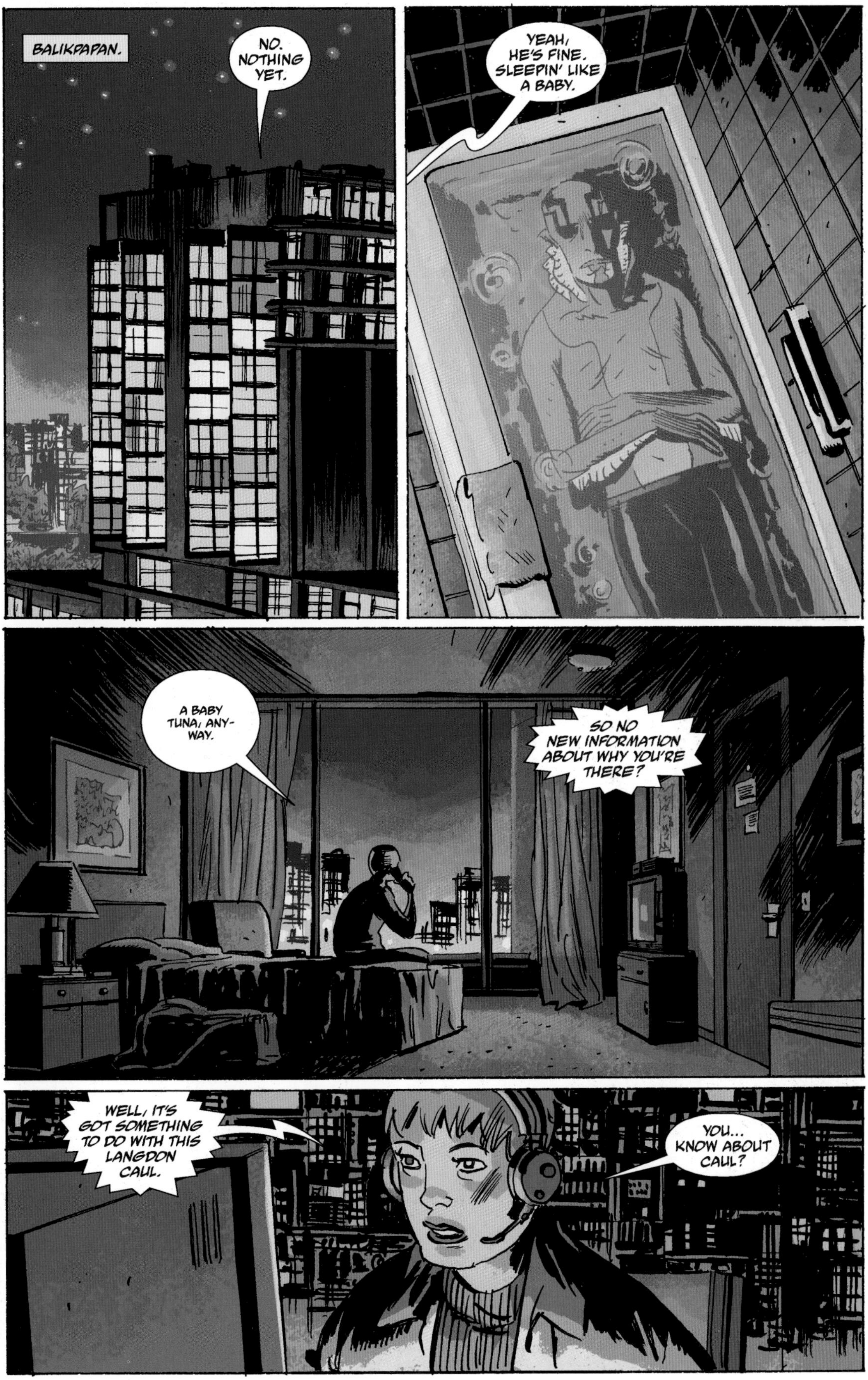
BALIKPAPAN.
NO. NOTHING YET.
YEAH, HE'S FINE. SLEEPIN' LIKE A BABY.
A BABY TUNA, ANY-WAY.
SO NO NEW INFORMATION ABOUT WHY YOU'RE THERE?
WELL, IT'S GOT SOMETHING TO DO WITH THIS LANGDON CAUL.
YOU... KNOW ABOUT CAUL?

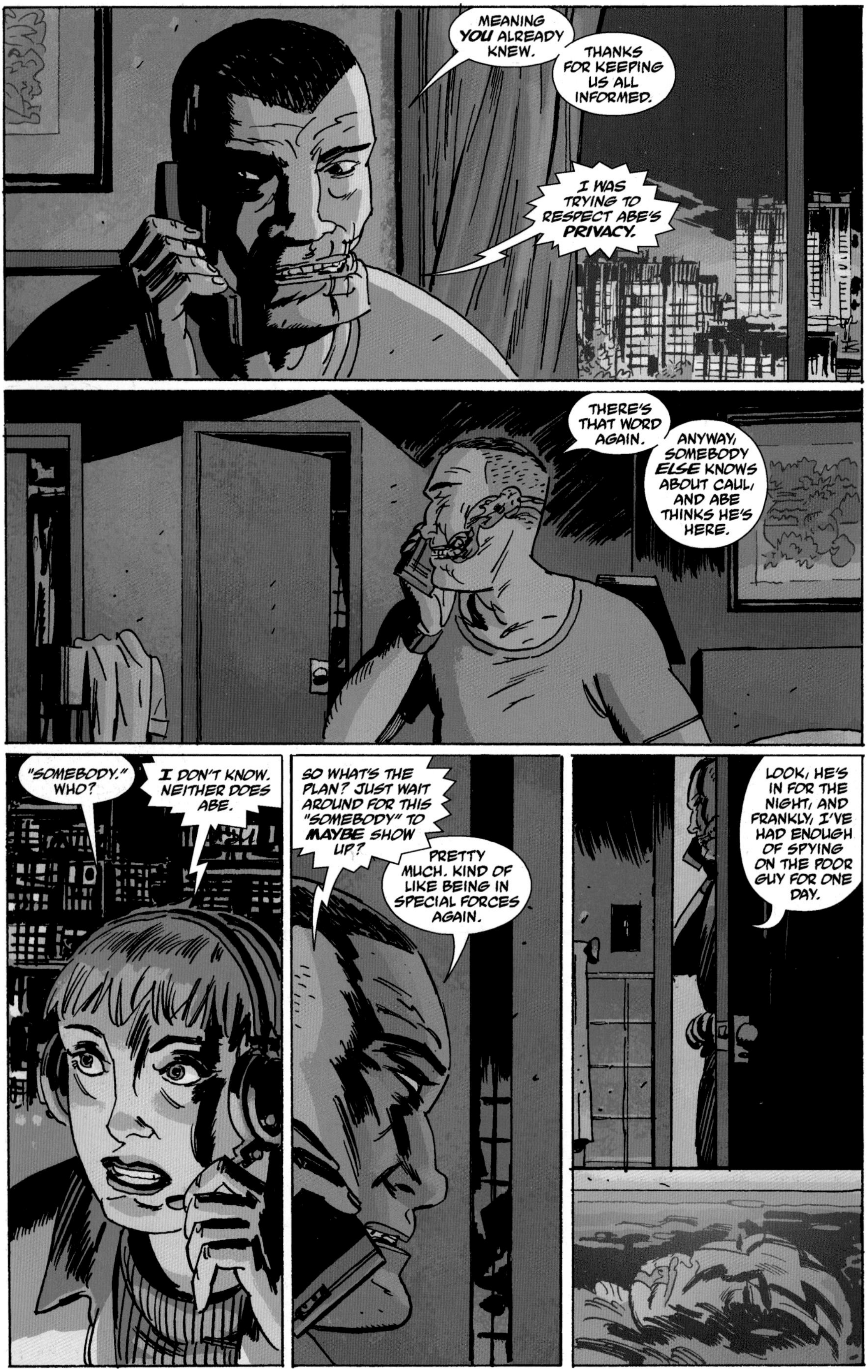
MEANING YOU ALREADY KNEW.
THANKS FOR KEEPING US ALL INFORMED.
I WAS TRYING TO RESPECT ABE'S PRIVACY.
THERE'S THAT WORD AGAIN.
ANYWAY, SOMEBODY ELSE KNOWS ABOUT CAUL, AND ABE THINKS HE'S HERE.
"SOMEBODY." WHO?
I DON'T KNOW. NEITHER DOES ABE.
SO WHAT'S THE PLAN? JUST WAIT AROUND FOR THIS "SOMEBODY" TO MAYBE SHOW UP?
PRETTY MUCH. KIND OF LIKE BEING IN SPECIAL FORCES AGAIN.
LOOK, HE'S IN FOR THE NIGHT, AND FRANKLY, I'VE HAD ENOUGH OF SPYING ON THE POOR GUY FOR ONE DAY.

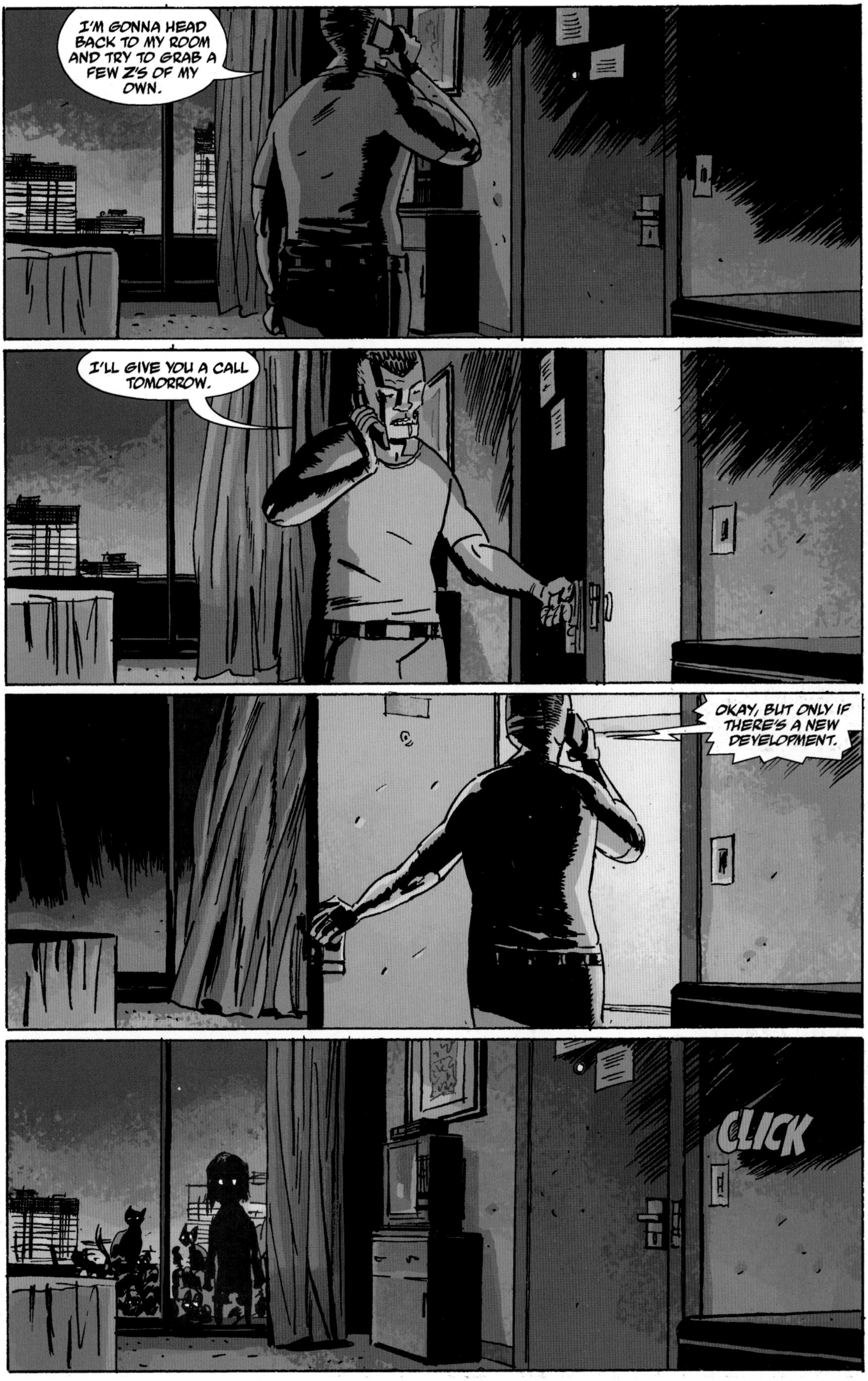
I'M GONNA HEAD BACK TO MY ROOM AND TRY TO GRAB A FEW Z'S OF MY OWN.
I'LL GIVE YOU A CALL TOMORROW.
OKAY, BUT ONLY IF THERE'S A NEW DEVELOPMENT.
CLICK

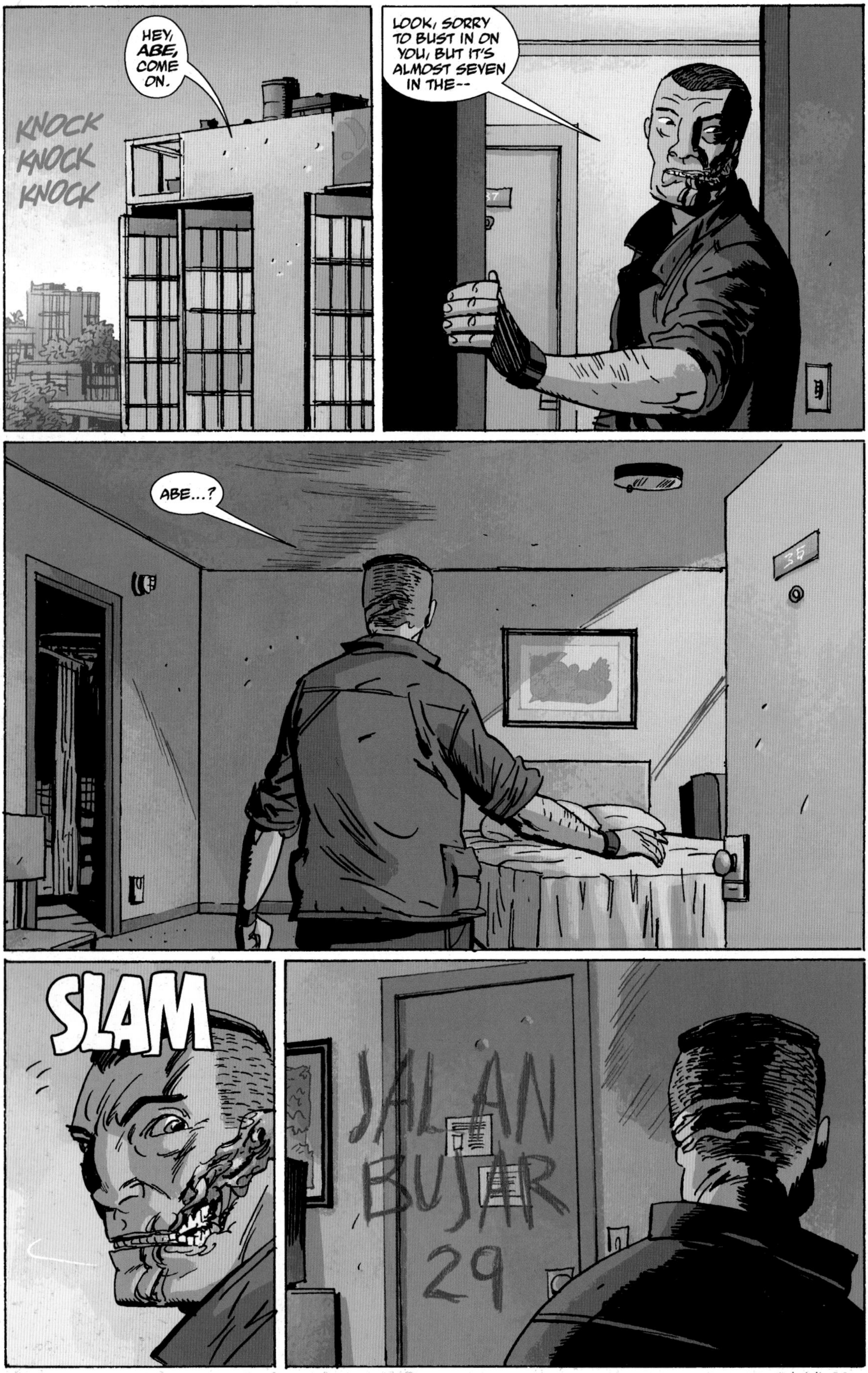
KNOCK
KNOCK
KNOCK
HEY, ABE, COME ON.
LOOK, SORRY TO BUST IN ON YOU, BUT IT'S ALMOST SEVEN IN THE--
ABE...?
SLAM
JALAN
BUJAR
29

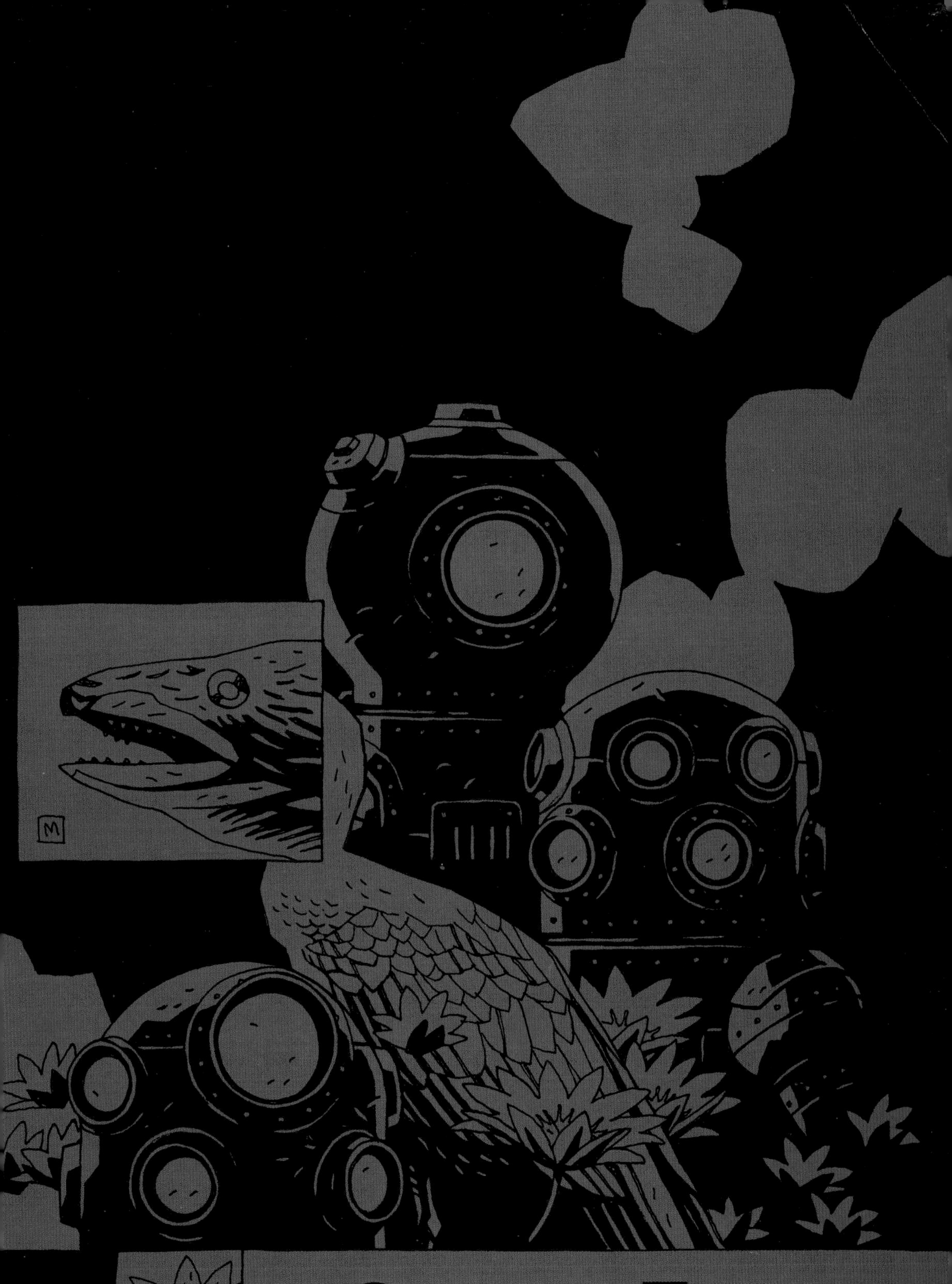

CHAPTER THREE

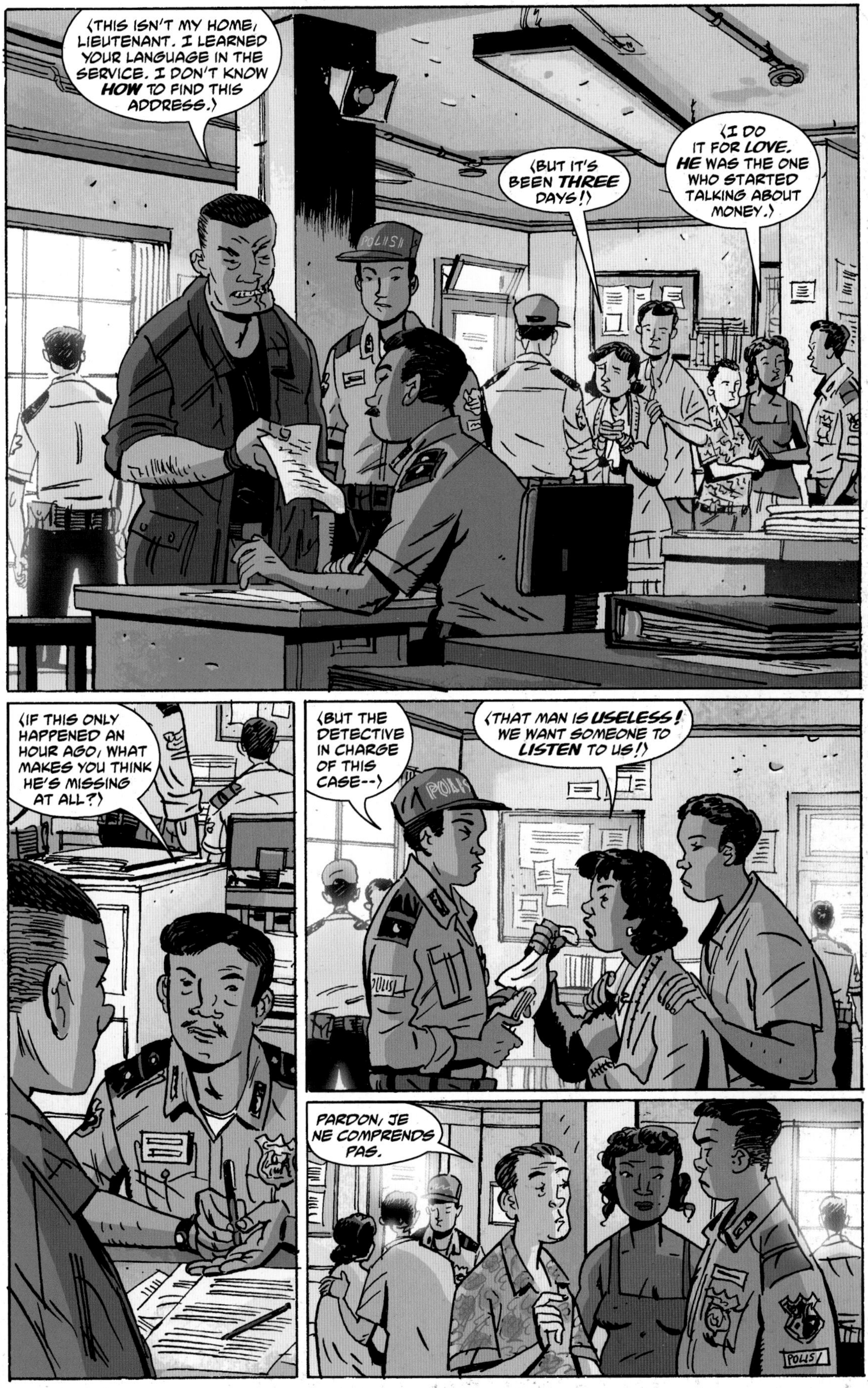
⟨THIS ISN'T MY HOME, LIEUTENANT. I LEARNED YOUR LANGUAGE IN THE SERVICE. I DON'T KNOW HOW TO FIND THIS ADDRESS.⟩
⟨BUT IT'S BEEN THREE DAYS!⟩
⟨I DO IT FOR LOVE. HE WAS THE ONE WHO STARTED TALKING ABOUT MONEY.⟩
POLISI
⟨IF THIS ONLY HAPPENED AN HOUR AGO, WHAT MAKES YOU THINK HE'S MISSING AT ALL?⟩
⟨BUT THE DETECTIVE IN CHARGE OF THIS CASE--⟩
⟨THAT MAN IS USELESS! WE WANT SOMEONE TO LISTEN TO US!⟩
PARDON, JE NE COMPRENDS PAS.
POLISI

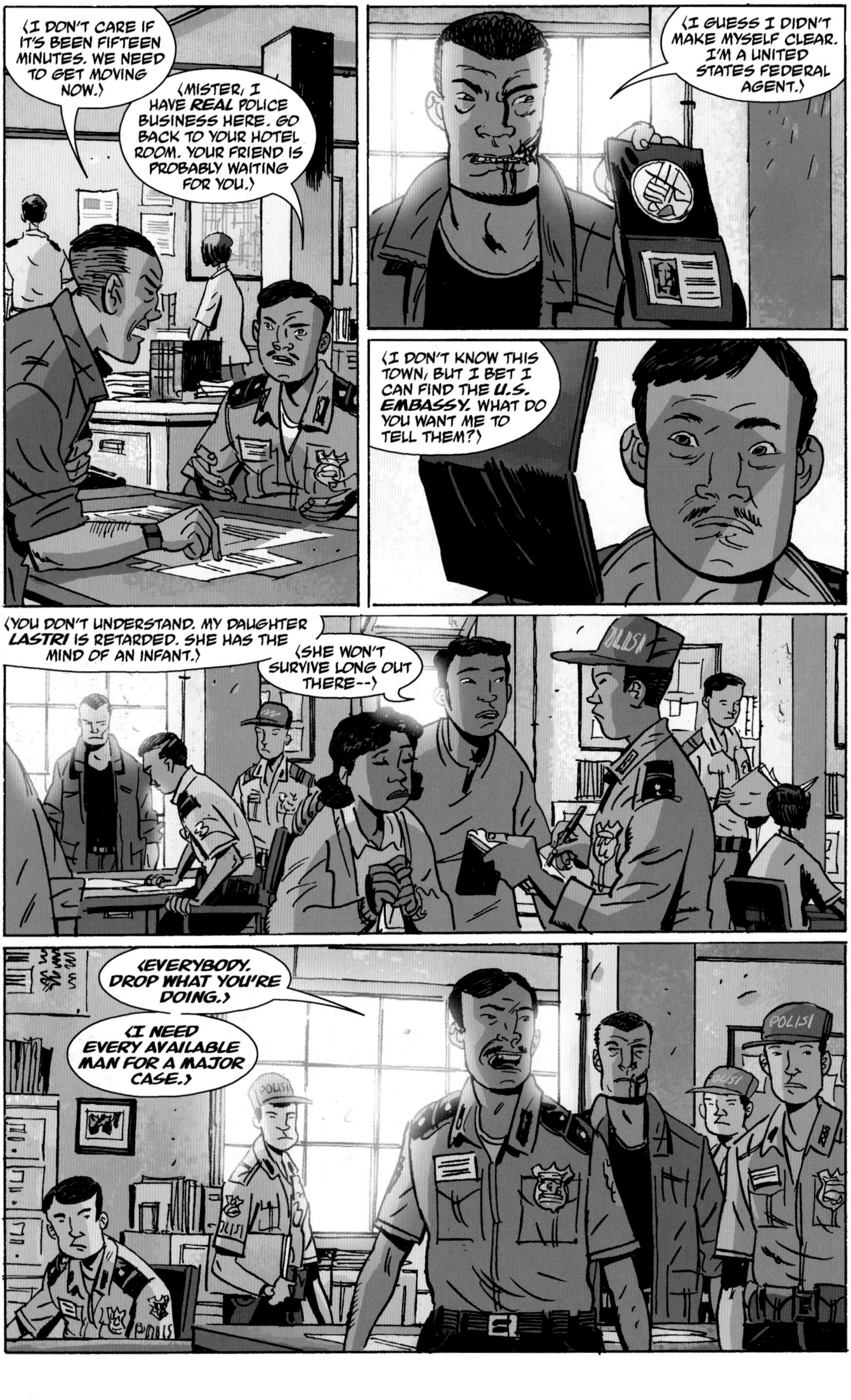
⟨I DON'T CARE IF IT'S BEEN FIFTEEN MINUTES. WE NEED TO GET MOVING NOW.⟩
⟨MISTER, I HAVE REAL POLICE BUSINESS HERE. GO BACK TO YOUR HOTEL ROOM. YOUR FRIEND IS PROBABLY WAITING FOR YOU.⟩
⟨I GUESS I DIDN'T MAKE MYSELF CLEAR. I'M A UNITED STATES FEDERAL AGENT.⟩
⟨I DON'T KNOW THIS TOWN, BUT I BET I CAN FIND THE U.S. EMBASSY. WHAT DO YOU WANT ME TO TELL THEM?⟩
⟨YOU DON'T UNDERSTAND. MY DAUGHTER LASTRI IS RETARDED. SHE HAS THE MIND OF AN INFANT.⟩
⟨SHE WON'T SURVIVE LONG OUT THERE--⟩
POLISI
⟨EVERYBODY. DROP WHAT YOU'RE DOING.⟩
⟨I NEED EVERY AVAILABLE MAN FOR A MAJOR CASE.⟩
POLISI
POLISI
POLISI

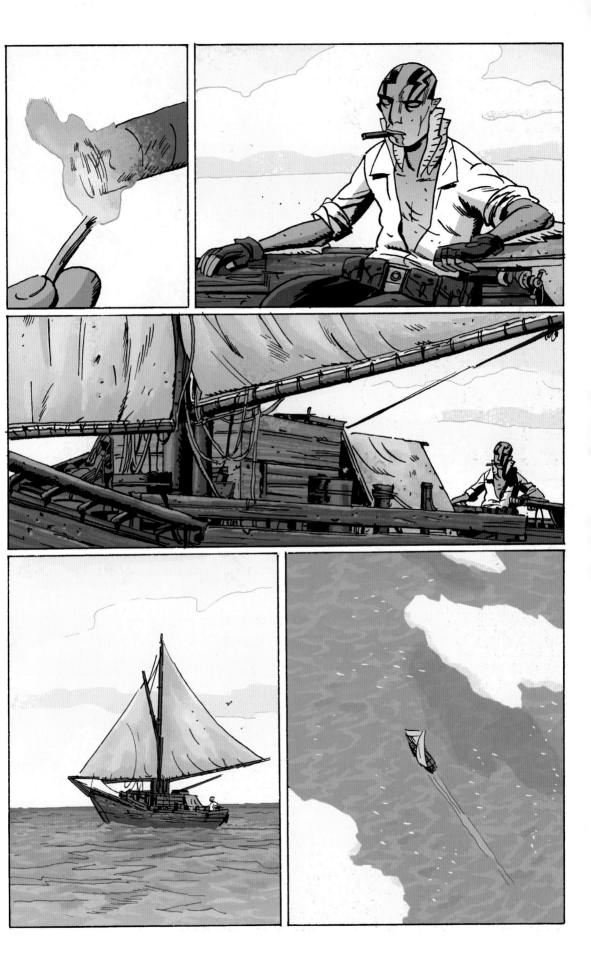

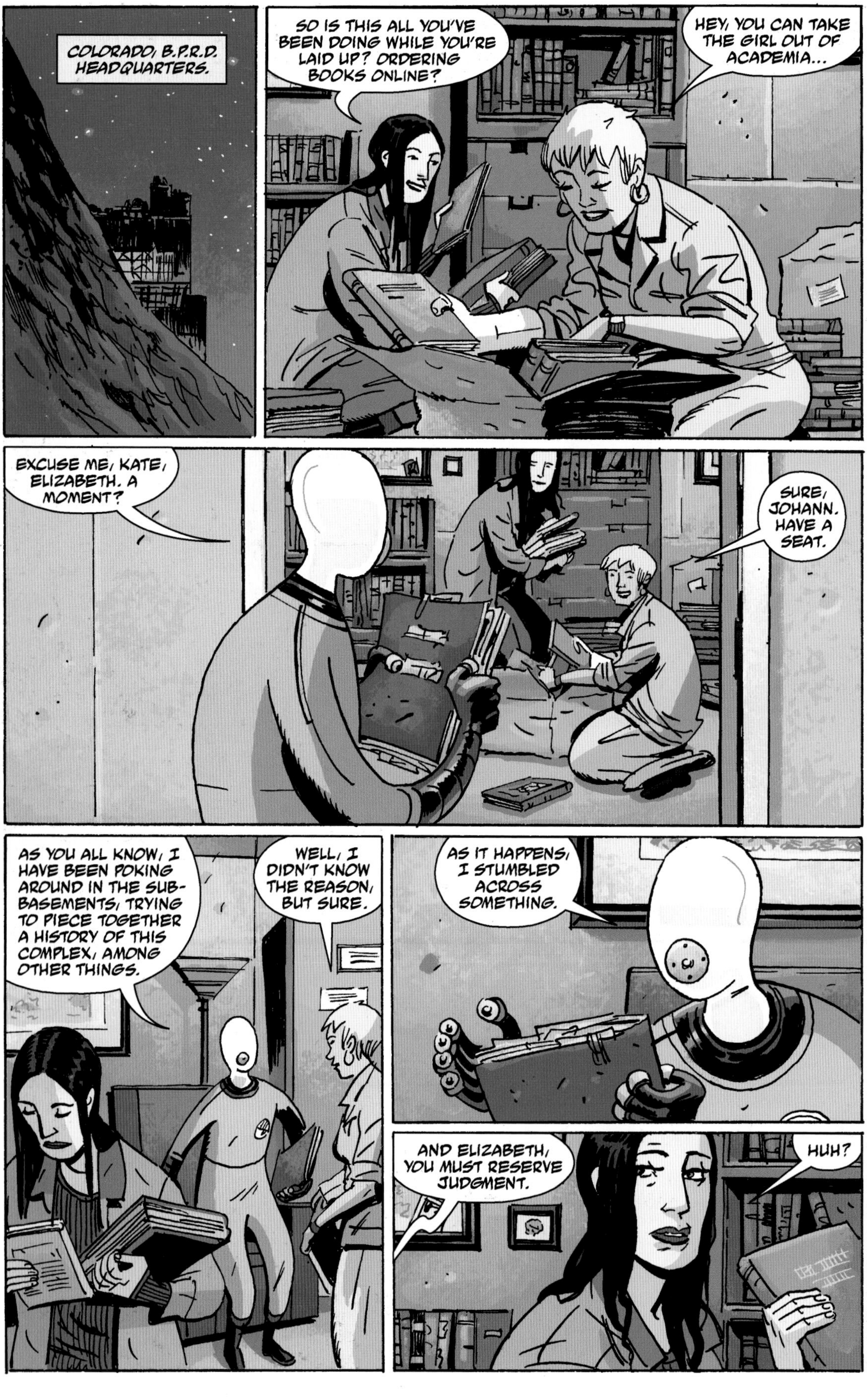
COLORADO; B.P.R.D. HEADQUARTERS.
SO IS THIS ALL YOU'VE BEEN DOING WHILE YOU'RE LAID UP? ORDERING BOOKS ONLINE?
HEY, YOU CAN TAKE THE GIRL OUT OF ACADEMIA...
EXCUSE ME, KATE, ELIZABETH. A MOMENT?
SURE, JOHANN. HAVE A SEAT.
AS YOU ALL KNOW, I HAVE BEEN POKING AROUND IN THE SUB-BASEMENTS, TRYING TO PIECE TOGETHER A HISTORY OF THIS COMPLEX, AMONG OTHER THINGS.
WELL, I DIDN'T KNOW THE REASON, BUT SURE.
AS IT HAPPENS, I STUMBLED ACROSS SOMETHING.
AND ELIZABETH, YOU MUST RESERVE JUDGMENT.
HUH?

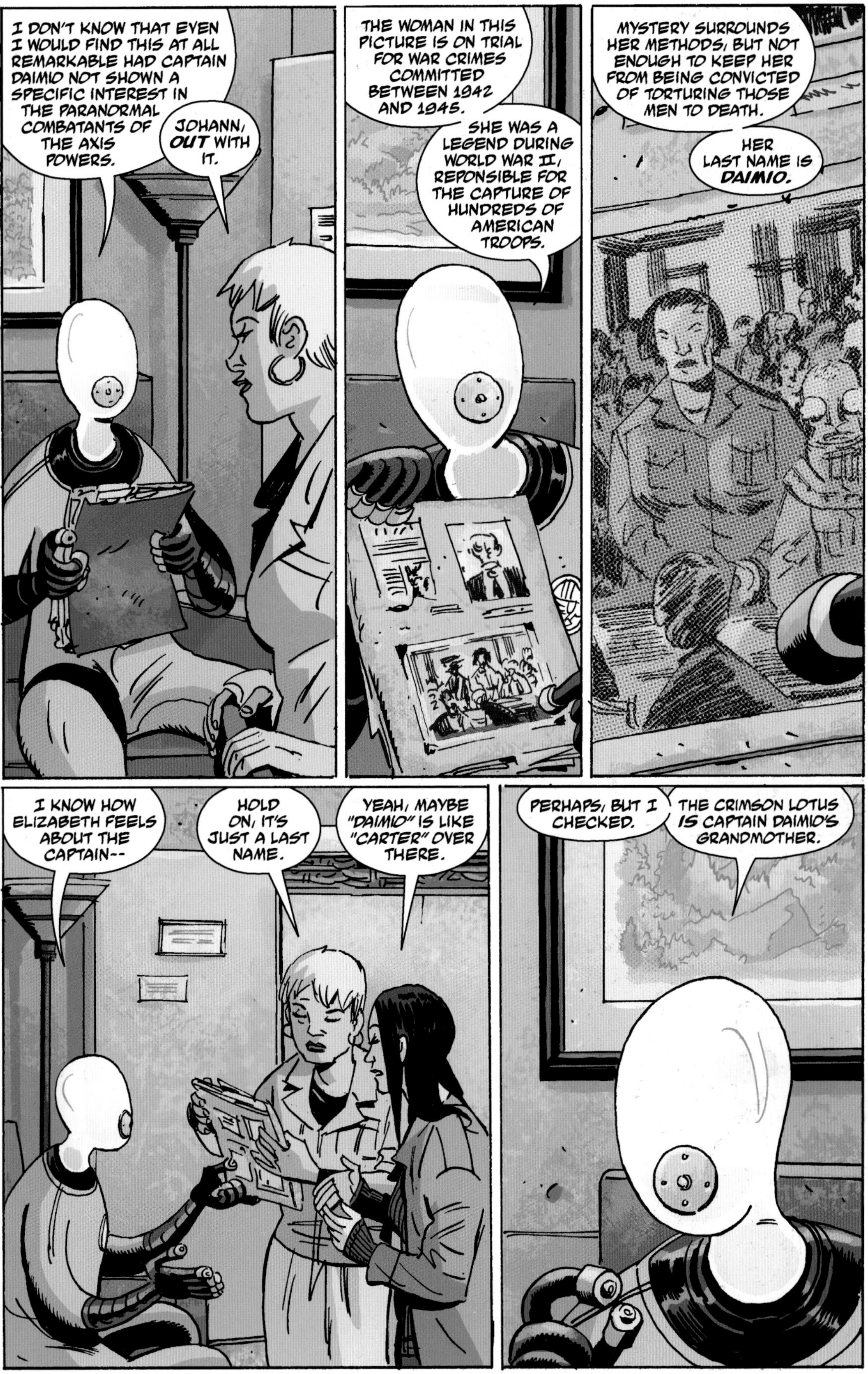
I DON'T KNOW THAT EVEN I WOULD FIND THIS AT ALL REMARKABLE HAD CAPTAIN DAIMIO NOT SHOWN A SPECIFIC INTEREST IN THE PARANORMAL COMBATANTS OF THE AXIS POWERS.
JOHANN, OUT WITH IT.
THE WOMAN IN THIS PICTURE IS ON TRIAL FOR WAR CRIMES COMMITTED BETWEEN 1942 AND 1945.
SHE WAS A LEGEND DURING WORLD WAR II, REPONSIBLE FOR THE CAPTURE OF HUNDREDS OF AMERICAN TROOPS.
MYSTERY SURROUNDS HER METHODS, BUT NOT ENOUGH TO KEEP HER FROM BEING CONVICTED OF TORTURING THOSE MEN TO DEATH.
HER LAST NAME IS DAIMIO.
I KNOW HOW ELIZABETH FEELS ABOUT THE CAPTAIN--
HOLD ON, IT'S JUST A LAST NAME.
YEAH, MAYBE "DAIMIO" IS LIKE "CARTER" OVER THERE.
PERHAPS, BUT I CHECKED.
THE CRIMSON LOTUS IS CAPTAIN DAIMIO'S GRANDMOTHER.

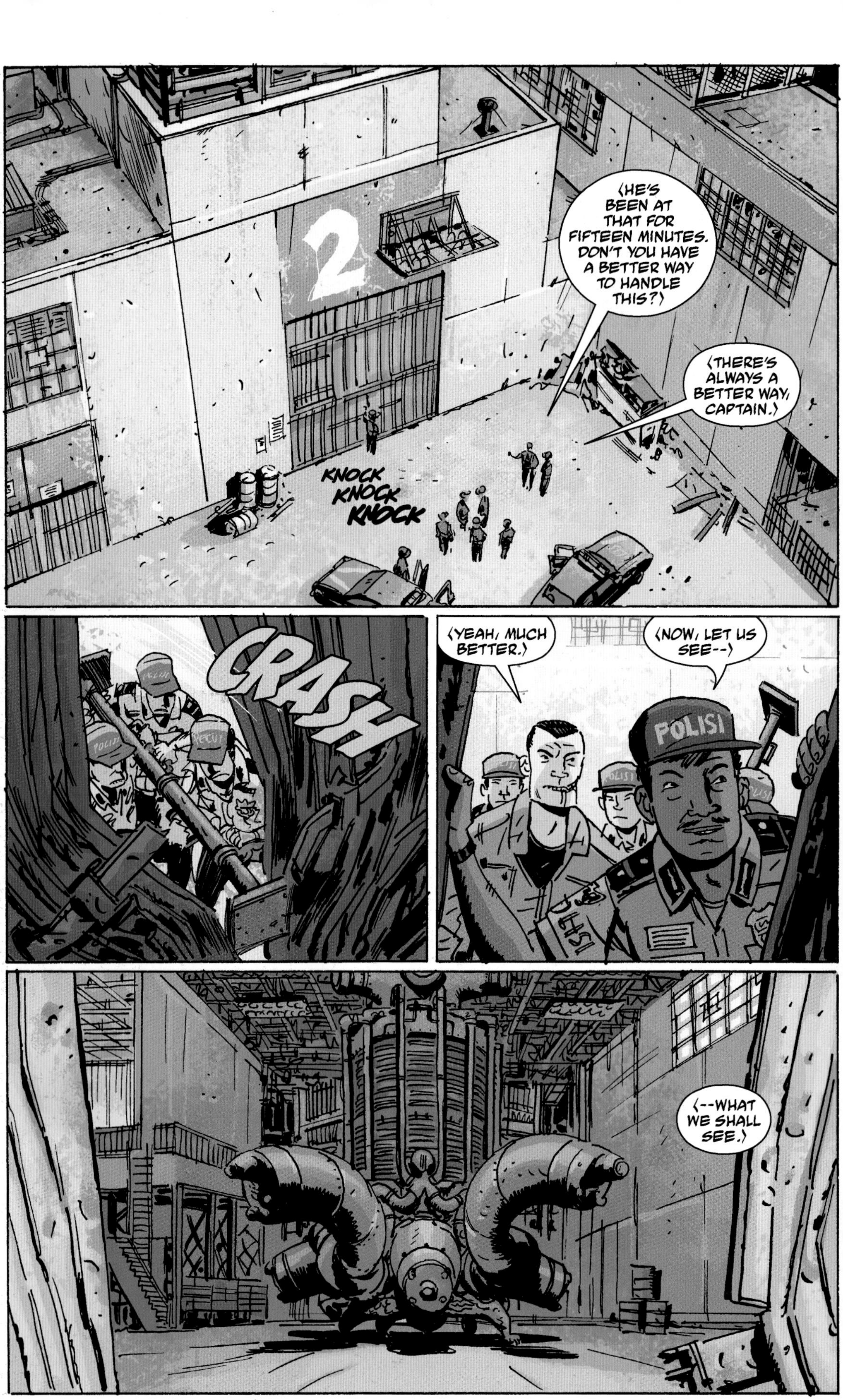
⟨HE'S BEEN AT THAT FOR FIFTEEN MINUTES. DON'T YOU HAVE A BETTER WAY TO HANDLE THIS?⟩
⟨THERE'S ALWAYS A BETTER WAY, CAPTAIN.⟩
KNOCK KNOCK KNOCK
CRASH
⟨YEAH, MUCH BETTER.⟩
⟨NOW, LET US SEE--⟩
POLISI
⟨--WHAT WE SHALL SEE.⟩

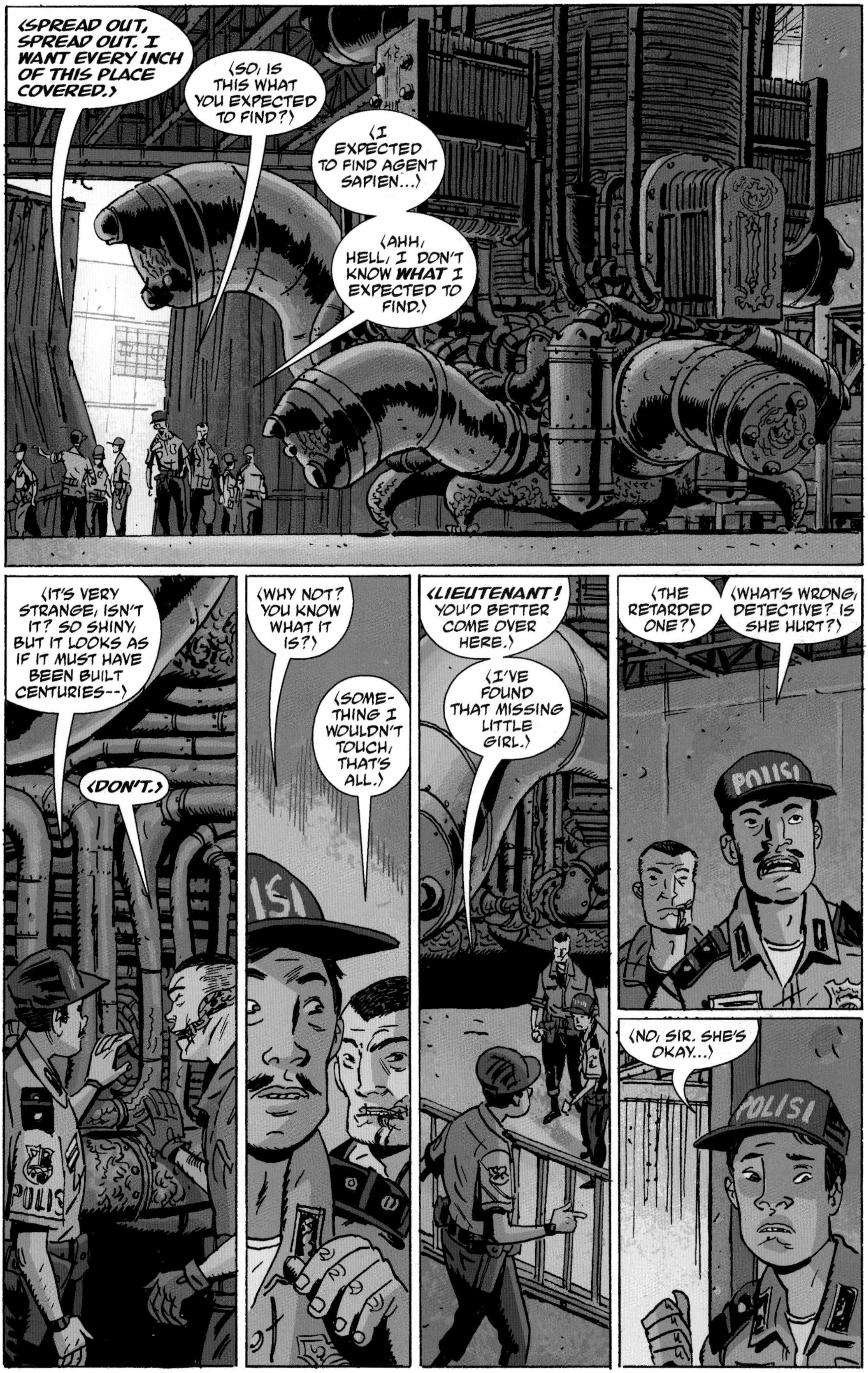
‹SPREAD OUT, SPREAD OUT. I WANT EVERY INCH OF THIS PLACE COVERED.›
‹SO, IS THIS WHAT YOU EXPECTED TO FIND?›
‹I EXPECTED TO FIND AGENT SAPIEN...›
‹AHH, HELL, I DON'T KNOW WHAT I EXPECTED TO FIND.›
‹IT'S VERY STRANGE, ISN'T IT? SO SHINY, BUT IT LOOKS AS IF IT MUST HAVE BEEN BUILT CENTURIES--›
‹DON'T.›
‹WHY NOT? YOU KNOW WHAT IT IS?›
‹SOMETHING I WOULDN'T TOUCH, THAT'S ALL.›
‹LIEUTENANT! YOU'D BETTER COME OVER HERE.›
‹I'VE FOUND THAT MISSING LITTLE GIRL.›
‹THE RETARDED ONE?›
‹WHAT'S WRONG, DETECTIVE? IS SHE HURT?›
‹NO, SIR. SHE'S OKAY...›
POLISI

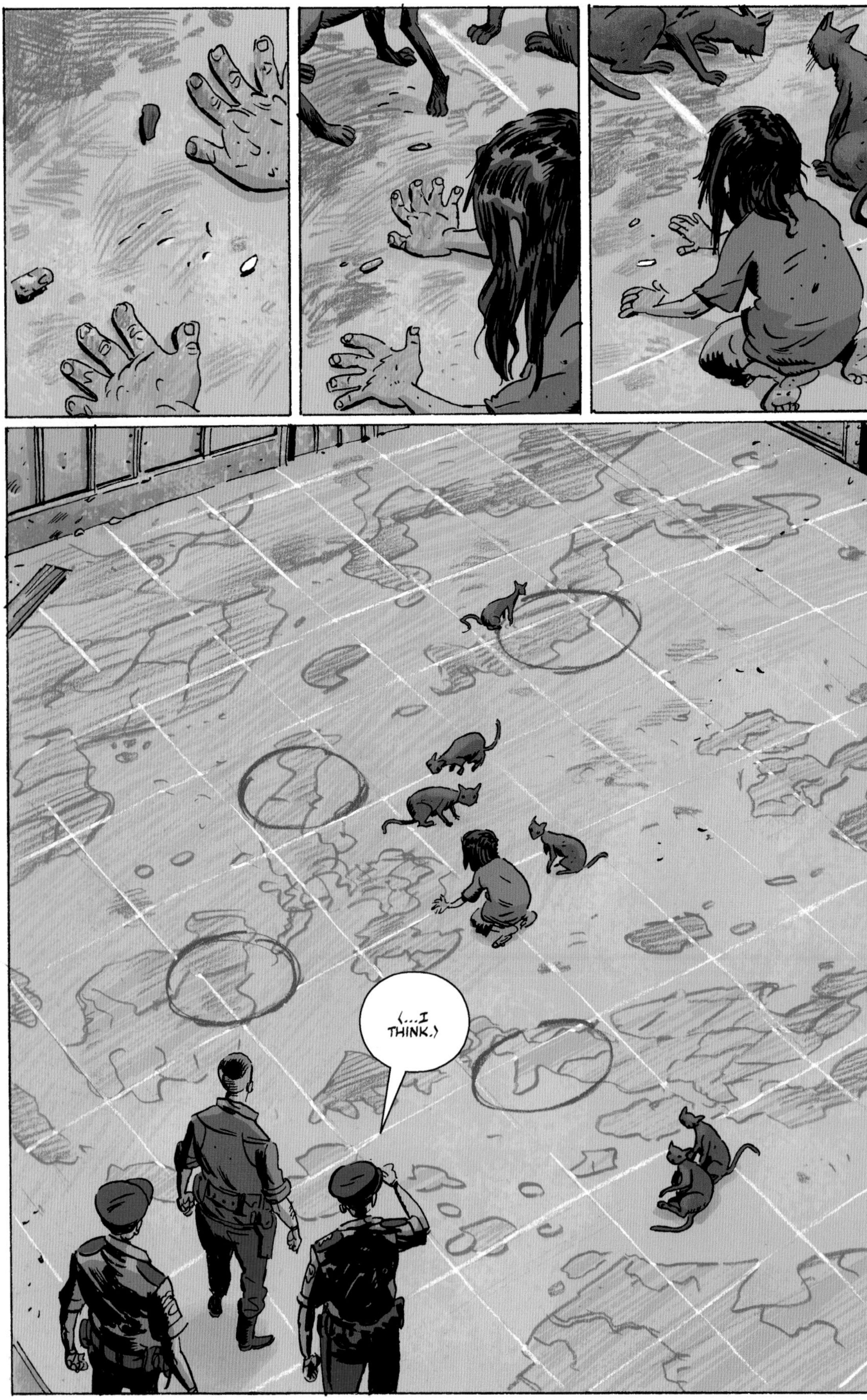
‹...I THINK.›

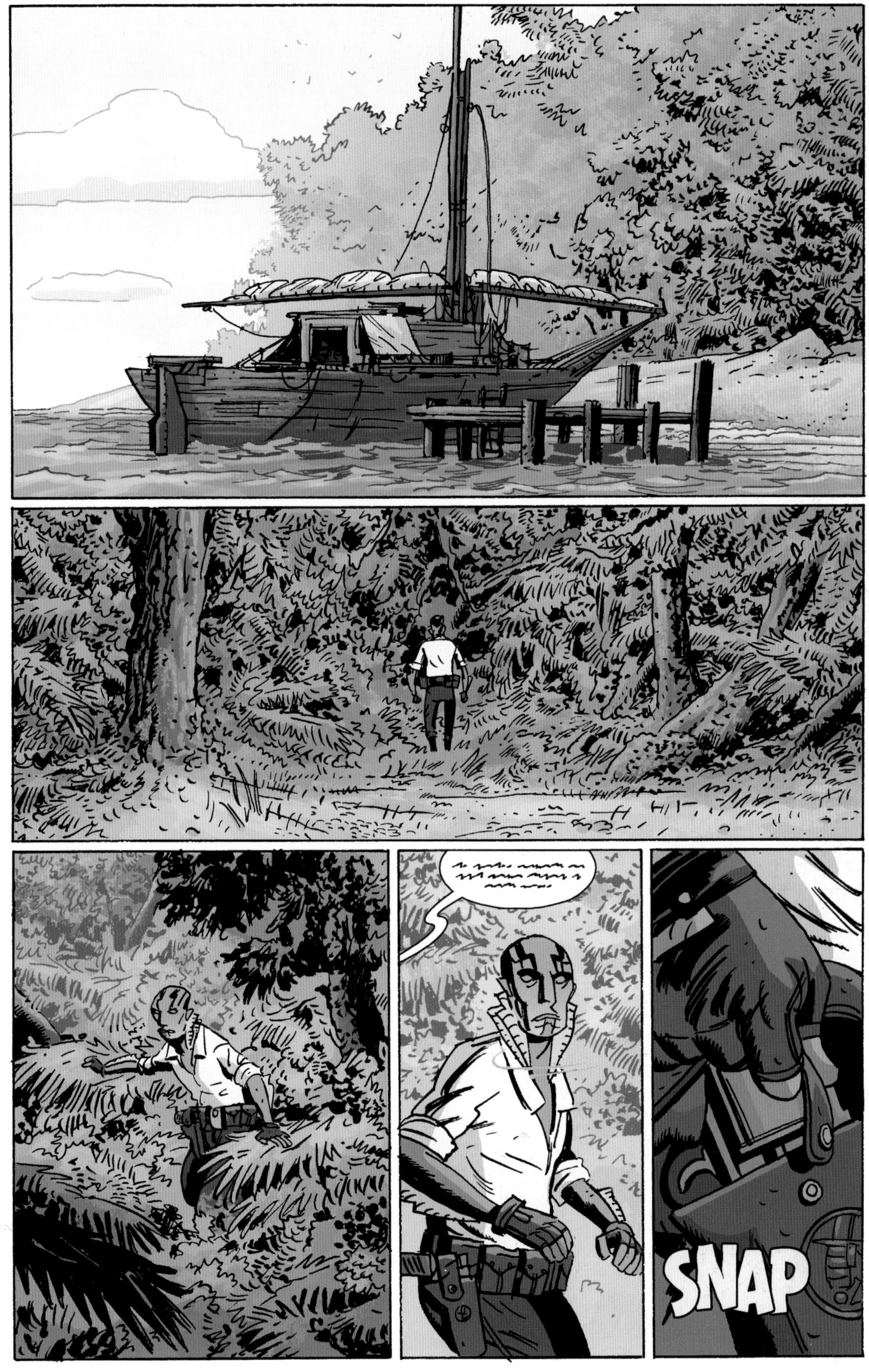
SNAP

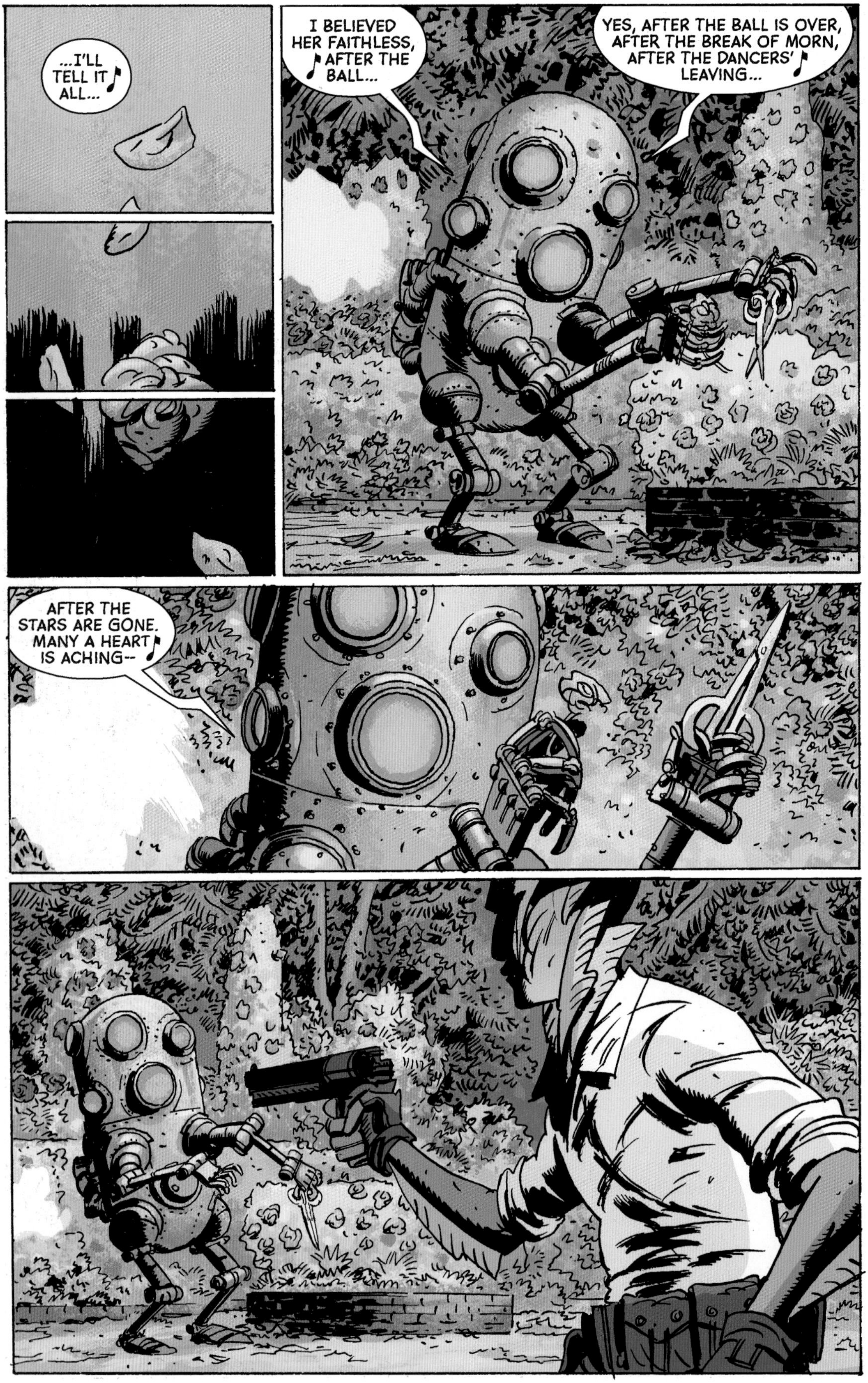
...I'LL TELL IT ALL...
I BELIEVED HER FAITHLESS, AFTER THE BALL...
YES, AFTER THE BALL IS OVER, AFTER THE BREAK OF MORN, AFTER THE DANCERS' LEAVING...
AFTER THE STARS ARE GONE. MANY A HEART IS ACHING--

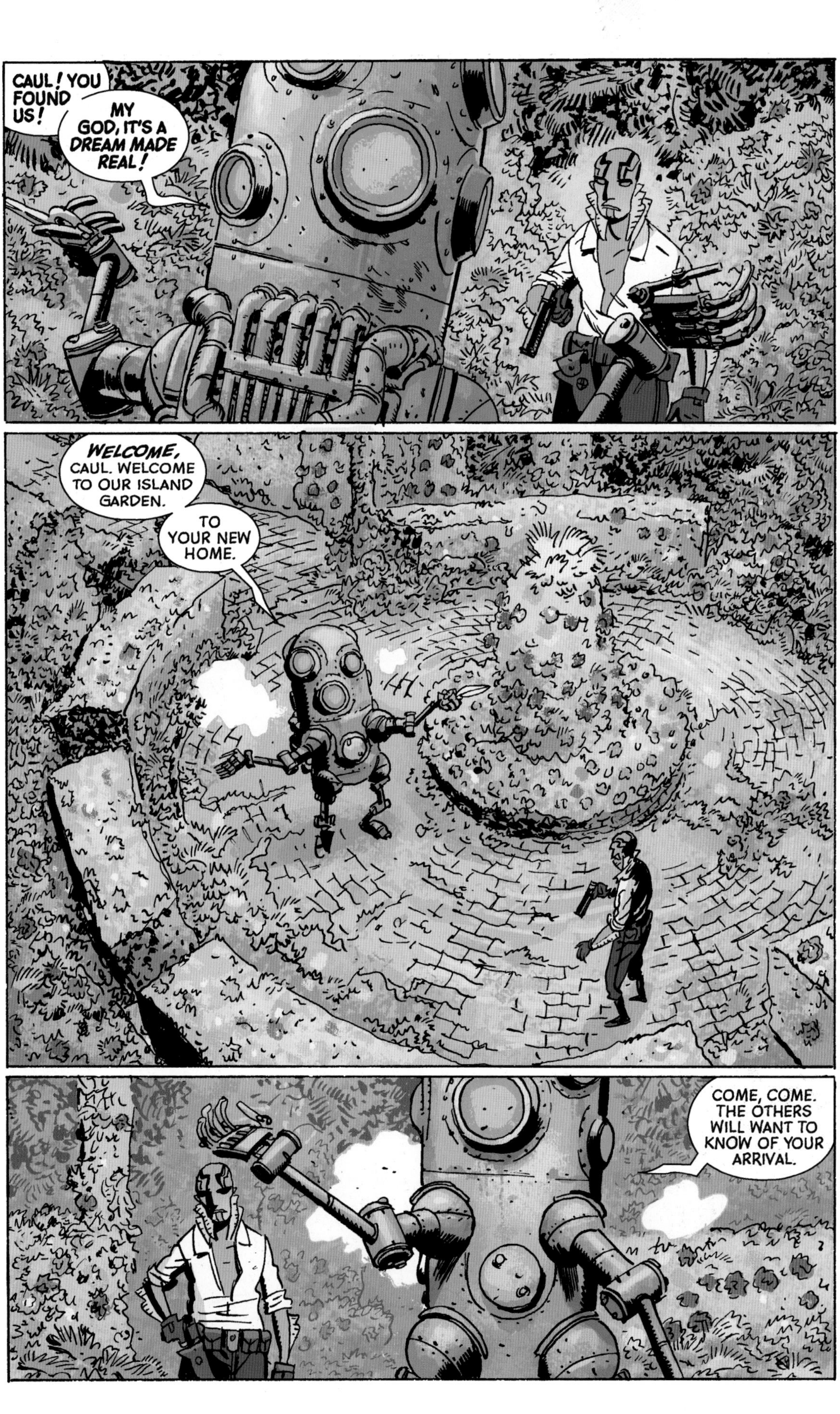
CAUL! YOU FOUND US!
MY GOD, IT'S A DREAM MADE REAL!
WELCOME, CAUL. WELCOME TO OUR ISLAND GARDEN.
TO YOUR NEW HOME.
COME, COME. THE OTHERS WILL WANT TO KNOW OF YOUR ARRIVAL.

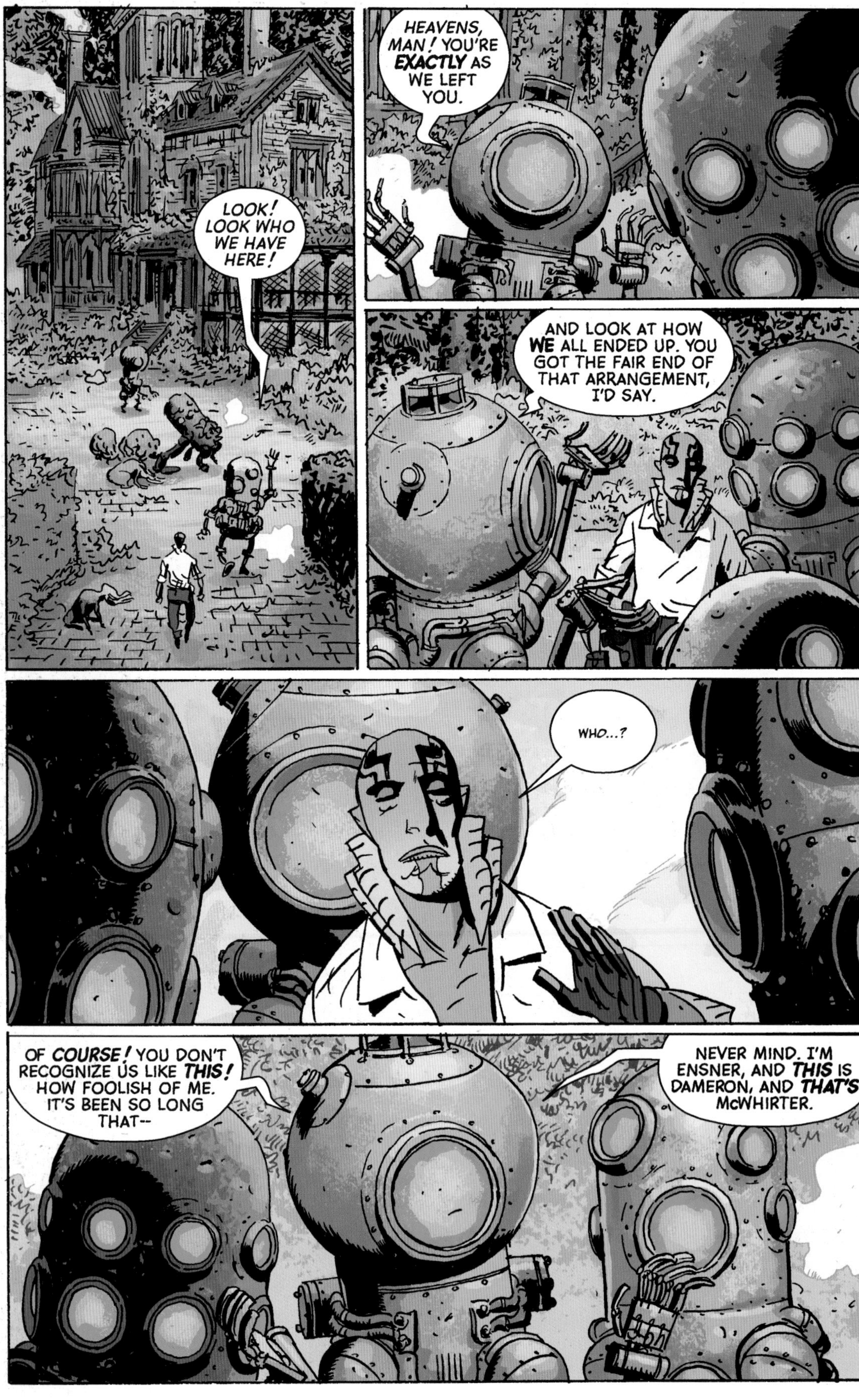
LOOK! LOOK WHO WE HAVE HERE!
HEAVENS, MAN! YOU'RE EXACTLY AS WE LEFT YOU.
AND LOOK AT HOW WE ALL ENDED UP. YOU GOT THE FAIR END OF THAT ARRANGEMENT, I'D SAY.
WHO...?
OF COURSE! YOU DON'T RECOGNIZE US LIKE THIS! HOW FOOLISH OF ME. IT'S BEEN SO LONG THAT--
NEVER MIND. I'M ENSNER, AND THIS IS DAMERON, AND THAT'S McWHIRTER.

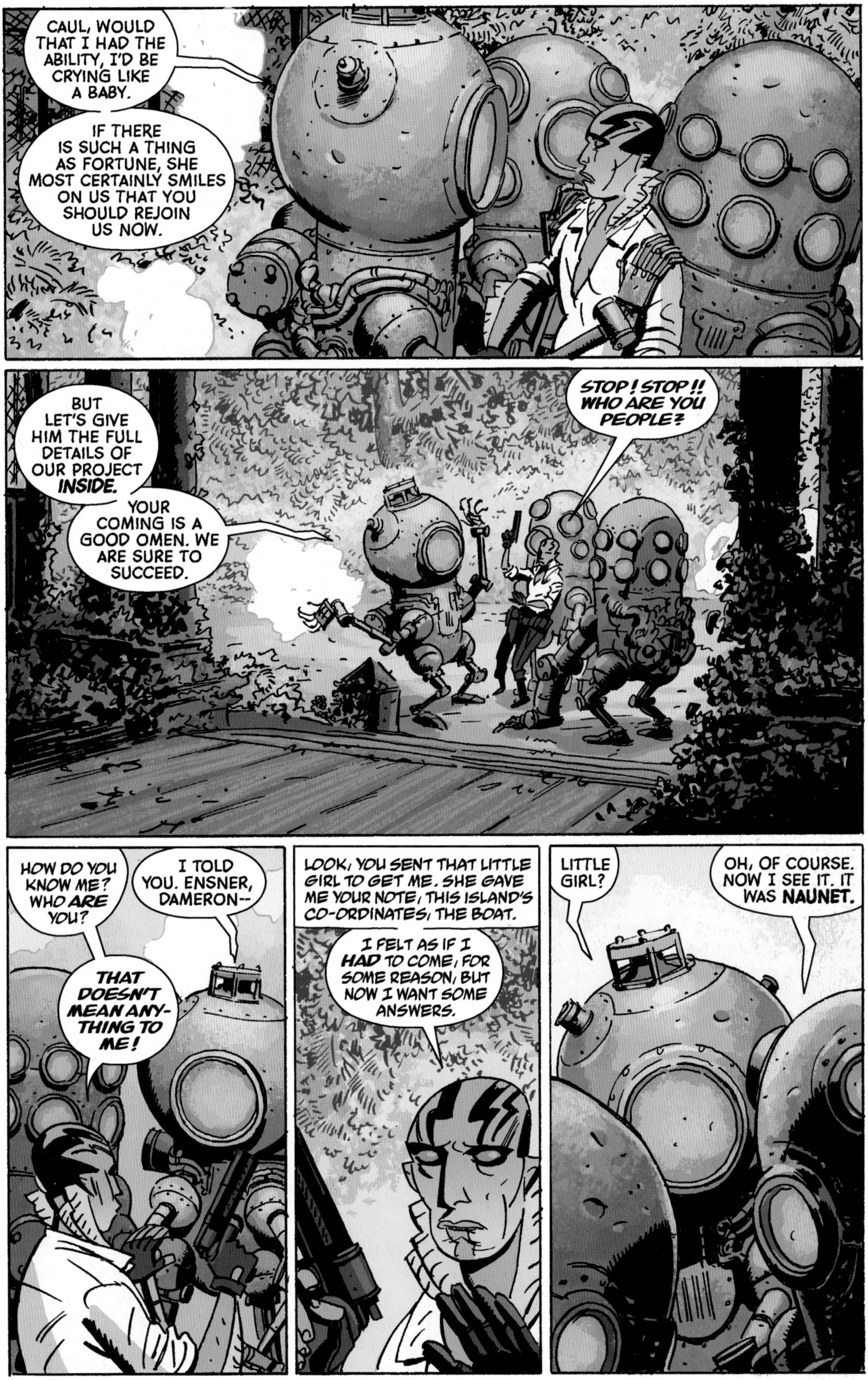
CAUL, WOULD THAT I HAD THE ABILITY, I'D BE CRYING LIKE A BABY.
IF THERE IS SUCH A THING AS FORTUNE, SHE MOST CERTAINLY SMILES ON US THAT YOU SHOULD REJOIN US NOW.
BUT LET'S GIVE HIM THE FULL DETAILS OF OUR PROJECT INSIDE.
YOUR COMING IS A GOOD OMEN. WE ARE SURE TO SUCCEED.
STOP! STOP!! WHO ARE YOU PEOPLE?
HOW DO YOU KNOW ME? WHO ARE YOU?
I TOLD YOU. ENSNER, DAMERON--
THAT DOESN'T MEAN ANY-THING TO ME!
LOOK, YOU SENT THAT LITTLE GIRL TO GET ME. SHE GAVE ME YOUR NOTE, THIS ISLAND'S CO-ORDINATES, THE BOAT.
I FELT AS IF I HAD TO COME, FOR SOME REASON, BUT NOW I WANT SOME ANSWERS.
LITTLE GIRL?
OH, OF COURSE. NOW I SEE IT. IT WAS NAUNET.

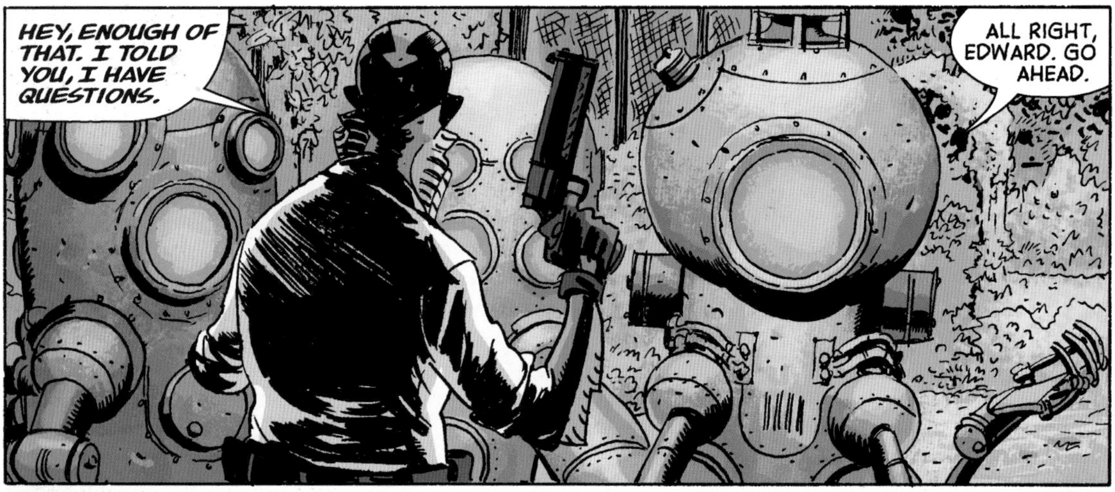
HEY, ENOUGH OF THAT. I TOLD YOU, I HAVE QUESTIONS.
ALL RIGHT, EDWARD. GO AHEAD.

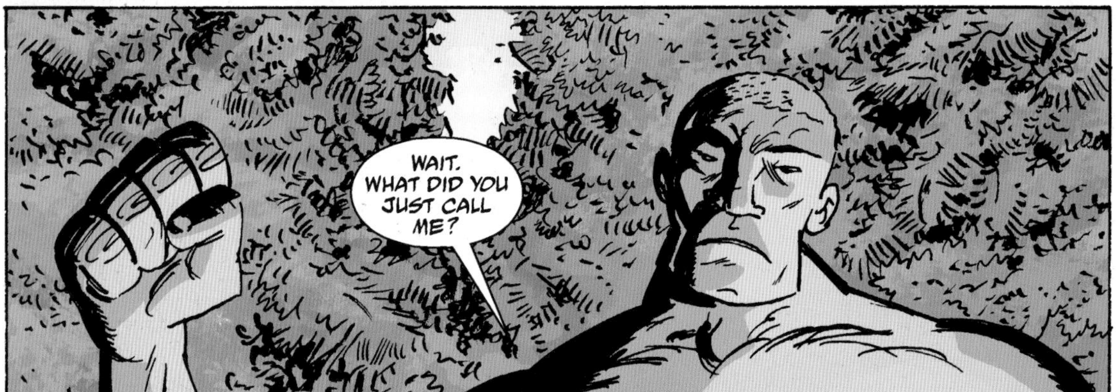
WAIT. WHAT DID YOU JUST CALL ME?

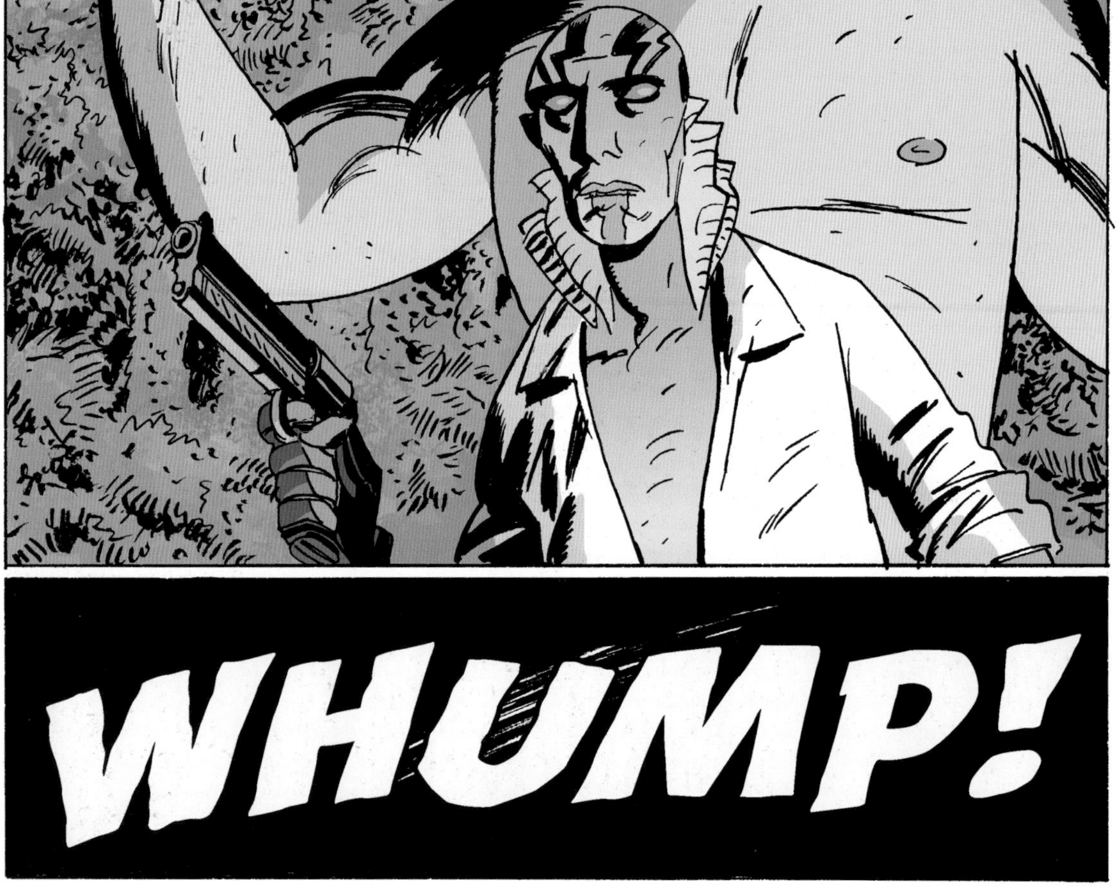
WHUMP!

--HAD A SON IN KAGOSHIMA, RIGHT BEFORE THE JAPANESE SIGNED THE TRIPARTITE TREATY WITH NAZI GERMANY AND FASCIST ITALY.

HER SISTER RAISED HIM WHILE SHE WAS IN THE EMPEROR'S SERVICE, AND THEY MOVED TO CALIFORNIA IN 1946 WHILE *THE LOTUS* WAS ON TRIAL.

HE GREW UP IN CONCORD, AND EVENTUALLY FATHERED A SON BY HIS SECOND WIFE. THAT SON IS BENJAMIN DAIMIO--OUR CAPTAIN.

IT'S ALL VERY PLAIN. A MATTER OF PUBLIC RECORD, AS YOU CAN SEE.

WELL, WHY NOT? IT'S NOT AS IF ANY OF THIS IS ILLEGAL.

NO, OF COURSE NOT, BUT HE'S NEVER MENTIONED ANY CONNECTION.

EVEN WHEN HE SAW ME READING THAT SCRAPBOOK I FOUND.

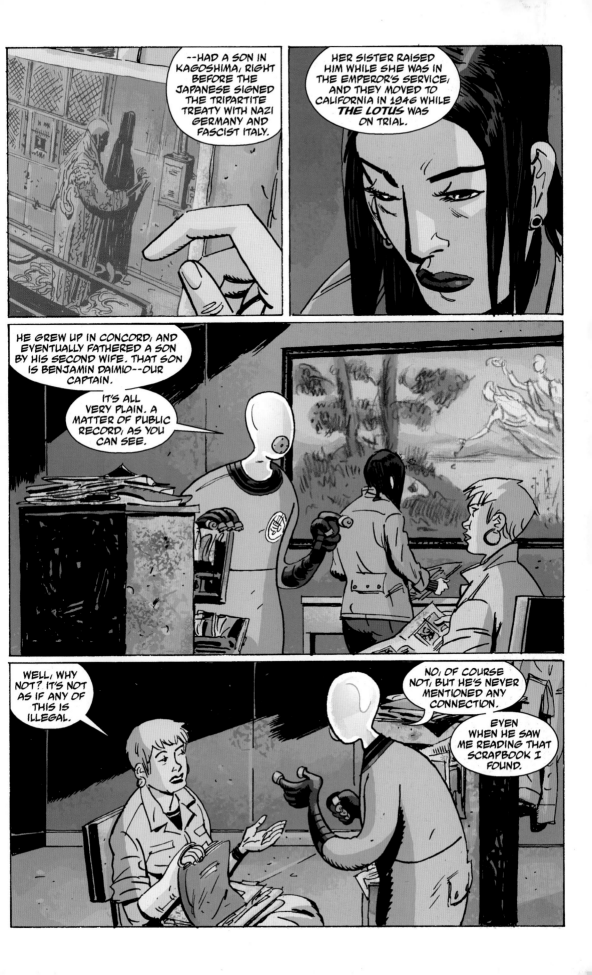

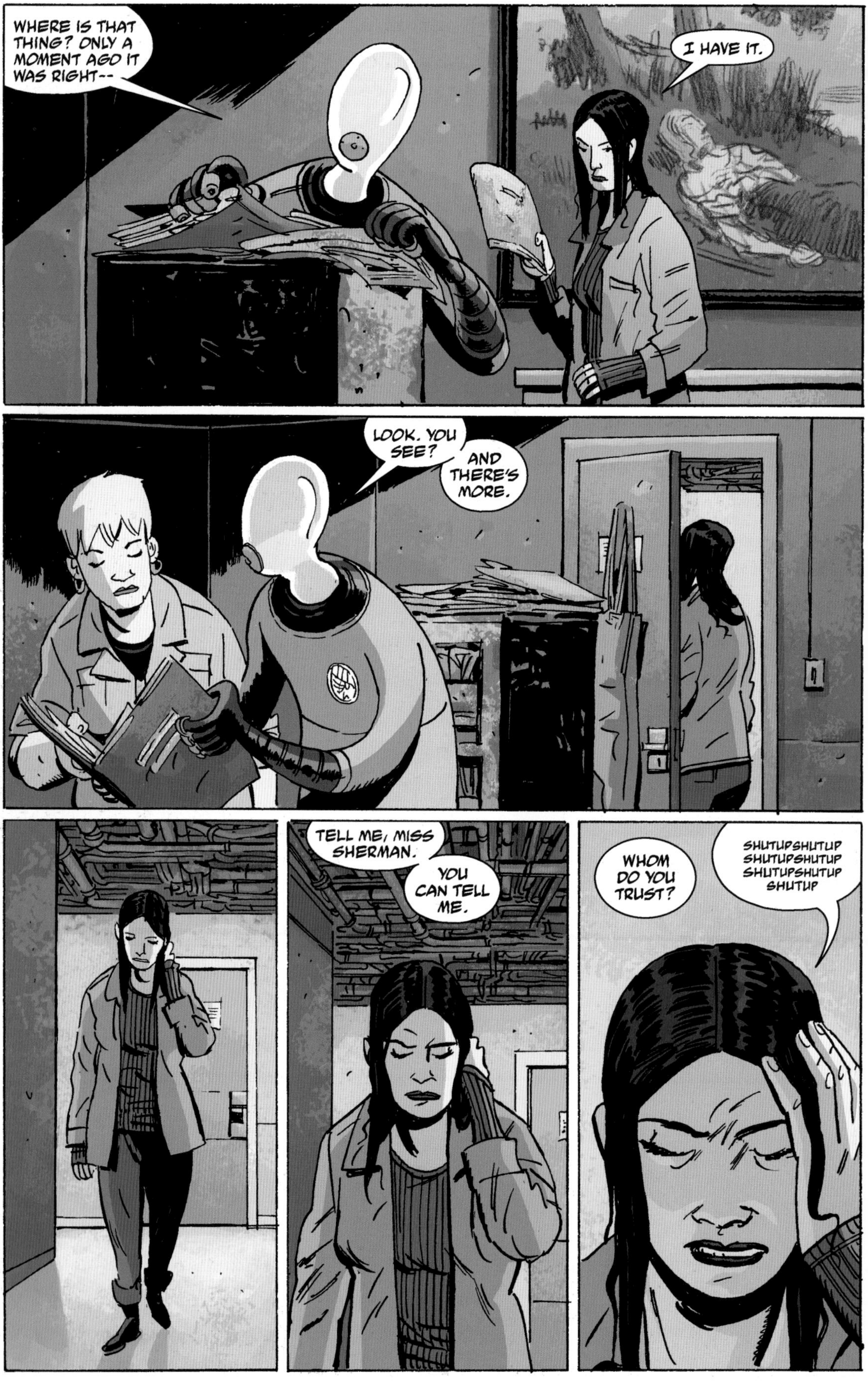
WHERE IS THAT THING? ONLY A MOMENT AGO IT WAS RIGHT--
I HAVE IT.
LOOK. YOU SEE?
AND THERE'S MORE.
TELL ME, MISS SHERMAN.
YOU CAN TELL ME.
WHOM DO YOU TRUST?
SHUTUPSHUTUP SHUTUPSHUTUP SHUTUPSHUTUP SHUTUP

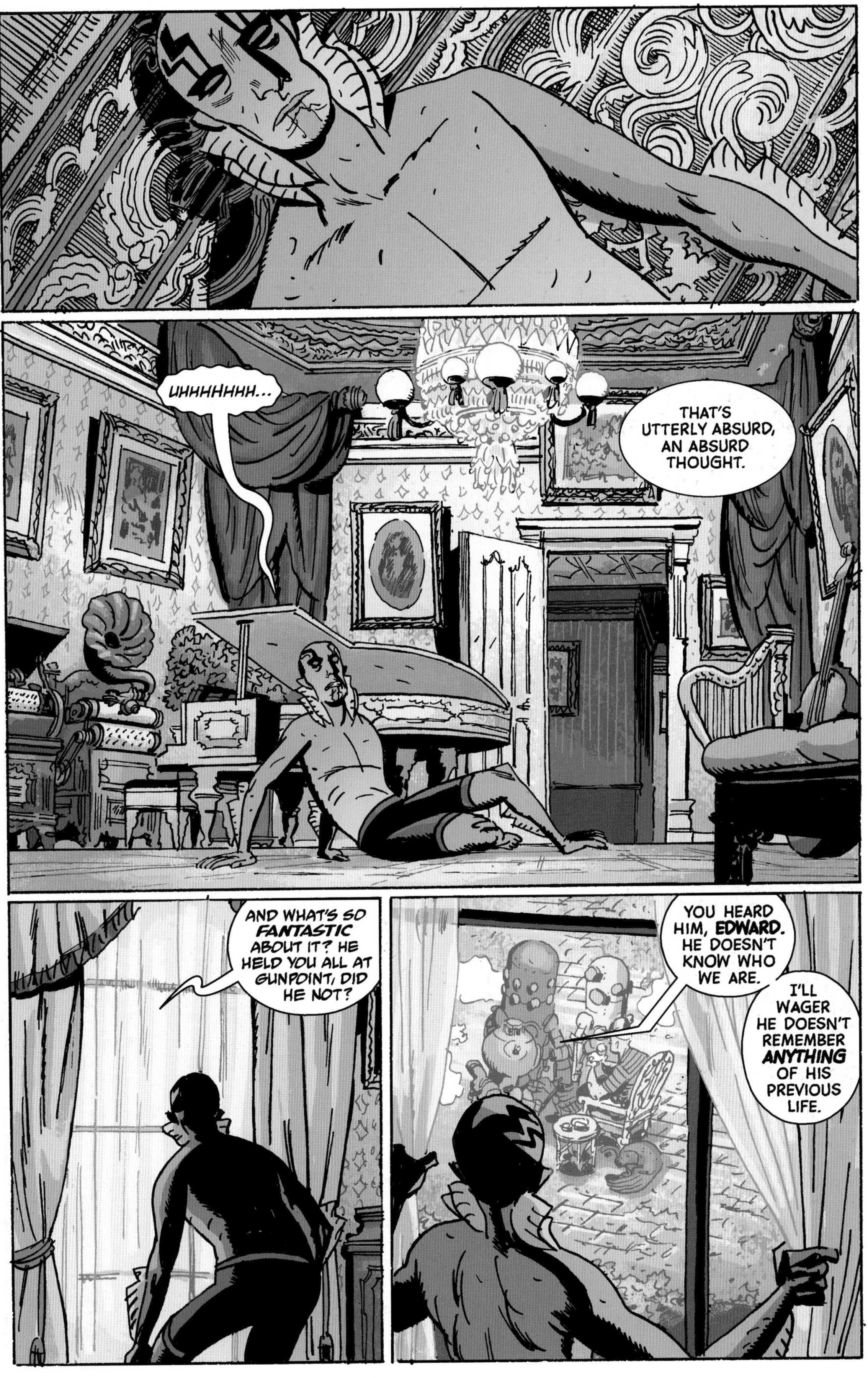
UHHHHHHH...
THAT'S UTTERLY ABSURD, AN ABSURD THOUGHT.
AND WHAT'S SO FANTASTIC ABOUT IT? HE HELD YOU ALL AT GUNPOINT, DID HE NOT?
YOU HEARD HIM, EDWARD. HE DOESN'T KNOW WHO WE ARE.
I'LL WAGER HE DOESN'T REMEMBER ANYTHING OF HIS PREVIOUS LIFE.

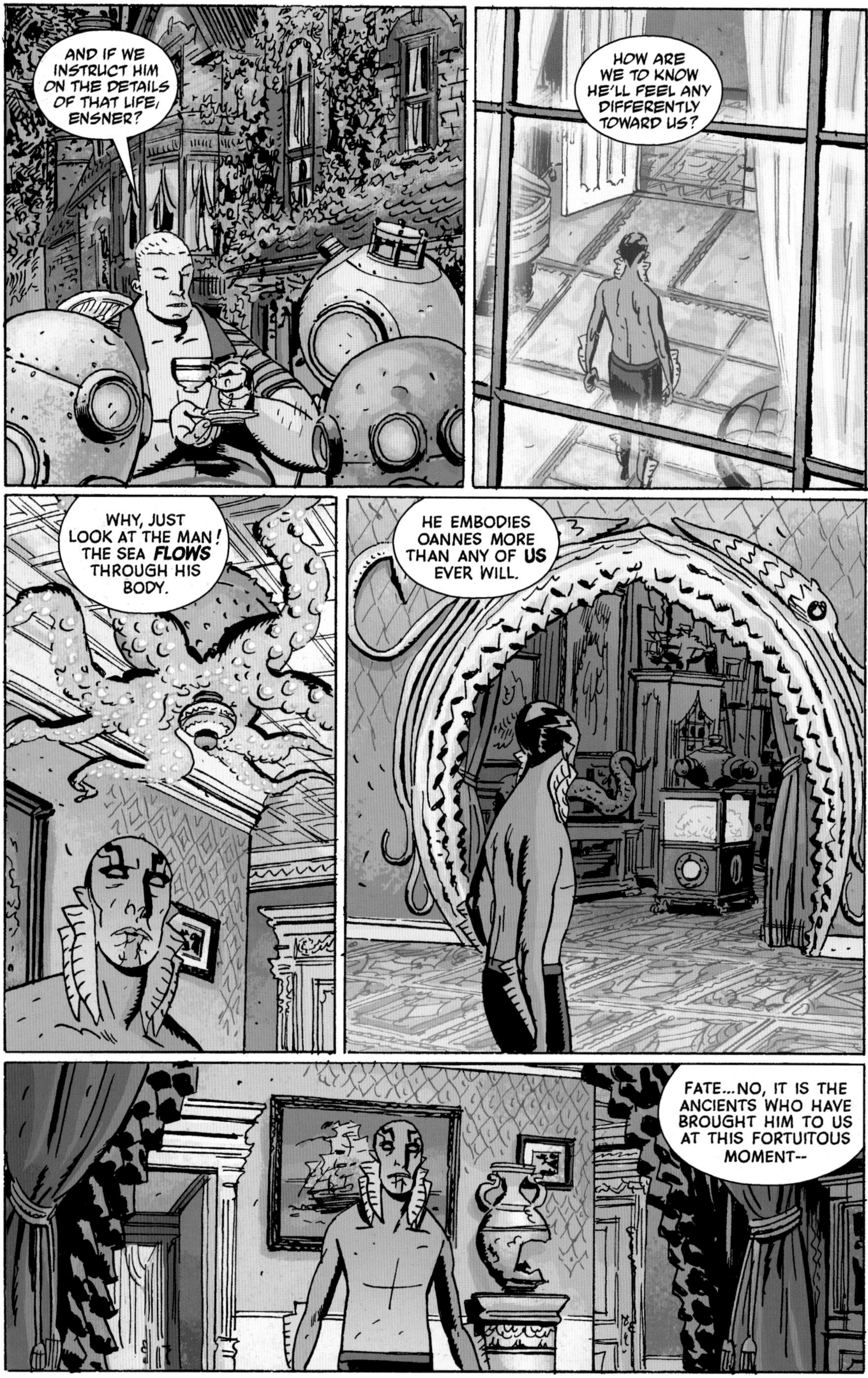
AND IF WE INSTRUCT HIM ON THE DETAILS OF THAT LIFE, ENSNER?
HOW ARE WE TO KNOW HE'LL FEEL ANY DIFFERENTLY TOWARD US?
WHY, JUST LOOK AT THE MAN! THE SEA FLOWS THROUGH HIS BODY.
HE EMBODIES OANNES MORE THAN ANY OF US EVER WILL.
FATE...NO, IT IS THE ANCIENTS WHO HAVE BROUGHT HIM TO US AT THIS FORTUITOUS MOMENT--

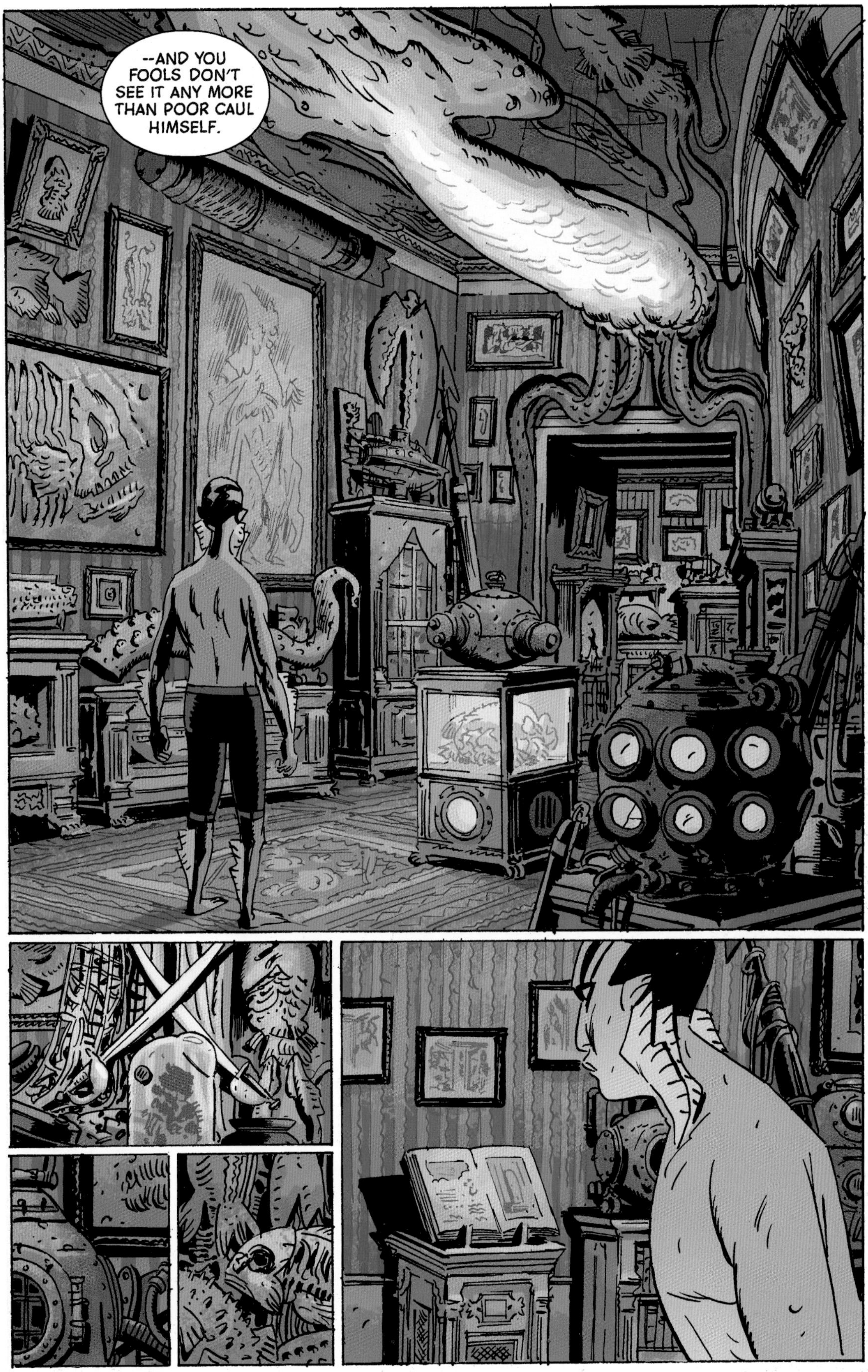
--AND YOU FOOLS DON'T SEE IT ANY MORE THAN POOR CAUL HIMSELF.

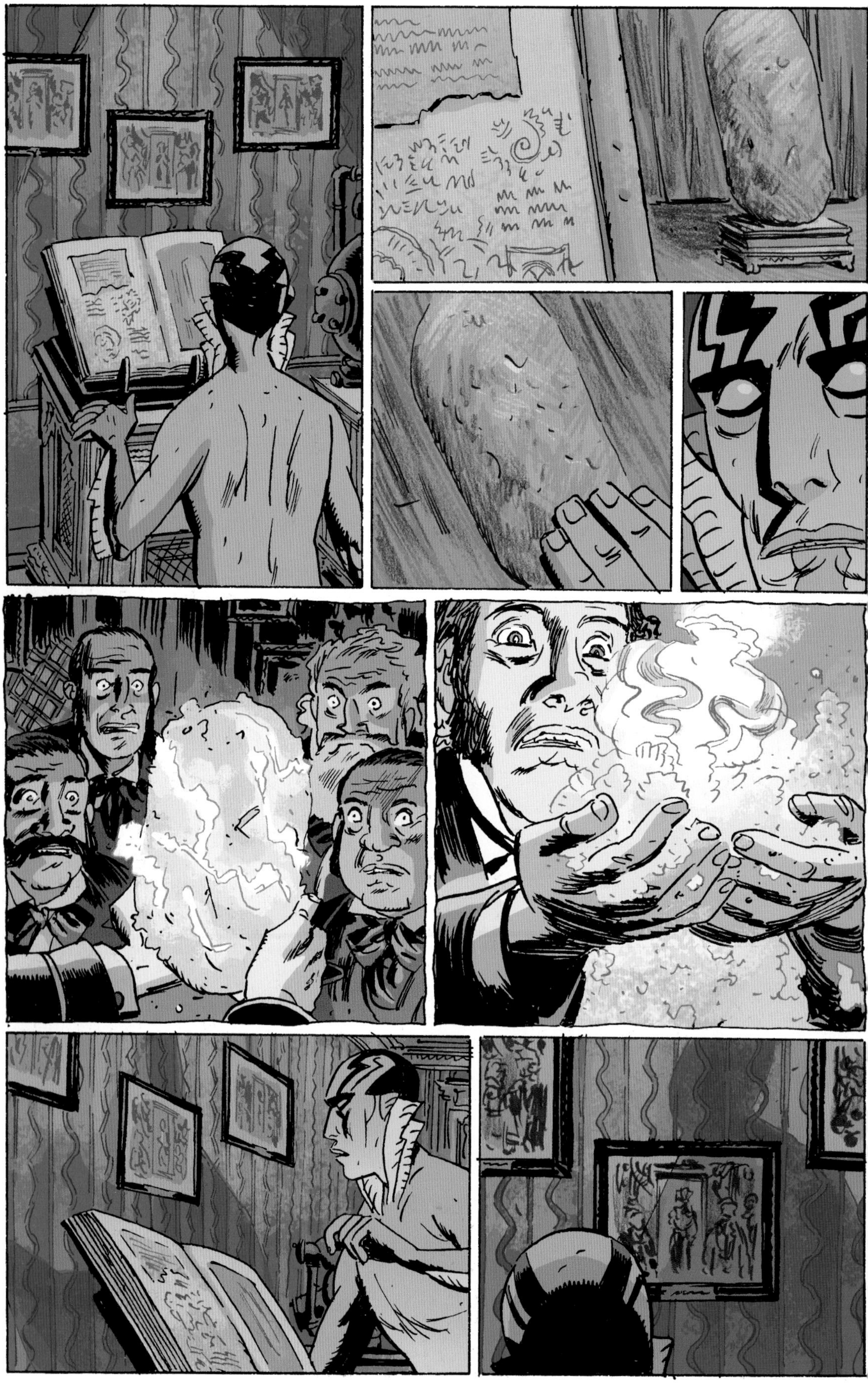

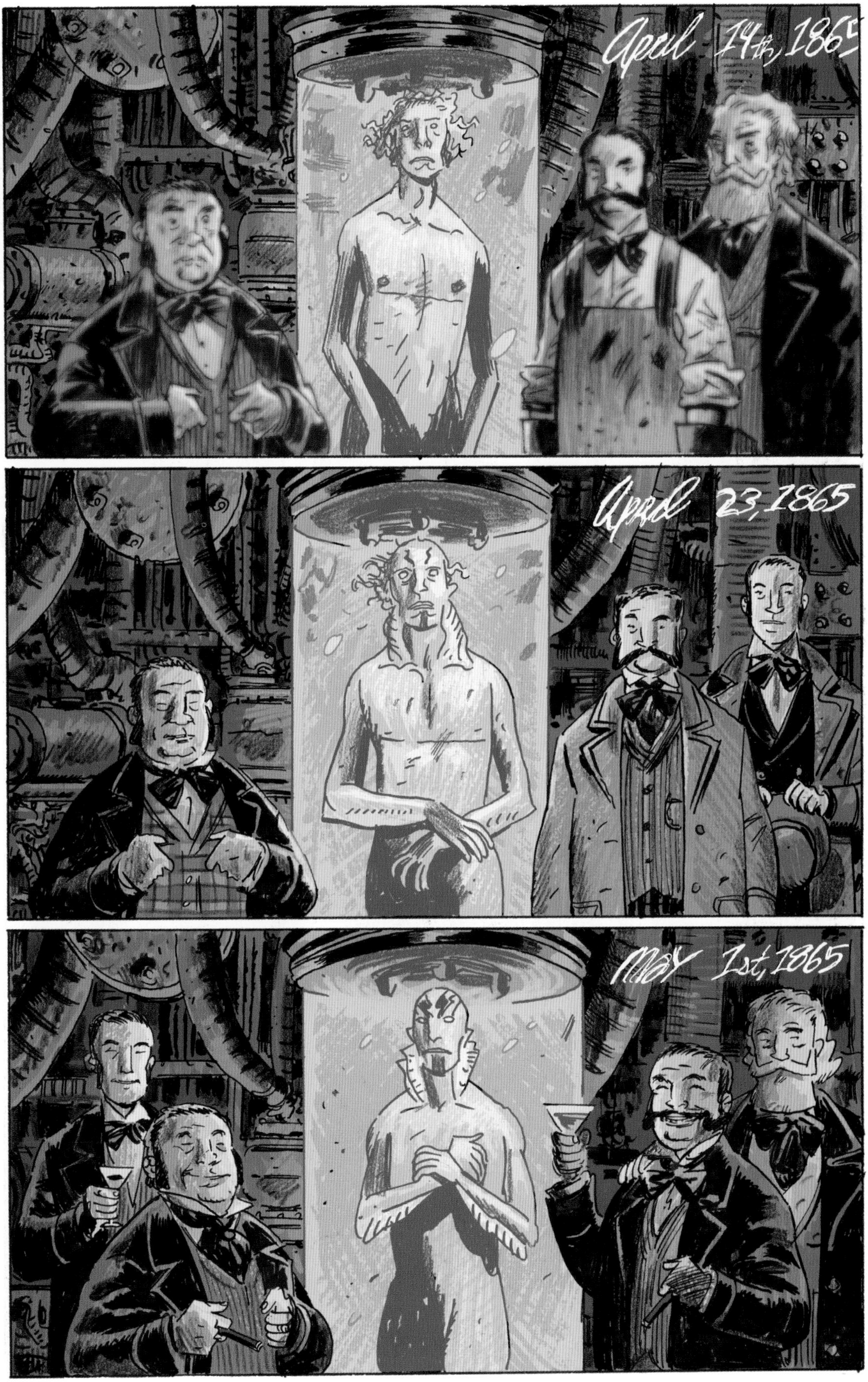
April 14th, 1865
April 23, 1865
May 1st, 1865

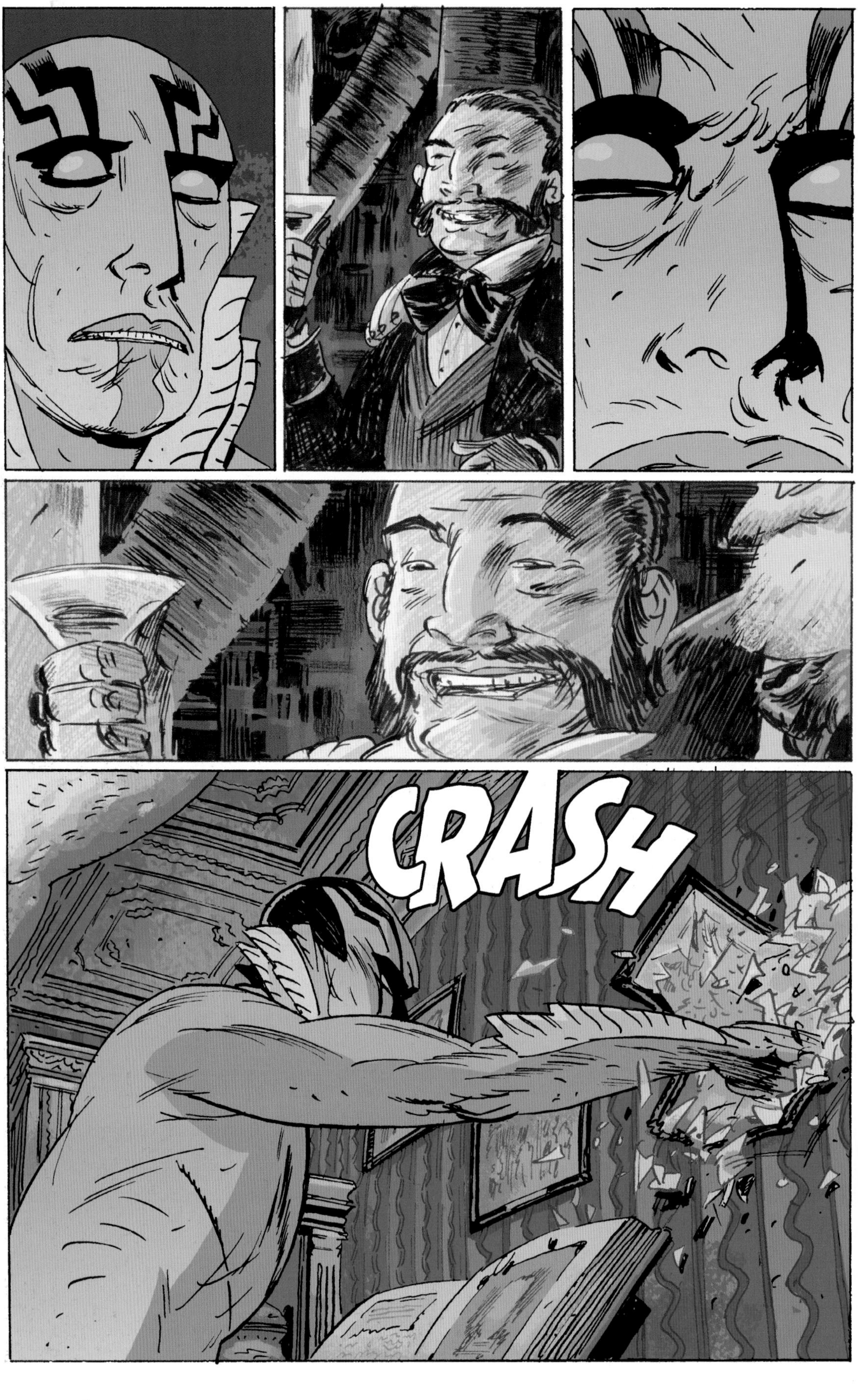
CRASH

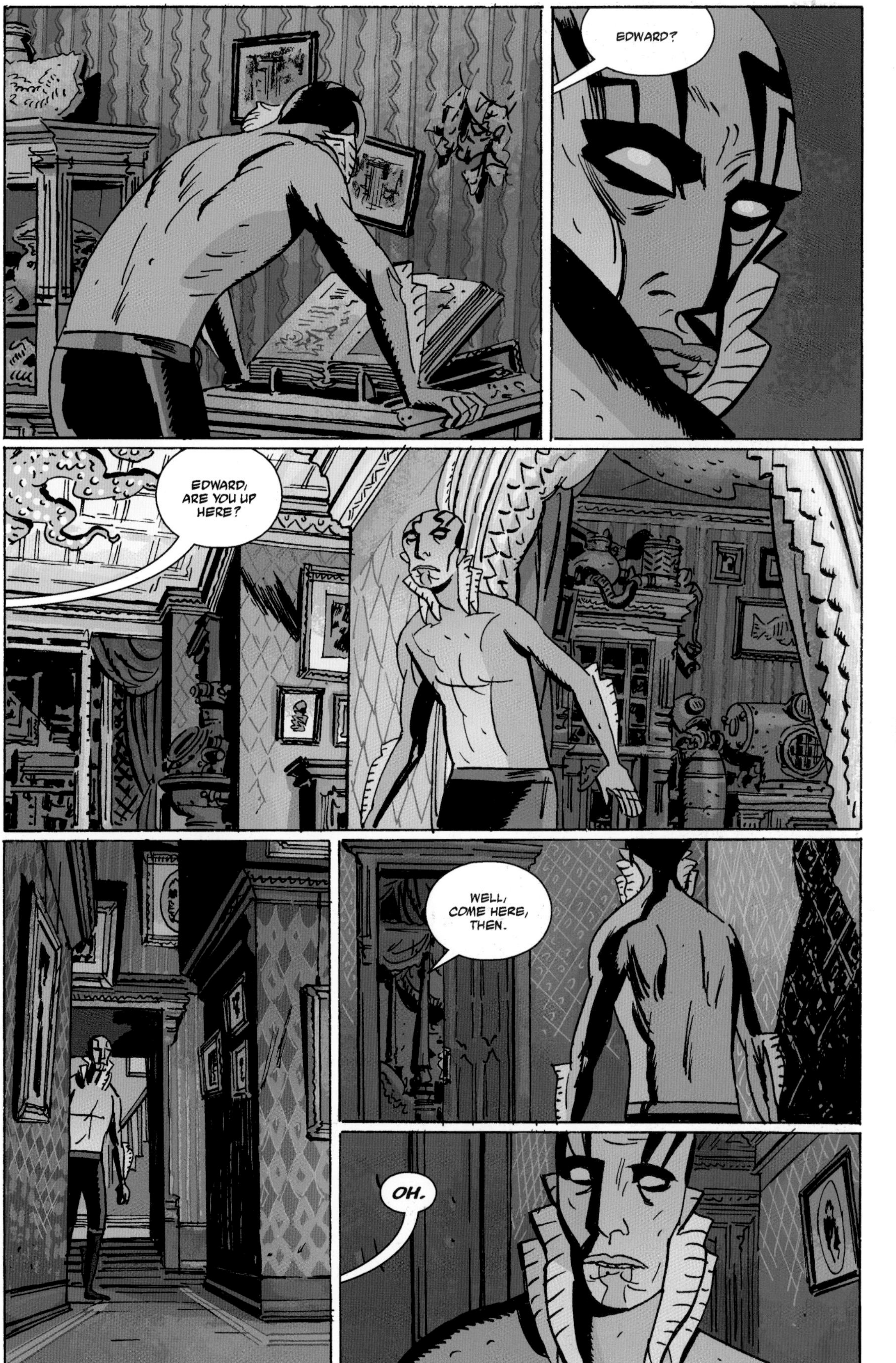
EDWARD?
EDWARD, ARE YOU UP HERE?
WELL, COME HERE, THEN.
OH.

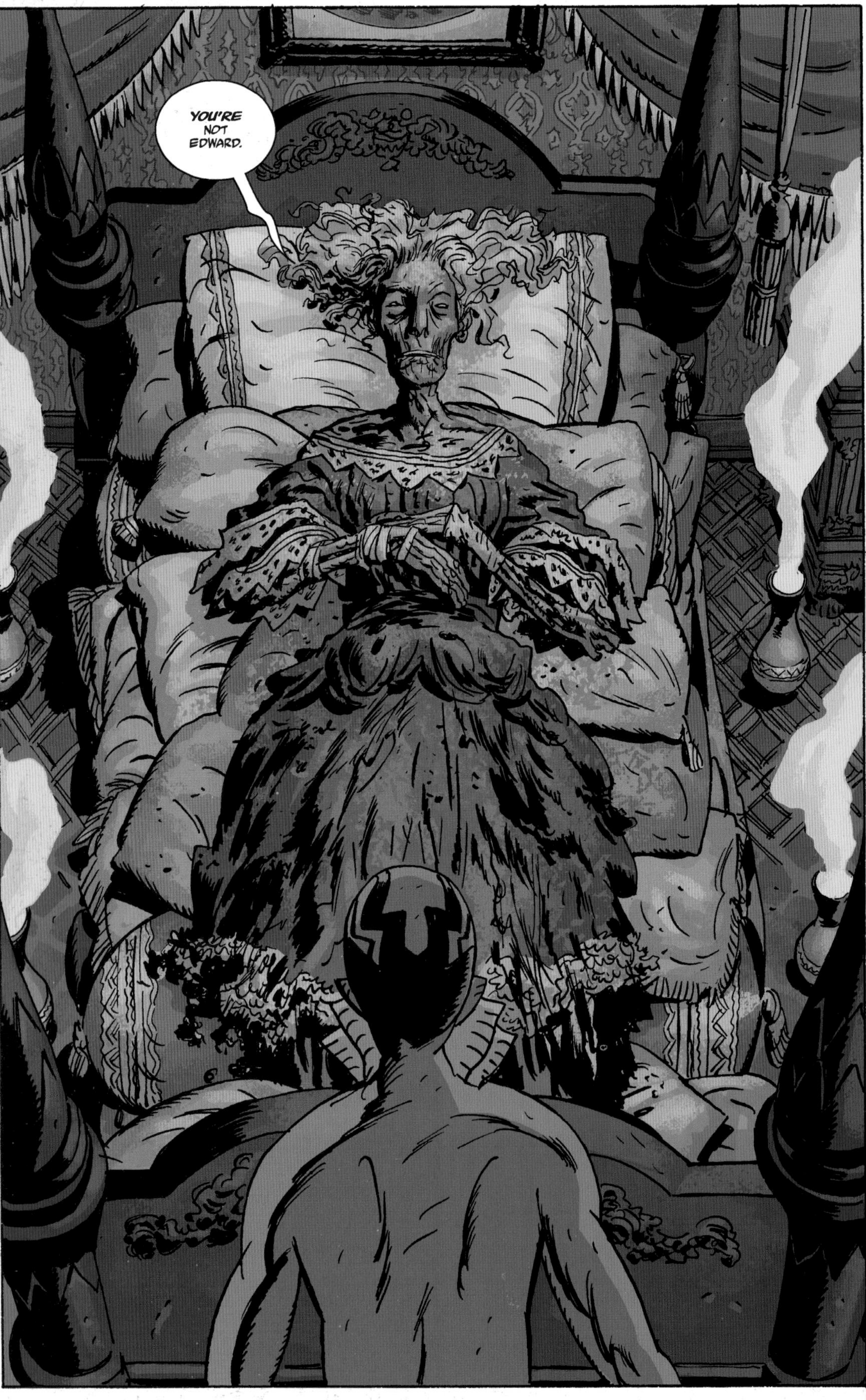
YOU'RE NOT EDWARD.

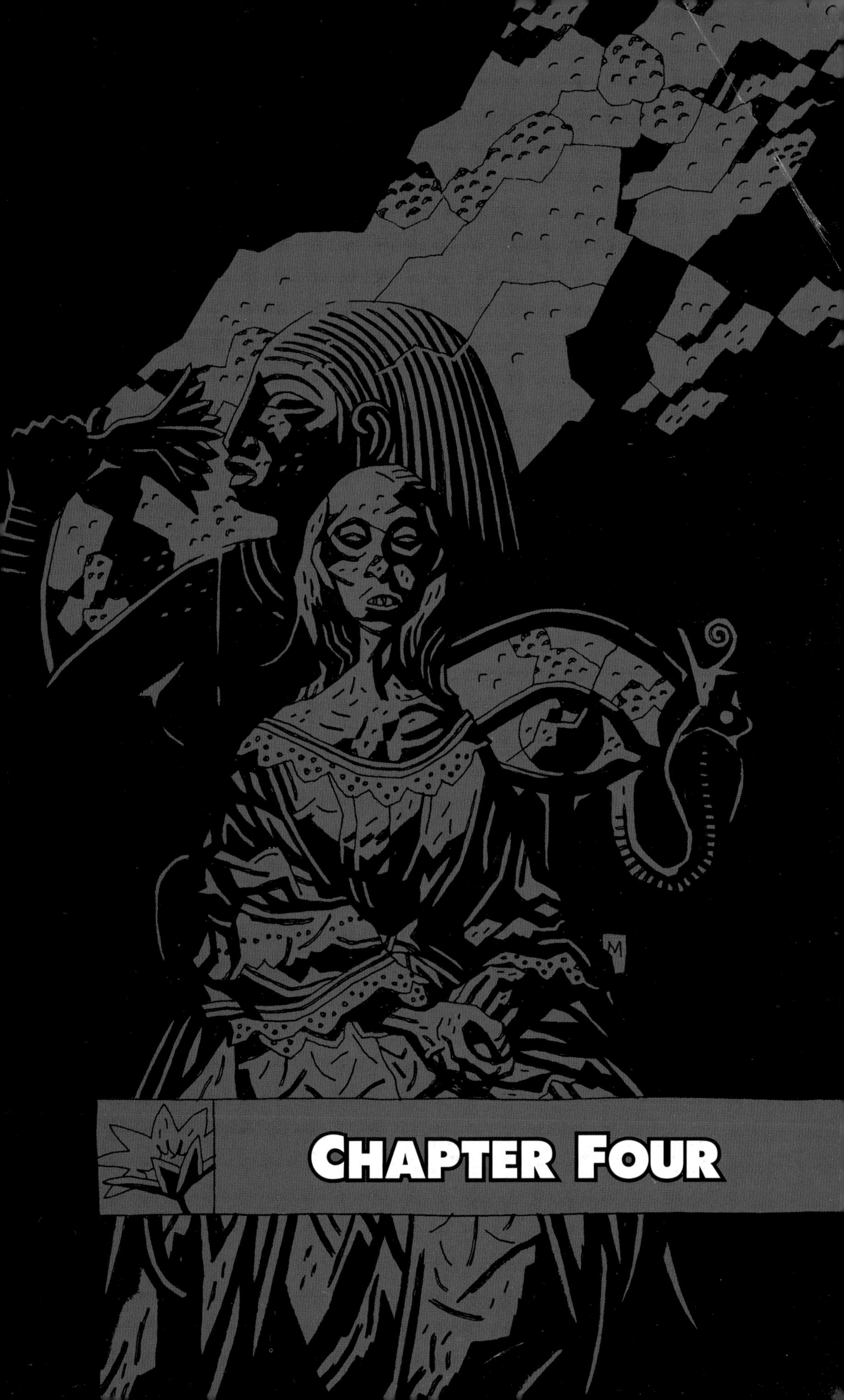

CHAPTER FOUR

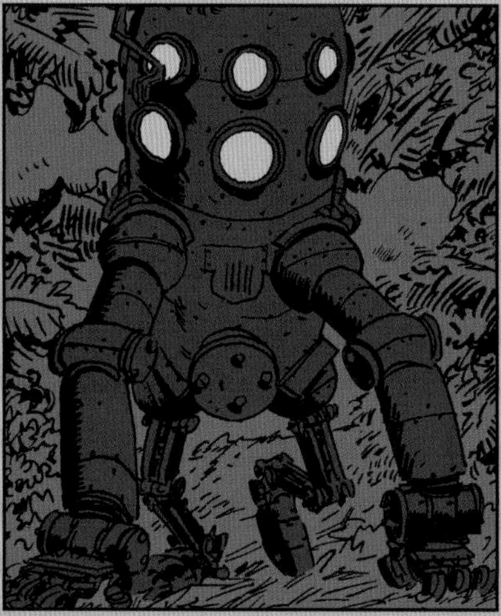

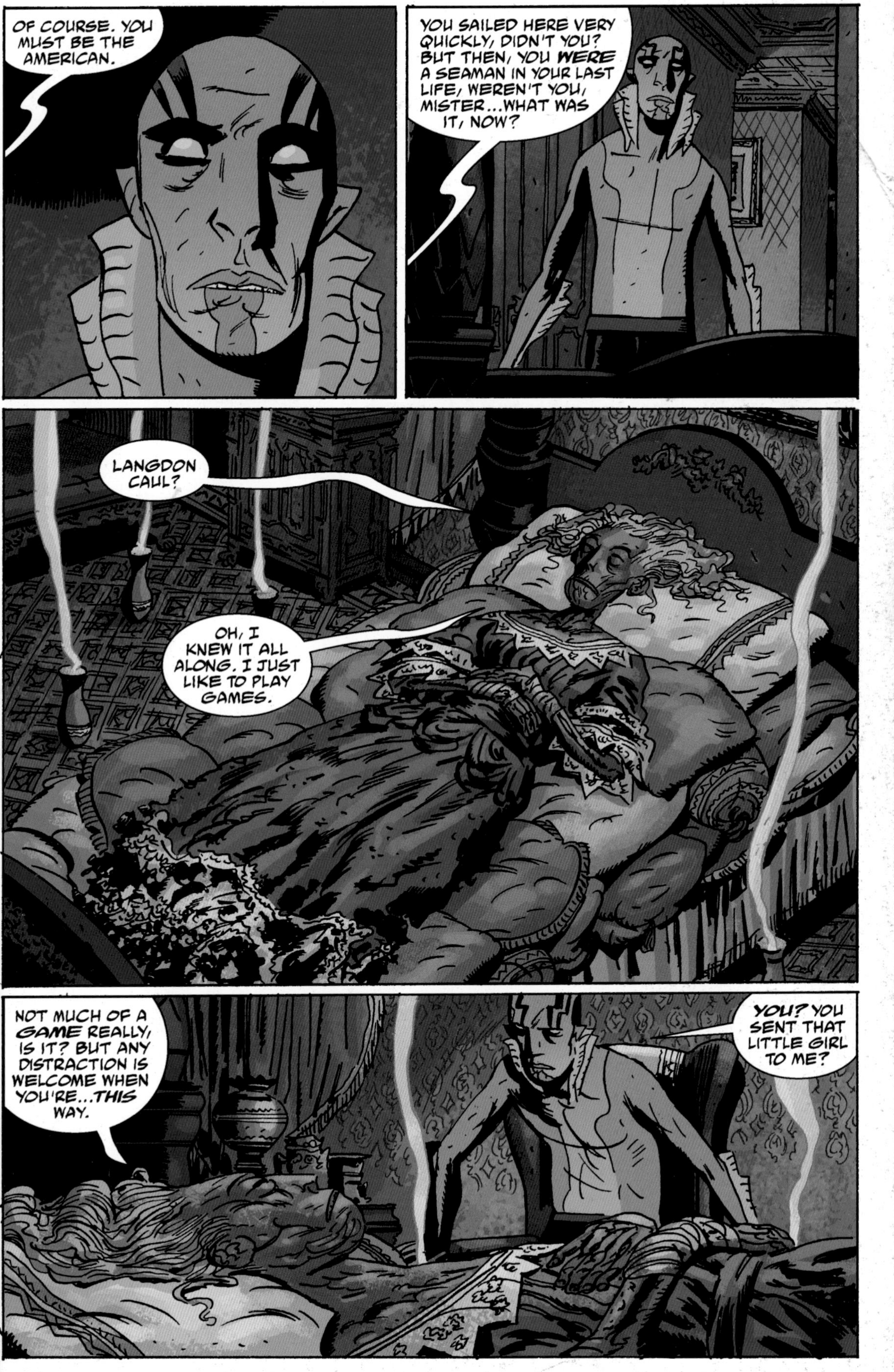

OF COURSE. YOU MUST BE THE AMERICAN.
YOU SAILED HERE VERY QUICKLY, DIDN'T YOU? BUT THEN, YOU *WERE* A SEAMAN IN YOUR LAST LIFE, WEREN'T YOU, MISTER...WHAT WAS IT, NOW?
LANGDON CAUL?
OH, I KNEW IT ALL ALONG. I JUST LIKE TO PLAY GAMES.
NOT MUCH OF A *GAME* REALLY, IS IT? BUT ANY DISTRACTION IS WELCOME WHEN YOU'RE...*THIS* WAY.
YOU? YOU SENT THAT LITTLE GIRL TO ME?

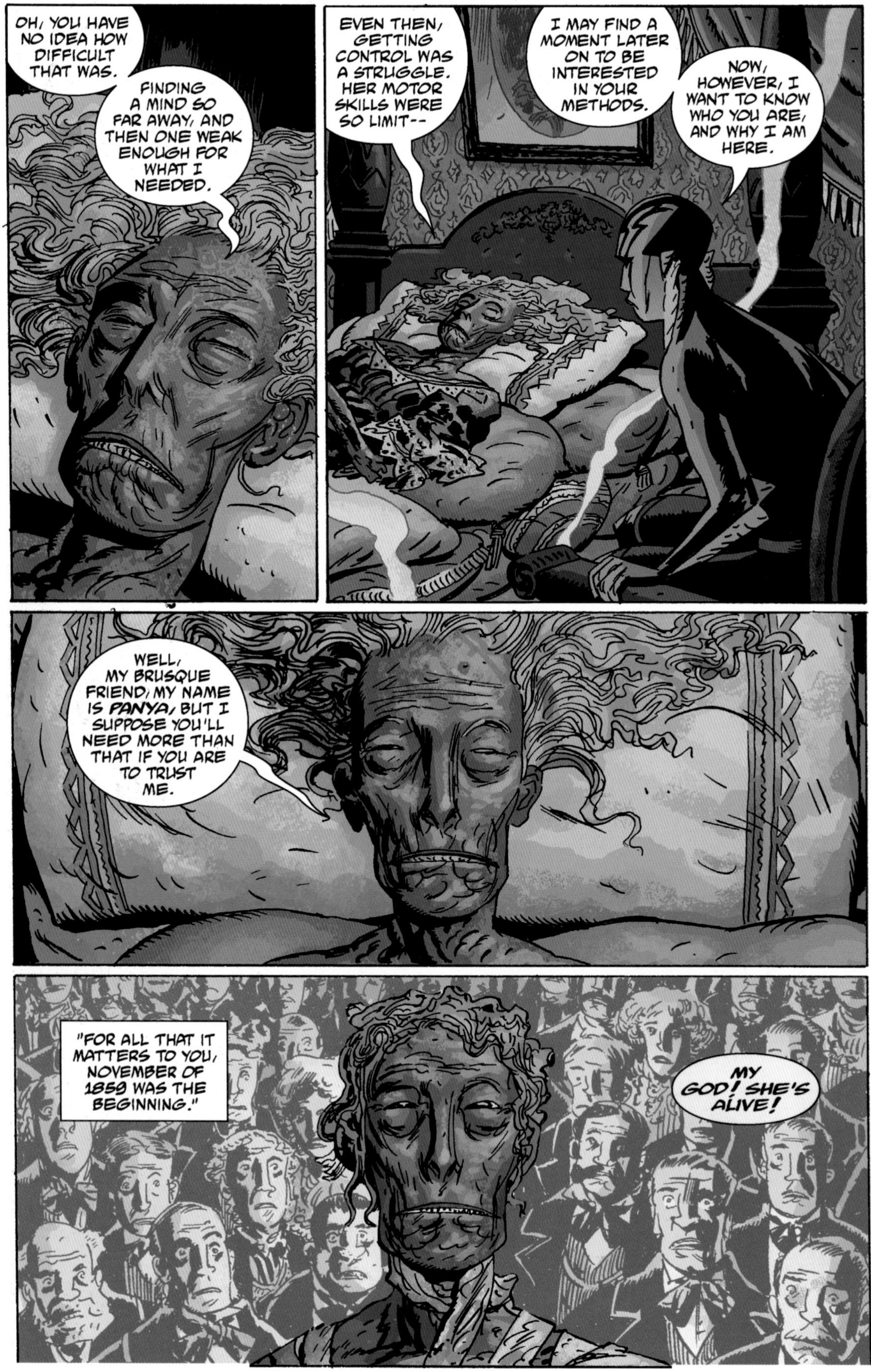
OH, YOU HAVE NO IDEA HOW DIFFICULT THAT WAS.
FINDING A MIND SO FAR AWAY, AND THEN ONE WEAK ENOUGH FOR WHAT I NEEDED.
EVEN THEN, GETTING CONTROL WAS A STRUGGLE. HER MOTOR SKILLS WERE SO LIMIT--
I MAY FIND A MOMENT LATER ON TO BE INTERESTED IN YOUR METHODS.
NOW, HOWEVER, I WANT TO KNOW WHO YOU ARE, AND WHY I AM HERE.
WELL, MY BRUSQUE FRIEND, MY NAME IS PANYA, BUT I SUPPOSE YOU'LL NEED MORE THAN THAT IF YOU ARE TO TRUST ME.
"FOR ALL THAT IT MATTERS TO YOU, NOVEMBER OF 1859 WAS THE BEGINNING."
MY GOD! SHE'S ALIVE!

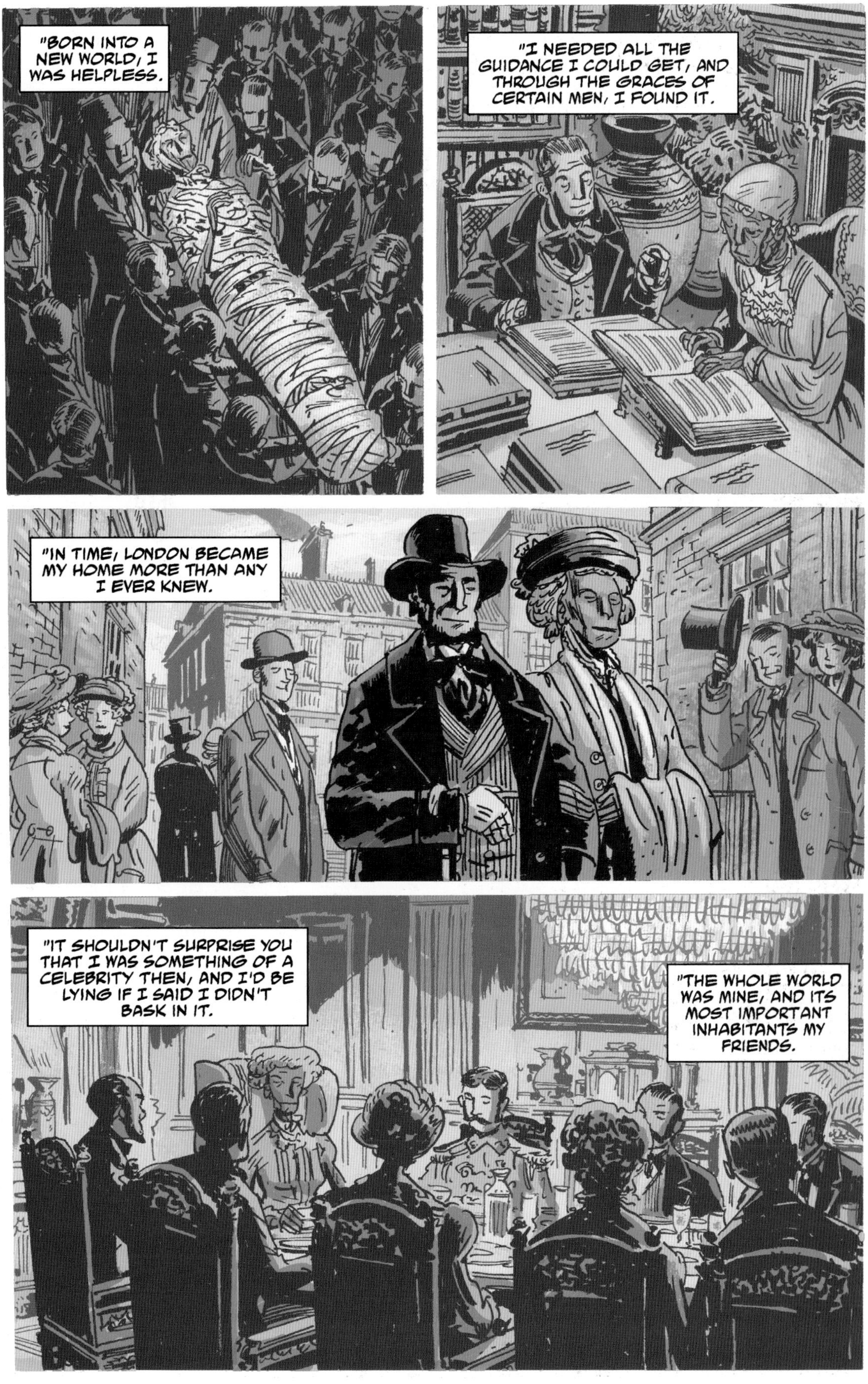
"BORN INTO A NEW WORLD, I WAS HELPLESS.
"I NEEDED ALL THE GUIDANCE I COULD GET, AND THROUGH THE GRACES OF CERTAIN MEN, I FOUND IT.
"IN TIME, LONDON BECAME MY HOME MORE THAN ANY I EVER KNEW.
"IT SHOULDN'T SURPRISE YOU THAT I WAS SOMETHING OF A CELEBRITY THEN, AND I'D BE LYING IF I SAID I DIDN'T BASK IN IT.
"THE WHOLE WORLD WAS MINE, AND ITS MOST IMPORTANT INHABITANTS MY FRIENDS.

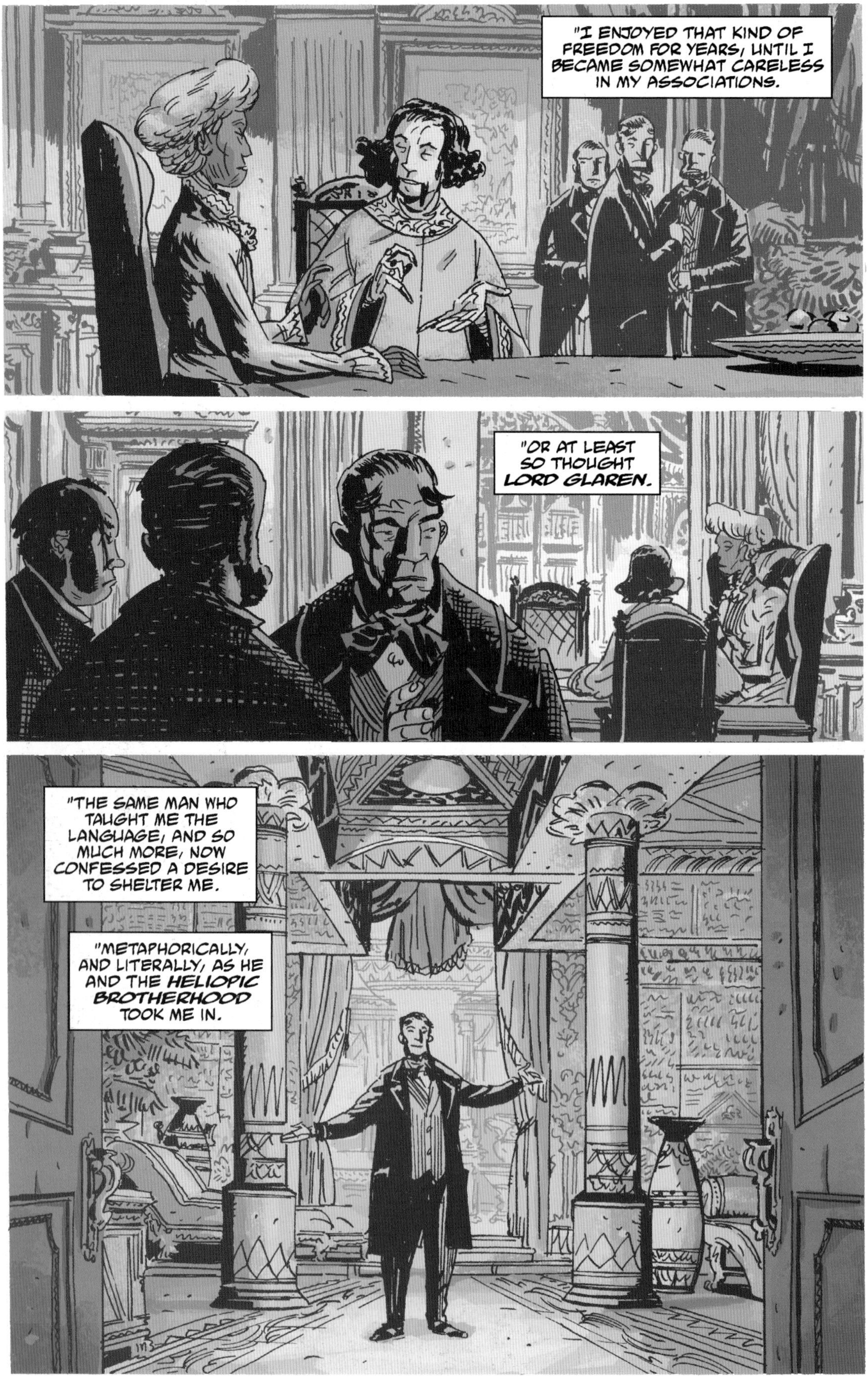
"I ENJOYED THAT KIND OF FREEDOM FOR YEARS, UNTIL I BECAME SOMEWHAT CARELESS IN MY ASSOCIATIONS.
"OR AT LEAST SO THOUGHT LORD GLAREN.
"THE SAME MAN WHO TAUGHT ME THE LANGUAGE, AND SO MUCH MORE, NOW CONFESSED A DESIRE TO SHELTER ME.
"METAPHORICALLY, AND LITERALLY, AS HE AND THE HELIOPIC BROTHERHOOD TOOK ME IN.

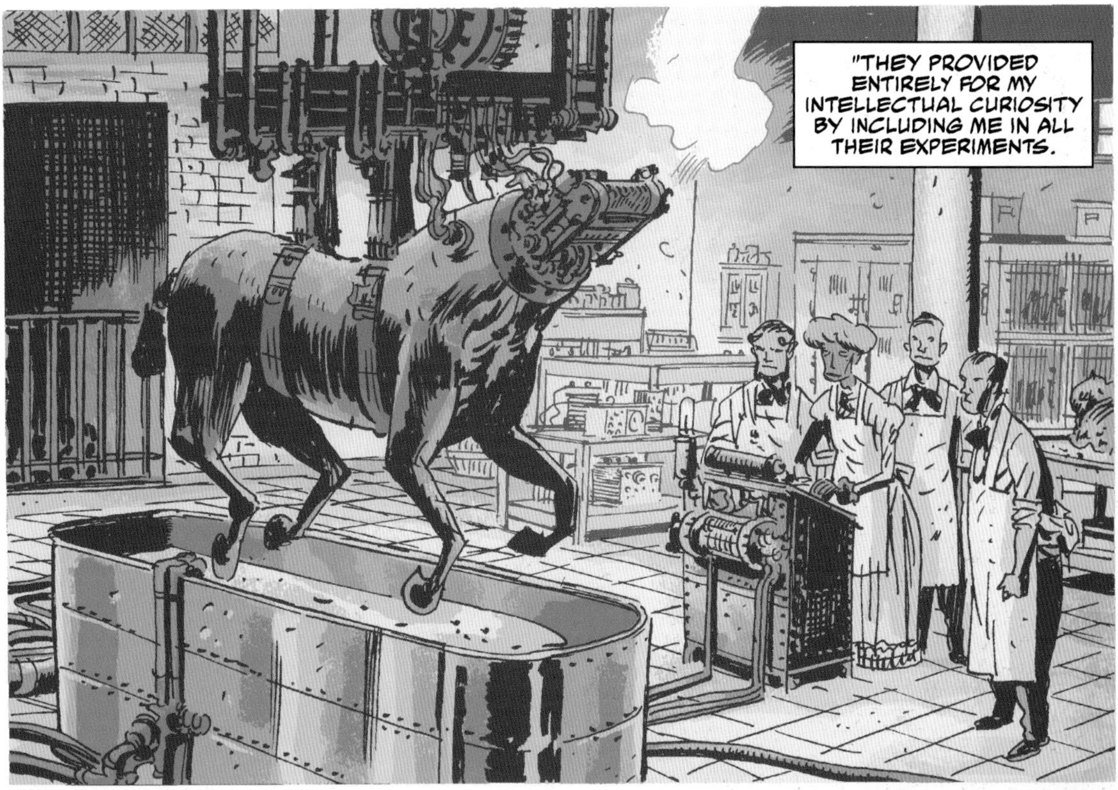
"THEY PROVIDED ENTIRELY FOR MY INTELLECTUAL CURIOSITY BY INCLUDING ME IN ALL THEIR EXPERIMENTS.

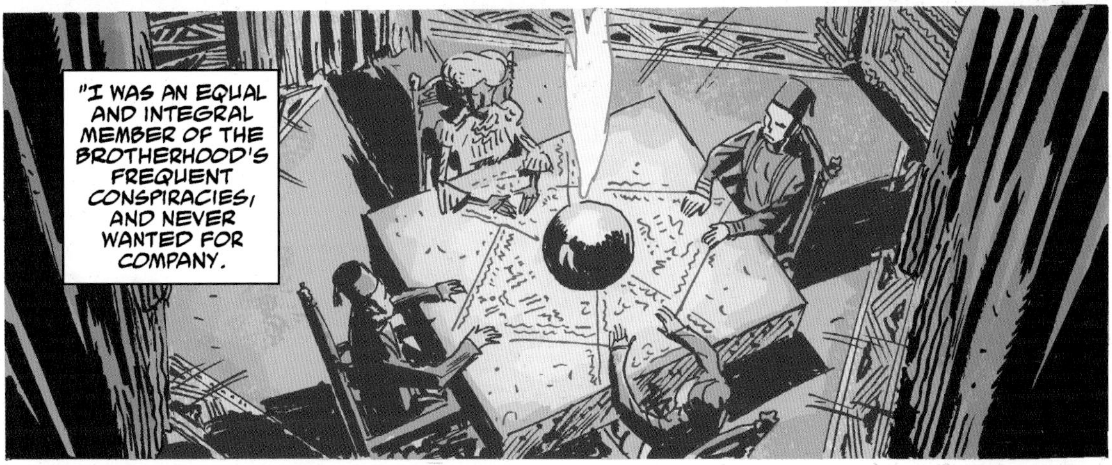
"I WAS AN EQUAL AND INTEGRAL MEMBER OF THE BROTHERHOOD'S FREQUENT CONSPIRACIES, AND NEVER WANTED FOR COMPANY.

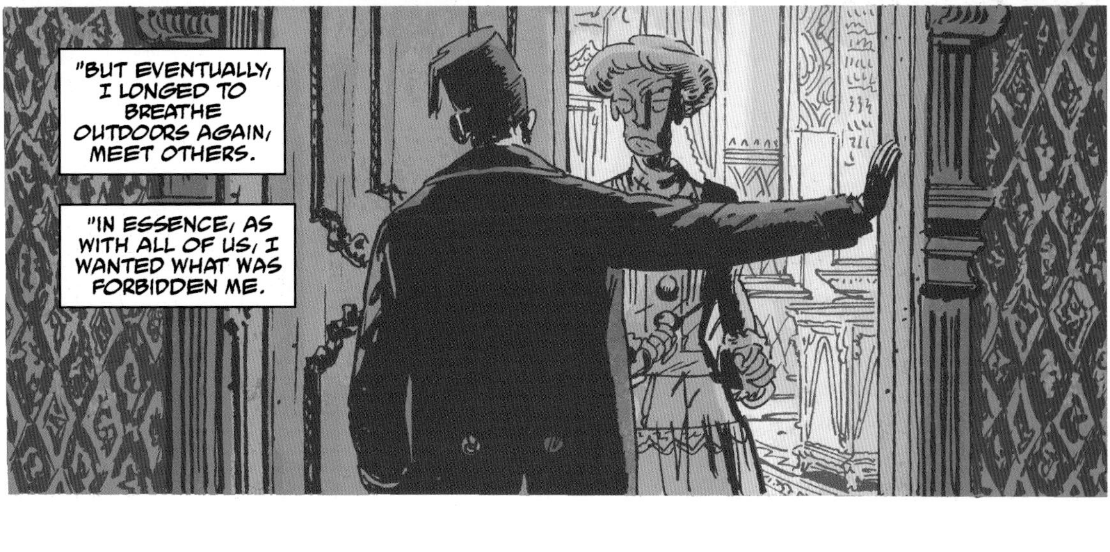
"BUT EVENTUALLY, I LONGED TO BREATHE OUTDOORS AGAIN, MEET OTHERS.
"IN ESSENCE, AS WITH ALL OF US, I WANTED WHAT WAS FORBIDDEN ME.

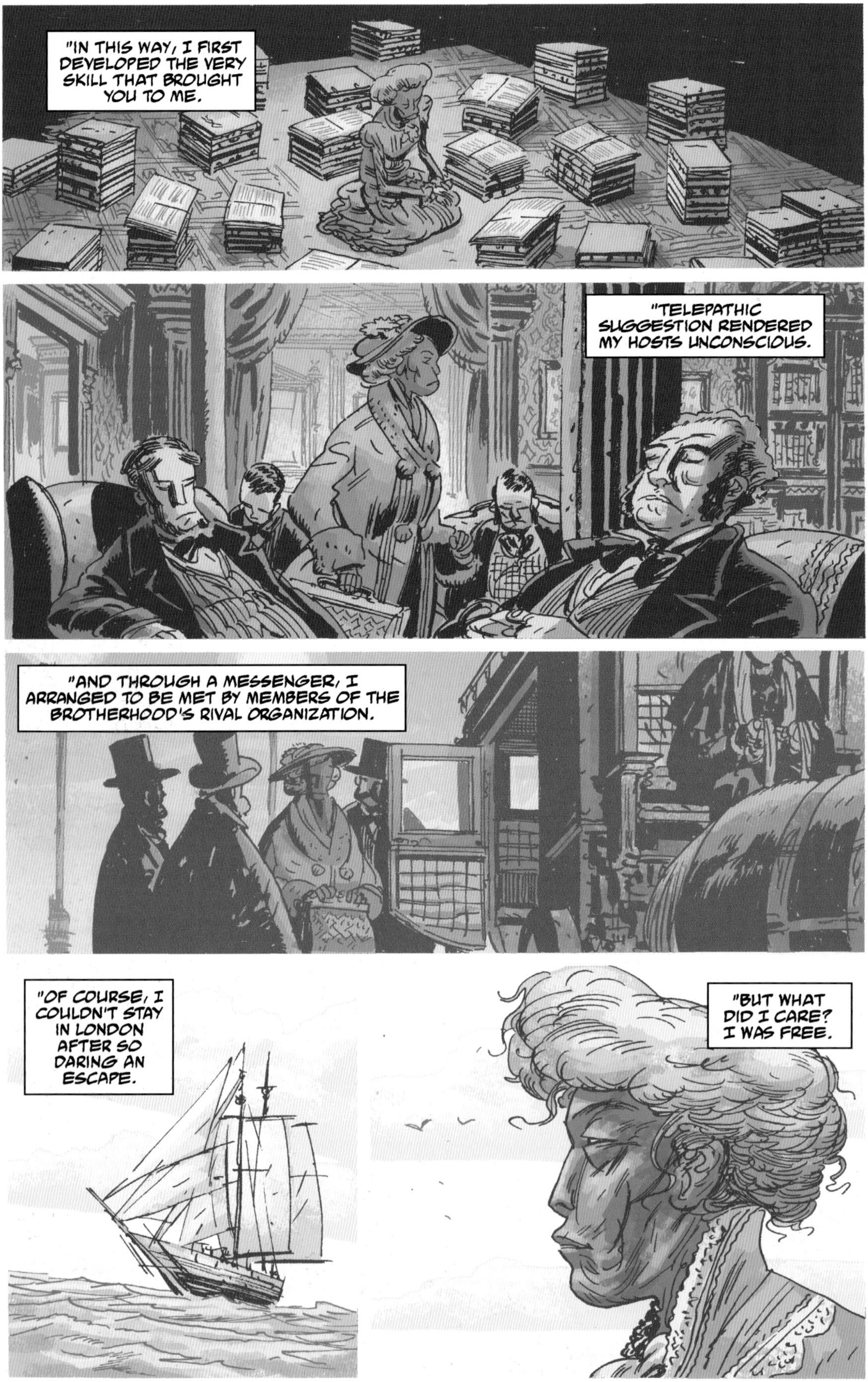
"IN THIS WAY, I FIRST DEVELOPED THE VERY SKILL THAT BROUGHT YOU TO ME.
"TELEPATHIC SUGGESTION RENDERED MY HOSTS UNCONSCIOUS.
"AND THROUGH A MESSENGER, I ARRANGED TO BE MET BY MEMBERS OF THE BROTHERHOOD'S RIVAL ORGANIZATION.
"OF COURSE, I COULDN'T STAY IN LONDON AFTER SO DARING AN ESCAPE.
"BUT WHAT DID I CARE? I WAS FREE.

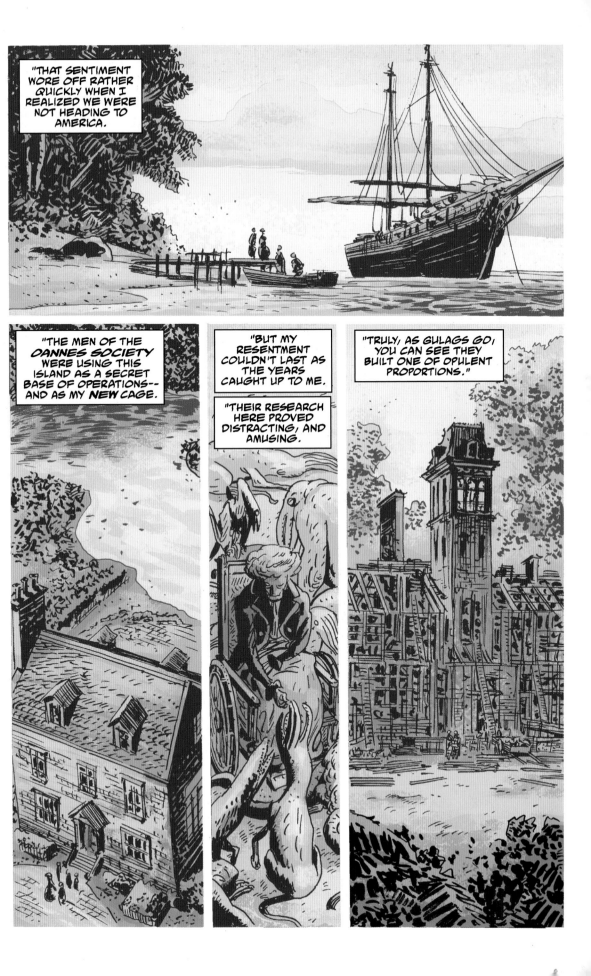

"THAT SENTIMENT WORE OFF RATHER QUICKLY WHEN I REALIZED WE WERE NOT HEADING TO AMERICA.

"THE MEN OF THE *OANNES SOCIETY* WERE USING THIS ISLAND AS A SECRET BASE OF OPERATIONS-- AND AS MY *NEW* CAGE.

"BUT MY RESENTMENT COULDN'T LAST AS THE YEARS CAUGHT UP TO ME.

"THEIR RESEARCH HERE PROVED DISTRACTING, AND AMUSING.

"TRULY, AS GULAGS GO, YOU CAN SEE THEY BUILT ONE OF OPULENT PROPORTIONS."

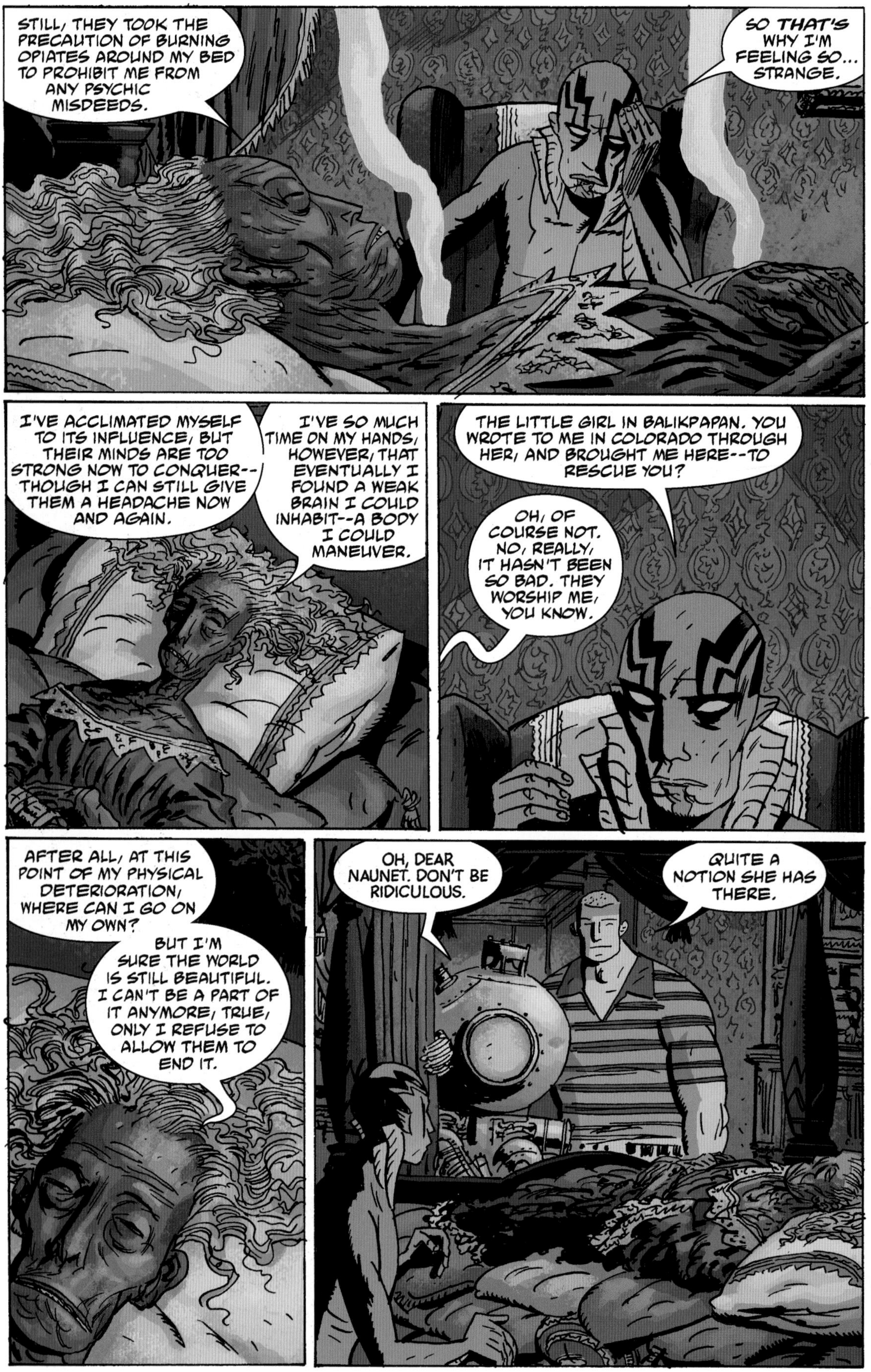
STILL, THEY TOOK THE PRECAUTION OF BURNING OPIATES AROUND MY BED TO PROHIBIT ME FROM ANY PSYCHIC MISDEEDS.
SO THAT'S WHY I'M FEELING SO... STRANGE.
I'VE ACCLIMATED MYSELF TO ITS INFLUENCE, BUT THEIR MINDS ARE TOO STRONG NOW TO CONQUER-- THOUGH I CAN STILL GIVE THEM A HEADACHE NOW AND AGAIN.
I'VE SO MUCH TIME ON MY HANDS, HOWEVER, THAT EVENTUALLY I FOUND A WEAK BRAIN I COULD INHABIT--A BODY I COULD MANEUVER.
THE LITTLE GIRL IN BALIKPAPAN. YOU WROTE TO ME IN COLORADO THROUGH HER, AND BROUGHT ME HERE--TO RESCUE YOU?
OH, OF COURSE NOT. NO, REALLY, IT HASN'T BEEN SO BAD. THEY WORSHIP ME, YOU KNOW.
AFTER ALL, AT THIS POINT OF MY PHYSICAL DETERIORATION, WHERE CAN I GO ON MY OWN?
BUT I'M SURE THE WORLD IS STILL BEAUTIFUL. I CAN'T BE A PART OF IT ANYMORE, TRUE, ONLY I REFUSE TO ALLOW THEM TO END IT.
OH, DEAR NAUNET. DON'T BE RIDICULOUS.
QUITE A NOTION SHE HAS THERE.

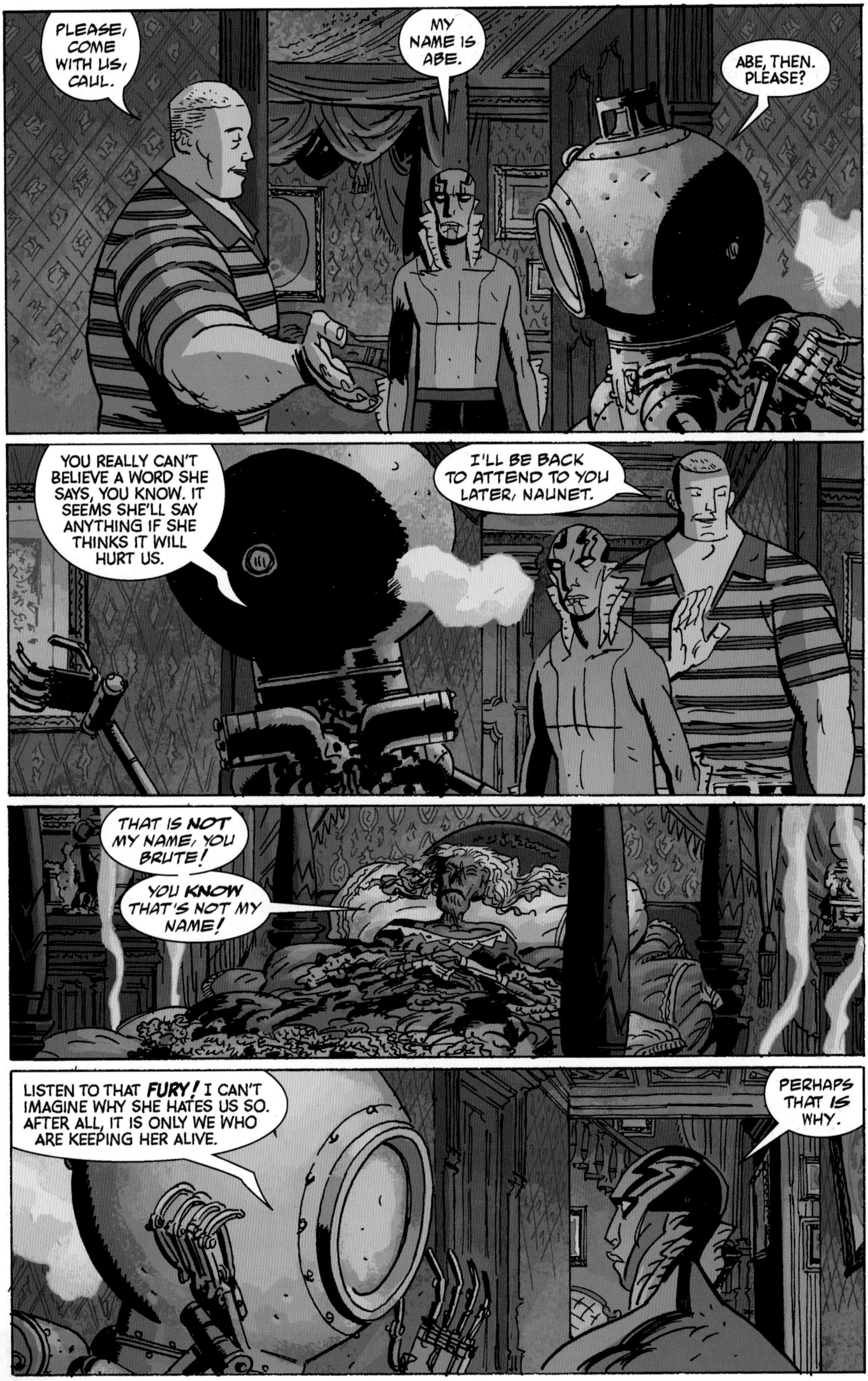
PLEASE, COME WITH US, CAUL.
MY NAME IS ABE.
ABE, THEN. PLEASE?
YOU REALLY CAN'T BELIEVE A WORD SHE SAYS, YOU KNOW. IT SEEMS SHE'LL SAY ANYTHING IF SHE THINKS IT WILL HURT US.
I'LL BE BACK TO ATTEND TO YOU LATER, NAUNET.
THAT IS **NOT** MY NAME, YOU BRUTE!
YOU **KNOW** THAT'S NOT MY NAME!
LISTEN TO THAT **FURY!** I CAN'T IMAGINE WHY SHE HATES US SO. AFTER ALL, IT IS ONLY WE WHO ARE KEEPING HER ALIVE.
PERHAPS THAT **IS** WHY.

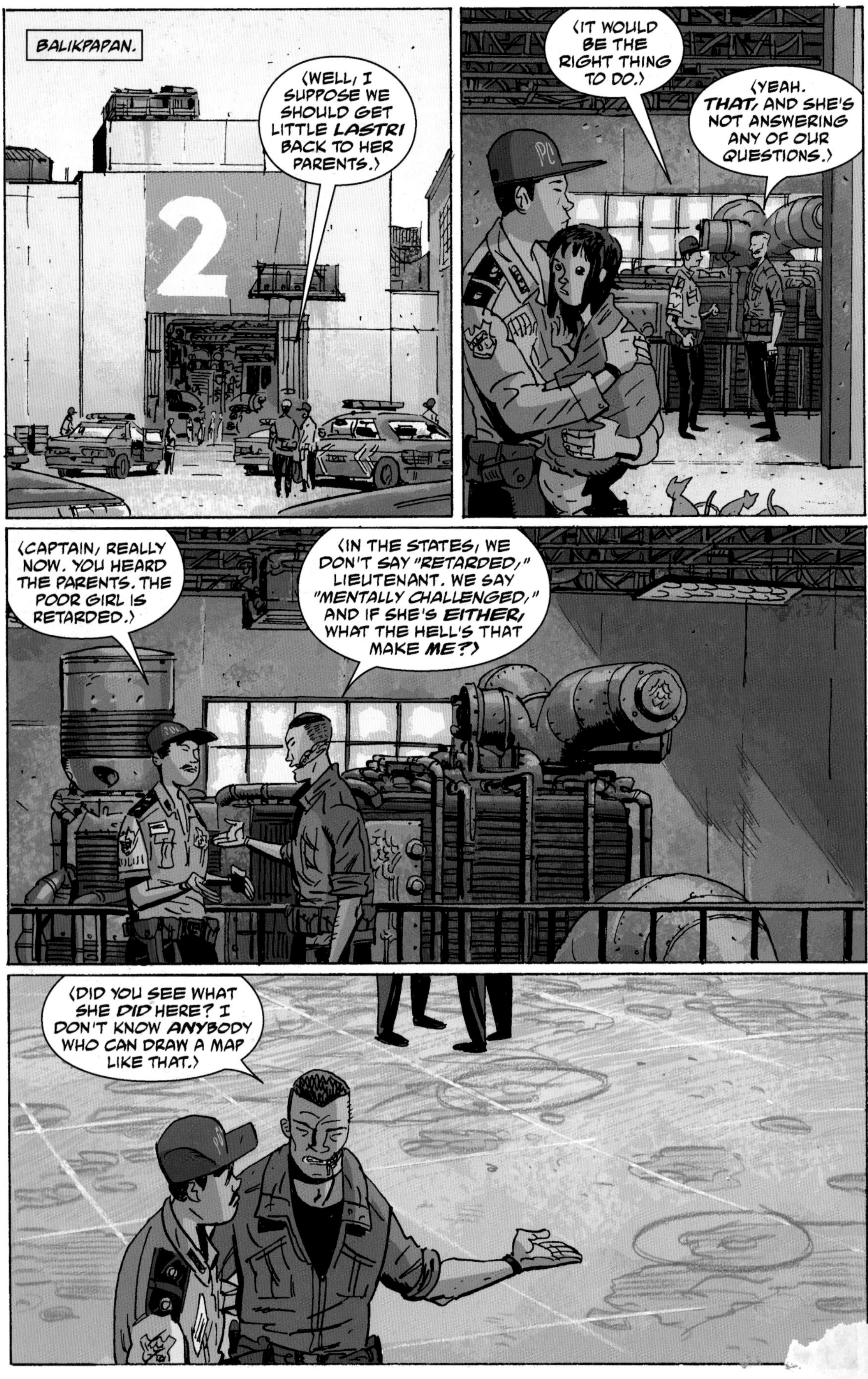
BALIKPAPAN.
‹WELL, I SUPPOSE WE SHOULD GET LITTLE LASTRI BACK TO HER PARENTS.›
‹IT WOULD BE THE RIGHT THING TO DO.›
‹YEAH. THAT, AND SHE'S NOT ANSWERING ANY OF OUR QUESTIONS.›
‹CAPTAIN, REALLY NOW. YOU HEARD THE PARENTS. THE POOR GIRL IS RETARDED.›
‹IN THE STATES, WE DON'T SAY "RETARDED," LIEUTENANT. WE SAY "MENTALLY CHALLENGED," AND IF SHE'S EITHER, WHAT THE HELL'S THAT MAKE ME?›
‹DID YOU SEE WHAT SHE DID HERE? I DON'T KNOW ANYBODY WHO CAN DRAW A MAP LIKE THAT.›

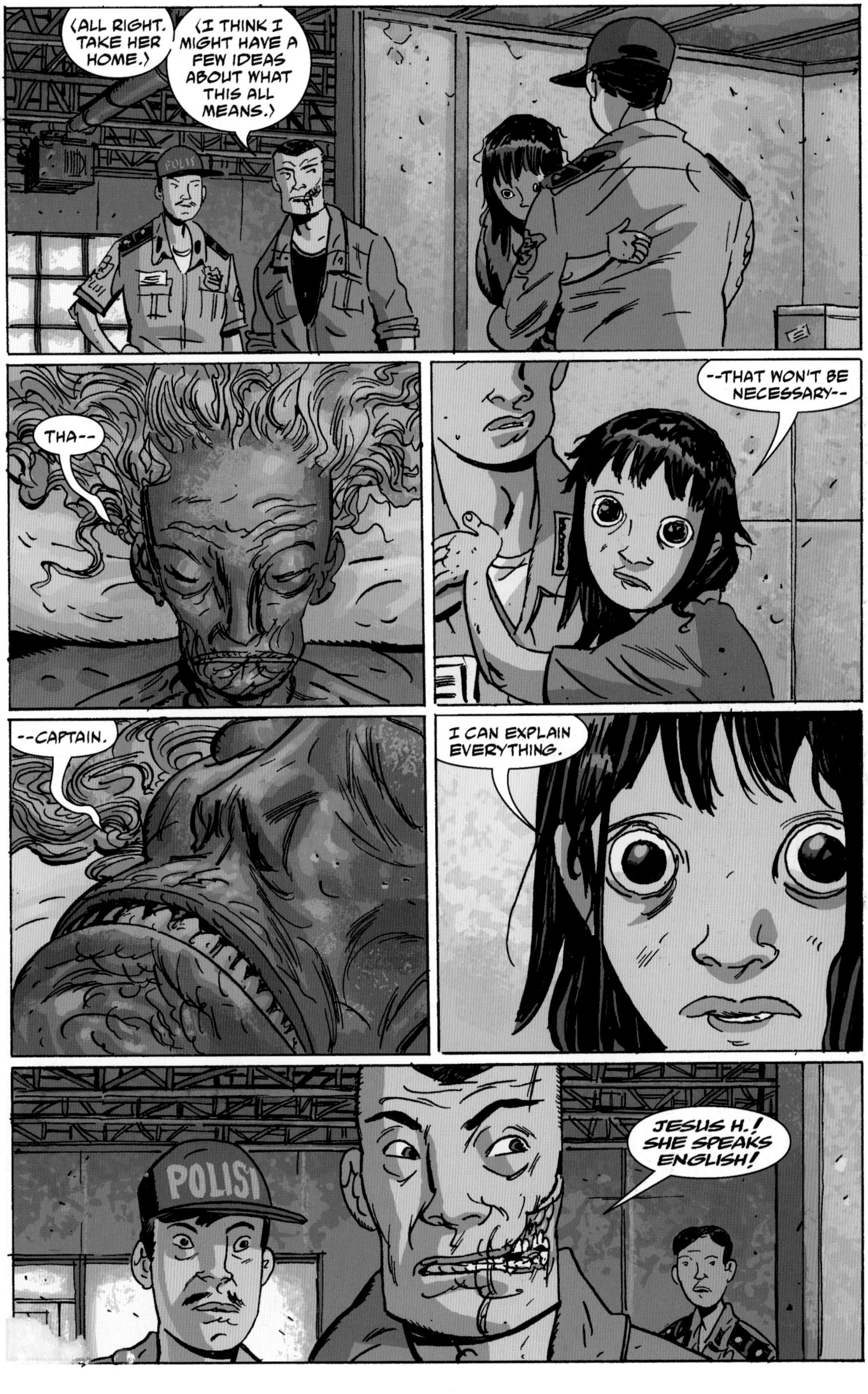
‹ALL RIGHT. TAKE HER HOME.›
‹I THINK I MIGHT HAVE A FEW IDEAS ABOUT WHAT THIS ALL MEANS.›
POLIS
THA--
--THAT WON'T BE NECESSARY--
--CAPTAIN.
I CAN EXPLAIN EVERYTHING.
POLIS
JESUS H.! SHE SPEAKS ENGLISH!

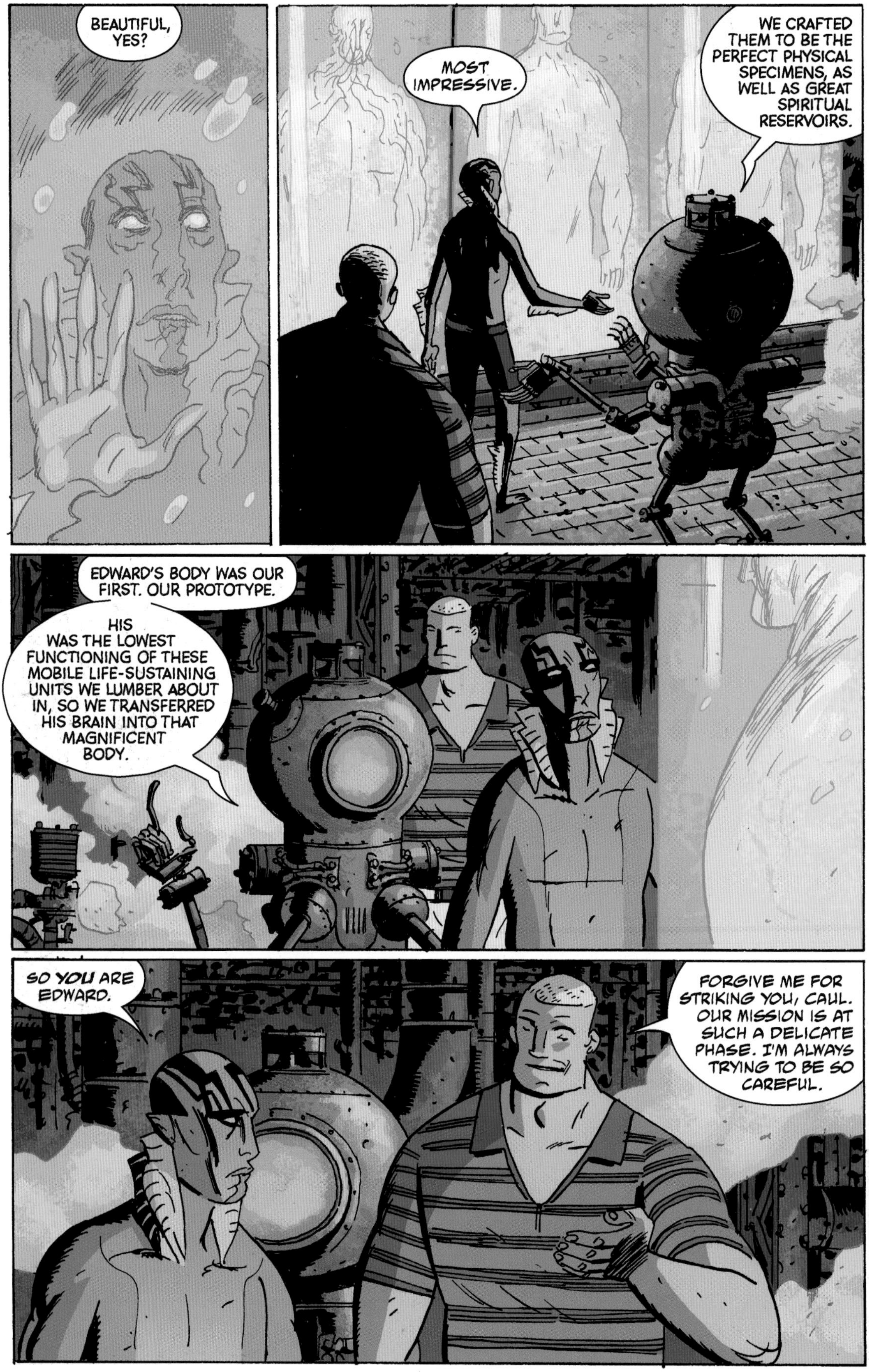
BEAUTIFUL, YES?
MOST IMPRESSIVE.
WE CRAFTED THEM TO BE THE PERFECT PHYSICAL SPECIMENS, AS WELL AS GREAT SPIRITUAL RESERVOIRS.
EDWARD'S BODY WAS OUR FIRST. OUR PROTOTYPE.
HIS WAS THE LOWEST FUNCTIONING OF THESE MOBILE LIFE-SUSTAINING UNITS WE LUMBER ABOUT IN, SO WE TRANSFERRED HIS BRAIN INTO THAT MAGNIFICENT BODY.
SO YOU ARE EDWARD.
FORGIVE ME FOR STRIKING YOU, CAUL. OUR MISSION IS AT SUCH A DELICATE PHASE. I'M ALWAYS TRYING TO BE SO CAREFUL.

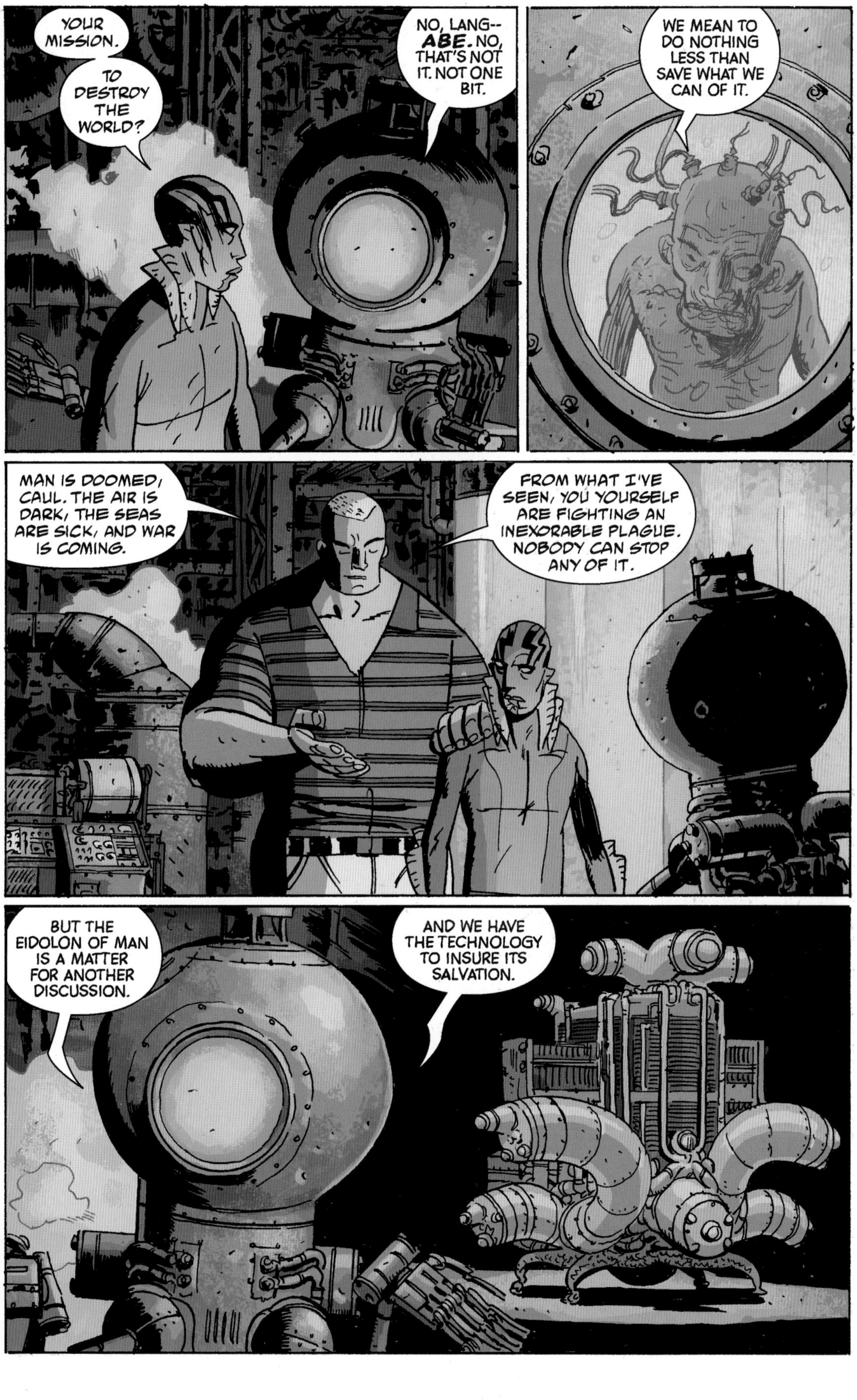
YOUR MISSION.
TO DESTROY THE WORLD?
NO, LANG-- ABE. NO, THAT'S NOT IT. NOT ONE BIT.
WE MEAN TO DO NOTHING LESS THAN SAVE WHAT WE CAN OF IT.
MAN IS DOOMED, CAUL. THE AIR IS DARK, THE SEAS ARE SICK, AND WAR IS COMING.
FROM WHAT I'VE SEEN, YOU YOURSELF ARE FIGHTING AN INEXORABLE PLAGUE. NOBODY CAN STOP ANY OF IT.
BUT THE EIDOLON OF MAN IS A MATTER FOR ANOTHER DISCUSSION.
AND WE HAVE THE TECHNOLOGY TO INSURE ITS SALVATION.

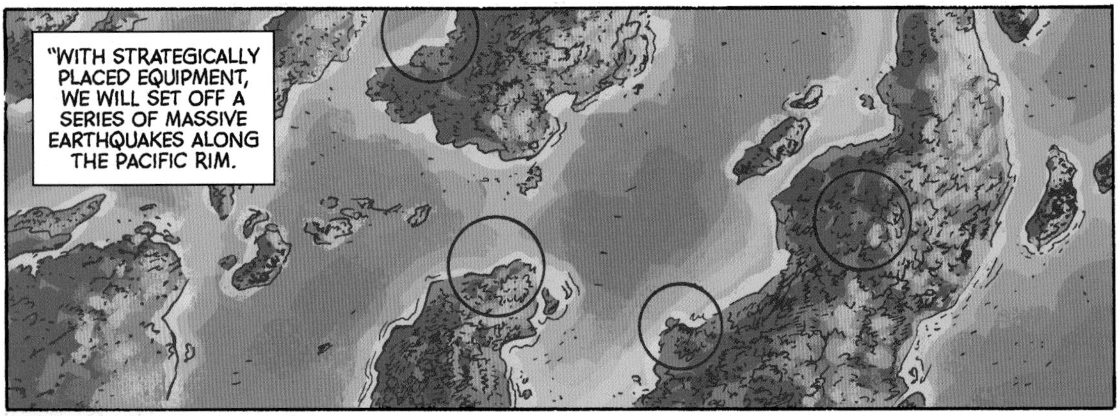
"WITH STRATEGICALLY PLACED EQUIPMENT, WE WILL SET OFF A SERIES OF MASSIVE EARTHQUAKES ALONG THE PACIFIC RIM.

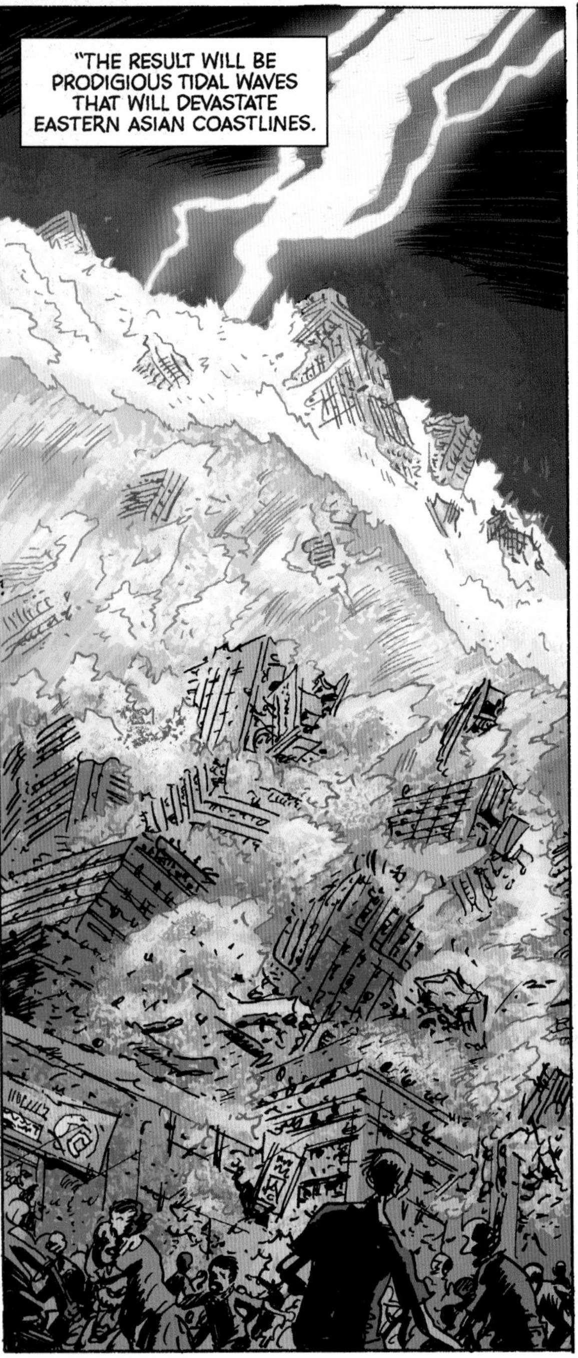
"THE RESULT WILL BE PRODIGIOUS TIDAL WAVES THAT WILL DEVASTATE EASTERN ASIAN COASTLINES.

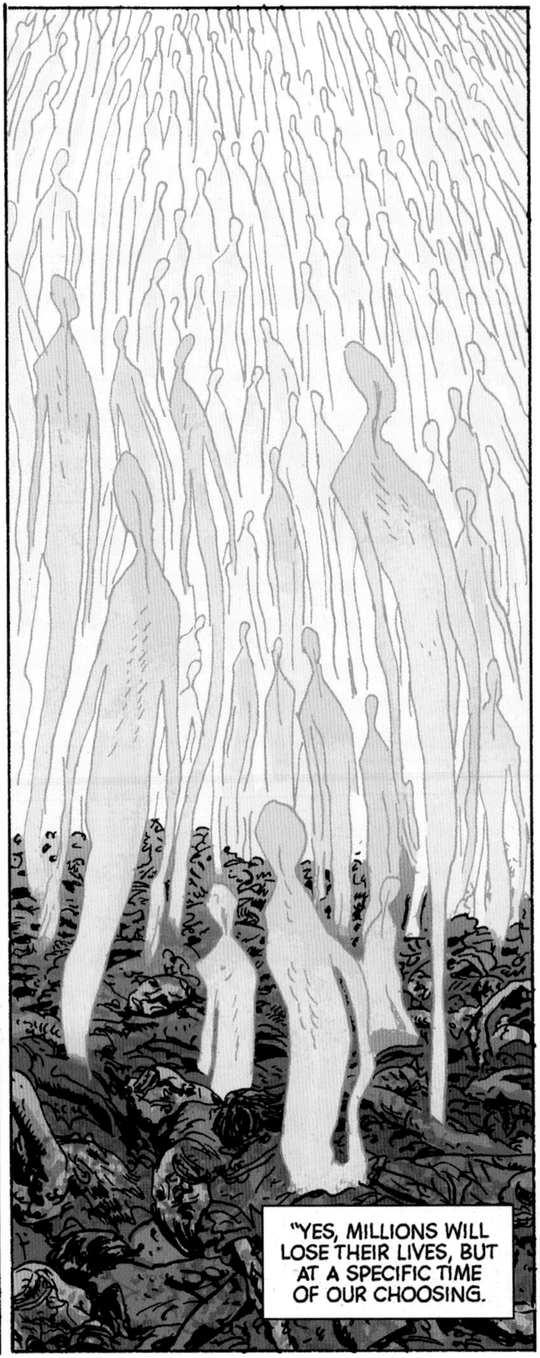
"YES, MILLIONS WILL LOSE THEIR LIVES, BUT AT A SPECIFIC TIME OF OUR CHOOSING.

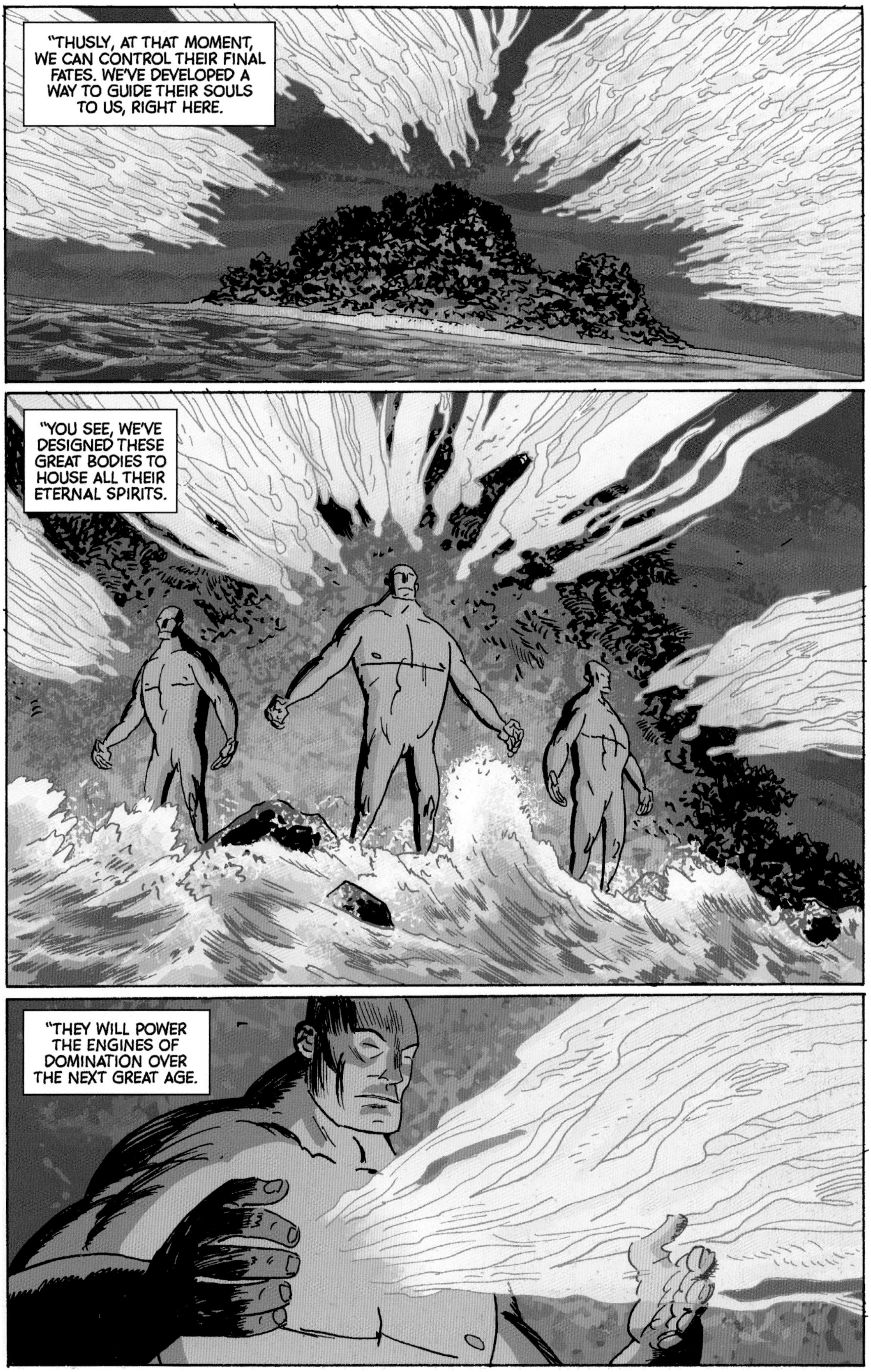
"THUSLY, AT THAT MOMENT, WE CAN CONTROL THEIR FINAL FATES. WE'VE DEVELOPED A WAY TO GUIDE THEIR SOULS TO US, RIGHT HERE.
"YOU SEE, WE'VE DESIGNED THESE GREAT BODIES TO HOUSE ALL THEIR ETERNAL SPIRITS.
"THEY WILL POWER THE ENGINES OF DOMINATION OVER THE NEXT GREAT AGE.

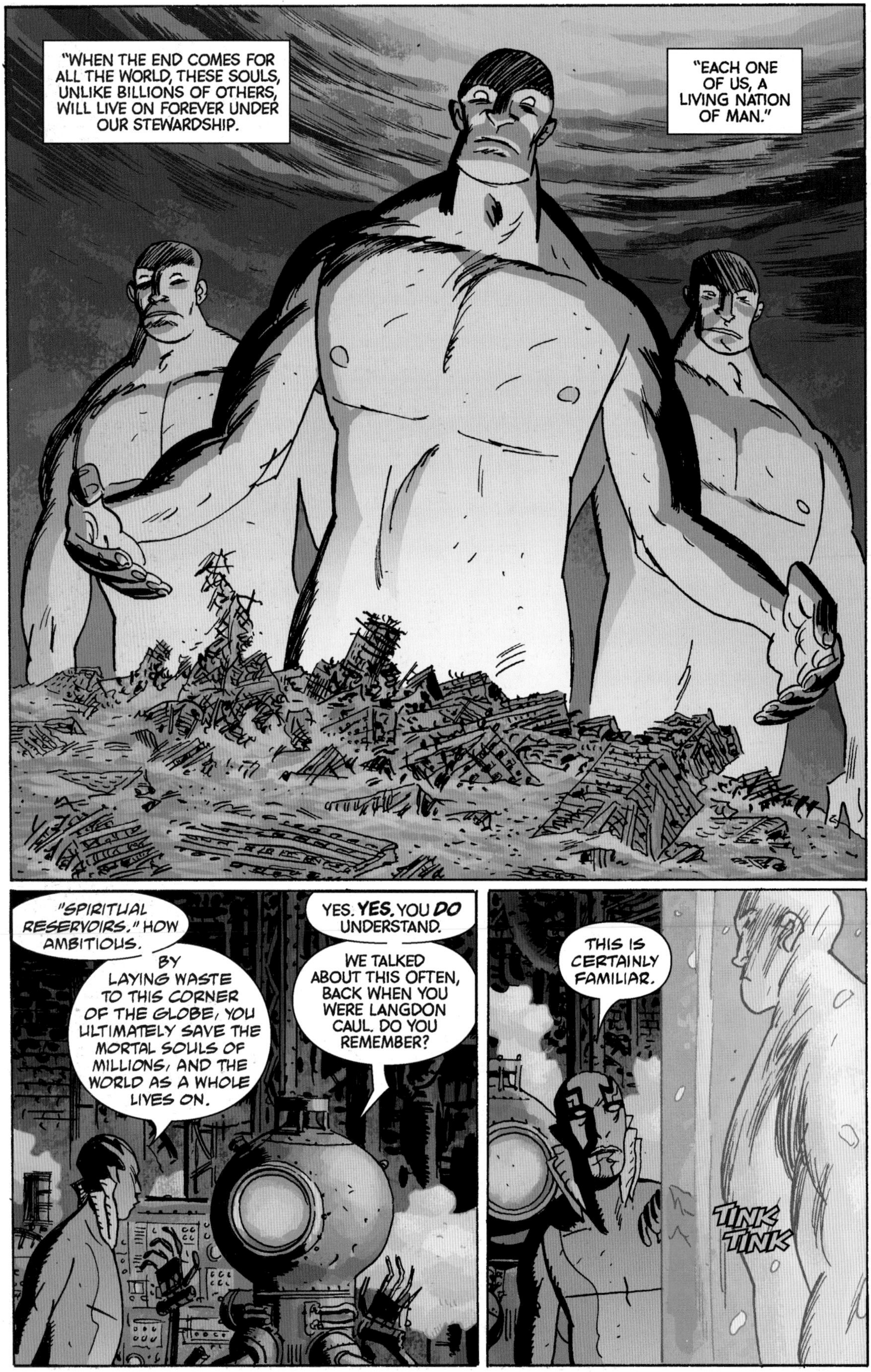
"WHEN THE END COMES FOR ALL THE WORLD, THESE SOULS, UNLIKE BILLIONS OF OTHERS, WILL LIVE ON FOREVER UNDER OUR STEWARDSHIP.
"EACH ONE OF US, A LIVING NATION OF MAN."
"SPIRITUAL RESERVOIRS." HOW AMBITIOUS.
BY LAYING WASTE TO THIS CORNER OF THE GLOBE, YOU ULTIMATELY SAVE THE MORTAL SOULS OF MILLIONS, AND THE WORLD AS A WHOLE LIVES ON.
YES. **YES.** YOU ***DO*** UNDERSTAND.
WE TALKED ABOUT THIS OFTEN, BACK WHEN YOU WERE LANGDON CAUL. DO YOU REMEMBER?
THIS IS CERTAINLY FAMILIAR.
TINK TINK

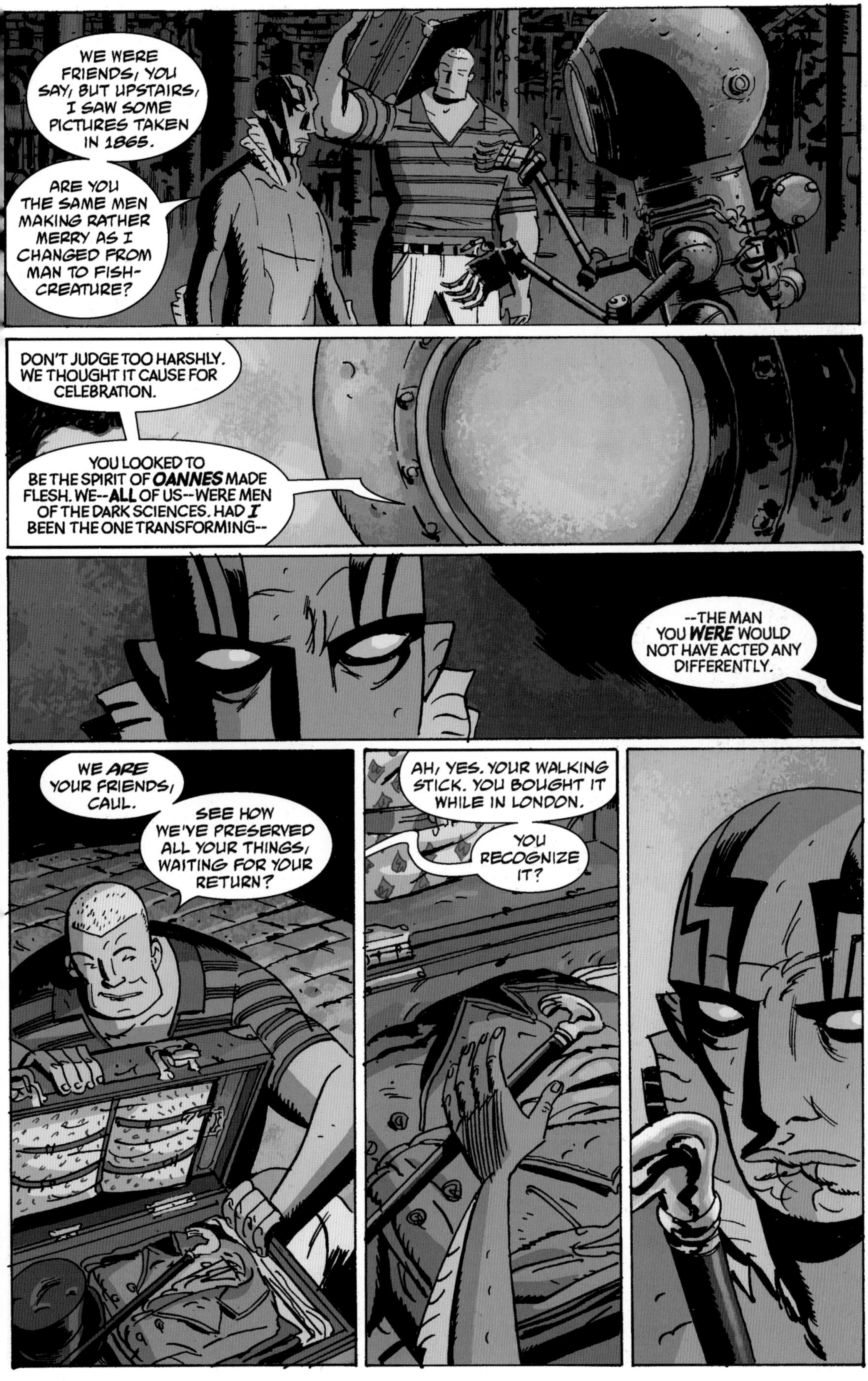
WE WERE FRIENDS, YOU SAY, BUT UPSTAIRS, I SAW SOME PICTURES TAKEN IN 1865.
ARE YOU THE SAME MEN MAKING RATHER MERRY AS I CHANGED FROM MAN TO FISH-CREATURE?
DON'T JUDGE TOO HARSHLY. WE THOUGHT IT CAUSE FOR CELEBRATION.
YOU LOOKED TO BE THE SPIRIT OF OANNES MADE FLESH. WE--ALL OF US--WERE MEN OF THE DARK SCIENCES. HAD I BEEN THE ONE TRANSFORMING--
--THE MAN YOU WERE WOULD NOT HAVE ACTED ANY DIFFERENTLY.
WE ARE YOUR FRIENDS, CAUL.
SEE HOW WE'VE PRESERVED ALL YOUR THINGS, WAITING FOR YOUR RETURN?
AH, YES. YOUR WALKING STICK. YOU BOUGHT IT WHILE IN LONDON.
YOU RECOGNIZE IT?

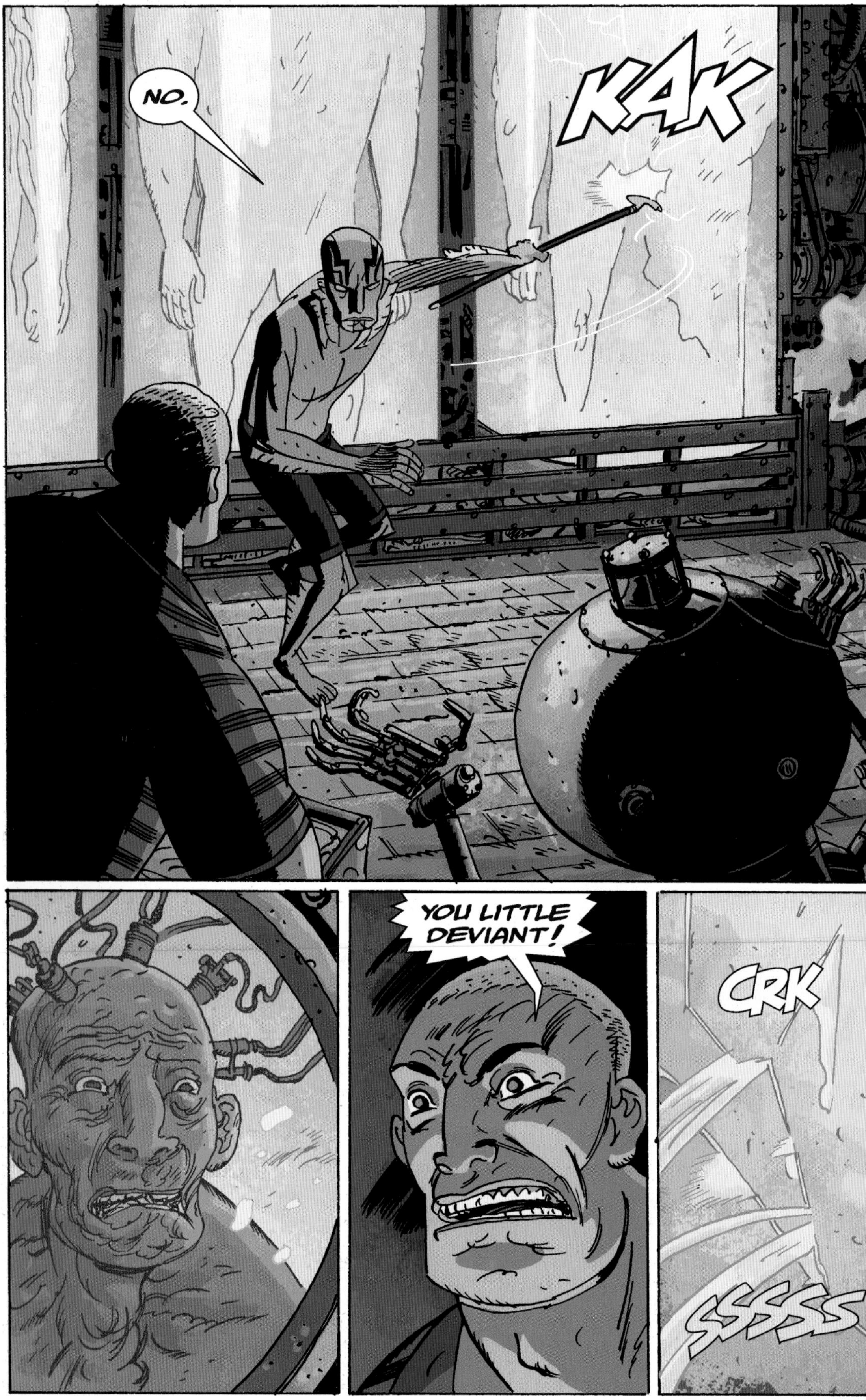
NO.
KAK
YOU LITTLE DEVIANT!
CRK
SSSSS

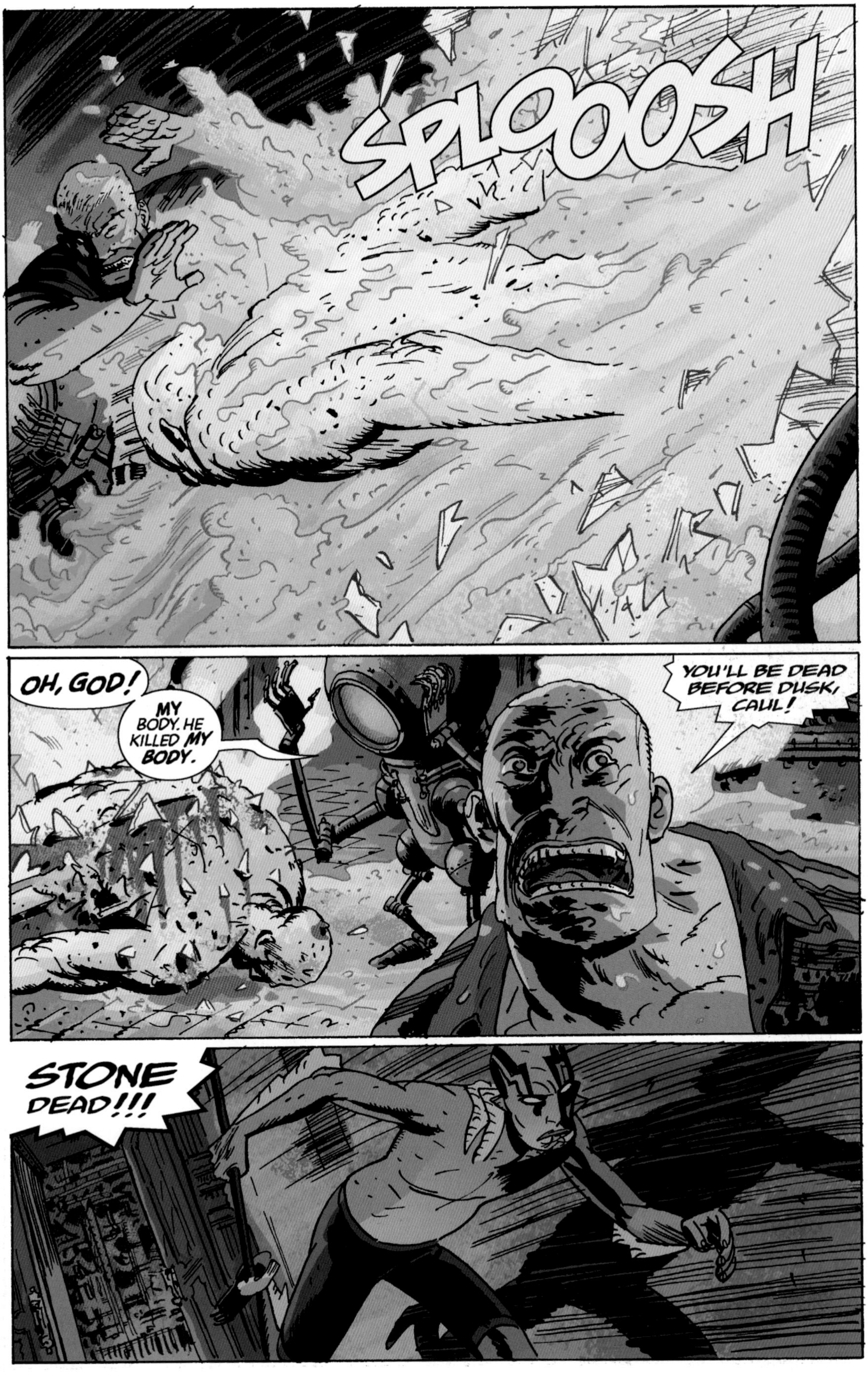
SPLOOOSH
OH, GOD!
MY BODY. HE KILLED MY BODY.
YOU'LL BE DEAD BEFORE DUSK, CAUL!
STONE DEAD!!!

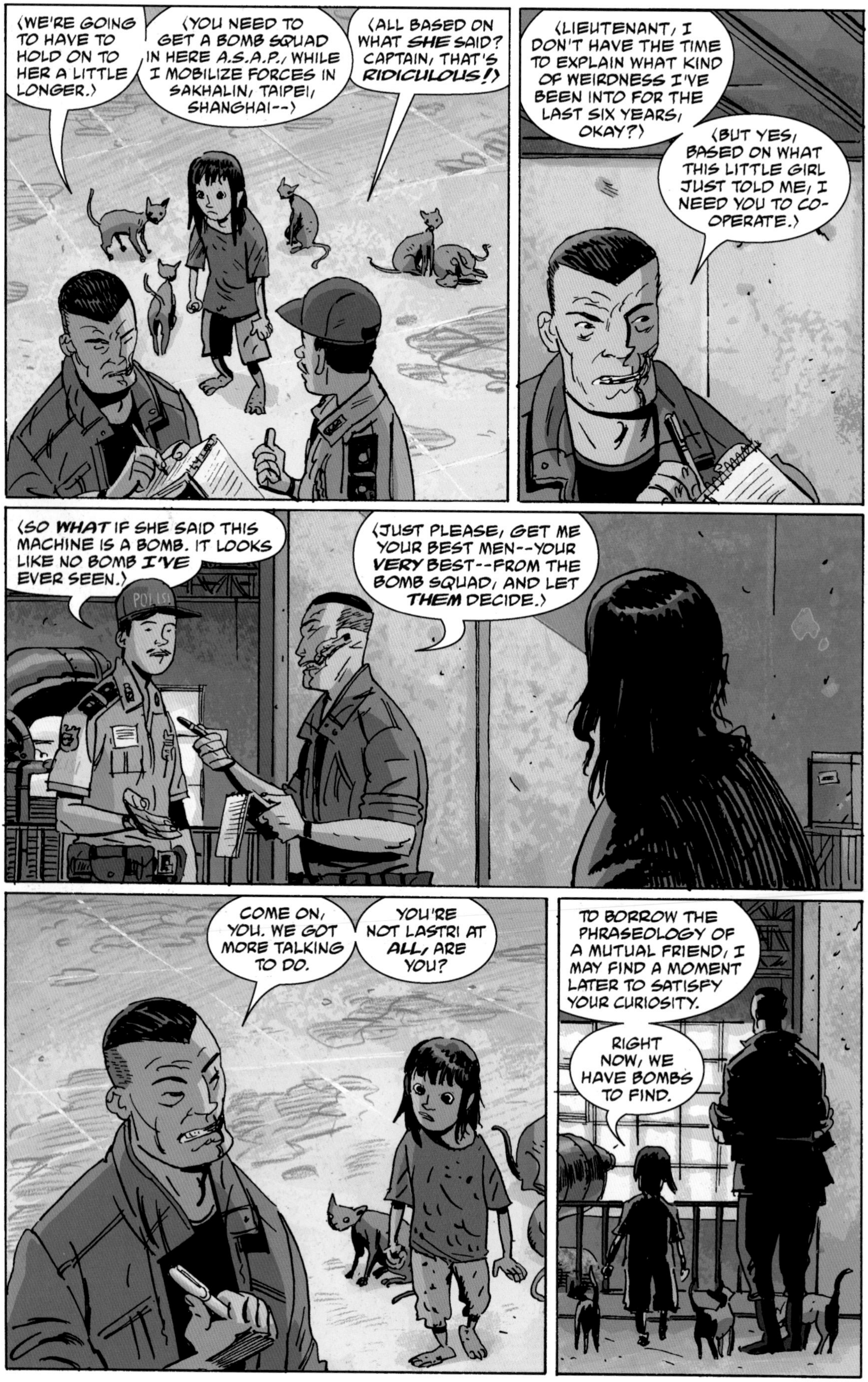
⟨WE'RE GOING TO HAVE TO HOLD ON TO HER A LITTLE LONGER.⟩
⟨YOU NEED TO GET A BOMB SQUAD IN HERE A.S.A.P., WHILE I MOBILIZE FORCES IN SAKHALIN, TAIPEI, SHANGHAI--⟩
⟨ALL BASED ON WHAT SHE SAID? CAPTAIN, THAT'S RIDICULOUS!⟩
⟨LIEUTENANT, I DON'T HAVE THE TIME TO EXPLAIN WHAT KIND OF WEIRDNESS I'VE BEEN INTO FOR THE LAST SIX YEARS, OKAY?⟩
⟨BUT YES, BASED ON WHAT THIS LITTLE GIRL JUST TOLD ME, I NEED YOU TO CO-OPERATE.⟩
⟨SO WHAT IF SHE SAID THIS MACHINE IS A BOMB. IT LOOKS LIKE NO BOMB I'VE EVER SEEN.⟩
POLISI
⟨JUST PLEASE, GET ME YOUR BEST MEN--YOUR VERY BEST--FROM THE BOMB SQUAD, AND LET THEM DECIDE.⟩
COME ON, YOU. WE GOT MORE TALKING TO DO.
YOU'RE NOT LASTRI AT ALL, ARE YOU?
TO BORROW THE PHRASEOLOGY OF A MUTUAL FRIEND, I MAY FIND A MOMENT LATER TO SATISFY YOUR CURIOSITY.
RIGHT NOW, WE HAVE BOMBS TO FIND.

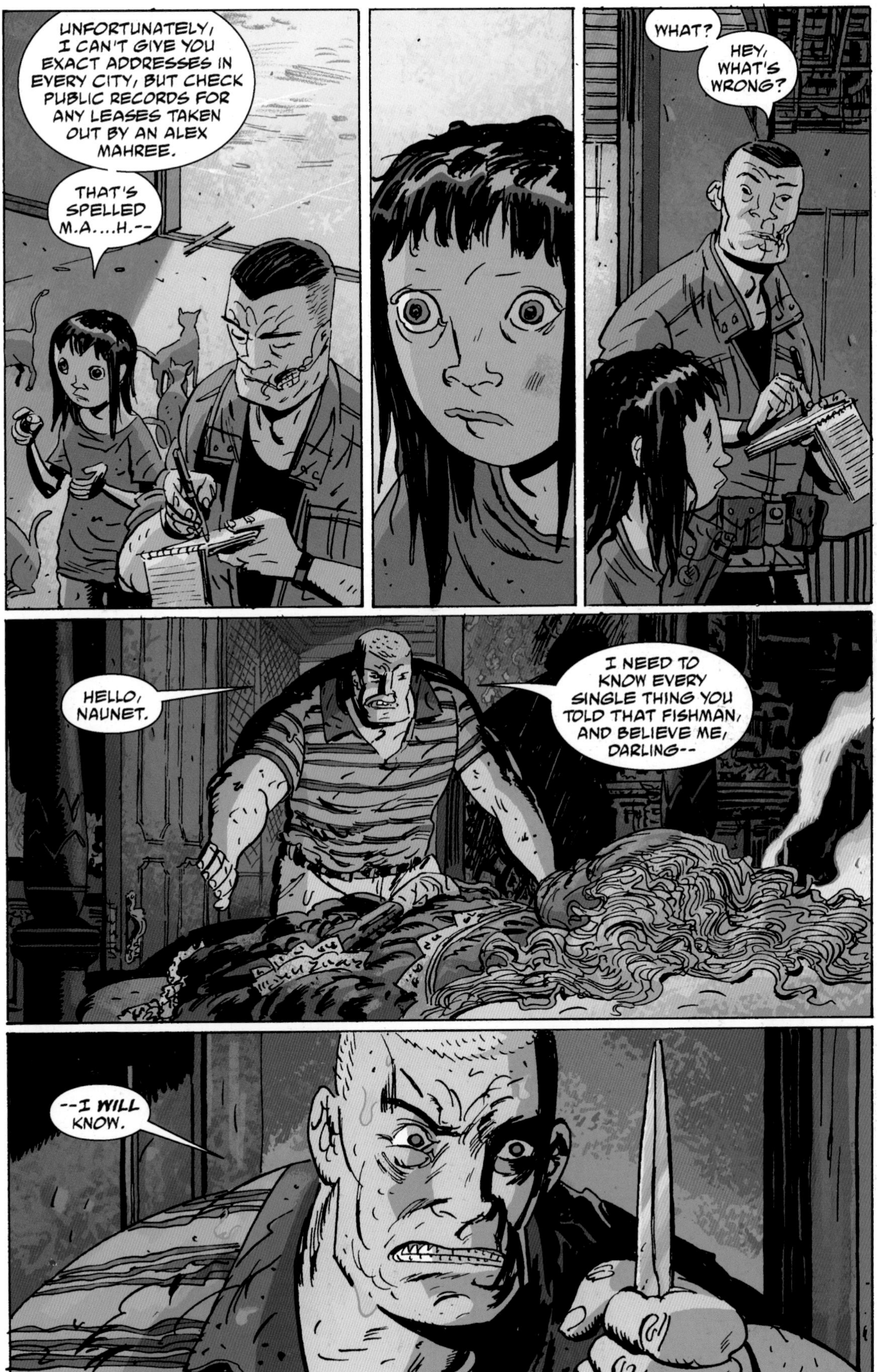
UNFORTUNATELY, I CAN'T GIVE YOU EXACT ADDRESSES IN EVERY CITY, BUT CHECK PUBLIC RECORDS FOR ANY LEASES TAKEN OUT BY AN ALEX MAHREE.
THAT'S SPELLED M.A....H.--
WHAT?
HEY, WHAT'S WRONG?
HELLO, NAUNET.
I NEED TO KNOW EVERY SINGLE THING YOU TOLD THAT FISHMAN, AND BELIEVE ME, DARLING--
--I *WILL* KNOW.

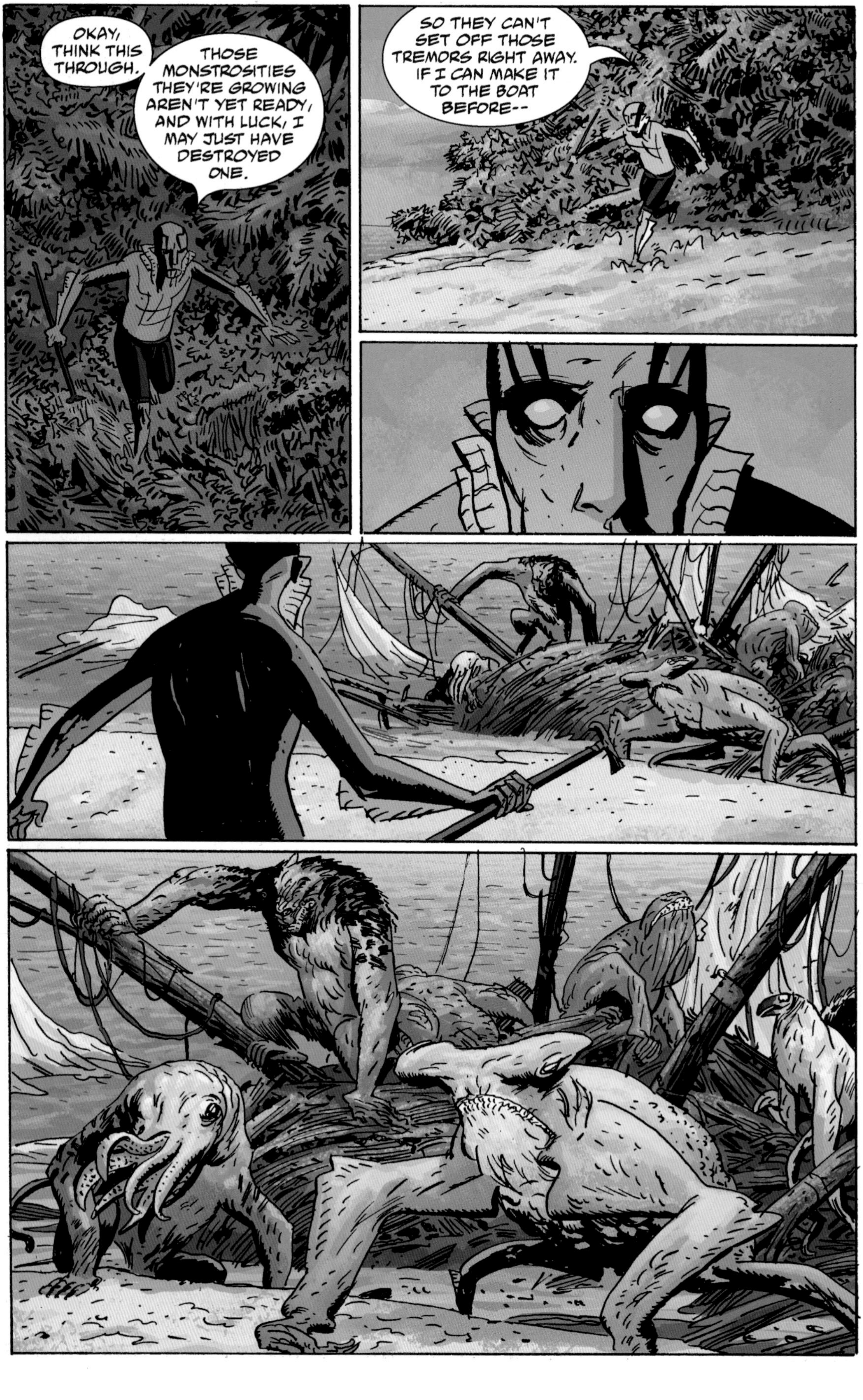
OKAY, THINK THIS THROUGH.
THOSE MONSTROSITIES THEY'RE GROWING AREN'T YET READY, AND WITH LUCK, I MAY JUST HAVE DESTROYED ONE.
SO THEY CAN'T SET OFF THOSE TREMORS RIGHT AWAY. IF I CAN MAKE IT TO THE BOAT BEFORE--

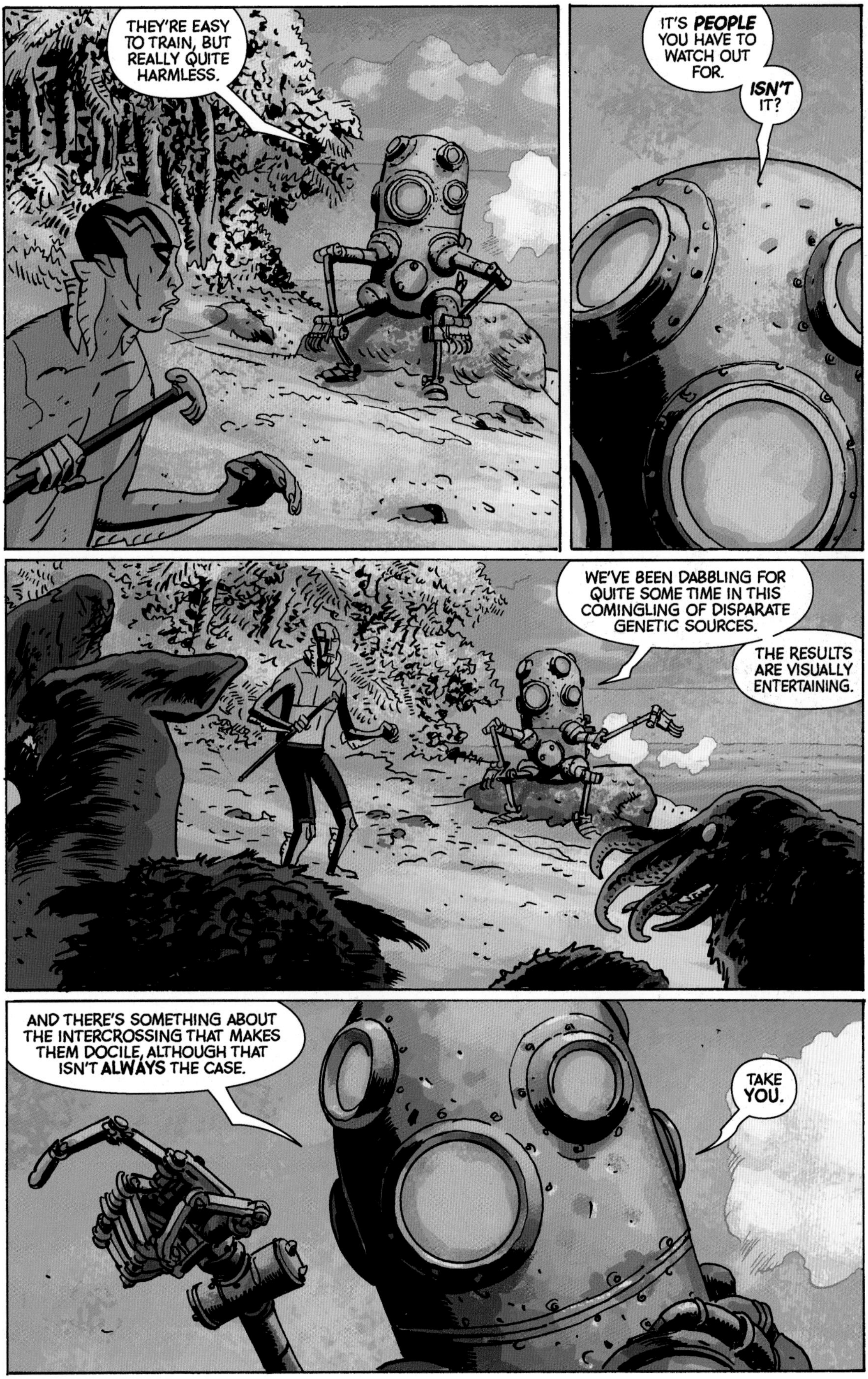
THEY'RE EASY TO TRAIN, BUT REALLY QUITE HARMLESS.
IT'S PEOPLE YOU HAVE TO WATCH OUT FOR.
ISN'T IT?
WE'VE BEEN DABBLING FOR QUITE SOME TIME IN THIS COMINGLING OF DISPARATE GENETIC SOURCES.
THE RESULTS ARE VISUALLY ENTERTAINING.
AND THERE'S SOMETHING ABOUT THE INTERCROSSING THAT MAKES THEM DOCILE, ALTHOUGH THAT ISN'T ALWAYS THE CASE.
TAKE YOU.

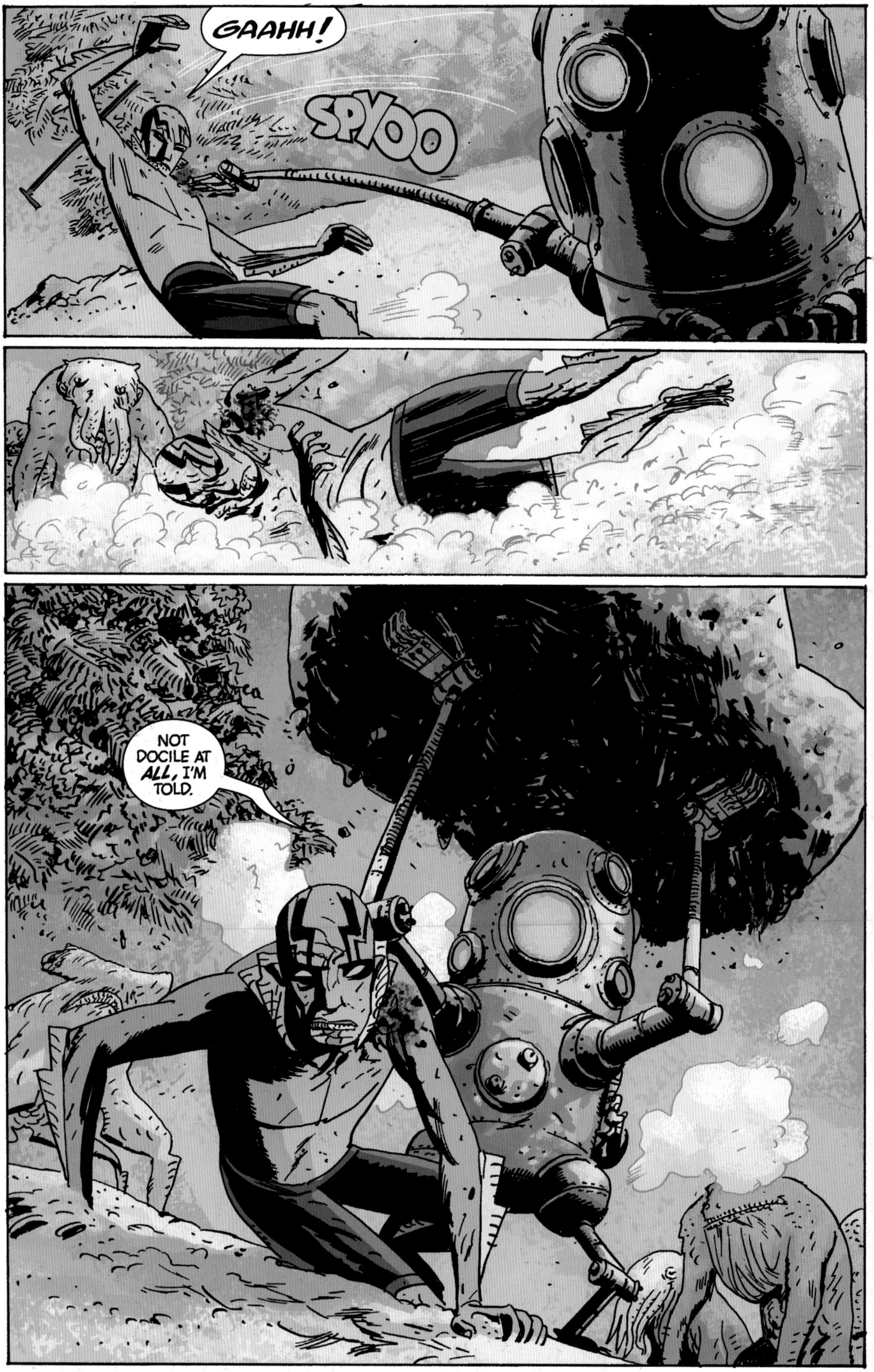
GAAHH!
SPYOO
NOT DOCILE AT ALL, I'M TOLD.

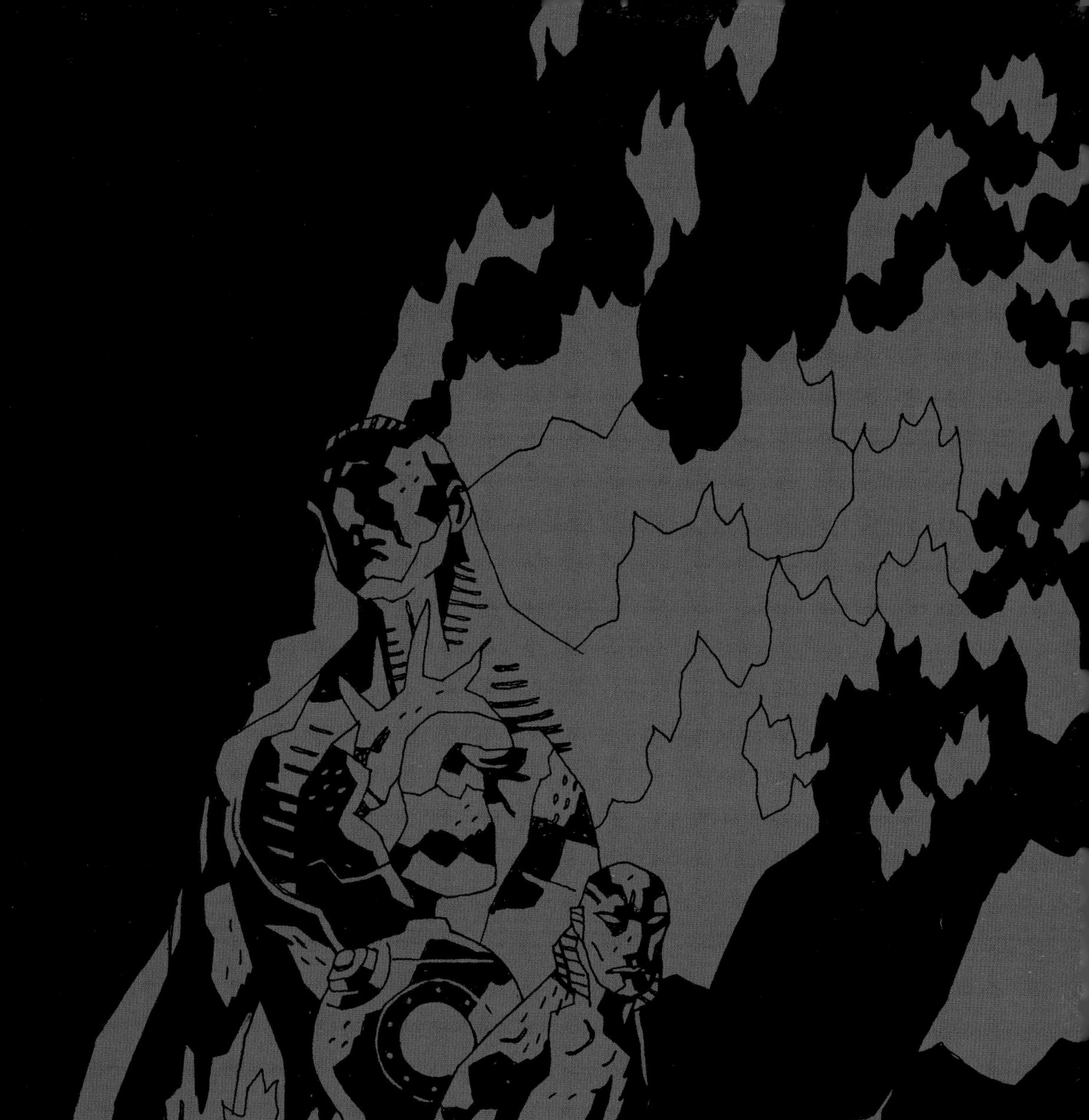

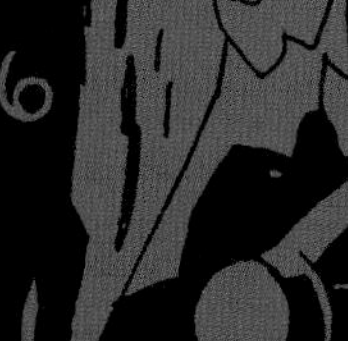

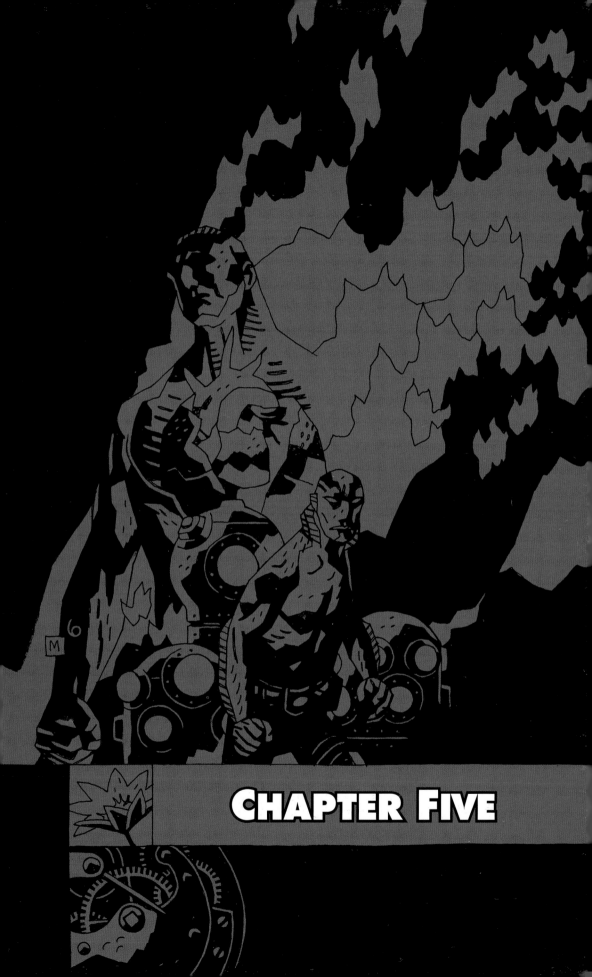

CHAPTER FIVE

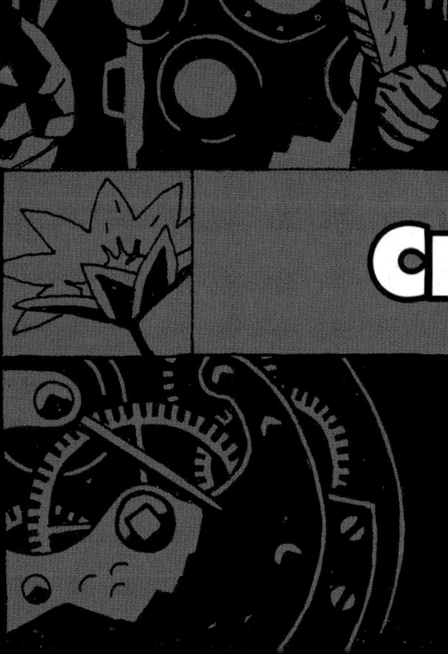

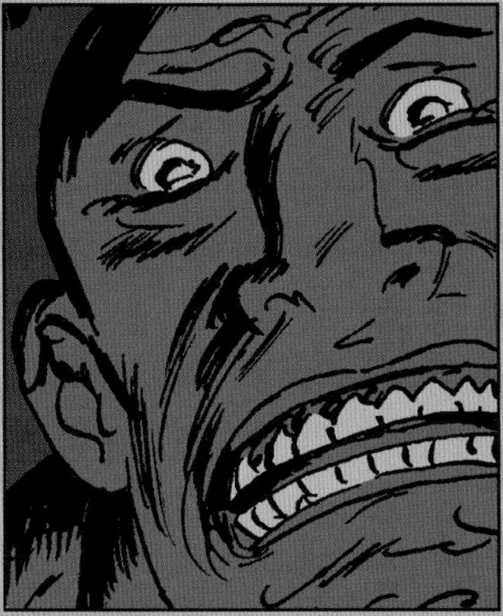

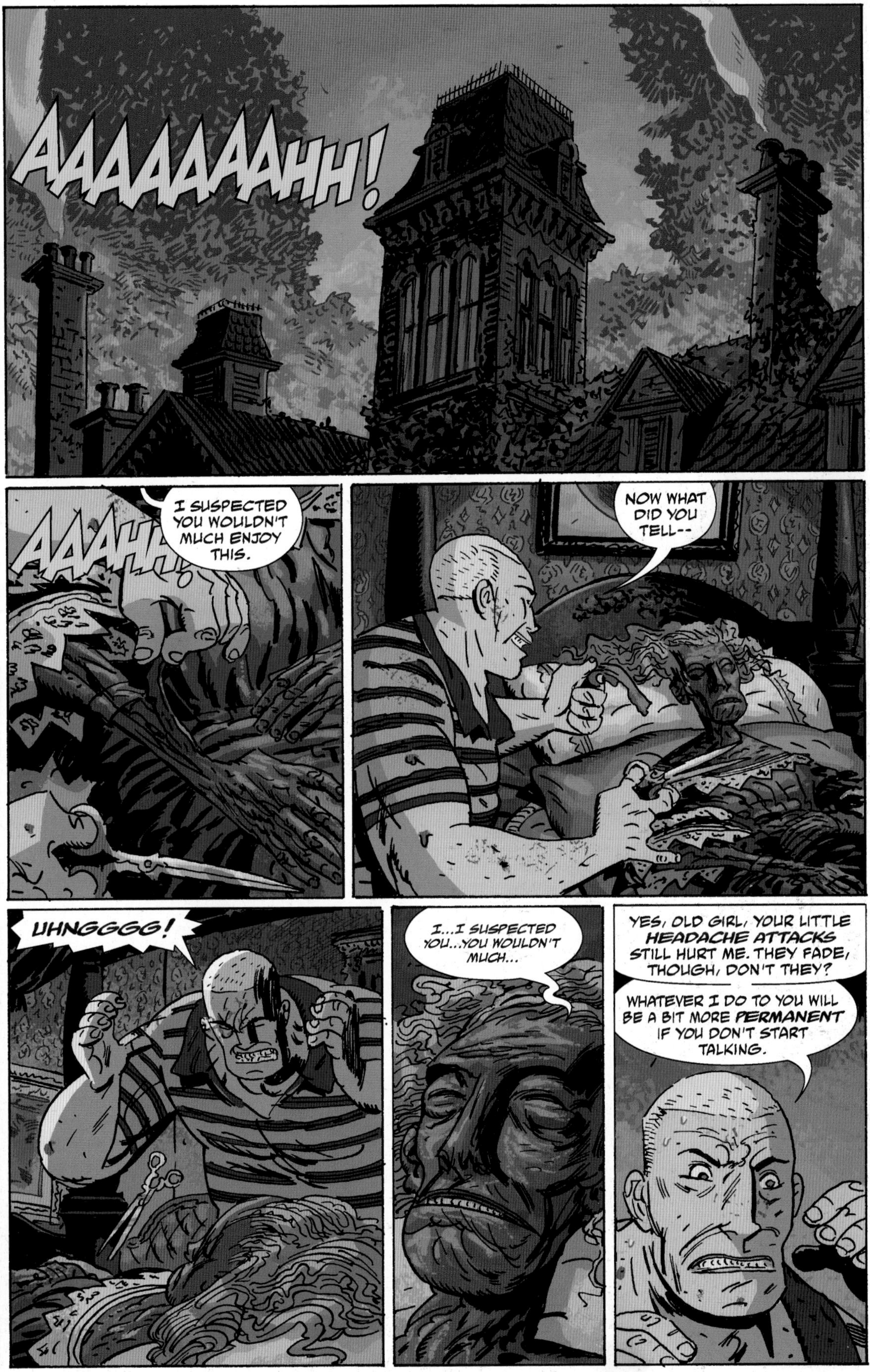
AAAAAAAHH!
AAAHH
I SUSPECTED YOU WOULDN'T MUCH ENJOY THIS.
NOW WHAT DID YOU TELL--
UHNGGGG!
I...I SUSPECTED YOU...YOU WOULDN'T MUCH...
YES, OLD GIRL, YOUR LITTLE HEADACHE ATTACKS STILL HURT ME. THEY FADE, THOUGH, DON'T THEY?
WHATEVER I DO TO YOU WILL BE A BIT MORE PERMANENT IF YOU DON'T START TALKING.

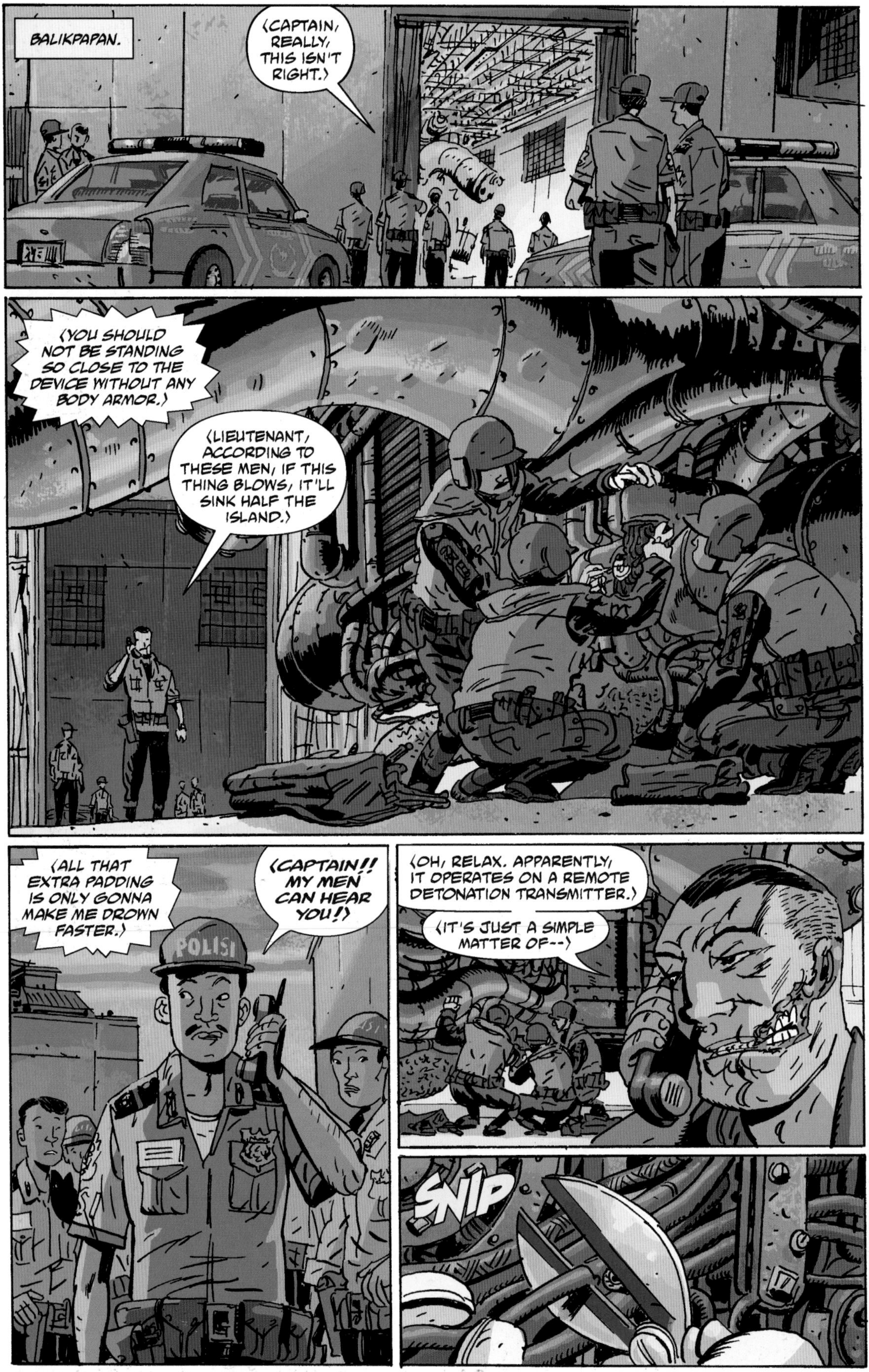
BALIKPAPAN.
⟨CAPTAIN, REALLY, THIS ISN'T RIGHT.⟩
⟨YOU SHOULD NOT BE STANDING SO CLOSE TO THE DEVICE WITHOUT ANY BODY ARMOR.⟩
⟨LIEUTENANT, ACCORDING TO THESE MEN, IF THIS THING BLOWS, IT'LL SINK HALF THE ISLAND.⟩
⟨ALL THAT EXTRA PADDING IS ONLY GONNA MAKE ME DROWN FASTER.⟩
⟨CAPTAIN!! MY MEN CAN HEAR YOU!⟩
POLISI
⟨OH, RELAX. APPARENTLY, IT OPERATES ON A REMOTE DETONATION TRANSMITTER.⟩
⟨IT'S JUST A SIMPLE MATTER OF--⟩
SNIP

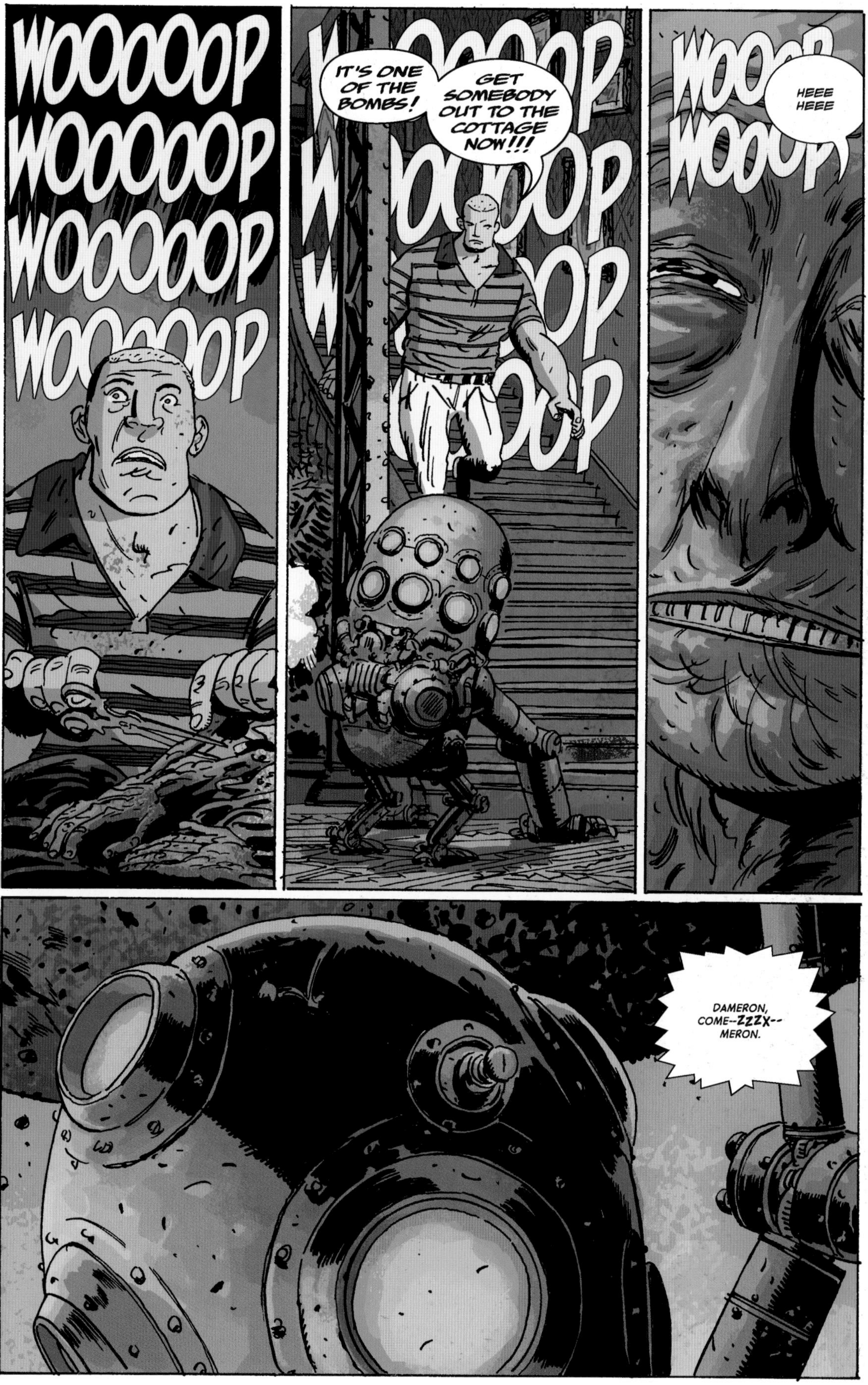
WOOOOOP
WOOOOOP
WOOOOOP
WOOOOOP
IT'S ONE OF THE BOMBS!
GET SOMEBODY OUT TO THE COTTAGE NOW!!!
HEEE HEEE
DAMERON, COME--ZZZX--MERON.

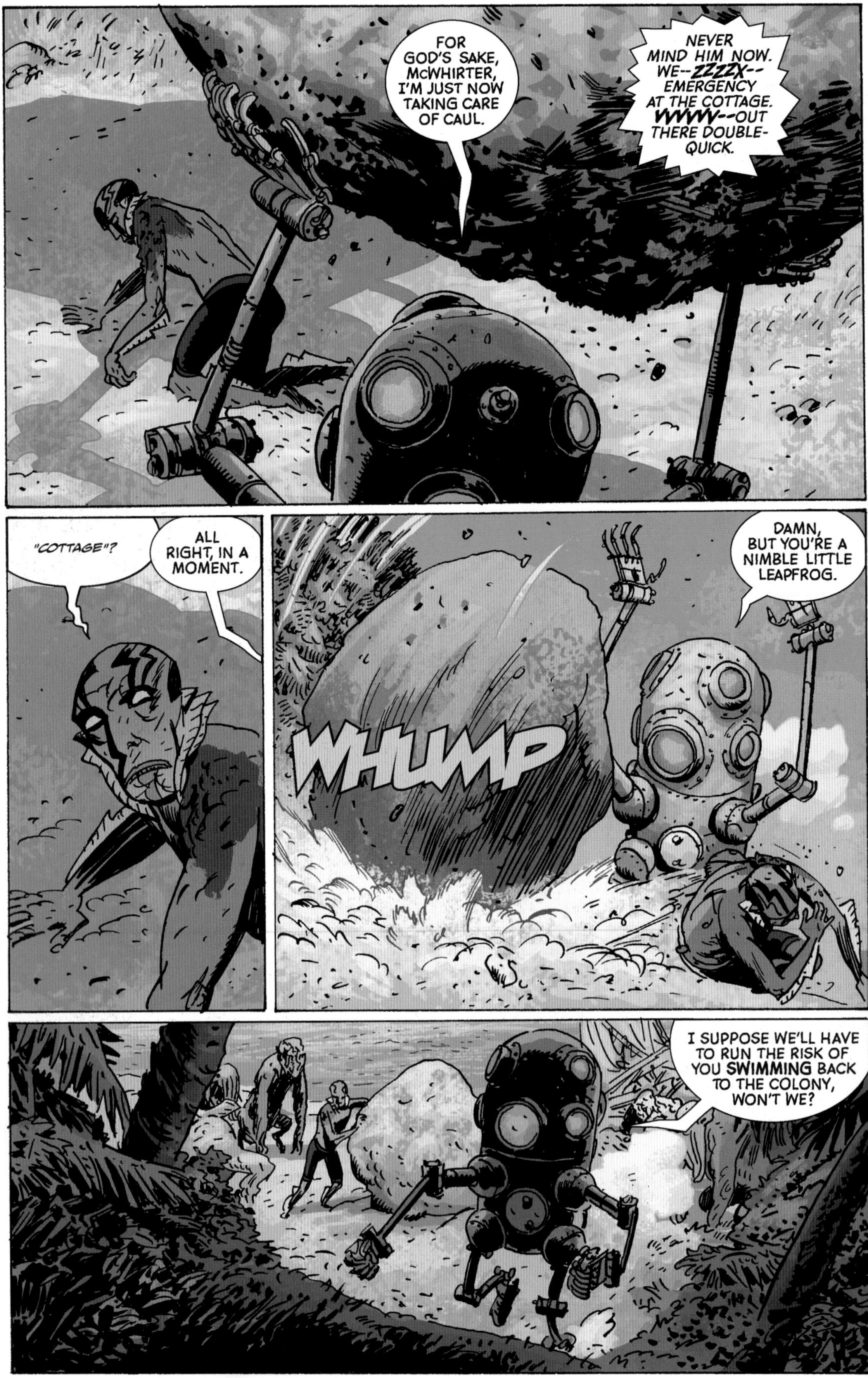
FOR GOD'S SAKE, McWHIRTER, I'M JUST NOW TAKING CARE OF CAUL.
NEVER MIND HIM NOW. WE--ZZZZX--EMERGENCY AT THE COTTAGE. VVVVV--OUT THERE DOUBLE-QUICK.
"COTTAGE"?
ALL RIGHT, IN A MOMENT.
WHUMP
DAMN, BUT YOU'RE A NIMBLE LITTLE LEAPFROG.
I SUPPOSE WE'LL HAVE TO RUN THE RISK OF YOU SWIMMING BACK TO THE COLONY, WON'T WE?

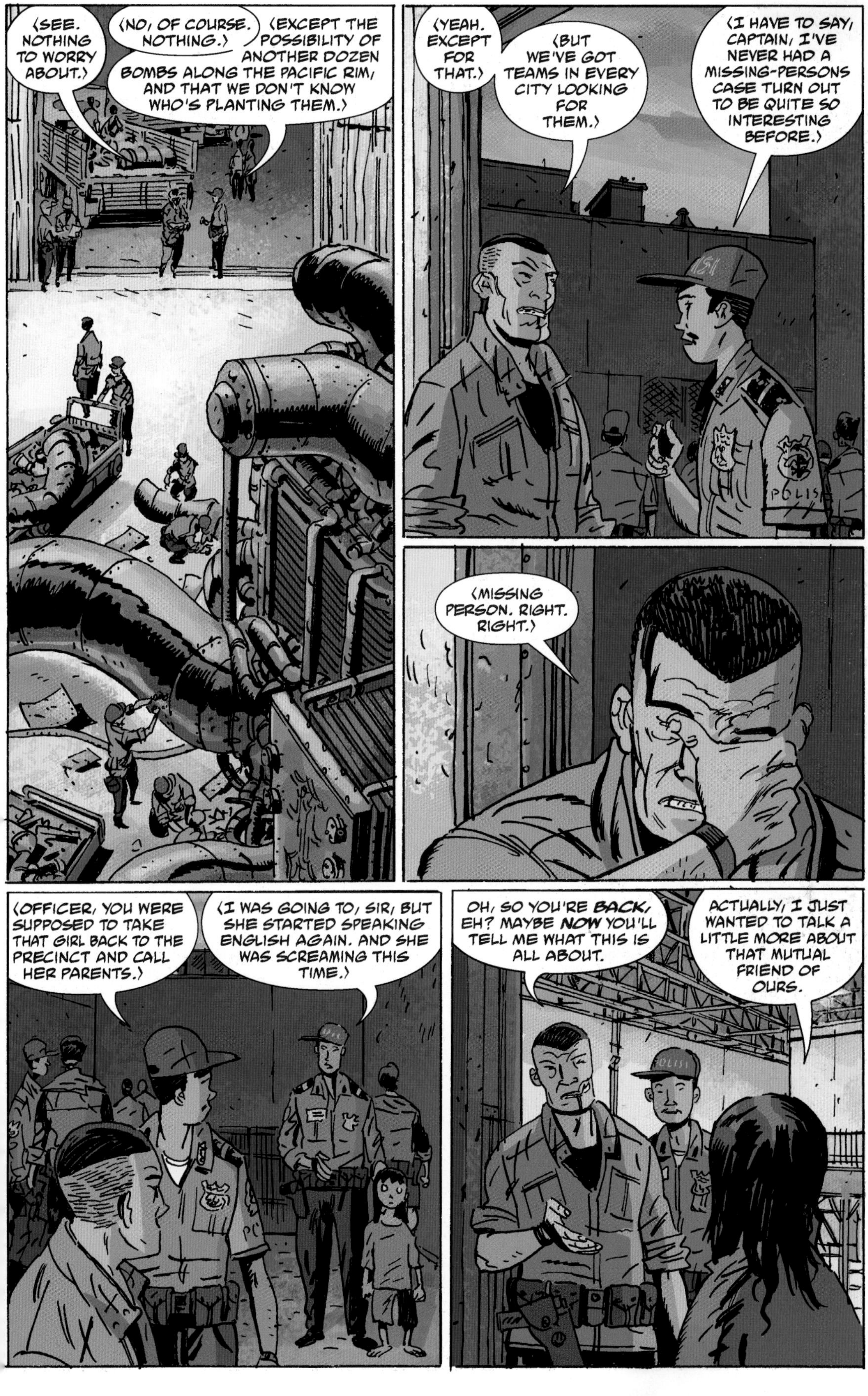

‹SEE. NOTHING TO WORRY ABOUT.›
‹NO, OF COURSE. NOTHING.›
‹EXCEPT THE POSSIBILITY OF ANOTHER DOZEN BOMBS ALONG THE PACIFIC RIM, AND THAT WE DON'T KNOW WHO'S PLANTING THEM.›
‹YEAH. EXCEPT FOR THAT.›
‹BUT WE'VE GOT TEAMS IN EVERY CITY LOOKING FOR THEM.›
‹I HAVE TO SAY, CAPTAIN, I'VE NEVER HAD A MISSING-PERSONS CASE TURN OUT TO BE QUITE SO INTERESTING BEFORE.›
POLIS
‹MISSING PERSON. RIGHT. RIGHT.›
‹OFFICER, YOU WERE SUPPOSED TO TAKE THAT GIRL BACK TO THE PRECINCT AND CALL HER PARENTS.›
‹I WAS GOING TO, SIR, BUT SHE STARTED SPEAKING ENGLISH AGAIN. AND SHE WAS SCREAMING THIS TIME.›
OH, SO YOU'RE **BACK**, EH? MAYBE **NOW** YOU'LL TELL ME WHAT THIS IS ALL ABOUT.
ACTUALLY, I JUST WANTED TO TALK A LITTLE MORE ABOUT THAT MUTUAL FRIEND OF OURS.

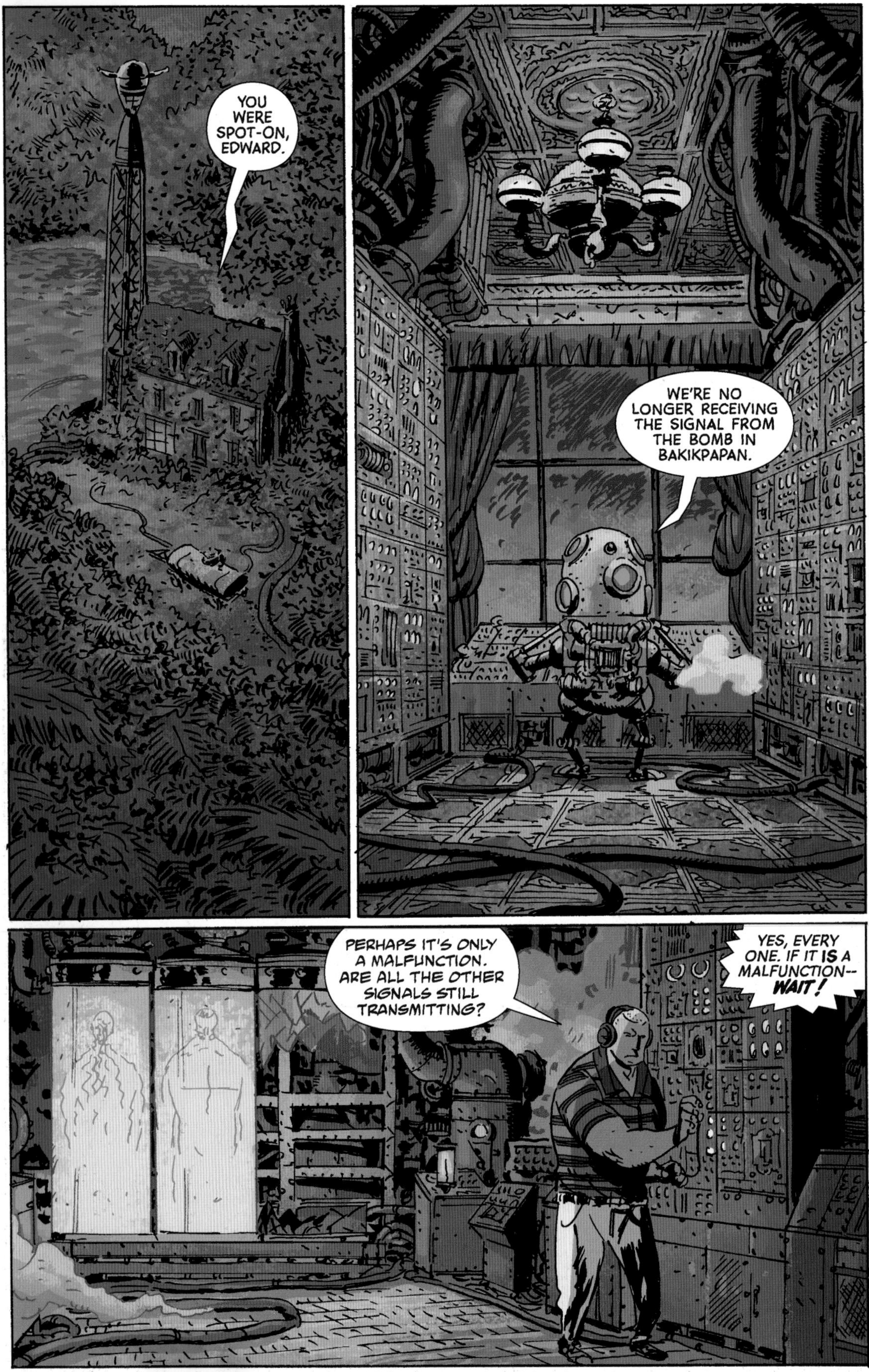
YOU WERE SPOT-ON, EDWARD.
WE'RE NO LONGER RECEIVING THE SIGNAL FROM THE BOMB IN BAKIKPAPAN.
PERHAPS IT'S ONLY A MALFUNCTION. ARE ALL THE OTHER SIGNALS STILL TRANSMITTING?
YES, EVERY ONE. IF IT **IS** A MALFUNCTION-- ***WAIT!***

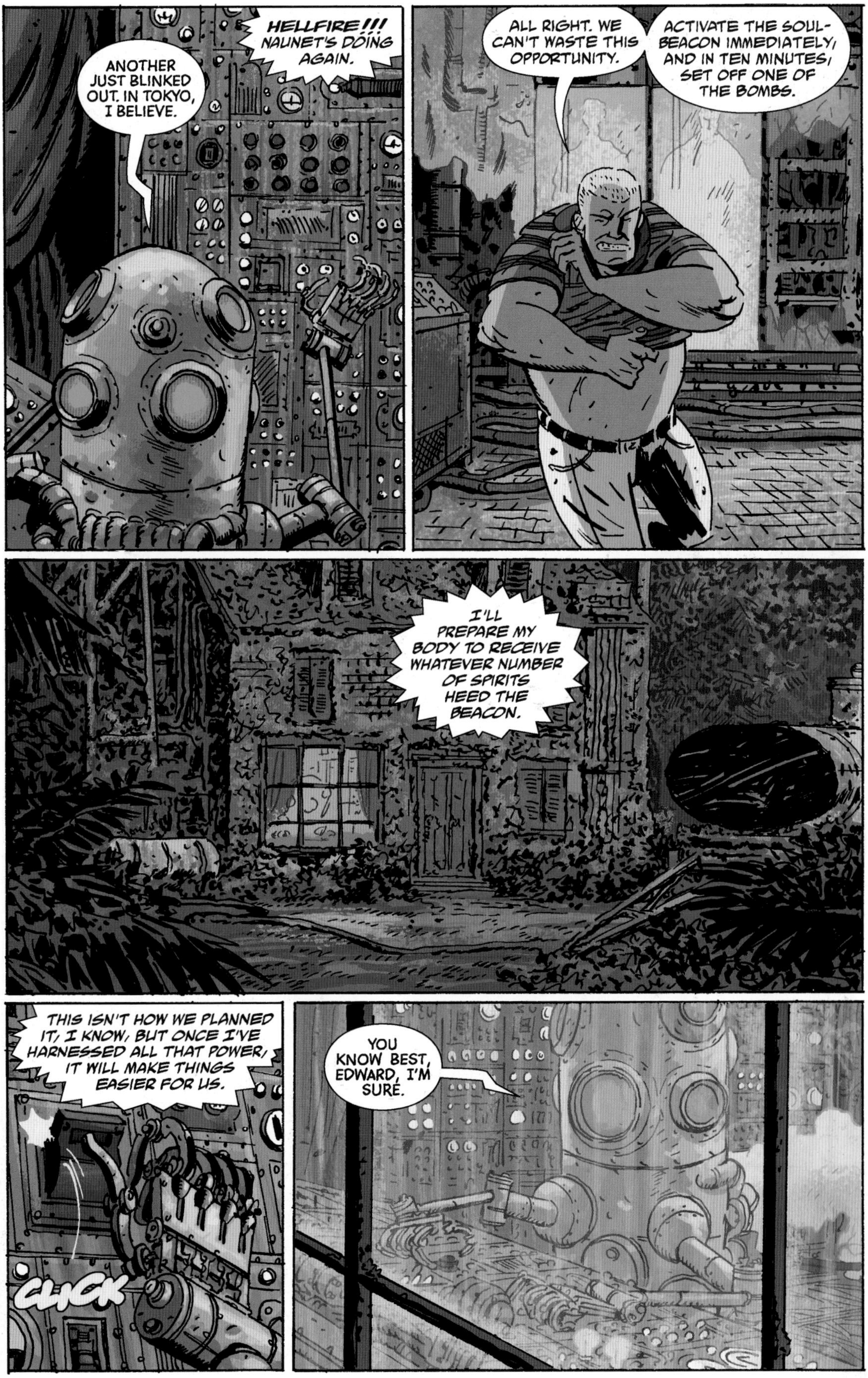
ANOTHER JUST BLINKED OUT. IN TOKYO, I BELIEVE.
HELLFIRE!!! NAUNET'S DOING AGAIN.
ALL RIGHT. WE CAN'T WASTE THIS OPPORTUNITY.
ACTIVATE THE SOUL-BEACON IMMEDIATELY, AND IN TEN MINUTES, SET OFF ONE OF THE BOMBS.
I'LL PREPARE MY BODY TO RECEIVE WHATEVER NUMBER OF SPIRITS HEED THE BEACON.
THIS ISN'T HOW WE PLANNED IT, I KNOW, BUT ONCE I'VE HARNESSED ALL THAT POWER, IT WILL MAKE THINGS EASIER FOR US.
CLICK
YOU KNOW BEST, EDWARD, I'M SURE.

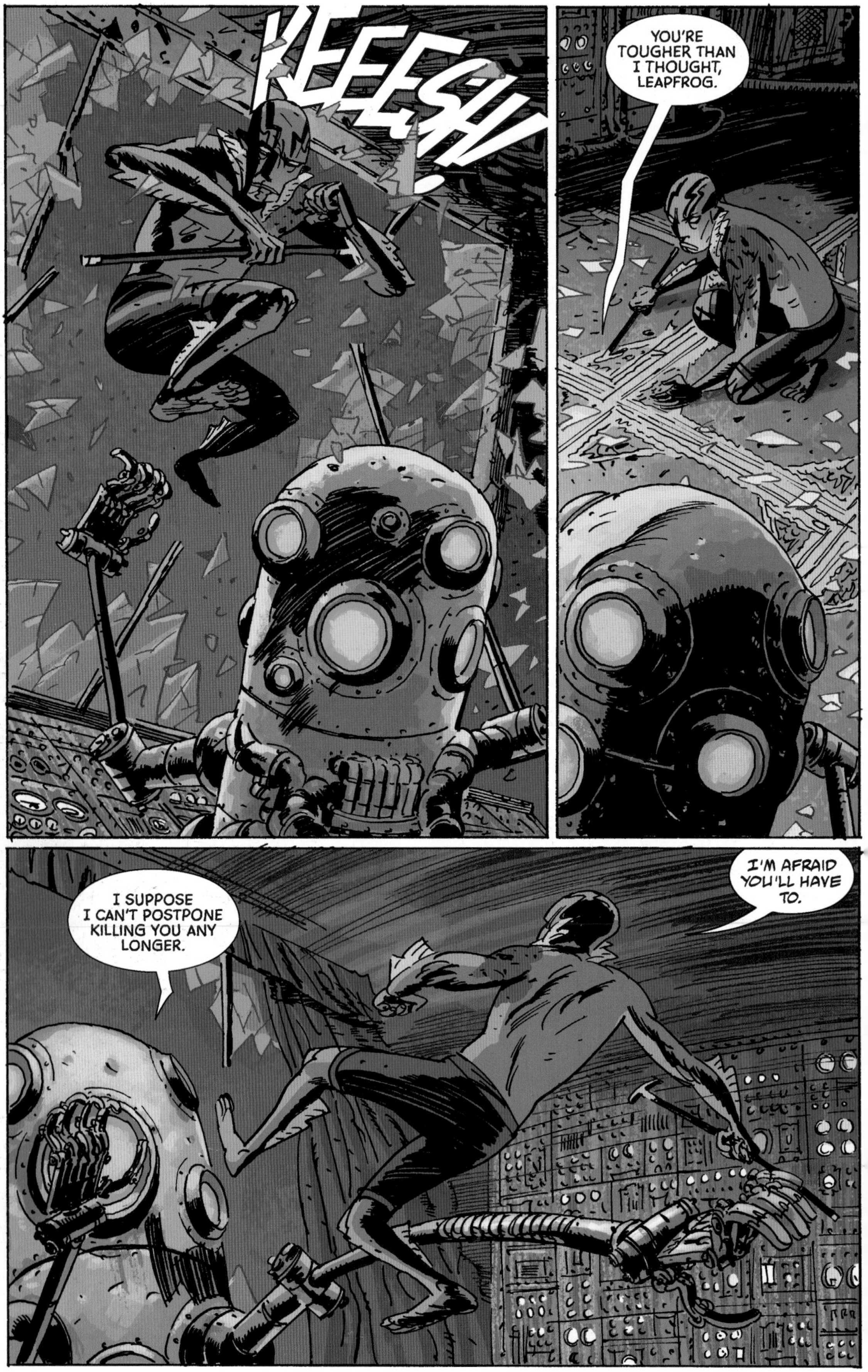
KLEESH!
YOU'RE TOUGHER THAN I THOUGHT, LEAPFROG.
I SUPPOSE I CAN'T POSTPONE KILLING YOU ANY LONGER.
I'M AFRAID YOU'LL HAVE TO.

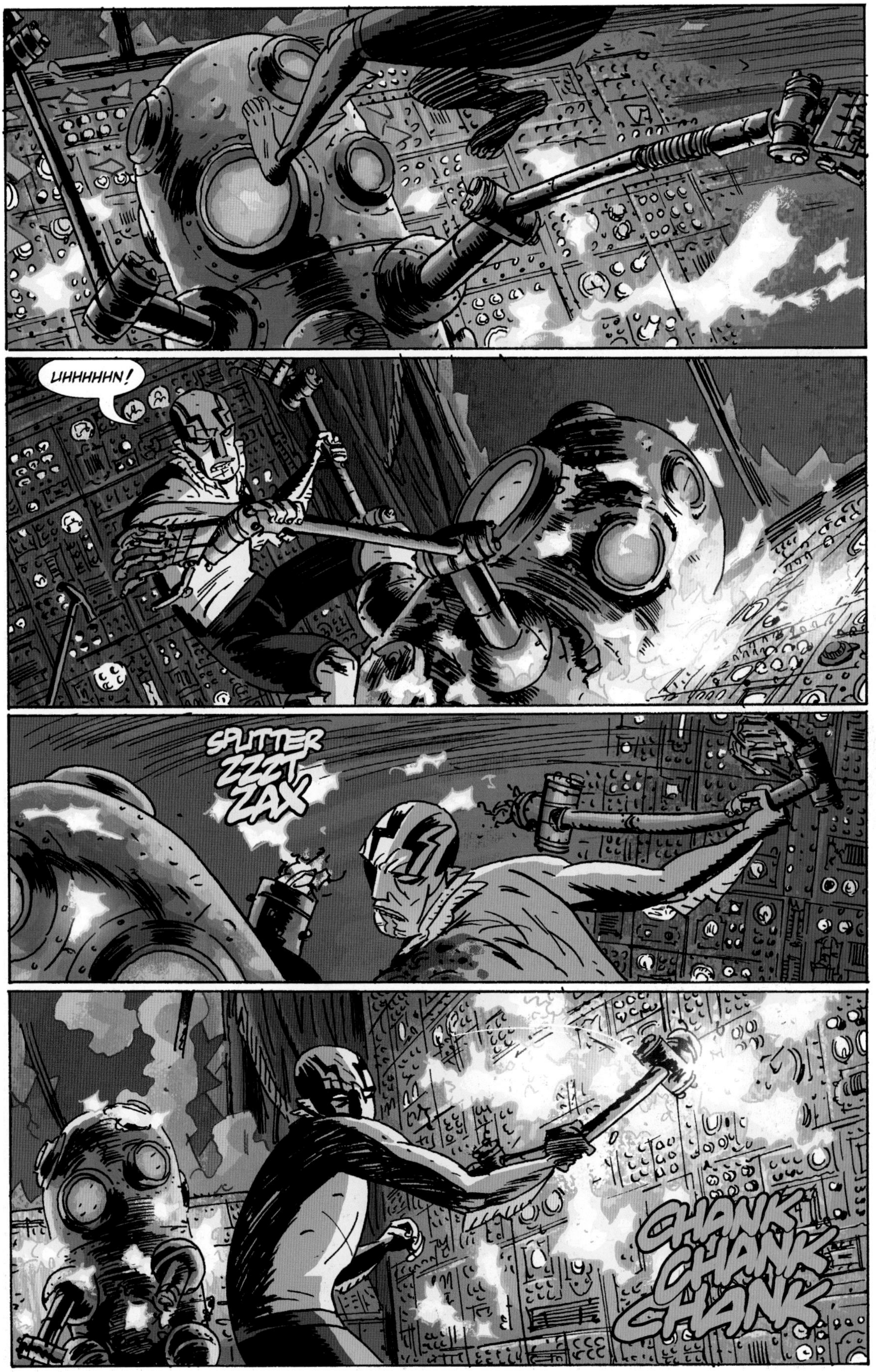
UHHHHHN!
SPUTTER ZZZT ZAX
CHANK CHANK CHANK

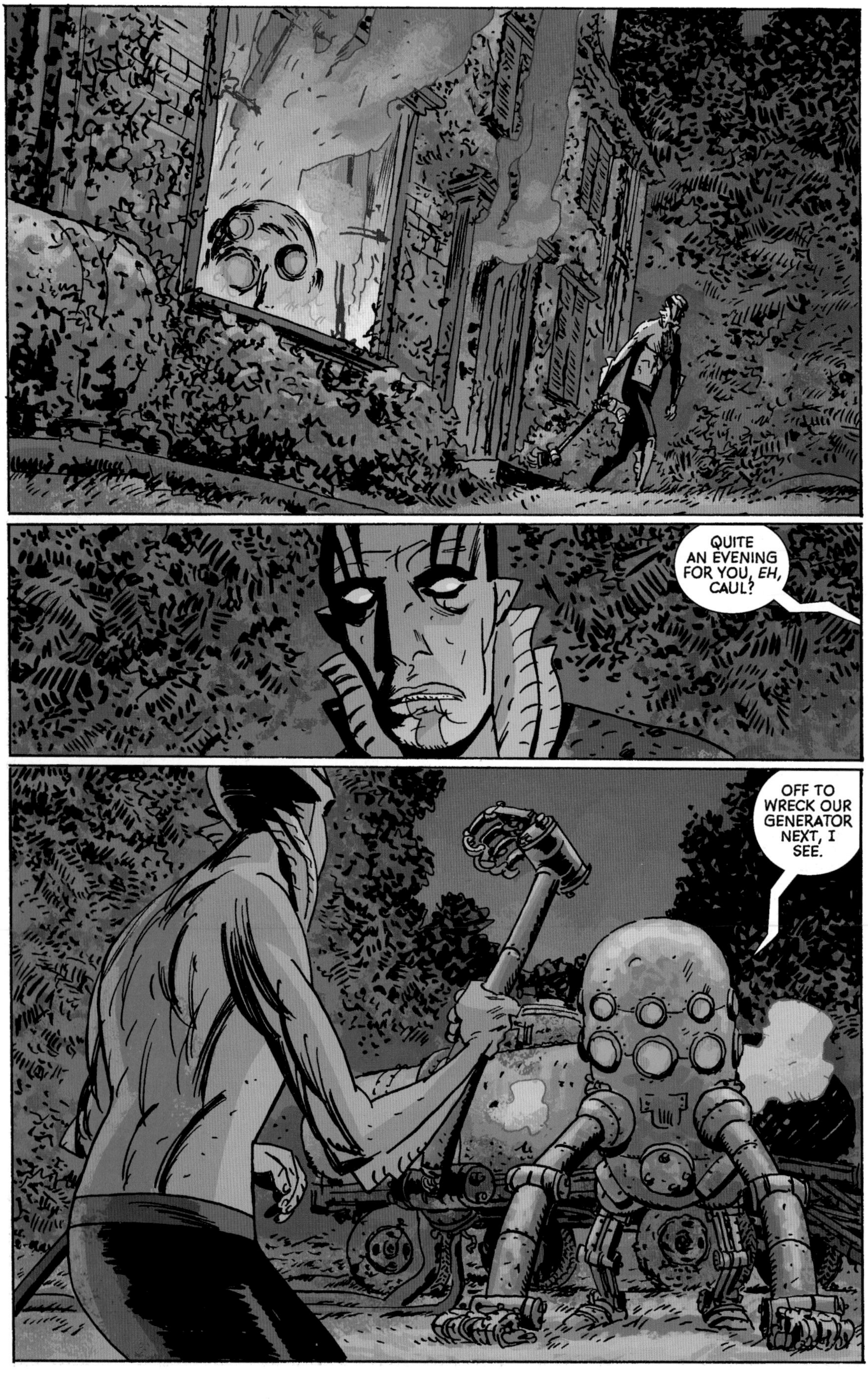
QUITE AN EVENING FOR YOU, EH, CAUL?
OFF TO WRECK OUR GENERATOR NEXT, I SEE.

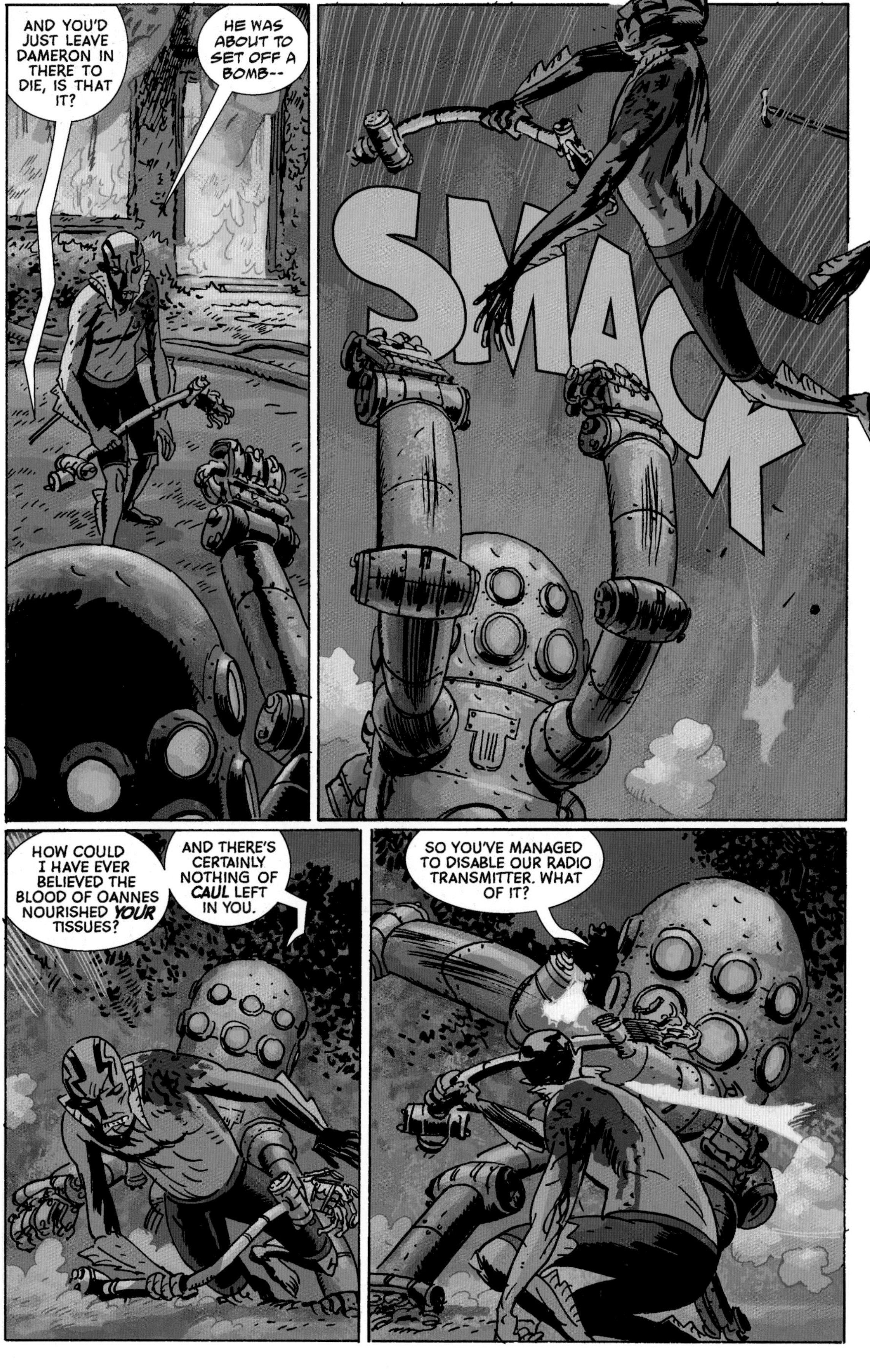
AND YOU'D JUST LEAVE DAMERON IN THERE TO DIE, IS THAT IT?
HE WAS ABOUT TO SET OFF A BOMB--
SMACK
HOW COULD I HAVE EVER BELIEVED THE BLOOD OF OANNES NOURISHED *YOUR* TISSUES?
AND THERE'S CERTAINLY NOTHING OF *CAUL* LEFT IN YOU.
SO YOU'VE MANAGED TO DISABLE OUR RADIO TRANSMITTER. WHAT OF IT?

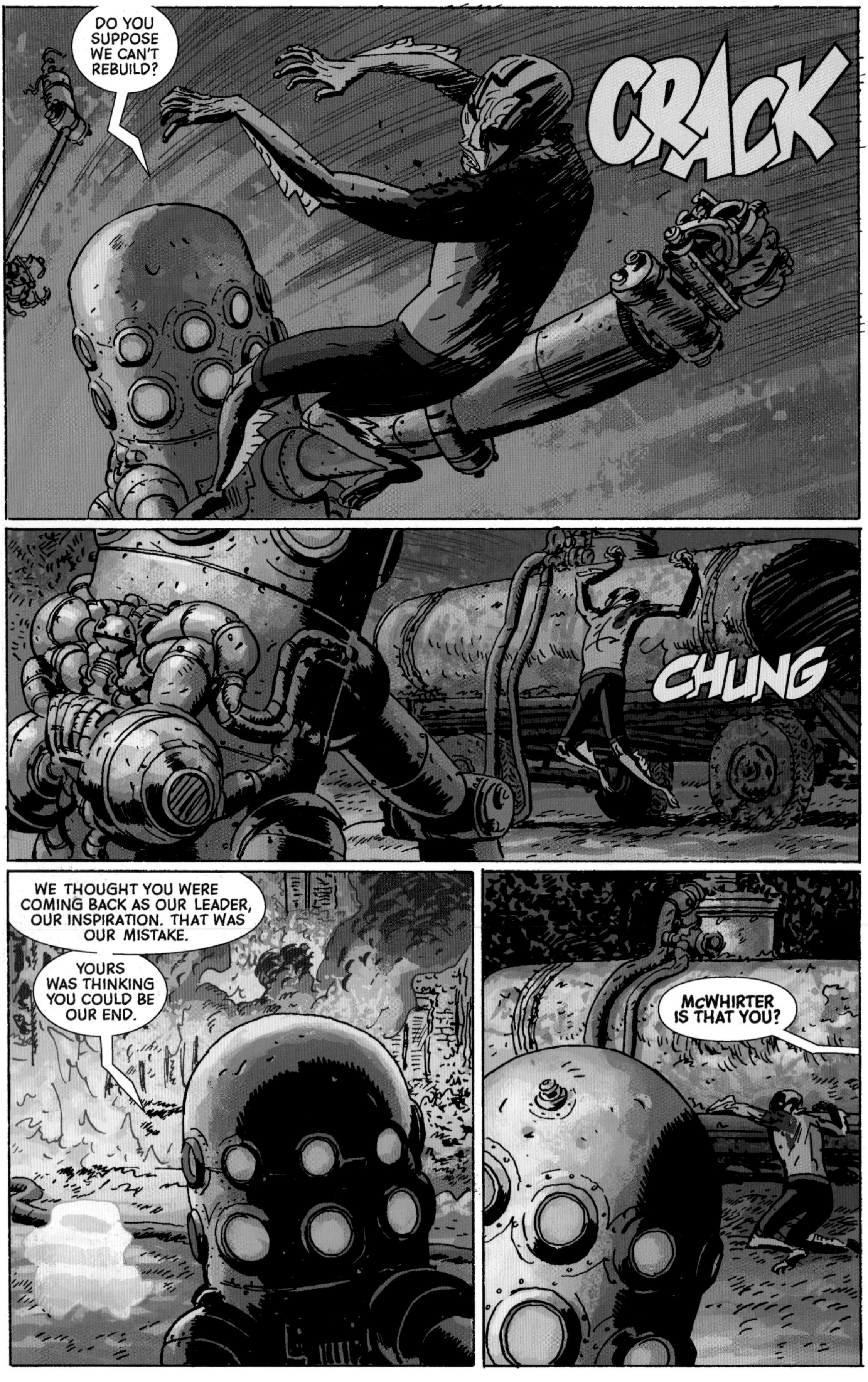
DO YOU SUPPOSE WE CAN'T REBUILD?
CRACK
CHUNG
WE THOUGHT YOU WERE COMING BACK AS OUR LEADER, OUR INSPIRATION. THAT WAS OUR MISTAKE.
YOURS WAS THINKING YOU COULD BE OUR END.
McWHIRTER IS THAT YOU?

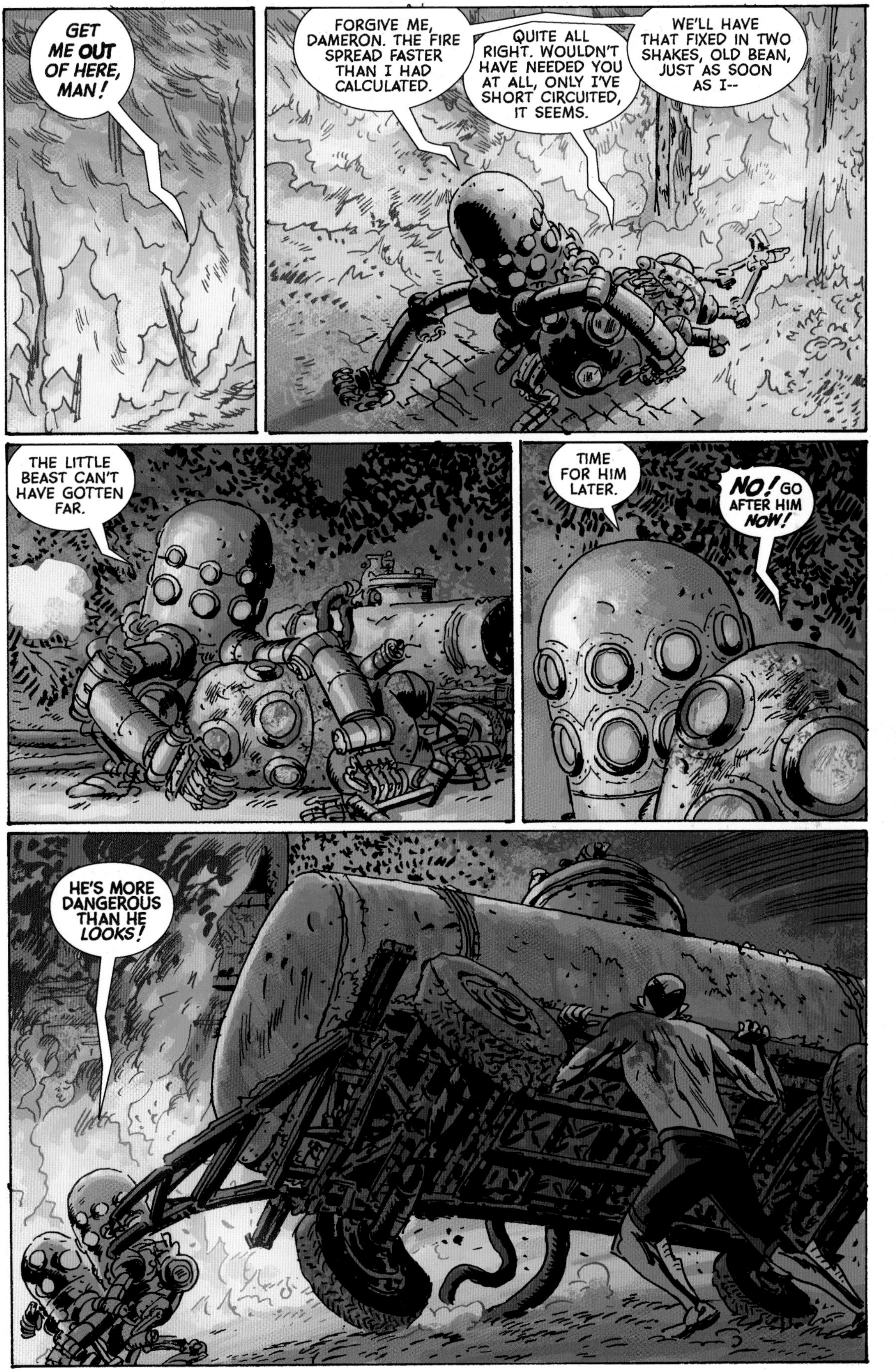
GET ME OUT OF HERE, MAN!
FORGIVE ME, DAMERON. THE FIRE SPREAD FASTER THAN I HAD CALCULATED.
QUITE ALL RIGHT. WOULDN'T HAVE NEEDED YOU AT ALL, ONLY I'VE SHORT CIRCUITED, IT SEEMS.
WE'LL HAVE THAT FIXED IN TWO SHAKES, OLD BEAN, JUST AS SOON AS I--
THE LITTLE BEAST CAN'T HAVE GOTTEN FAR.
TIME FOR HIM LATER.
NO! GO AFTER HIM NOW!
HE'S MORE DANGEROUS THAN HE LOOKS!

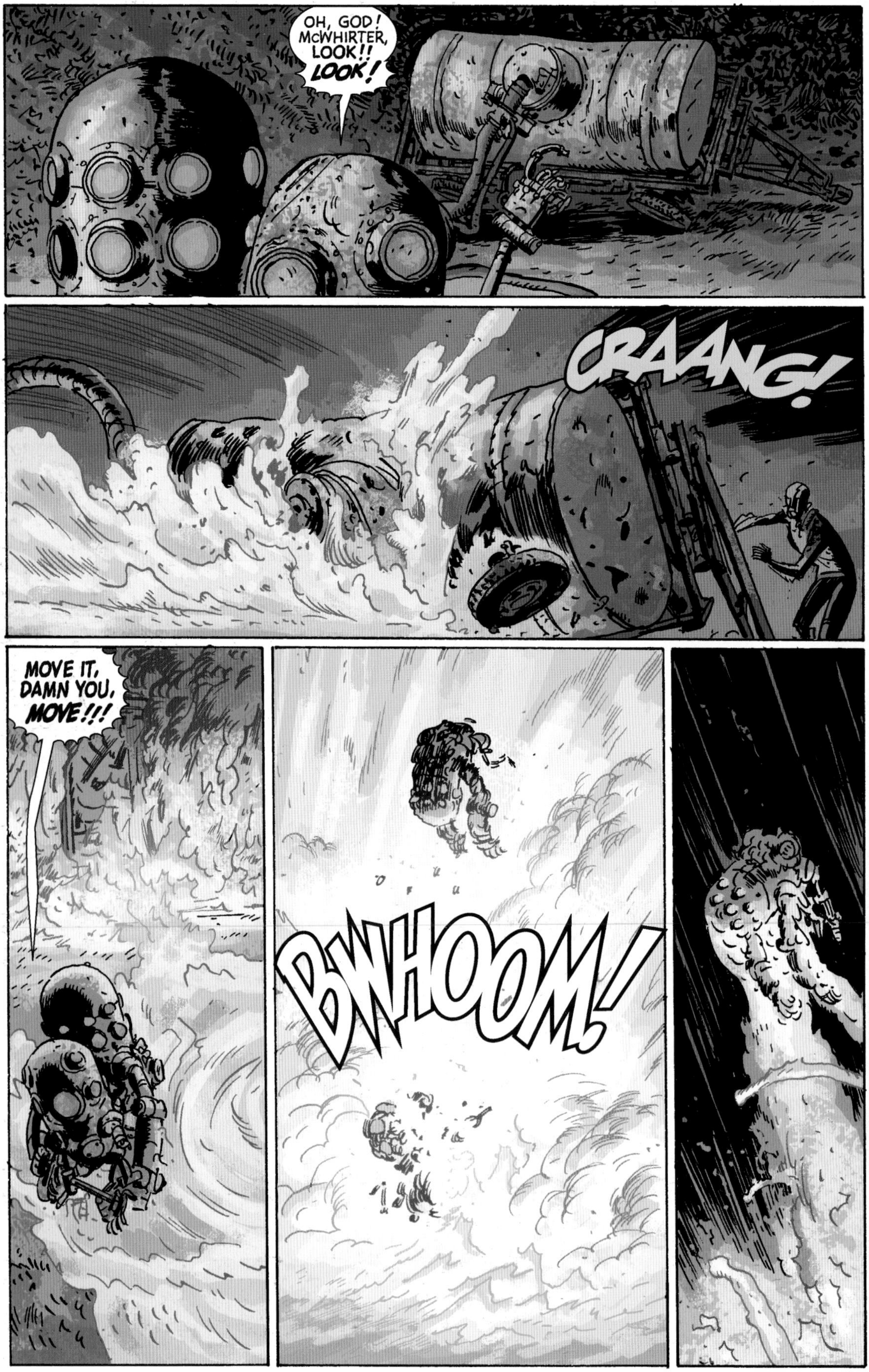
OH, GOD! McWHIRTER, LOOK!! LOOK!
CRAAANG!
MOVE IT, DAMN YOU, MOVE!!!
BWHOOM!

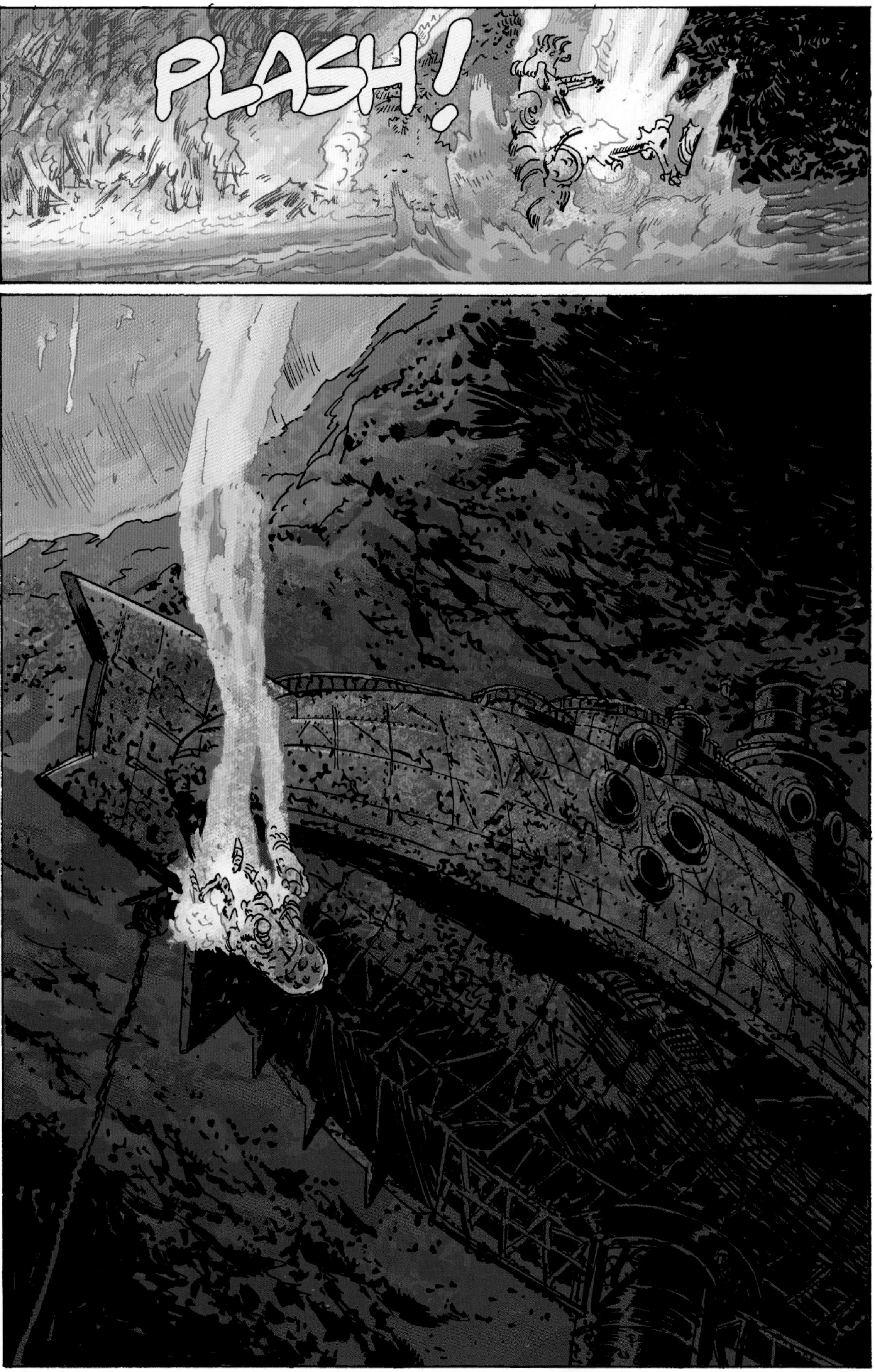
PLASH!

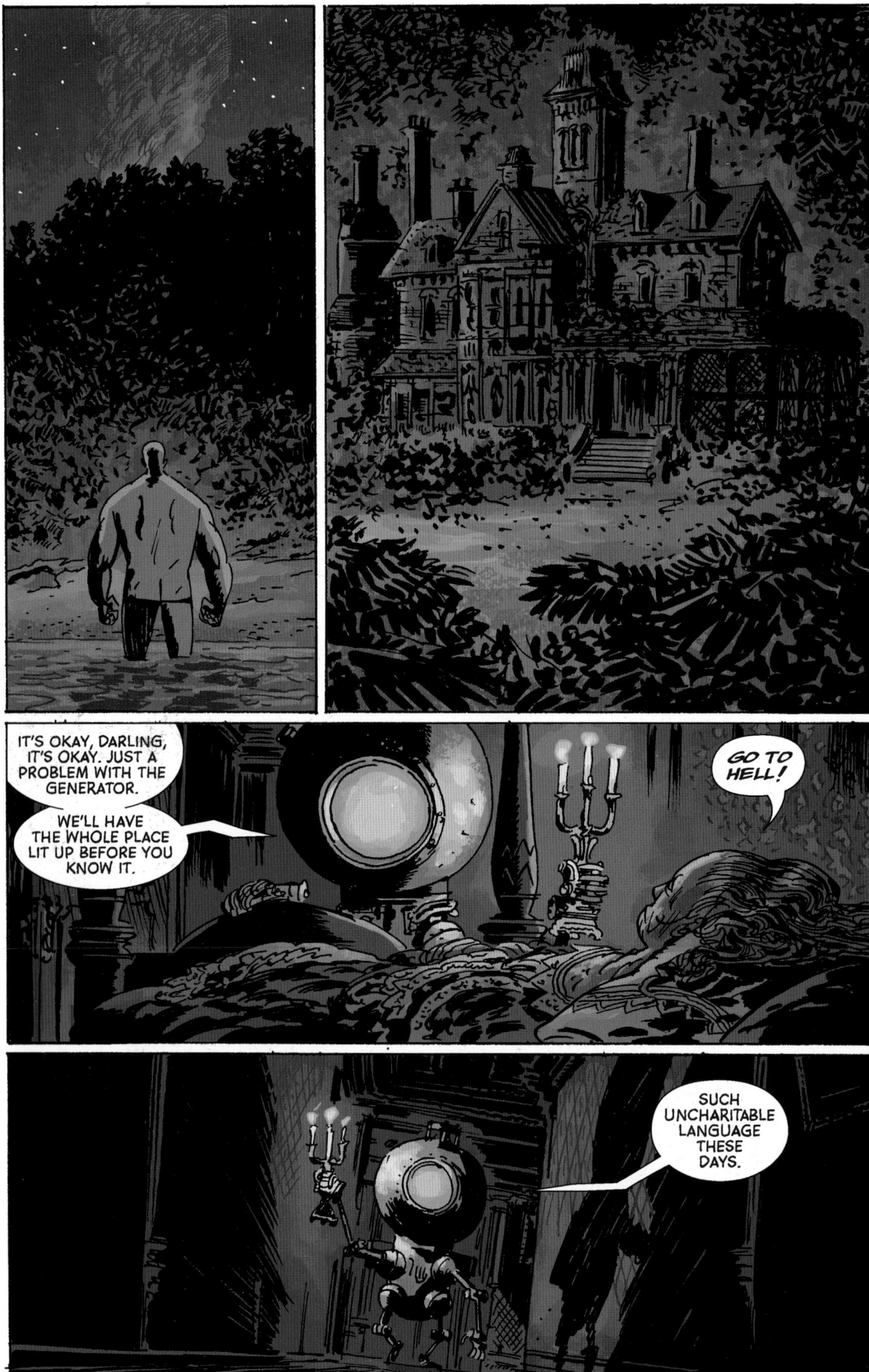
IT'S OKAY, DARLING, IT'S OKAY. JUST A PROBLEM WITH THE GENERATOR.
WE'LL HAVE THE WHOLE PLACE LIT UP BEFORE YOU KNOW IT.
GO TO HELL!
SUCH UNCHARITABLE LANGUAGE THESE DAYS.

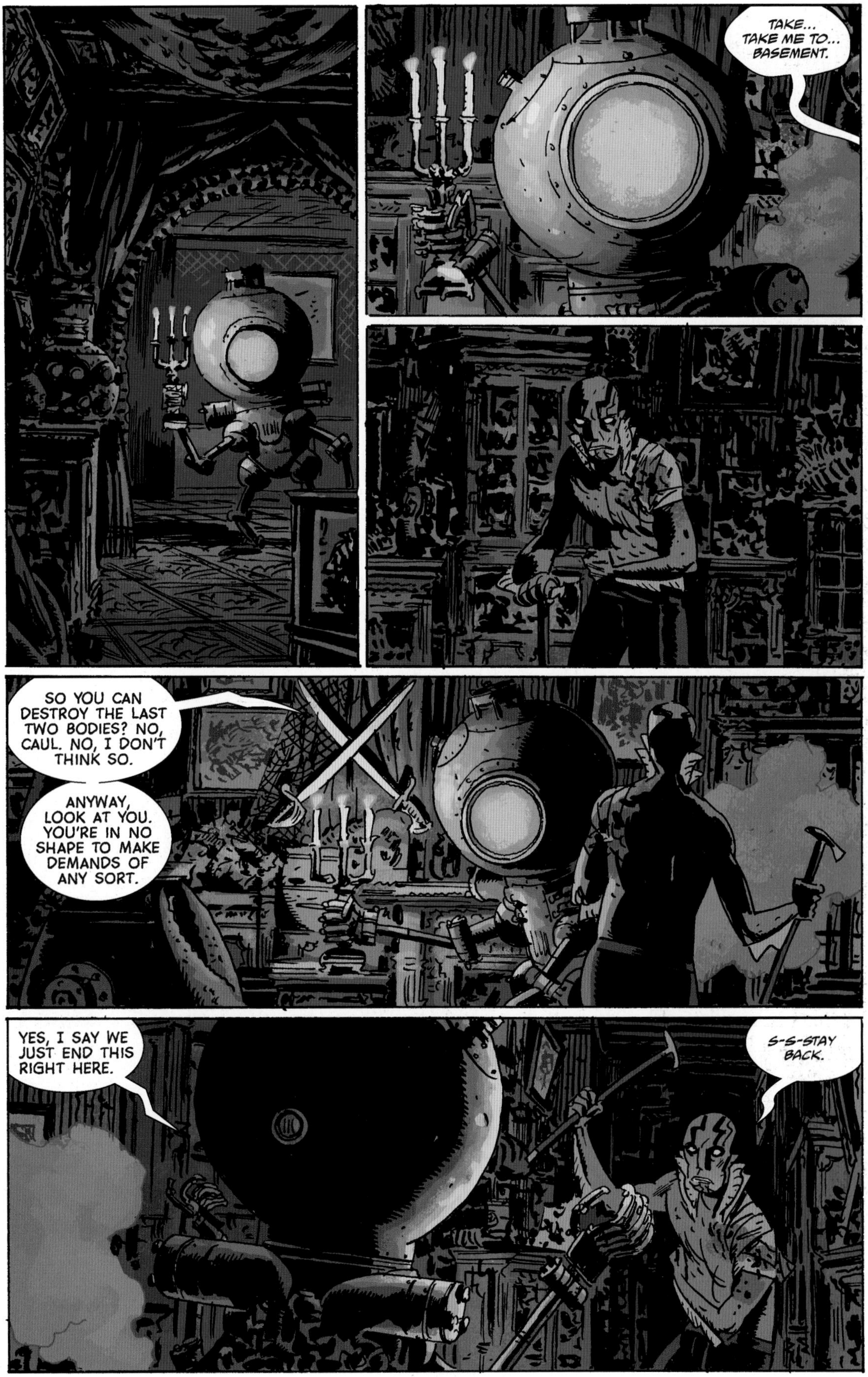
TAKE... TAKE ME TO... BASEMENT.
SO YOU CAN DESTROY THE LAST TWO BODIES? NO, CAUL. NO, I DON'T THINK SO.
ANYWAY, LOOK AT YOU. YOU'RE IN NO SHAPE TO MAKE DEMANDS OF ANY SORT.
YES, I SAY WE JUST END THIS RIGHT HERE.
S-S-STAY BACK.

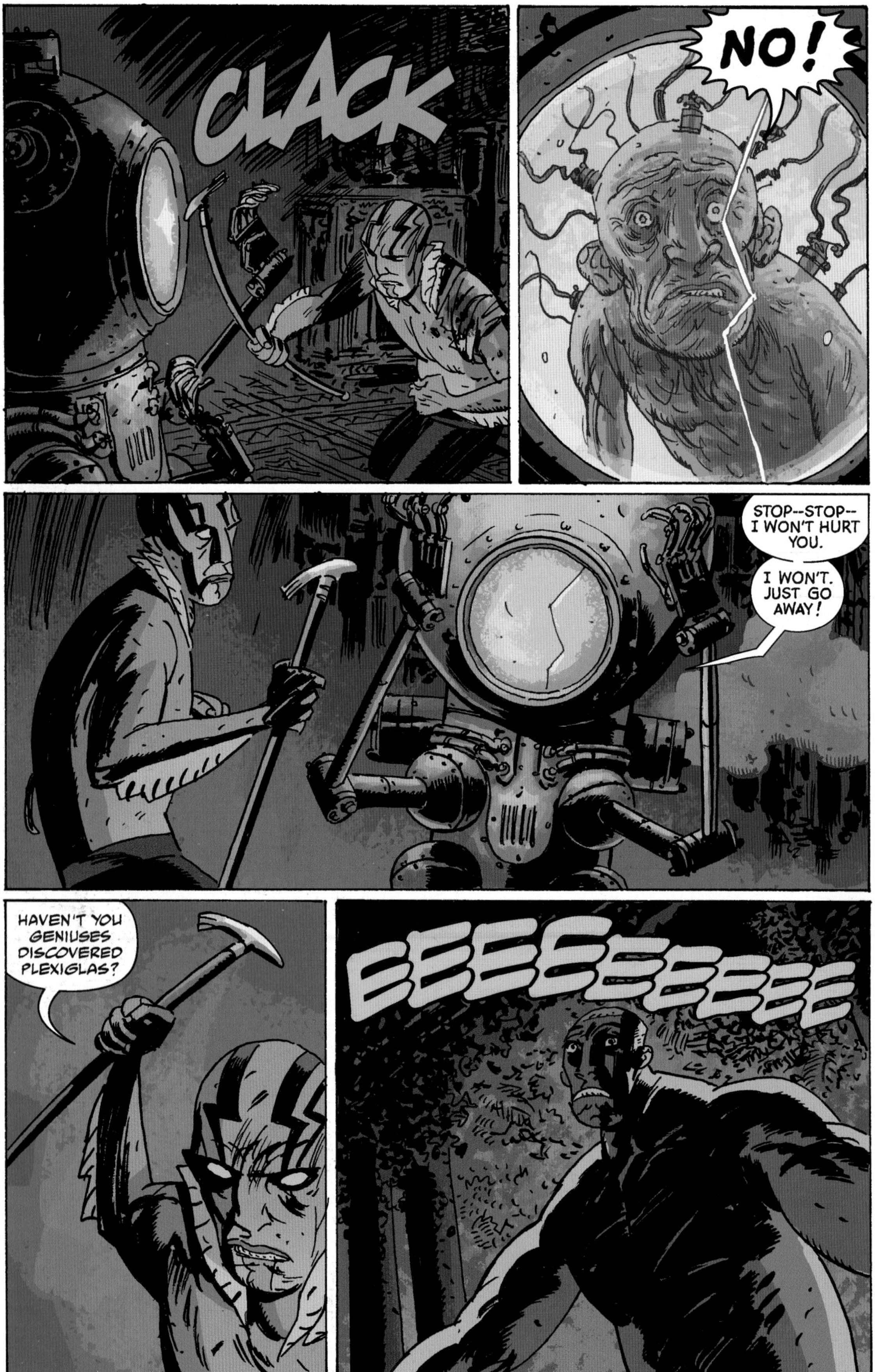
CLACK
NO!
STOP--STOP-- I WON'T HURT YOU.
I WON'T. JUST GO AWAY!
HAVEN'T YOU GENIUSES DISCOVERED PLEXIGLAS?
EEEEEEEEEEEE

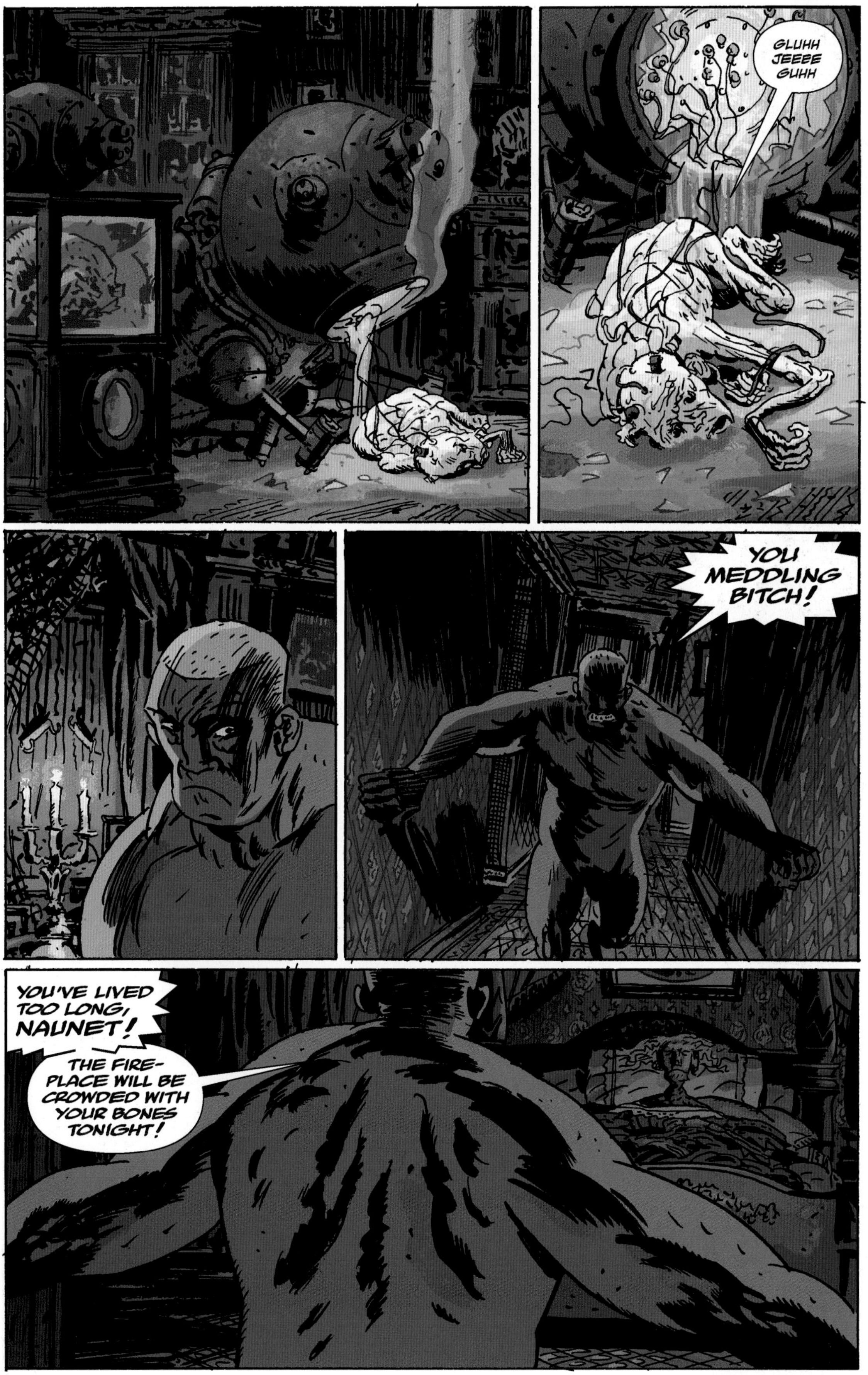
GLUHH JEEEE GUHH
YOU MEDDLING BITCH!
YOU'VE LIVED TOO LONG, NAUNET!
THE FIRE-PLACE WILL BE CROWDED WITH YOUR BONES TONIGHT!

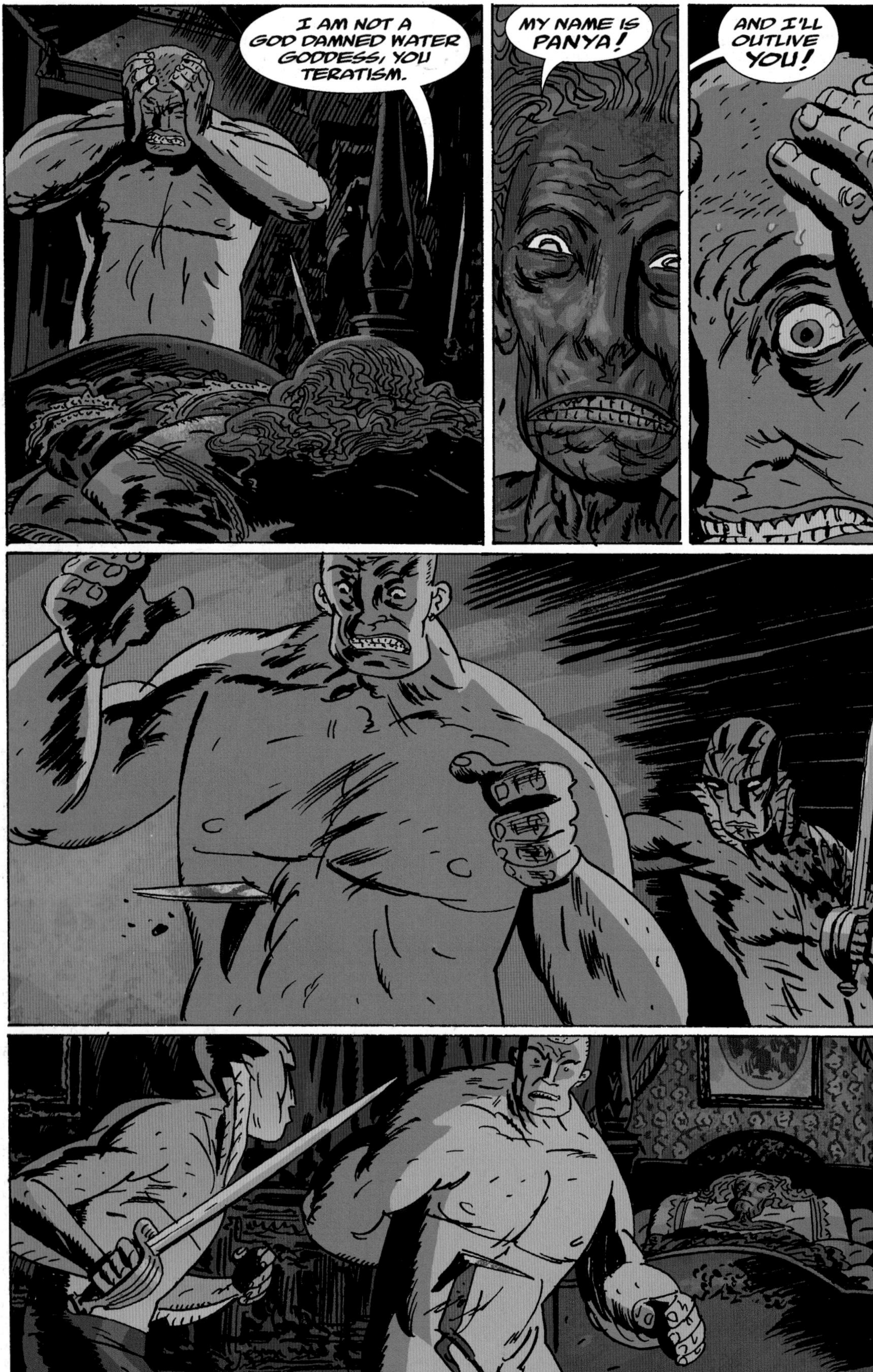
I AM NOT A GOD DAMNED WATER GODDESS, YOU TERATISM.
MY NAME IS PANYA!
AND I'LL OUTLIVE YOU!

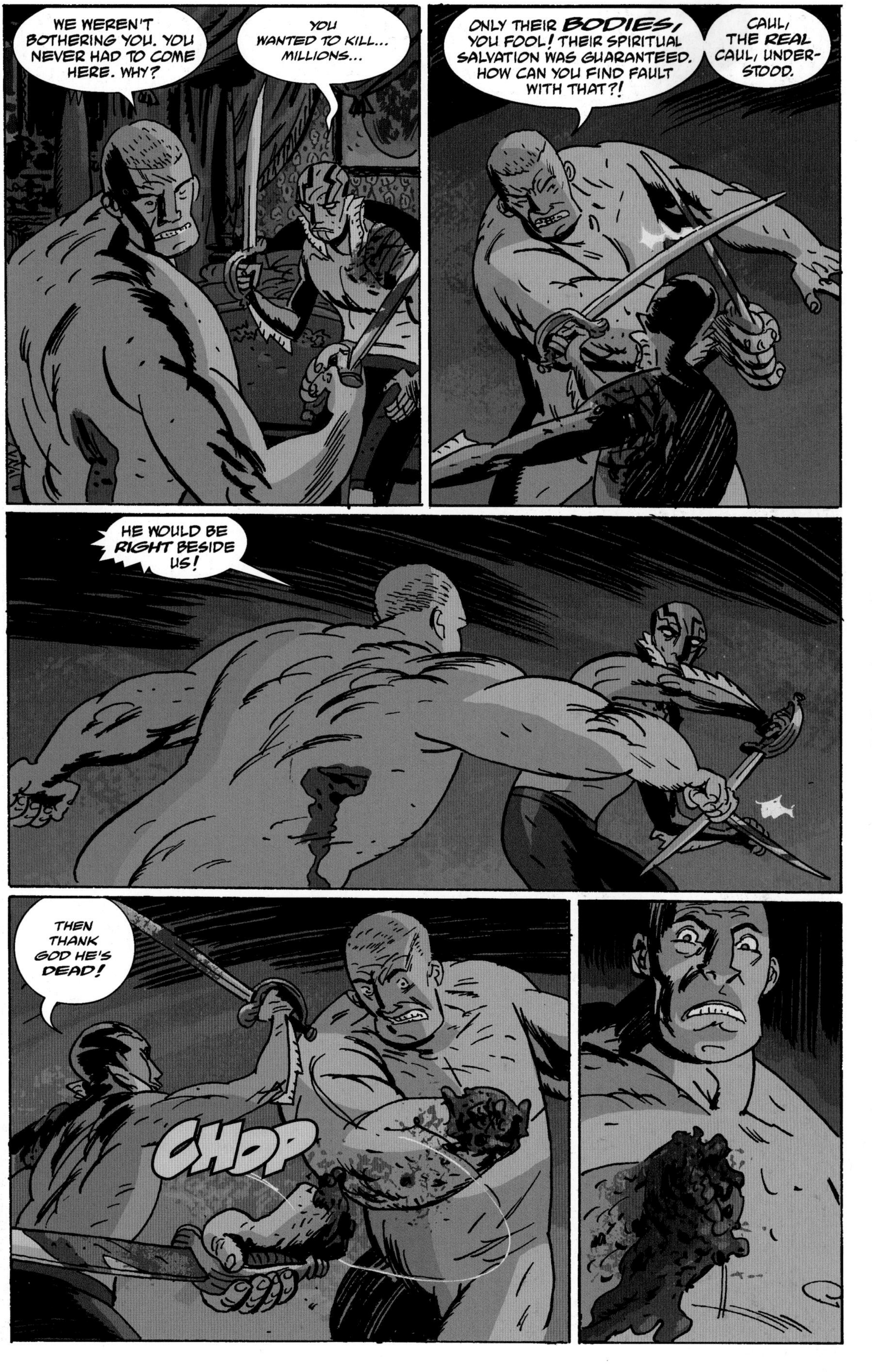
WE WEREN'T BOTHERING YOU. YOU NEVER HAD TO COME HERE. WHY?
YOU WANTED TO KILL... MILLIONS...
ONLY THEIR BODIES, YOU FOOL! THEIR SPIRITUAL SALVATION WAS GUARANTEED. HOW CAN YOU FIND FAULT WITH THAT?!
CAUL, THE REAL CAUL, UNDER-STOOD.
HE WOULD BE RIGHT BESIDE US!
THEN THANK GOD HE'S DEAD!
CHOP

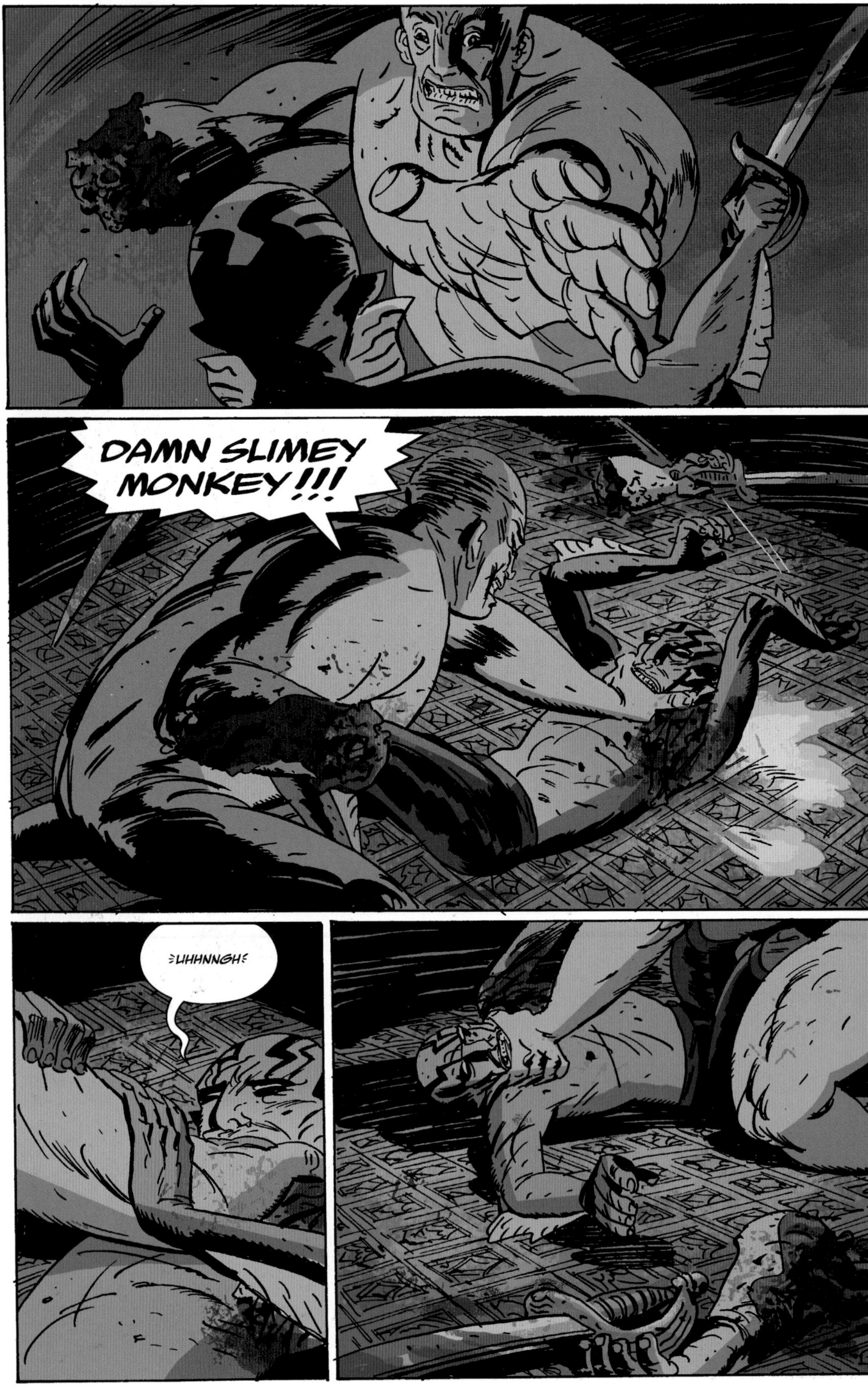
DAMN SLIMEY MONKEY!!!
UHHNNGH

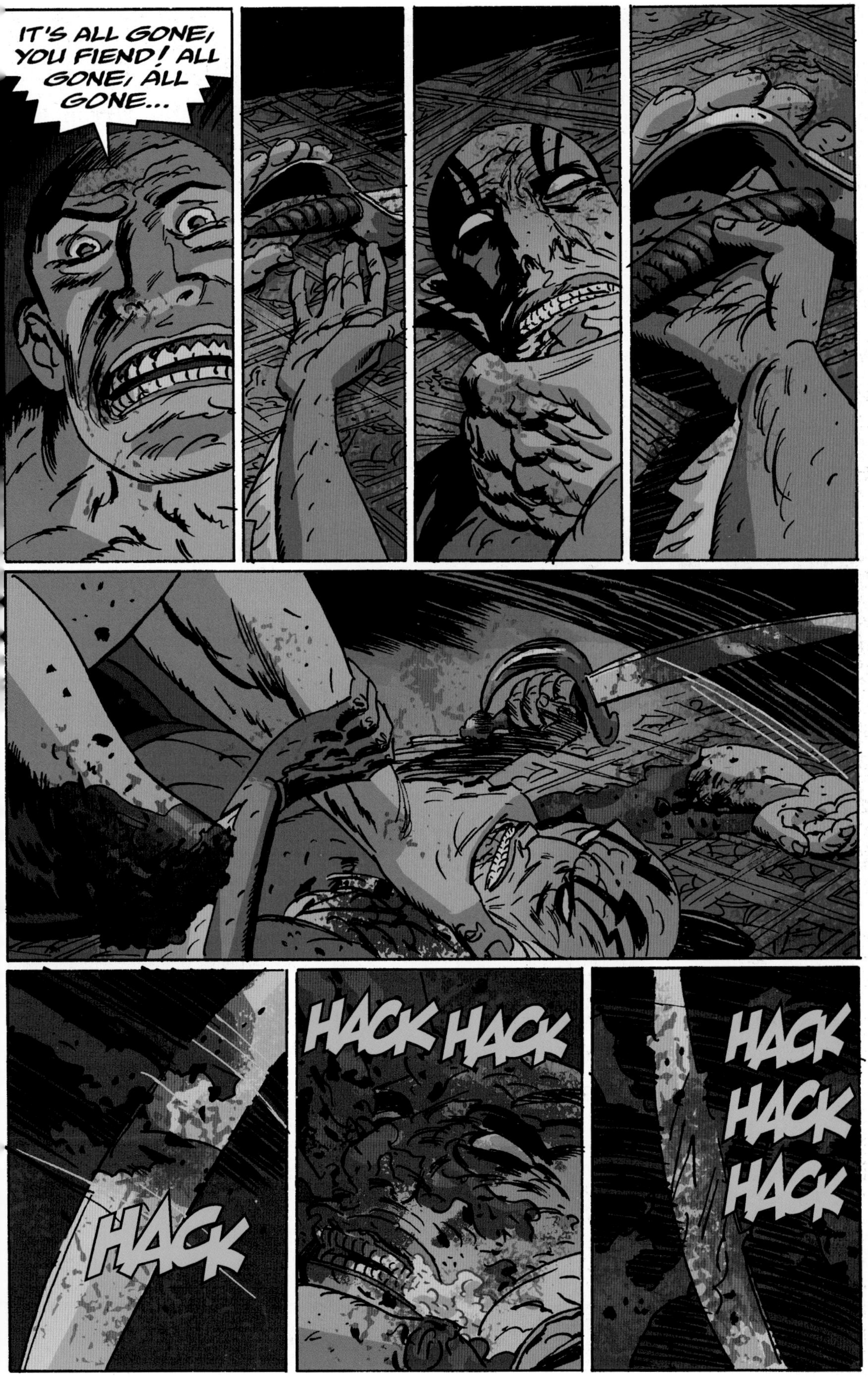
IT'S ALL GONE, YOU FIEND! ALL GONE, ALL GONE...
HACK
HACK HACK
HACK
HACK
HACK

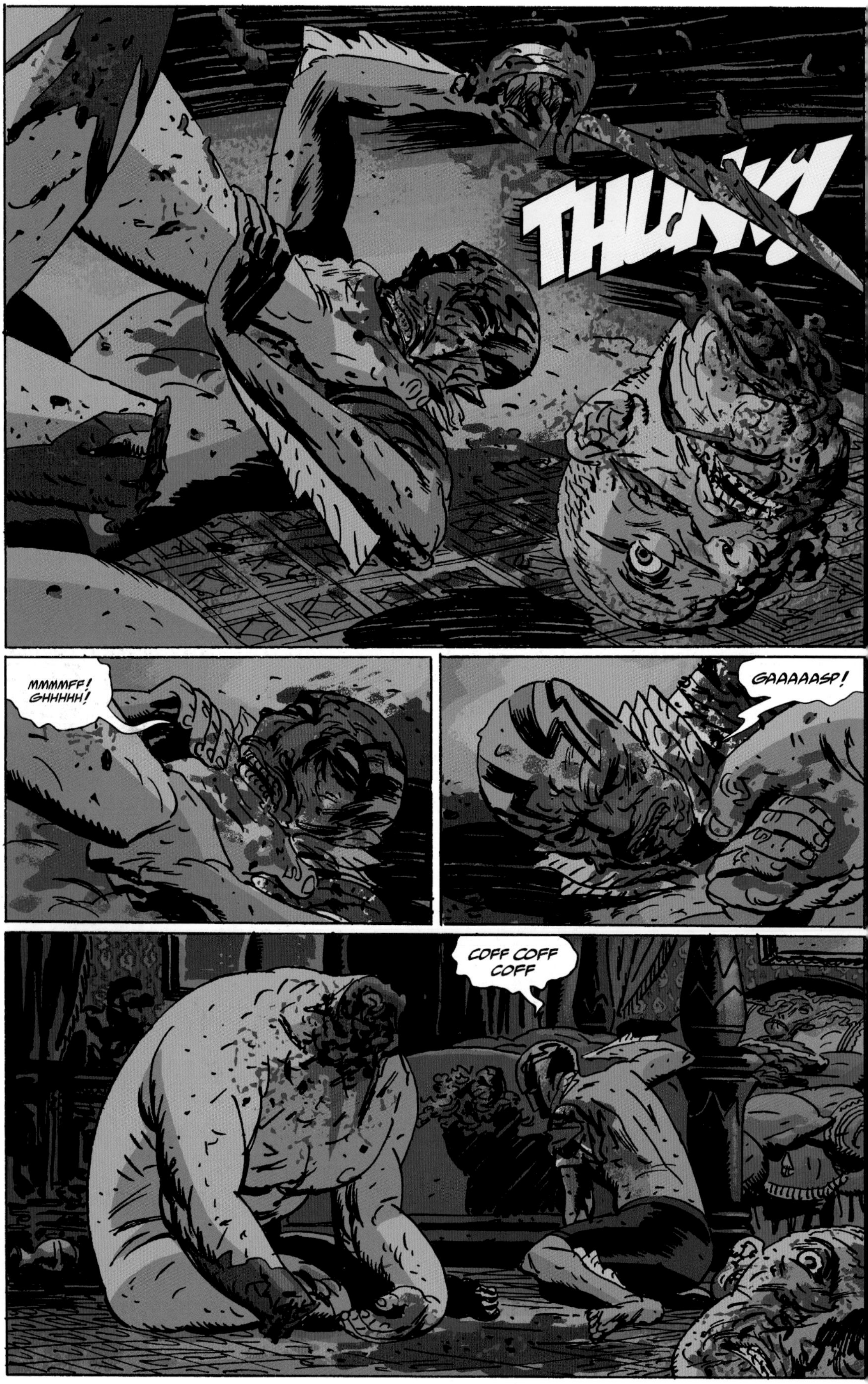
THUNK!
MMMMFF! GHHHHH!
GAAAAASP!
COFF COFF COFF

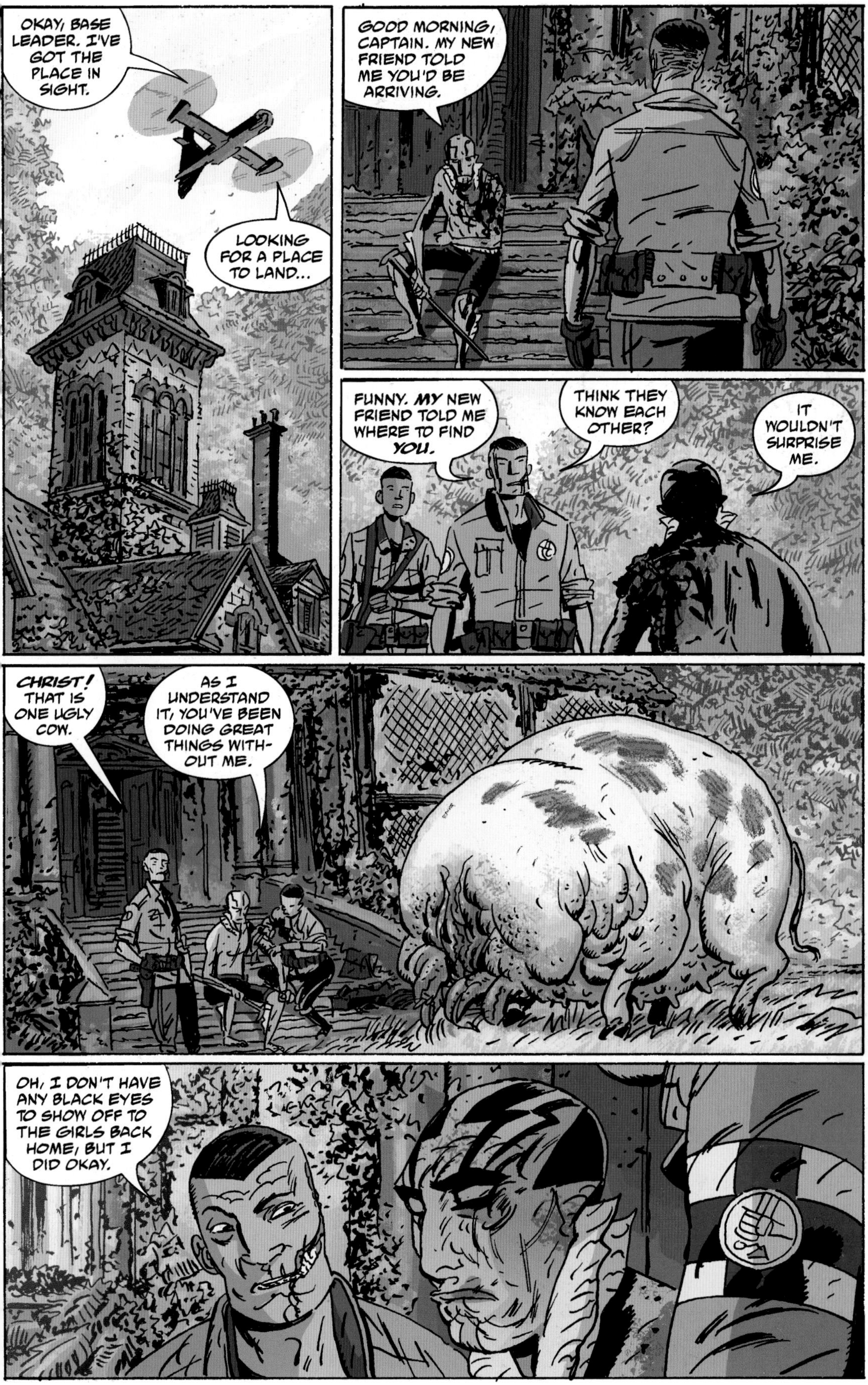
OKAY, BASE LEADER. I'VE GOT THE PLACE IN SIGHT.
LOOKING FOR A PLACE TO LAND...
GOOD MORNING, CAPTAIN. MY NEW FRIEND TOLD ME YOU'D BE ARRIVING.
FUNNY. MY NEW FRIEND TOLD ME WHERE TO FIND YOU.
THINK THEY KNOW EACH OTHER?
IT WOULDN'T SURPRISE ME.
CHRIST! THAT IS ONE UGLY COW.
AS I UNDERSTAND IT, YOU'VE BEEN DOING GREAT THINGS WITHOUT ME.
OH, I DON'T HAVE ANY BLACK EYES TO SHOW OFF TO THE GIRLS BACK HOME, BUT I DID OKAY.

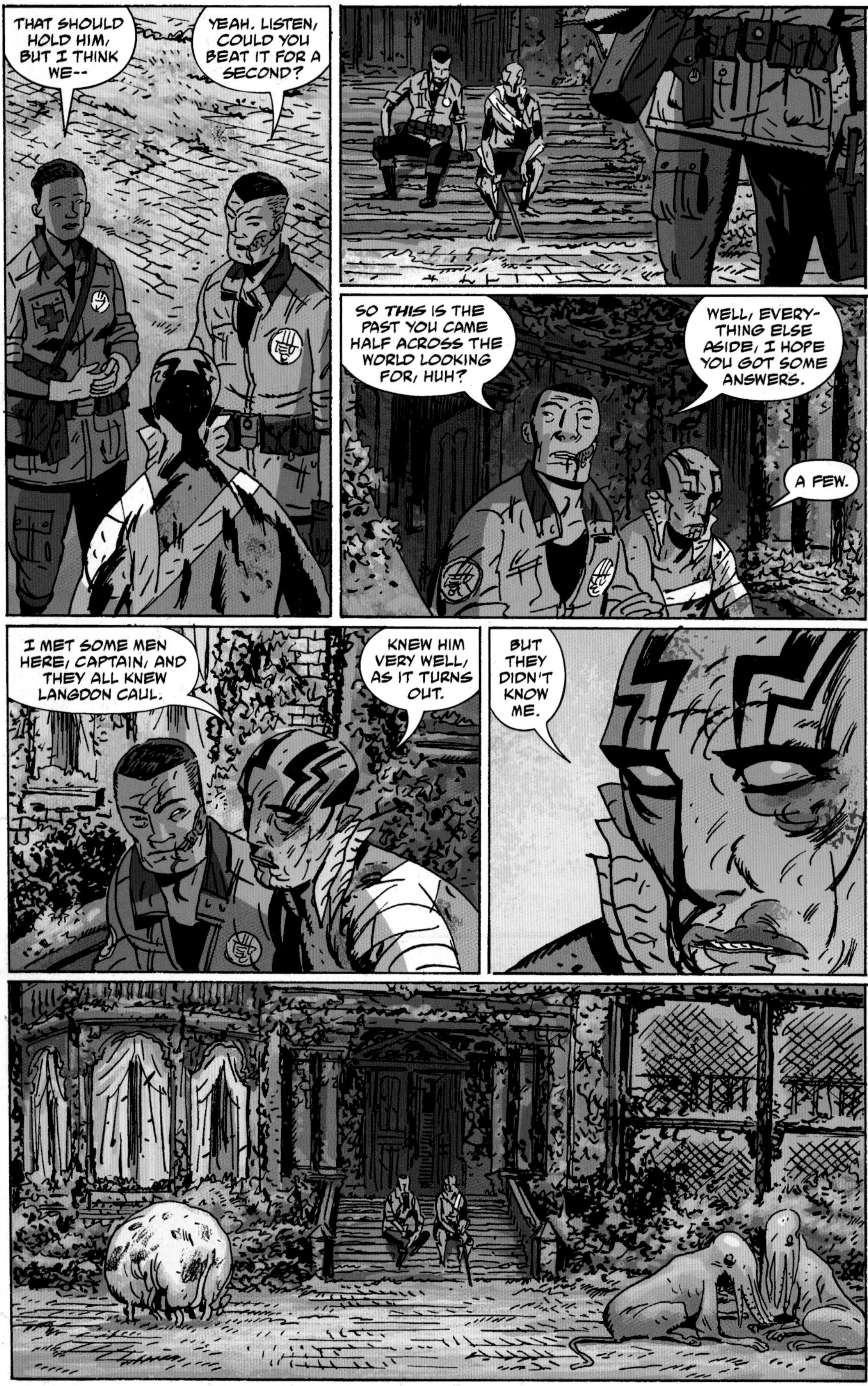
THAT SHOULD HOLD HIM, BUT I THINK WE--
YEAH. LISTEN, COULD YOU BEAT IT FOR A SECOND?
SO THIS IS THE PAST YOU CAME HALF ACROSS THE WORLD LOOKING FOR, HUH?
WELL, EVERY-THING ELSE ASIDE, I HOPE YOU GOT SOME ANSWERS.
A FEW.
I MET SOME MEN HERE, CAPTAIN, AND THEY ALL KNEW LANGDON CAUL.
KNEW HIM VERY WELL, AS IT TURNS OUT.
BUT THEY DIDN'T KNOW ME.

THE END

Afterword

It all started where every good story starts: in failure.

Years ago, back when Mike and I still lived within spitting distance of each other, we were having lunch one day discussing, I think, plot points on *The Black Flame*. As usual, we got off-topic, and Mike asked me what else I was working on. I was writing a series for another company at the time, so I told him about a story element I was planning to introduce; the Victorian, sub-aquatic cyborg of Captain Nemo (Nemo being a public-domain character, and all). He said, in his inimitably enthusiastic fashion, "That's *great!*" but then added after a pause, "Think they'll let you do it? 'Cause if they don't, you have to do it for *B.P.R.D.*" And we laughed about that for a little bit. I don't think I'm ruining any surprises here when I tell you that, in fact, they did not let me do it.

Months later, Mike and I started talking about bringing back the Oannes Society. We knew we needed Abe to confront the past that he'd been made aware of in *The Dead*. It just had to be part of the natural progression to getting Abe back to being the guy who we, and every reader out there, knew him to be. But what was the story? Yeah, that's where you always run into problems in this business; you need a plot. And a blank computer screen is no more fun to stare at than a blank canvas, but then, from the bottom of the sea, tiny bubbles started to trail up and into my consciousness, and suddenly, we had a starting place. Of course, *Garden of Souls* was built from a whole bunch of pieces that came from all over, and as it happens, that "big idea" ended up morphing into a pretty minor element. A minor element that helped to make *Garden of Souls* a larger, richer story, but a minor element nonetheless. And yet, really, it couldn't have been more important.

So what's the lesson to be learned from this little anecdote? I don't know. Somethin', probably.

—John Arcudi
Philadelphia

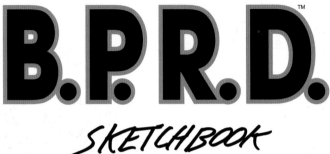

B.P.R.D.™

SKETCHBOOK

With a slew of new characters, an island full of cobbled-together menageries, and a trio of Victorian-era cyborgs, *Garden of Souls* turned out to be one of the most design-heavy *B.P.R.D.* stories to date—and a personal favorite! A major new character in the story is the mummy Panya—originally, it was to be a male character, and to the right are the first couple designs. When John changed her to female, the basic face design remained the same, with the addition of mud-caked hair that later changed to her long withered locks.

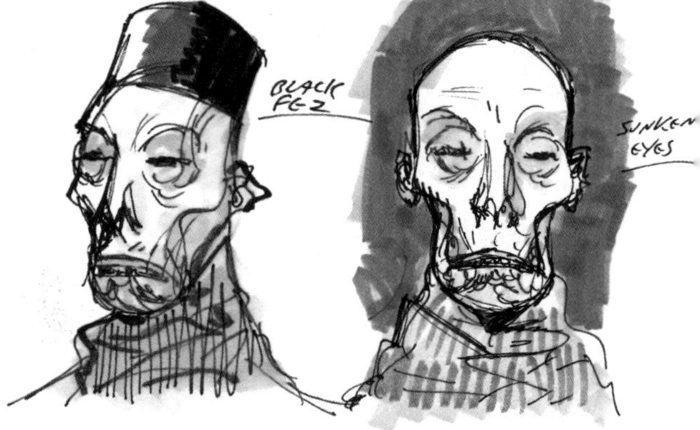
BLACK FEZ
SUNKEN EYES

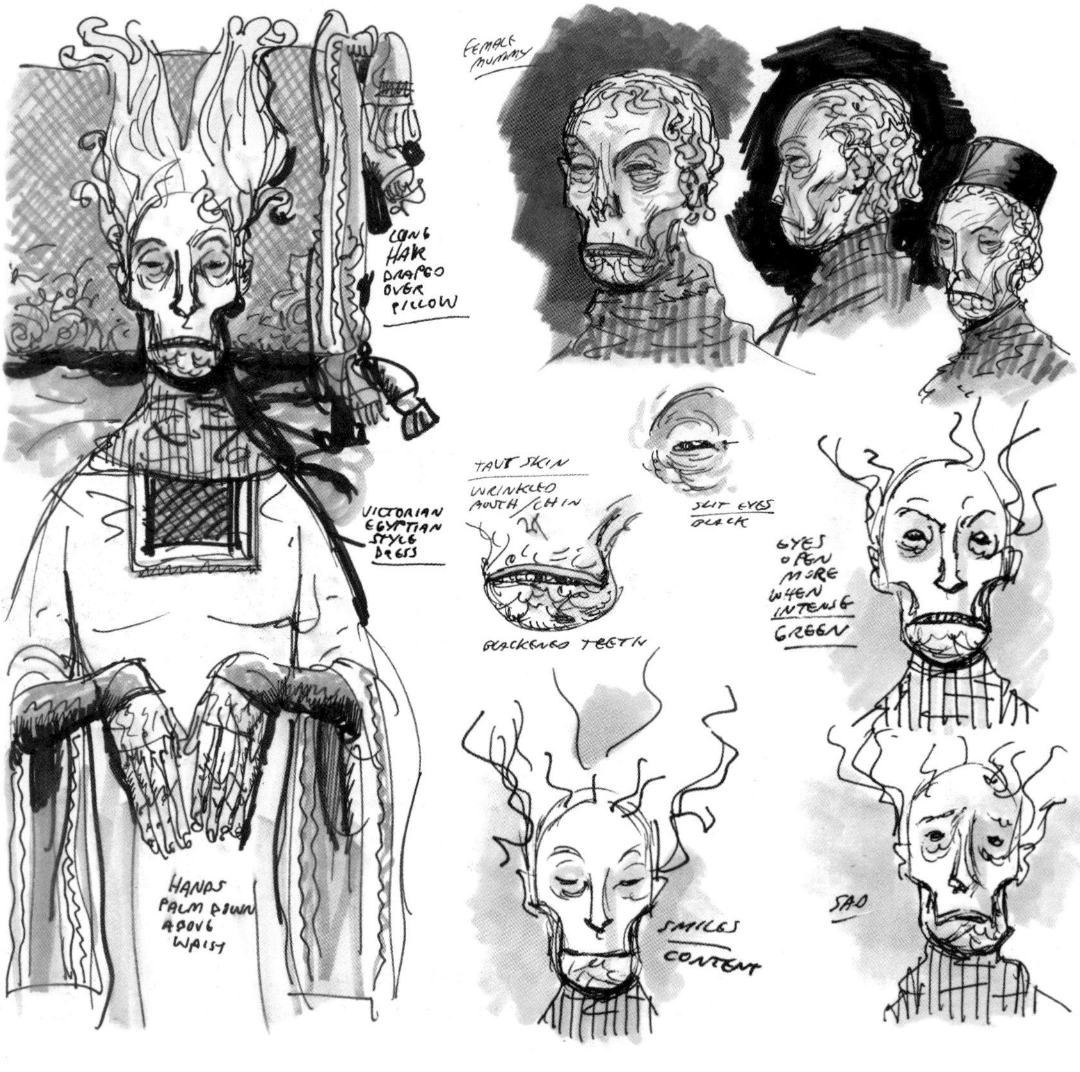
FEMALE MUMMY
LONG HAIR DRAPED OVER PILLOW
VICTORIAN EGYPTIAN STYLE DRESS
HANDS PALM DOWN ABOVE WAIST
TAUT SKIN
WRINKLED MOUTH/CHIN
BLACKENED TEETH
SLIT EYES BLACK
EYES OPEN MORE WHEN INTENSE GREEN
SMILES CONTENT
SAD

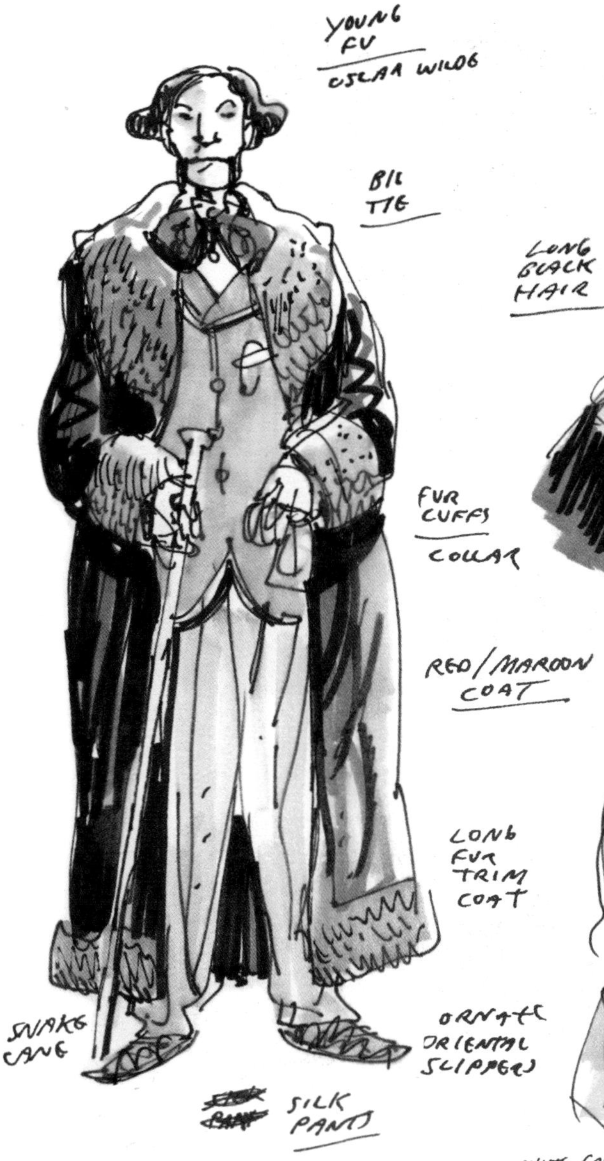
YOUNG FU
OSCAR WILDE
BIG TIE
FUR CUFFS
COLLAR
RED/MAROON COAT
LONG FUR TRIM COAT
SNAKE CANE
ORNATE ORIENTAL SLIPPERS
SILK PANTS

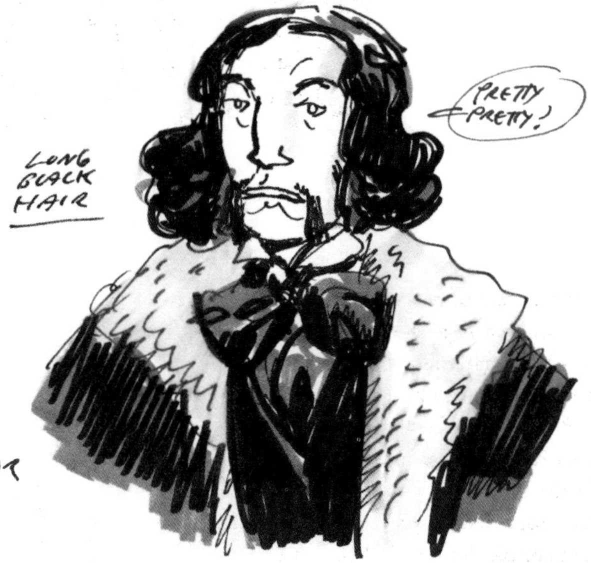
PRETTY PRETTY!
LONG BLACK HAIR

A troublesome character's youthful past, from one of Panya's flashbacks.

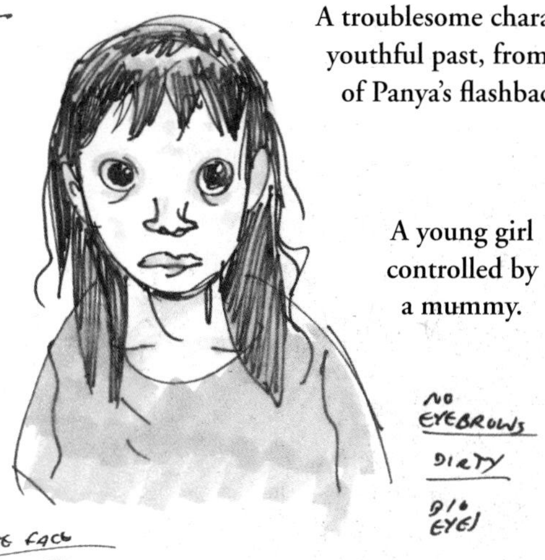
NO EYEBROWS
DIRTY
BIG EYES

A young girl controlled by a mummy.

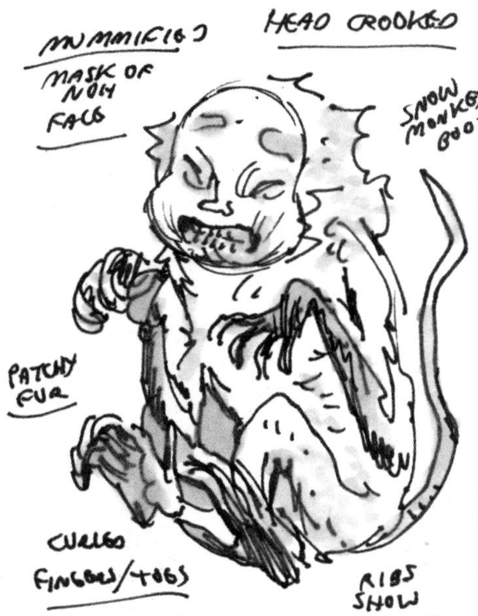
HEAD CROOKED
MUMMIFIED
MASK OF NOH FACE
PATCHY FUR
CURLED FINGERS/TOES
RIBS SHOW

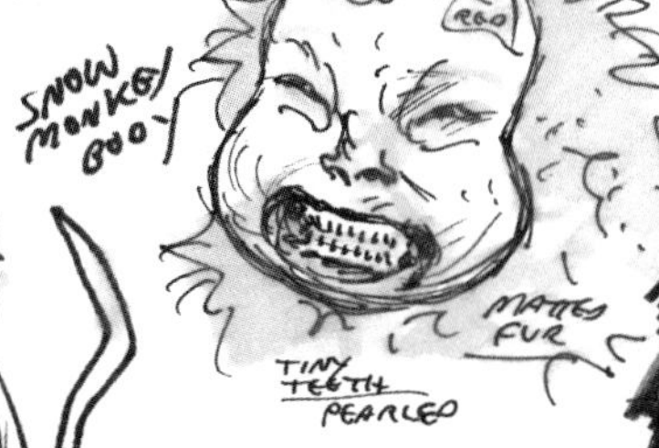
WHITE FACE
SNOW MONKEY BODY
RED
RED
MATTED FUR
TINY TEETH PEARLED

The *Noh* monkey is a favorite that seems to pop up all over the place in *B.P.R.D.*

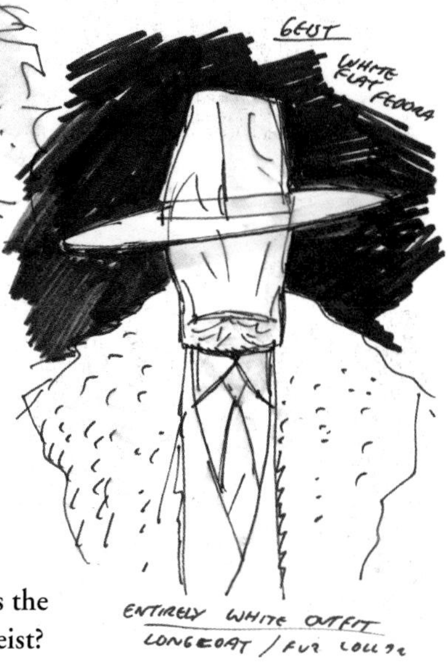
GEIST
WHITE FLAT FEDORA
ENTIRELY WHITE OUTFIT
LONGCOAT / FUR COLLAR

Geist!? Who is the mysterious Geist?

A lot of the fun designing *Garden of Souls* came from thinking up all the bizarre cobbled-together critters that fill the island jungles. Both Mike and John wanted them to look as natural and unmenacing as possible—they should feel like animals and not monsters. Below are some early designs for some critters like the "monkey-tiger" and "eel-bird" (but the "alligator-gazelle" never made it into the final story).

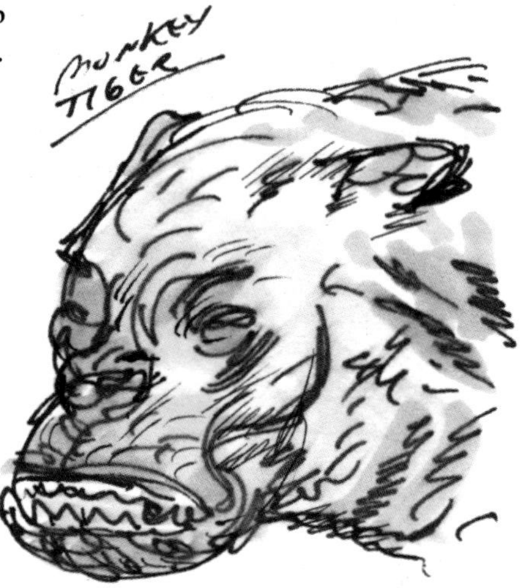
MONKEY TIGER

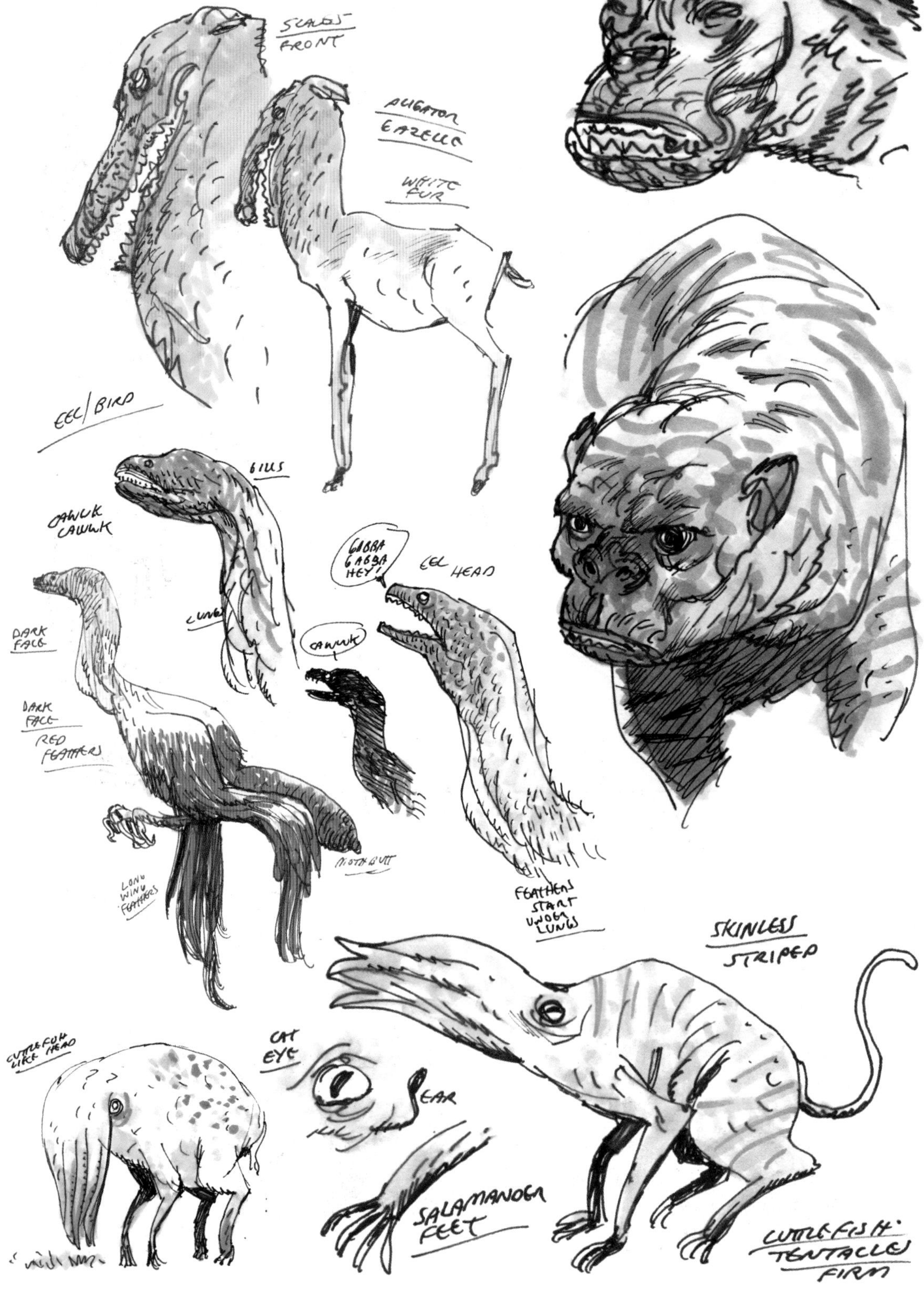
SCALES FRONT
ALLIGATOR GAZELLE
WHITE FUR
EEL/BIRD
GILLS
CAWWK CAWWK
DARK FACE
LUNGS
DARK FACE
RED FEATHERS
GABBA GABBA HEY!
EEL HEAD
CAWWK
MOTH BUTT
LONG WING FEATHERS
FEATHERS START UNDER LUNGS
SKINLESS
STRIPED
CUTTLEFISH LIKE HEAD
CAT EYE
EAR
SALAMANDER FEET
CUTTLEFISH TENTACLES FIRM

An early idea was to have a bunch of smaller critters running around the jungle mansion and getting into mischief as Abe explores the rooms. But with all the ornate Victorian details to the rooms themselves, I thought it would be distracting or they would get lost in the clutter, and abandoned the idea.

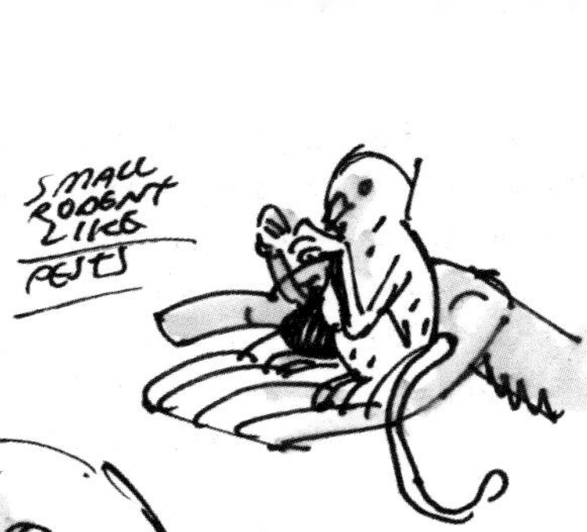
SMALL RODENT LIKE PETS

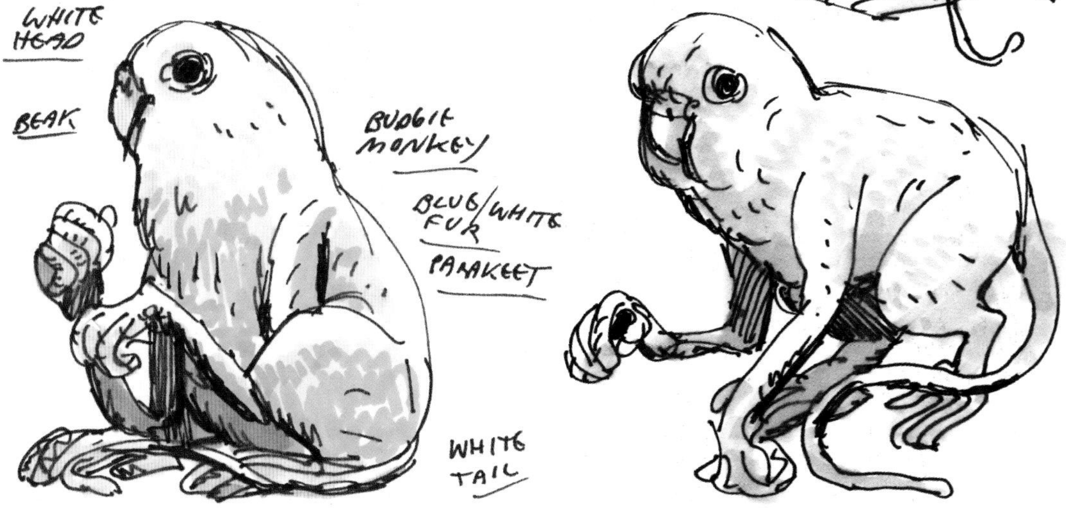
WHITE HEAD
BEAK
BUDGIE MONKEY
BLUE/WHITE FUR
PARAKEET
WHITE TAIL

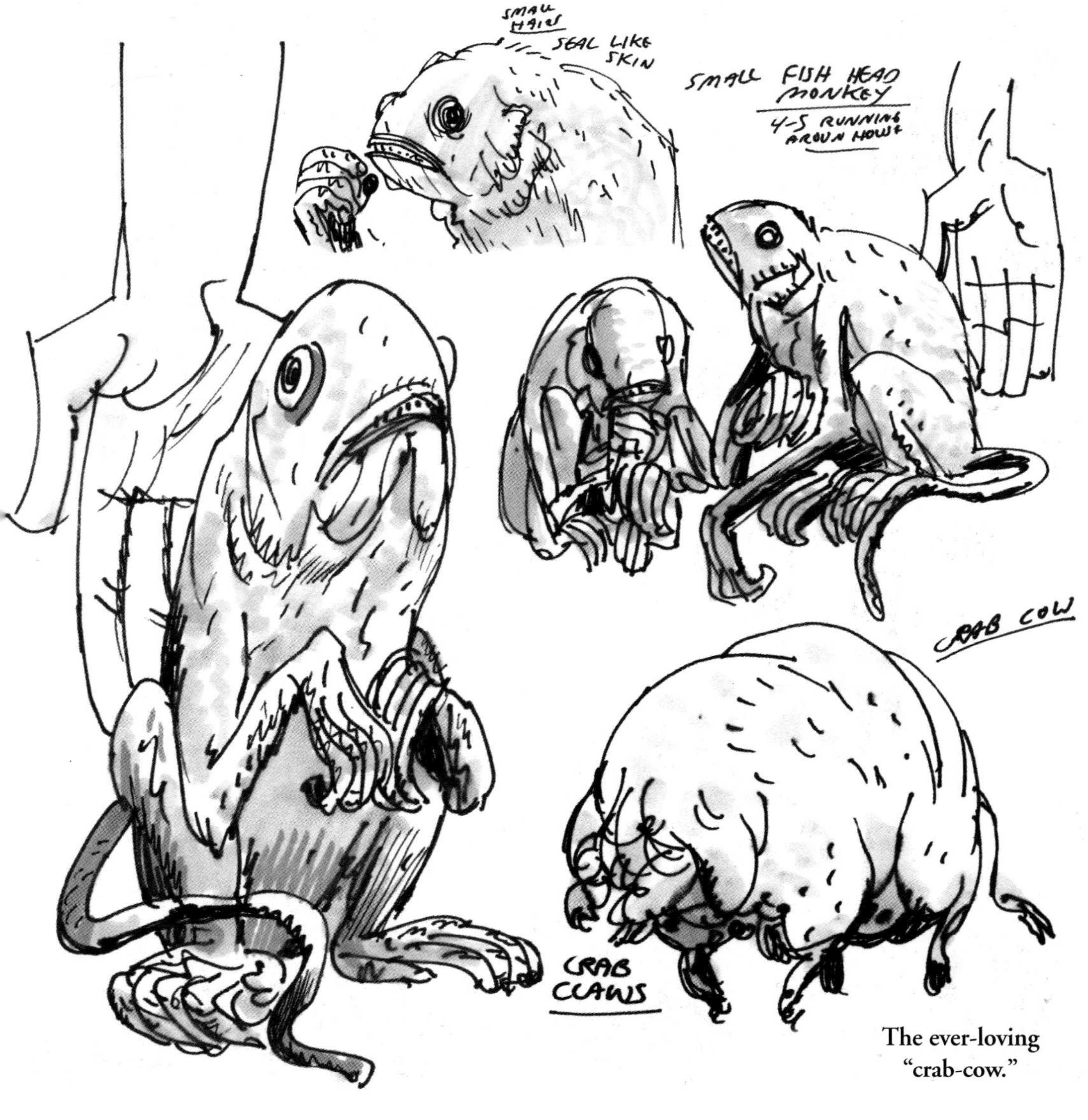
SMALL HAIRS
SEAL LIKE SKIN
SMALL FISH HEAD MONKEY
4-5 RUNNING AROUN HOUSE
CRAB COW
CRAB CLAWS

The ever-loving "crab-cow."

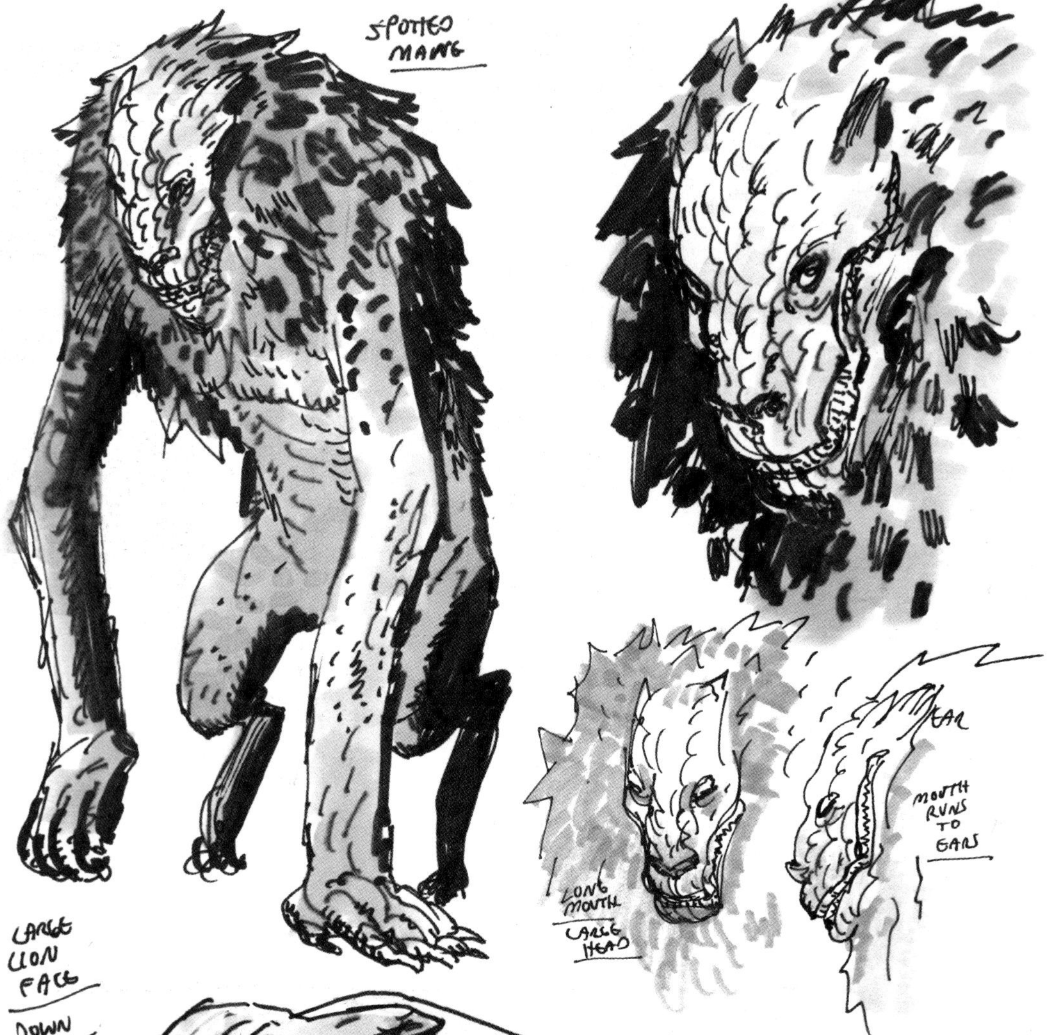
SPOTTED MANE
LARGE LION FACE
DOWN CHEST
EAR
MOUTH RUNS TO EARS
LONG MOUTH
LARGE HEAD

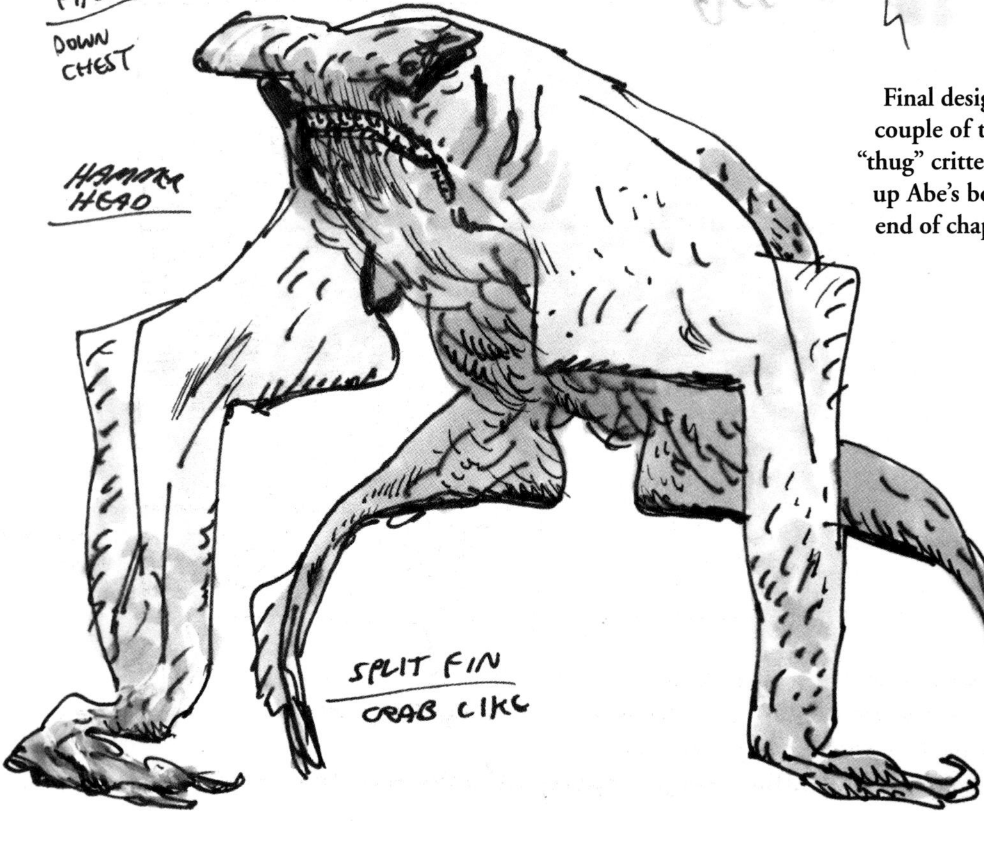
HAMMER HEAD
SPLIT FIN
CRAB LIKE

Final designs for a couple of the larger "thug" critters that tear up Abe's boat at the end of chapter four.

Eddie the god!
I thought it might be fun to give Eddie and his henchmen ornate get-ups for their visions of conquest in chapter four, but as John pointed out—Gods don't need fancy hats and the idealized bodies, and nudity would play against the restrained Victorian values of the group's past and hint at freedoms and powers reborn.

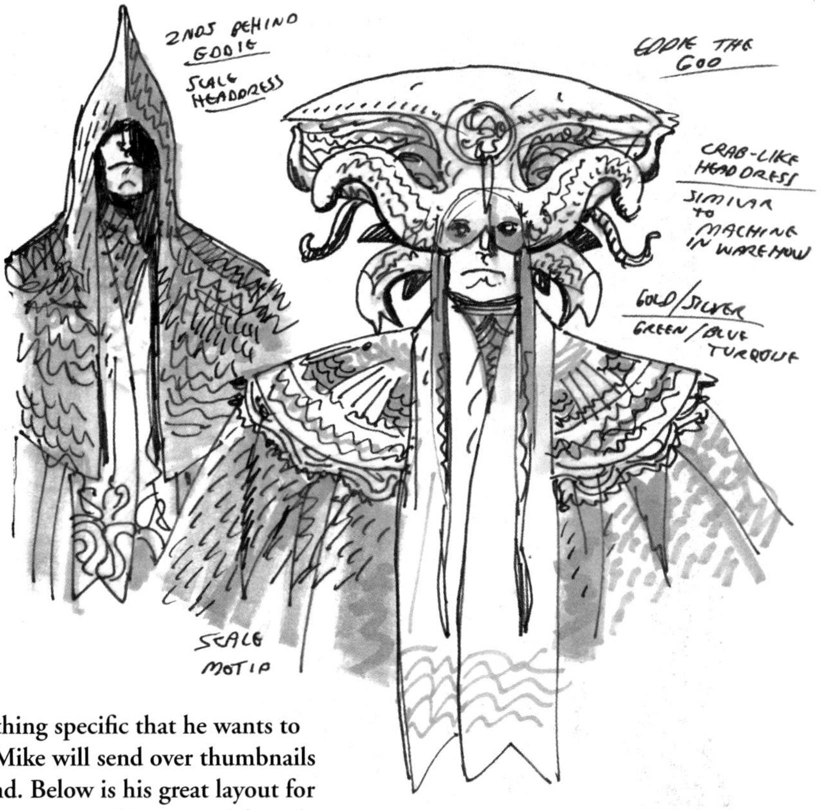
2NDS BEHIND EDDIE
SCALE HEADDRESS
EDDIE THE GOD
CRAB-LIKE HEAD DRESS
SIMILAR TO MACHINE IN WAREHOUSE
GOLD/SILVER
GREEN/BLUE TURQUOISE
SCALE MOTIF

Sometimes if he has something specific that he wants to come across in a sequence, Mike will send over thumbnails showing what he has in mind. Below is his great layout for the vision of doom in chapter two, working out a life cycle from frog creature to Ogdru-Hem.

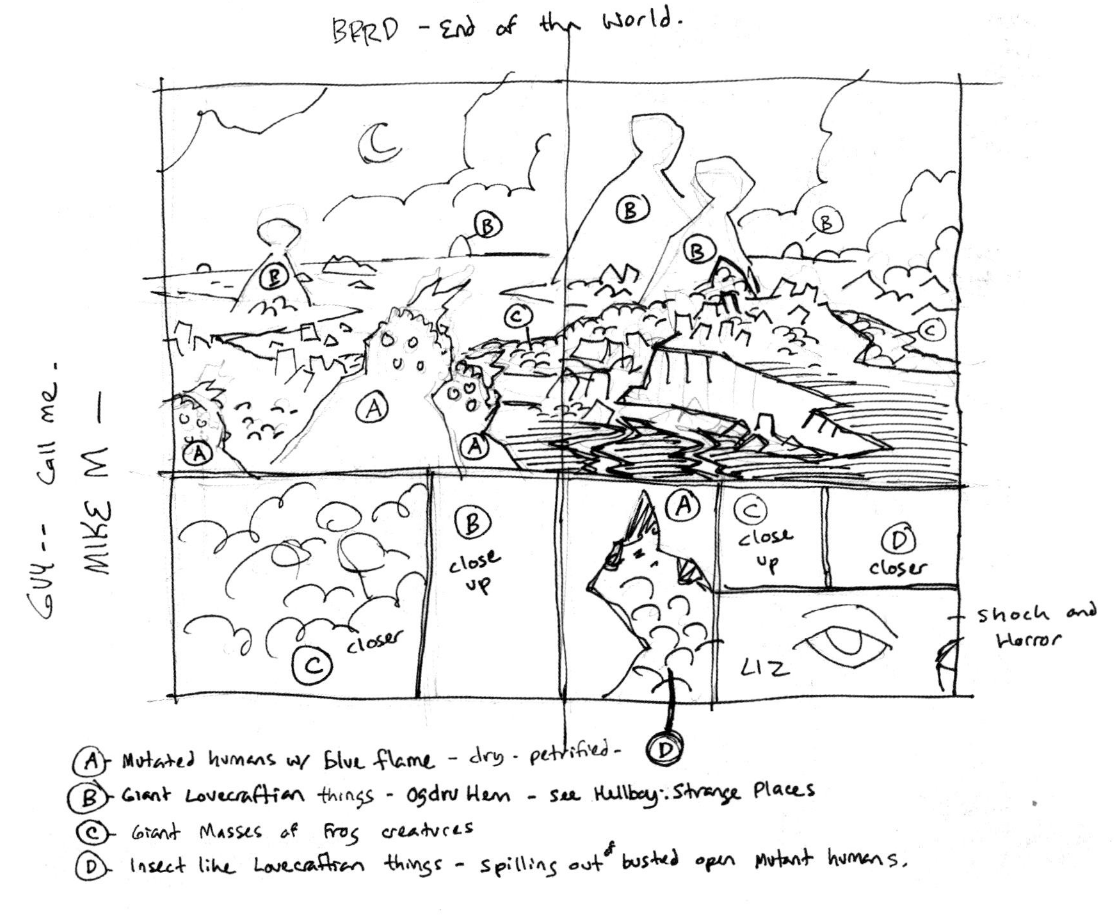
BPRD - End of the World.
GUY -- Call me. MIKE M —
B
A
C
close up
closer
D
LIZ
Shock and Horror
A - Mutated humans w/ blue flame - dry - petrified -
B - Giant Lovecraftian things - Ogdru Hem - see Hellboy: Strange Places
C - Giant Masses of Frog creatures
D - Insect like Lovecraftian things - spilling out of busted open Mutant humans.

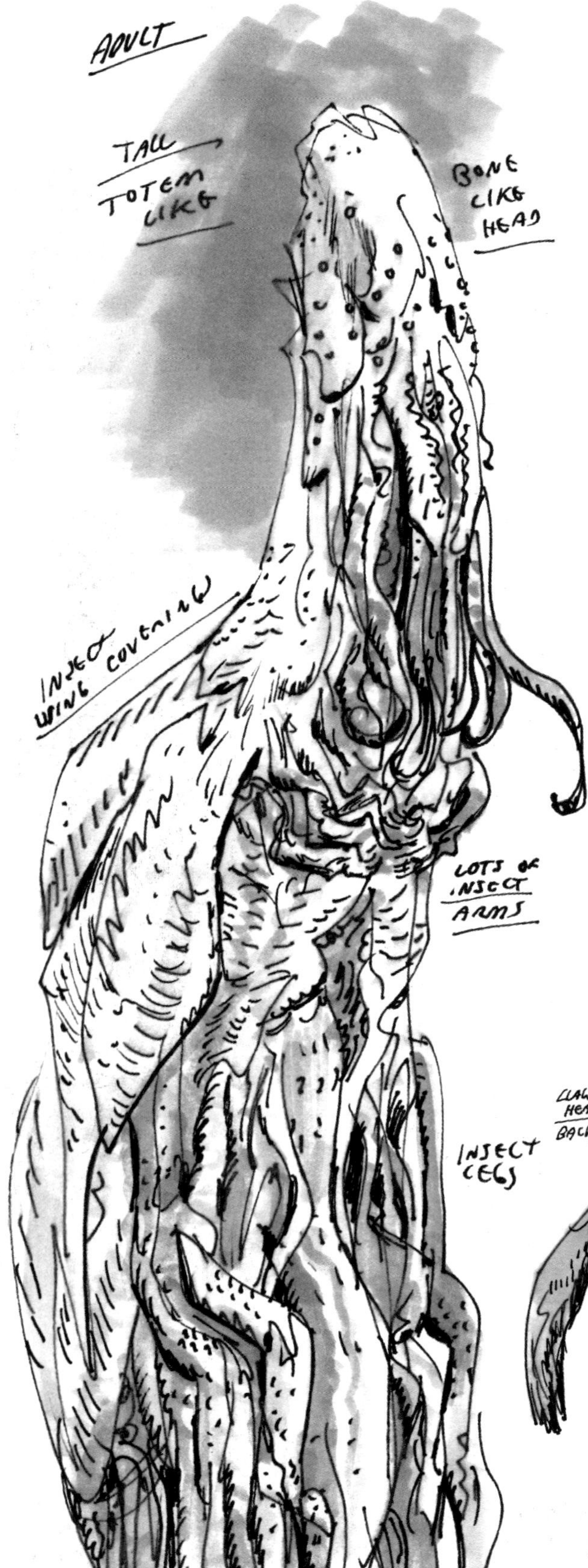
ADULT
TALL
TOTEM LIKE
BONE LIKE HEAD
INSECT WING COVERING
LOTS OF INSECT ARMS
INSECT LEGS
LARGE TENTACLE

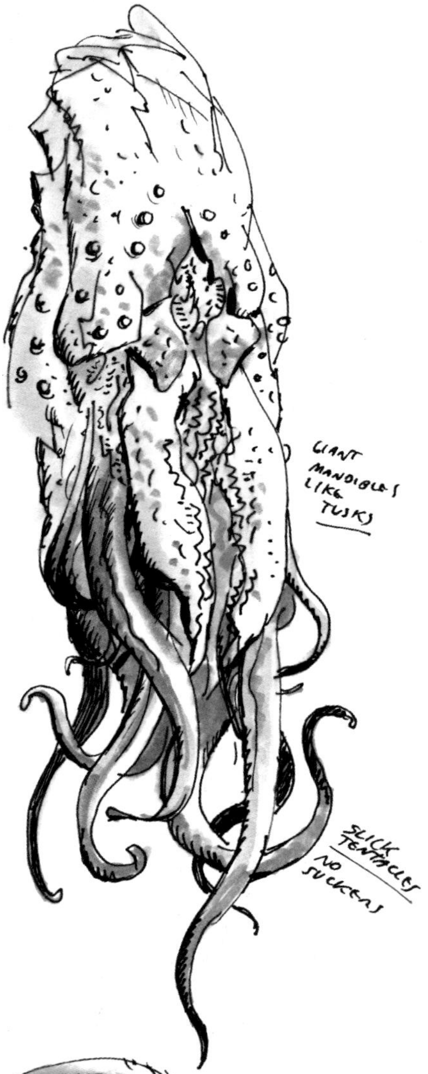
GIANT MANDIBLES LIKE TUSKS
SLICK TENTACLES
NO SUCKERS

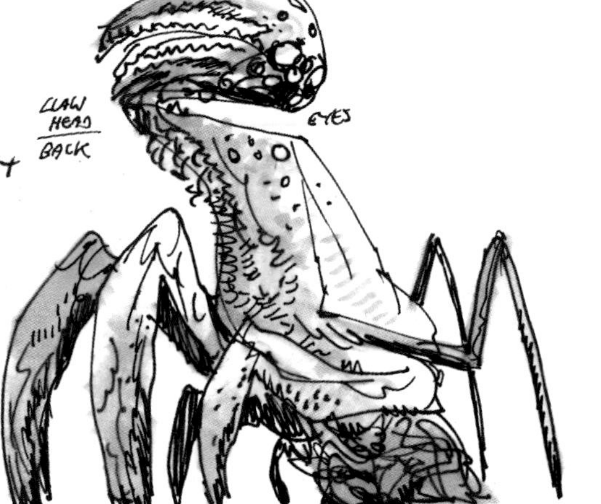
CLAW HEAD
BACK
EYES
MASS OF HERMIT CRAB LEGS

A couple early designs for the giant creatures populating the "doom spread" in chapter two that were too Lovecraftian for the Hellboy universe—which should be more insect-like than tentacled.

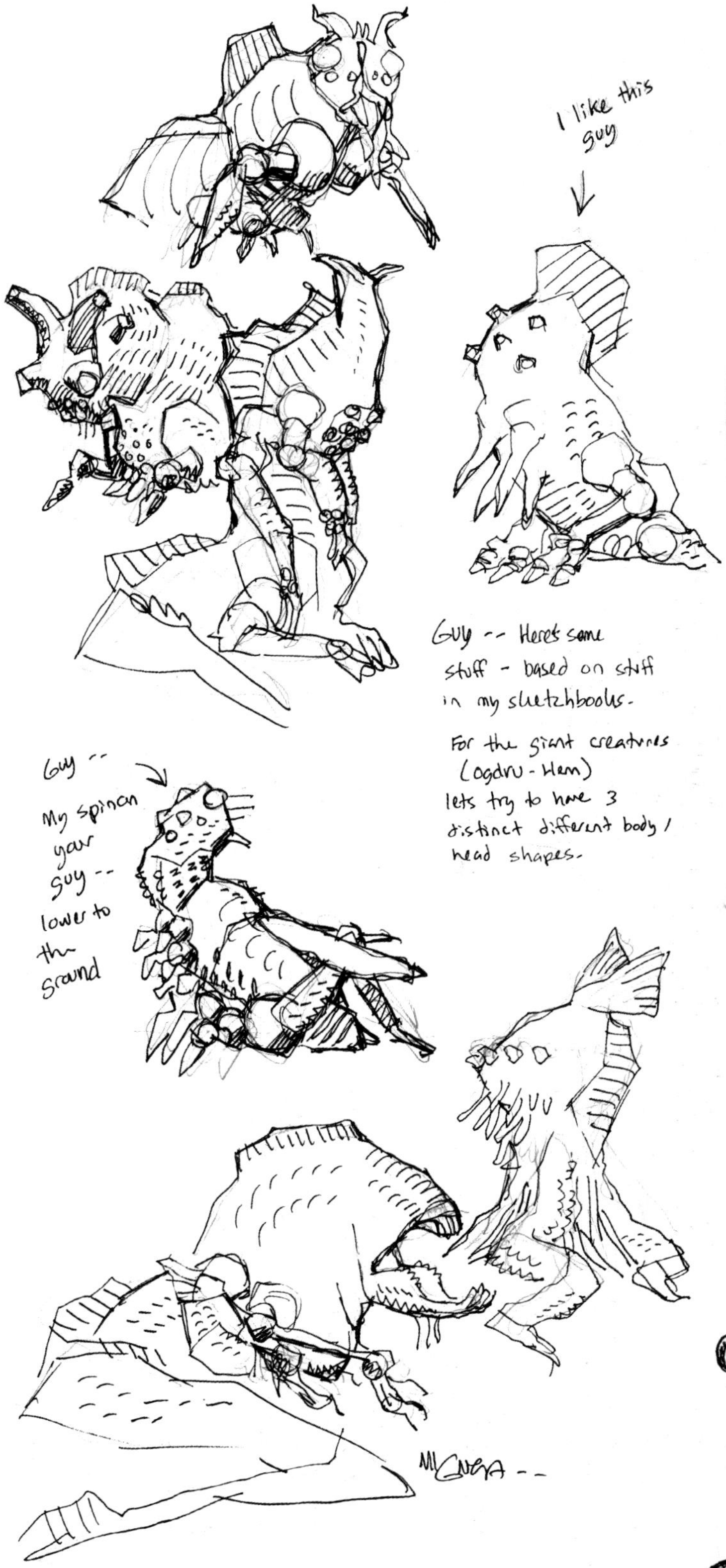
I like this guy
Guy -- Here's some stuff - based on stuff in my sketchbooks.
For the giant creatures (Ogdru-Hem) lets try to have 3 distinct different body / head shapes.
Guy -- My spin on your guy -- lower to the ground
MIGNOLA --

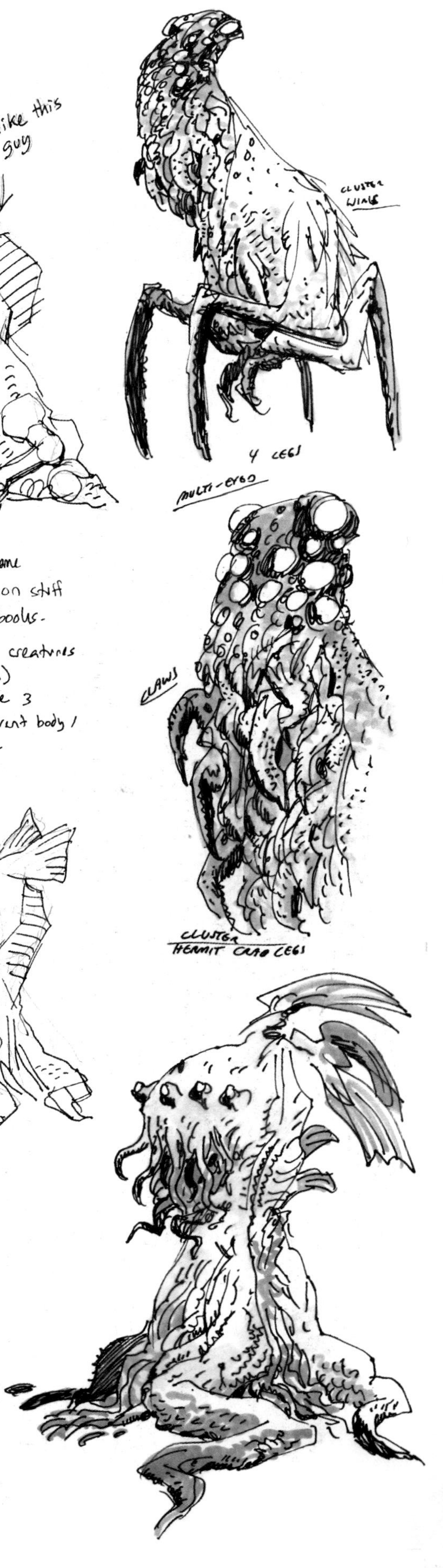
CLUSTER WINGS
4 LEGS
MULTI-EYED
CLAWS
CLUSTER HERMIT CRAB LEGS

Above are some of Mike's incredible designs for the Ogdru-Hem. To the right are a couple more insect-like creatures and my take on one of Mike's designs. The rest of his designs are all featured in the final "doom spread" itself.

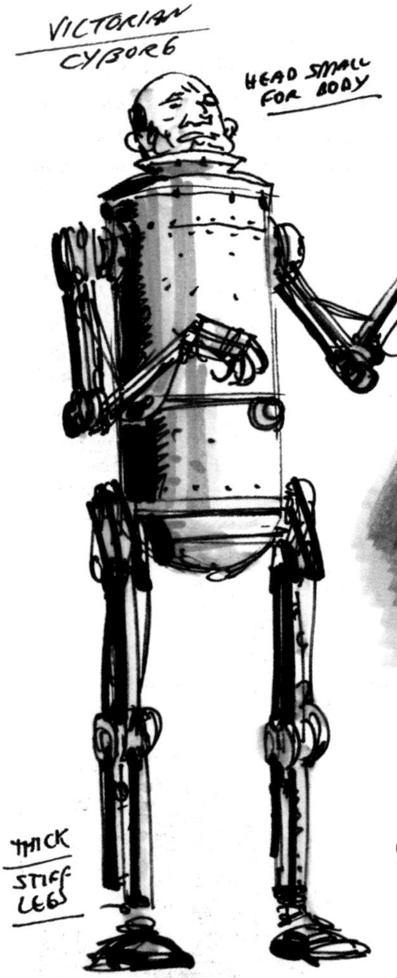
VICTORIAN CYBORG
HEAD SMALL FOR BODY
THIN ARMS
CORDS/PULLEYS
THICK
STIFF LEGS

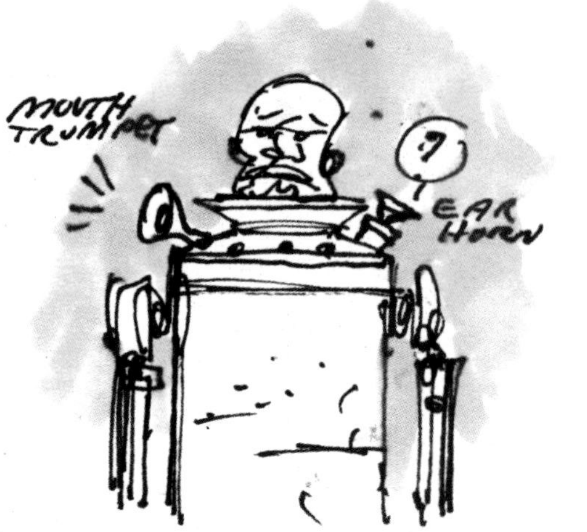
MOUTH TRUMPET
?
EAR HORN

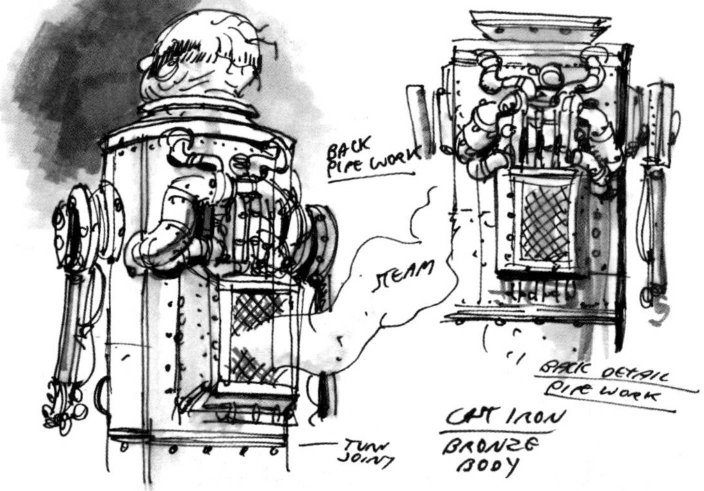
BACK PIPE WORK
STEAM
BACK DETAIL PIPE WORK
CAST IRON
BRONZE BODY

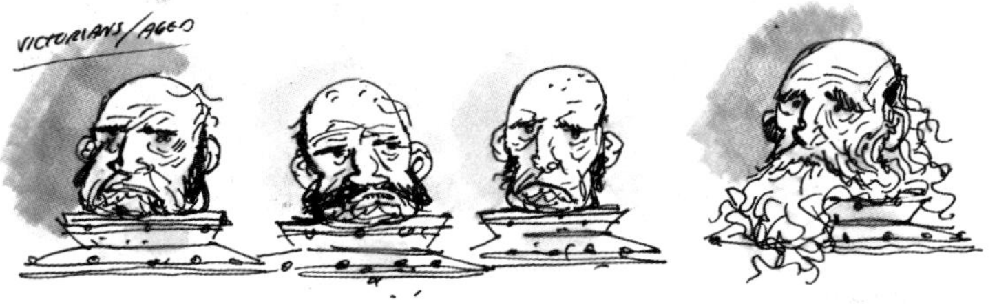
VICTORIANS/AGED

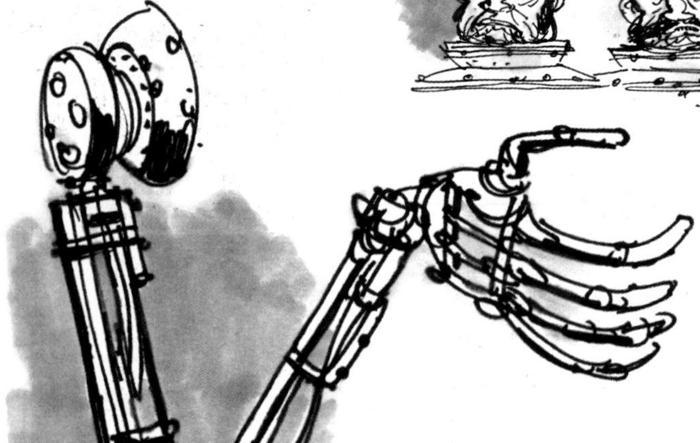

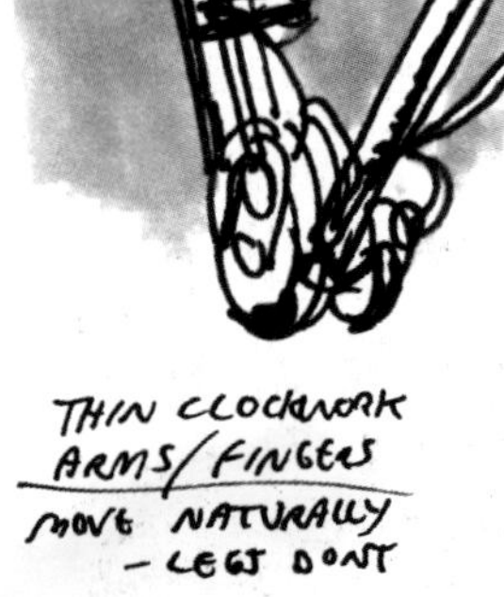
THIN CLOCKWORK ARMS/FINGERS
MOVE NATURALLY
– LEGS DONT

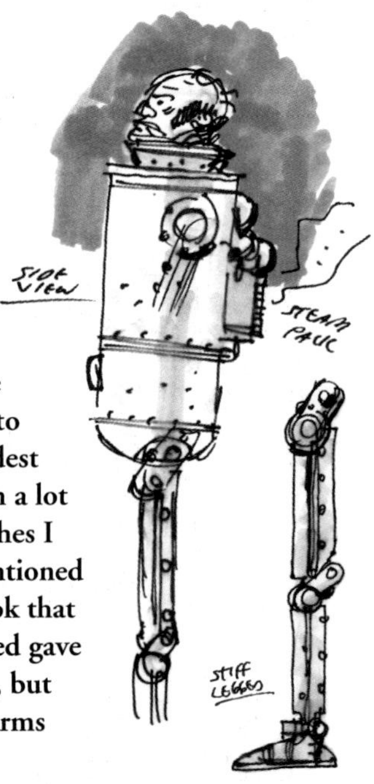
SIDE VIEW
STEAM PACK
STIFF LEGGED

The Victorian cyborg suits are my favorite part of *Garden of Souls,* and the most fun to draw—rivets and all! They were also the hardest ones to finalize in the designs and went through a lot of changes. On this page are the original sketches I came up with after talking to Mike—he had mentioned their suits are like a walking iron lung, and I took that a bit too literally. Also, having their heads exposed gave away who the characters were upon first sight, but the power pack on the back and mechanical arms would carry over to the final designs.

Next, it was suggested that they should have the feel of the Victorian diving suit from the end of *Plague of Frogs*—each one, a progression of technology, starting with a coal burner, then steam, and then electrical. And the images of deep-sea divers treading around the jungle would be a fun visual. Closer to the final design, but still too human-like and normal a form.

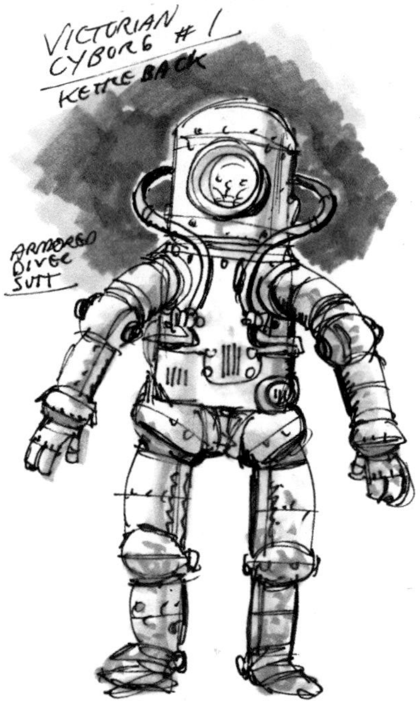
VICTORIAN CYBORG #1
KETTLE BACK
ARMORED DIVER SUIT

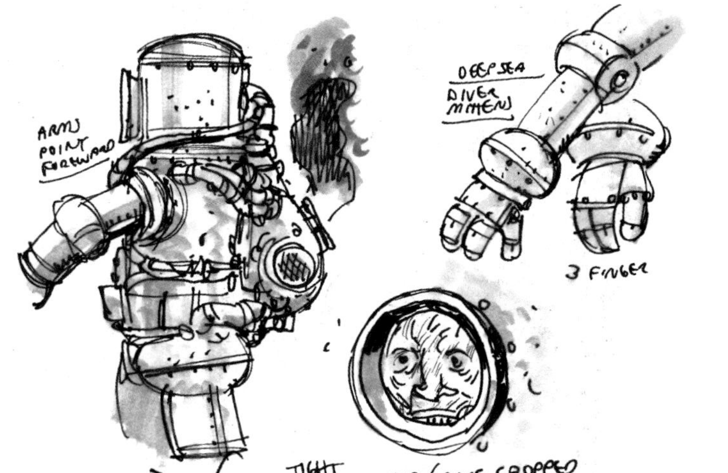
ARMS POINT FORWARD
DEEP SEA DIVER MITTENS
3 FINGER

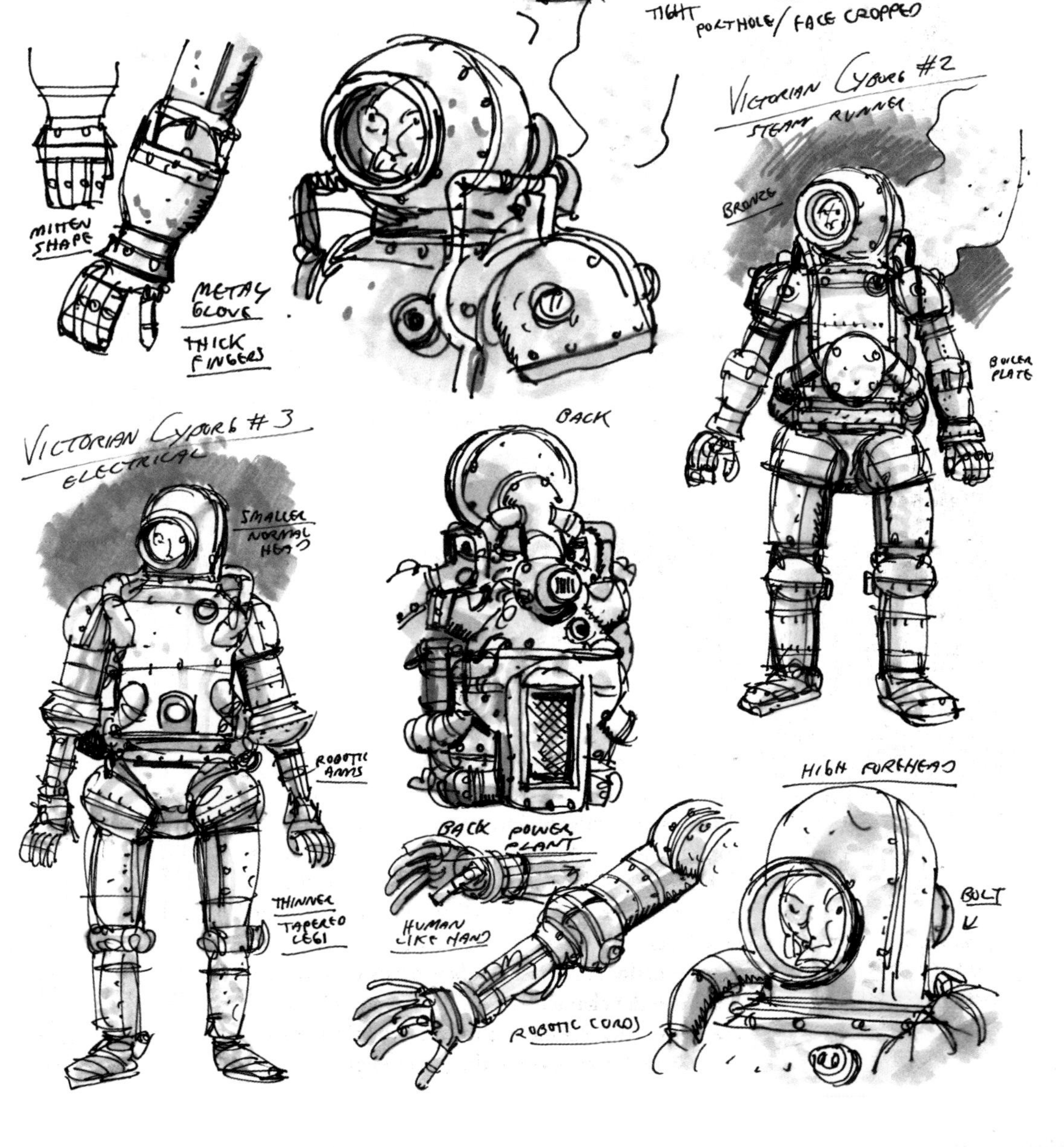
TIGHT PORTHOLE/ FACE CROPPED
MITTEN SHAPE
METAL GLOVE
THICK FINGERS
VICTORIAN CYBORG #2
STEAM RUNNER
BRONZE
BOILER PLATE
VICTORIAN CYBORG #3
ELECTRICAL
SMALLER NORMAL HEAD
ROBOTIC ARMS
THINNER
TAPERED LEGS
BACK
BACK POWER PLANT
HUMAN LIKE HAND
ROBOTIC CORDS
HIGH FOREHEAD
BOLT

Mike had the idea to make them each a unique shape with non-human positioning of the arms and legs, so the body would be curled up like a fetus in the torso of each suit, with the arms and legs purely mechanical. To the right are his initial sketches that made the cyborg designs fall into place (and also prove again why he's the best!), with my takes on them far right and below.

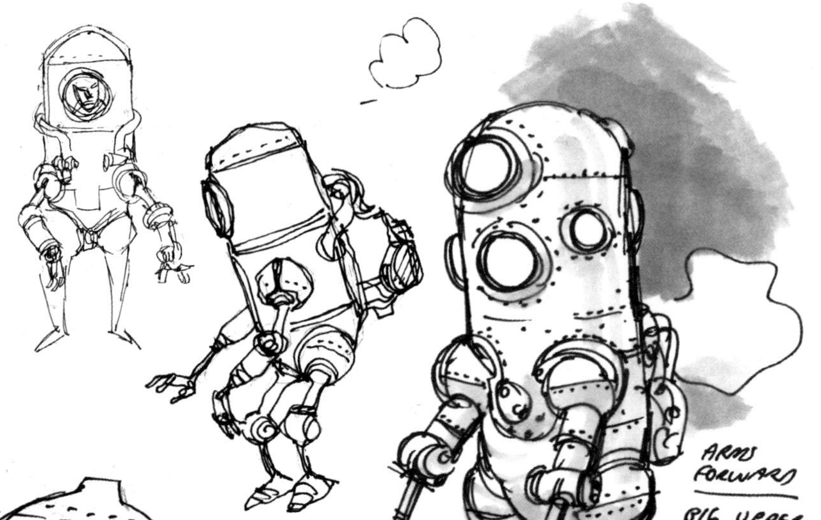
ARMS FORWARD
BIG UPPER
THIN LOWER
LONG UPPER LEG
SHORT

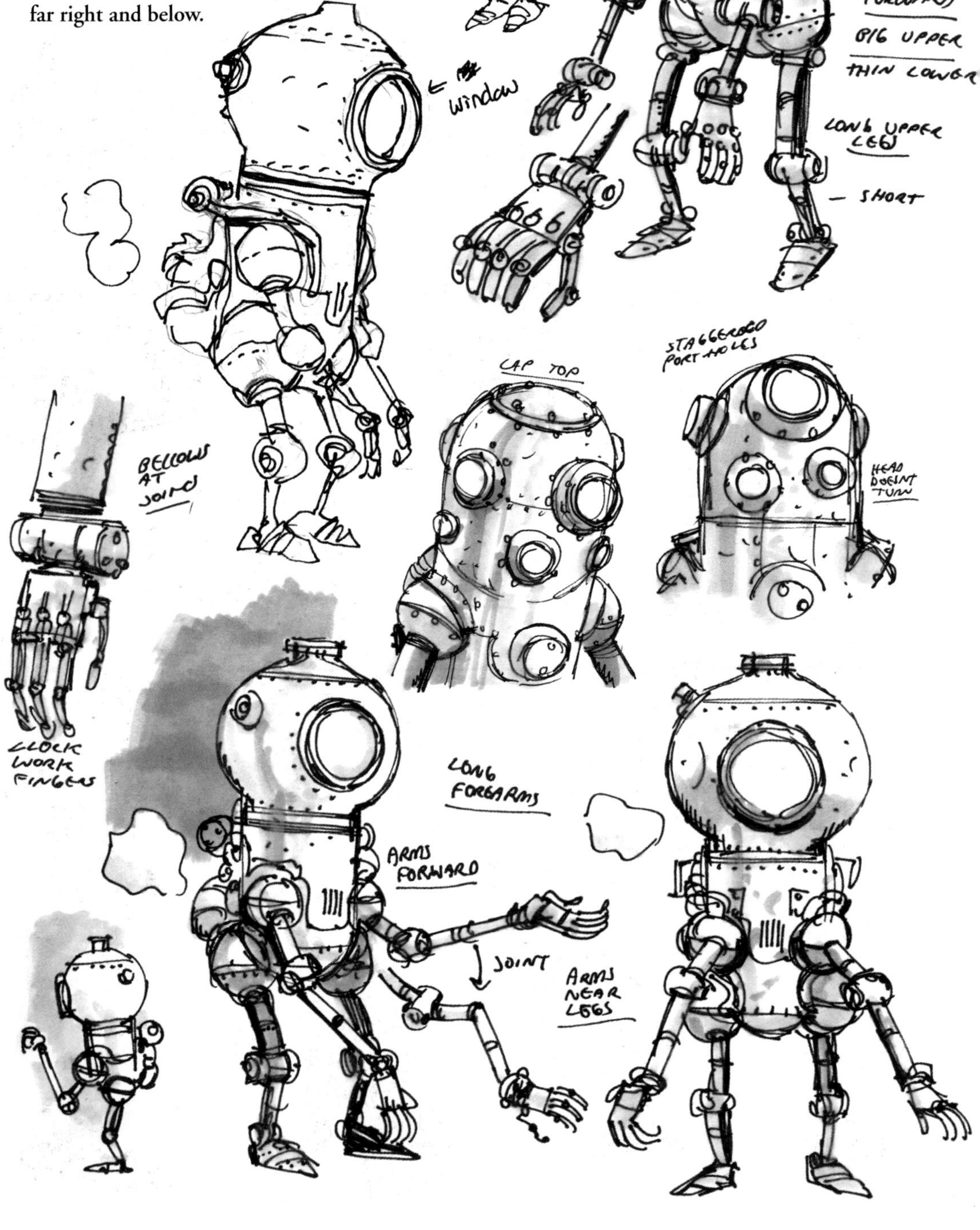
window
BELLOWS AT JOINT
CAP TOP
STAGGERED PORT HOLES
HEAD DOESN'T TURN
CLOCK WORK FINGERS
LONG FOREARMS
ARMS FORWARD
JOINT
ARMS NEAR LEGS

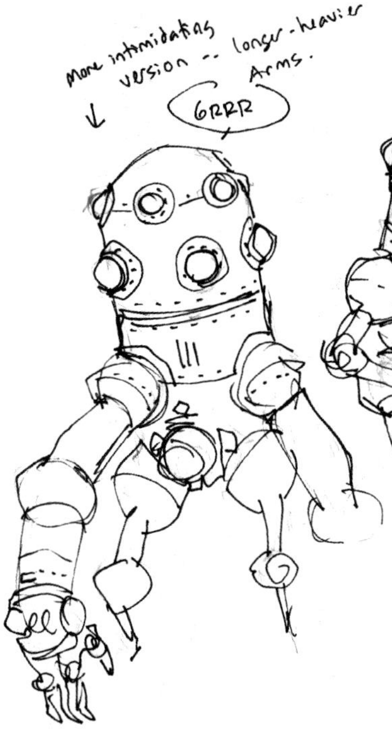
More intimidating version -- longer-heavier Arms.
GRRR

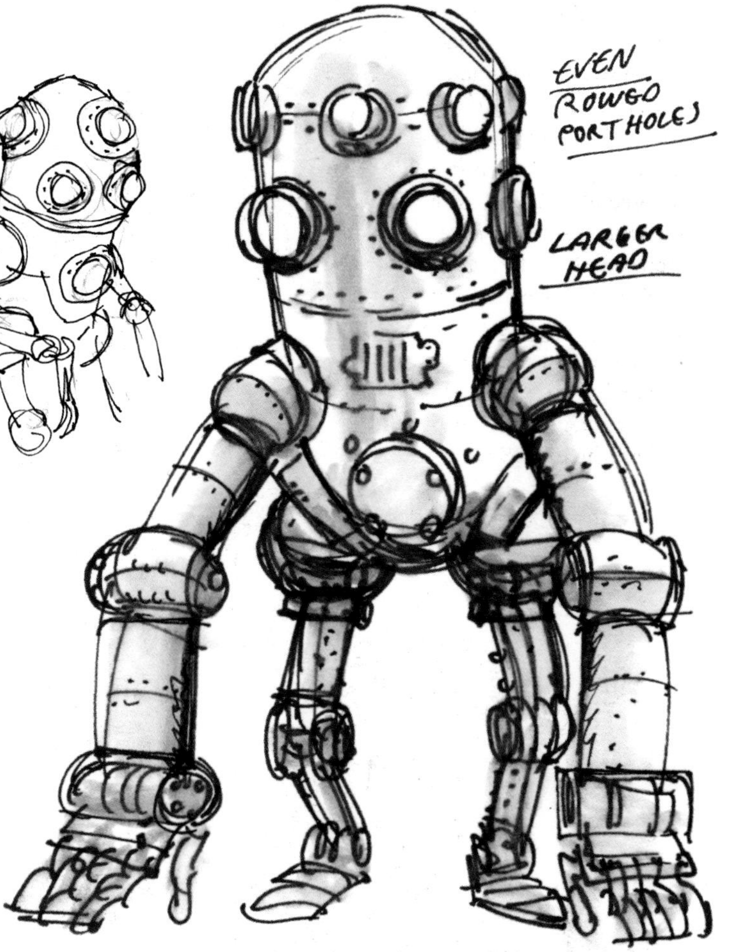
EVEN
PORTHOLES
LARGER HEAD

Above are Mike's sketches for the "gorilla-suit" cyborg, with my versions of his design fleshing out some details and mechanics to the right and below.

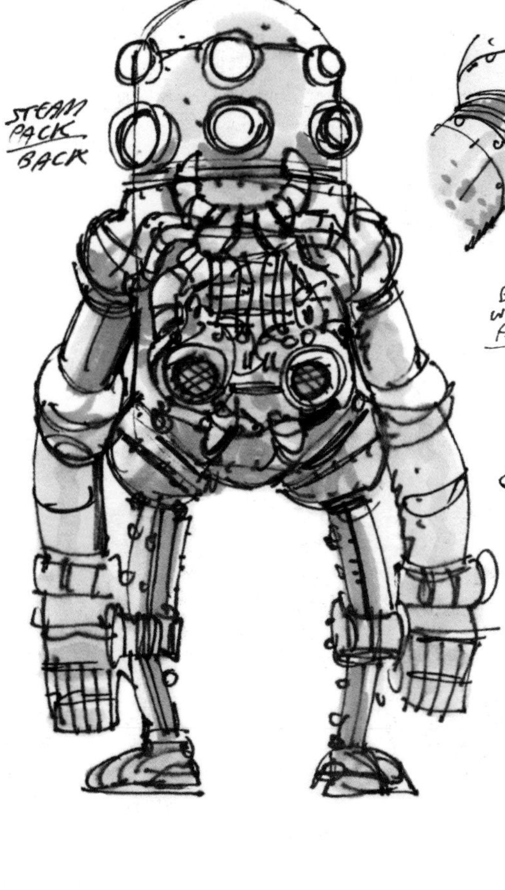
STEAM PACK BACK

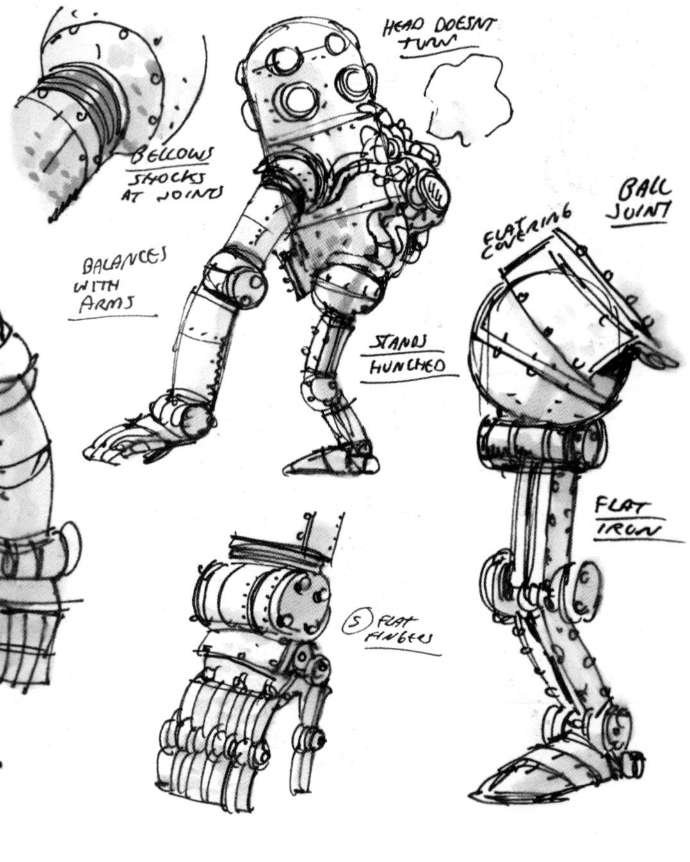
HEAD DOESNT TURN
BELLOWS SHOCKS AT JOINTS
BALANCES WITH ARMS
STANDS HUNCHED
BALL JOINT
FLAT IRON
5 FLAT FINGERS

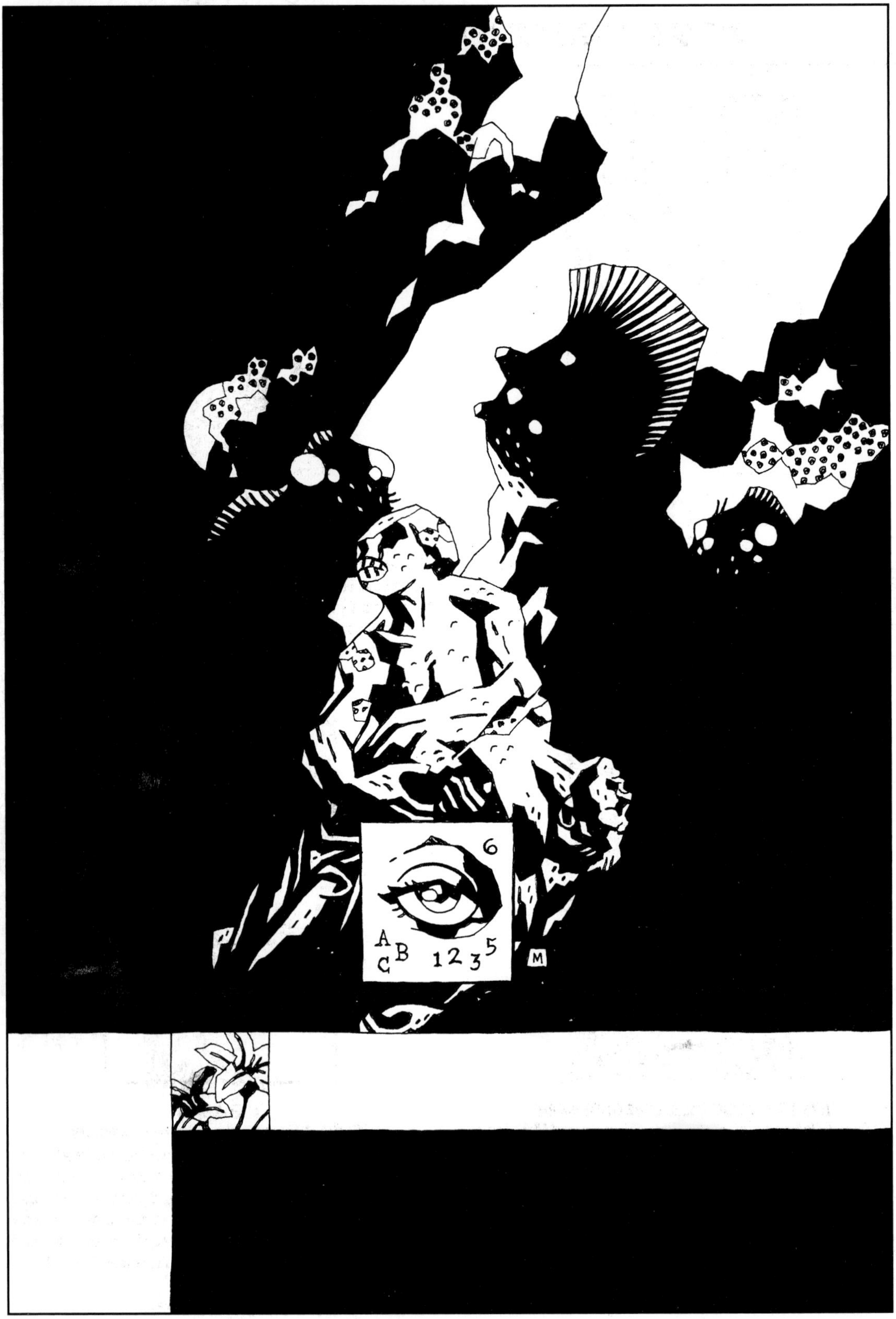

6
A
C B 1 2 3 5
M

Mike's wonderful but mystifying self-rejected cover to *Garden of Souls* #2.
Even he can't explain what this is supposed to be.

—Guy Davis
Crab Pointe, MI

ALSO FROM DARK HORSE BOOKS

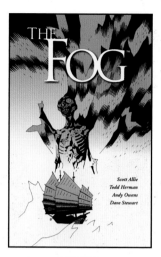

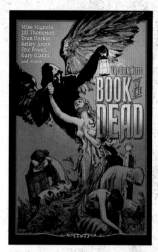

THE FOG™
Scott Allie
Todd Herman
Andy Owens
Dave Stewart

THE FOG
Scott Allie and Todd Herman
Fourteen years ago, a group of Shanghai traders fled their native land and the curse that haunted it. But the curse has found them again, as a sinister fog wreaks terrible changes on their small, seaside town in this chilling prequel to the 2005 film.
ISBN: 978-1-59307-423-4
$6.95

Mike Mignola
Jill Thompson
Evan Dorkin
Kelley Jones
Eric Powell
Gary Gianni
and others
The Dark Horse
BOOK OF THE DEAD

THE DARK HORSE BOOK OF THE DEAD
Kelley Jones, Mike Mignola, Jill Thompson, Evan Dorkin, Eric Powell, Gary Gianni, and others
The latest in Dark Horse's line of horror anthologies, *The Dark Horse Book of the Dead* features tales of the risen and hungry dead from comics notables including Mike Mignola, Gary Gianni, and *Conan* creator Robert E. Howard.
ISBN: 978-1-59307-281-0
$14.95

DWIGHT T. ALBATROSS'S
THE GOON NOIR
ERIC POWELL SCOTT ALLIE JOHN ARCUDI HILARY BARTA GUY DAVIS
TODD HERMAN ROGER LANGRIDGE THOMAS LENNON TONY MOORE BILL MORRISON
ARVID NELSON STEVE NILES KEVIN NOWLAN PATTON OSWALT MIKE PLOOG
BRIAN POSEHN HUMBERTO RAMOS THOMAS SNIEGOSKI RYAN SOOK

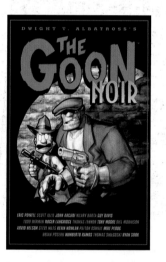

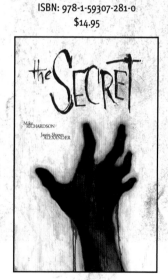

DWIGHT D. ALBATROSS'S THE GOON NOIR
Eric Powell, John Arcudi, Steve Niles, Ryan Sook, Mike Ploog, Todd Herman, and many more
Described as "EC by way of Looney Tunes," multiple award-winning cult hit The Goon has quickly risen to the forefront of hot creator-owned titles. Now a heapin' helping of the top names in comics and comedy put a new spin on their favorite characters, joining *The Goon*'s creator Eric Powell and erstwhile publisher Dwight D. Albatross to give you *The Goon* as you've never seen him before.
ISBN: 978-1-59307-785-3
$17.95

the SECRET
Mike RICHARDSON
Jason Shawn ALEXANDER

THE SECRET
Mike Richardson & Jason Shawn Alexander
Tonight is Tommy Morris's big chance: he's been invited to party with the social elite of Franklin High and maybe even hook up with Pam, the girl of his dreams. But when a prank call turns sour, Tommy gets sucked in deeper than he bargained for. A chilling coming-of-age mystery from Dark Horse founder Mike Richardson and Eisner-nominated artist Jason Shawn Alexander (*Damn Nation, The Escapists*).
ISBN: 978-1-59307-651-6
$15.95

AVAILABLE AT YOUR LOCAL COMICS SHOP OR BOOKSTORE! • To find a comics shop in your area, call 1-888-266-4226.
For more information or to order direct visit darkhorse.com or call 1-800-862-0052 Mon.–Fri. 9 A.M. to 5 P.M. Pacific Time. Prices and availability subject to change without notice.

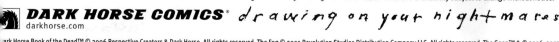

DARK HORSE COMICS® *drawing on your nightmares*
darkhorse.com